JOURNEY
TO
EDEN

AMBASSADOR

BELFAST, NORTHERN IRELAND
GREENVILLE, SOUTH CAROLINA

JOURNEY
TO
EDEN

a novel of love, faith and the origins of the universe

AMBASSADOR

BELFAST, NORTHERN IRELAND
GREENVILLE, SOUTH CAROLINA

Journey to Eden
© Copyright 2003 Richard Porter

ISBN 1 84030 143 0

Ambassador Publications
a division of
Ambassador Productions Ltd.
Providence House
Ardenlee Street,
Belfast,
BT6 8QJ
Northern Ireland
www.ambassador-productions.com

Emerald House
427 Wade Hampton Blvd.
Greenville
SC 29609, USA
www.emeraldhouse.com

BELFAST, NORTHERN IRELAND
GREENVILLE, SOUTH CAROLINA

ABOUT THE AUTHOR

Richard Porter was Professor of Orthopaedic Surgery at the University of Aberdeen in Scotland, and was also the Director of Education and Training at the Royal College of Surgeons of Edinburgh. He has had a strong academic career, conducting research into the physiology and pathology of the human spine. He has published over 120 medical papers in peer review journals, has written seven surgical text books and won two Volvo awards for basic science. He holds MD and DSc degrees from Edinburgh University and is Fellow of the Edinburgh and English Royal Colleges of Surgeons. This is his first novel, writing about time, origins and creation. He and his wife Christine live in South Yorkshire, England.

FOREWORD
by Jonathan Aitken

Professor Richard Porter has combined the skill of a good storyteller with the scholarship of an acclaimed scientist to produce a highly readable and original first novel.

"*Journey to Eden*" is an immediate page turner because of its compelling narrative and imaginative story line. Yet there is far more to this thought provoking novel than the action packed and romance filled drama that arrives like a whirlwind in the lives of the book's central characters. Jon a geological student from the island of Jersey falls in love with Sophie an Edinburgh University medical student. In the course of their courtship they meet and befriend Mohammed a research scientist from Baghdad who has been working on a top secret Iraqi space probe project of great interest to the Chinese, the Russians and the Americans.

Mohammed, whose pivotal role in the project turns him into a hunted man by espionage agents, shares his scientific secrets with Jon and Sophie. What he tells the young couple, is that the Iraqi space probe is on the brink of proving a revolutionary new hypothesis on time and the universe. Jon and Sophie become intensely excited with spiritual and scientific curiosity about this hypothesis which has mind blowing implications. They leave Mohammed and travel to Iraq to follow certain leads. The denouement of their journey is extraordinary.

This novel is electric in its pace and authentic in its backgrounds. Richard Porter knows his medicine, his geology, his locations, the latest scientific hypotheses on physical and biological time, and his biblical theology extremely well. He knows how to tell a good story, but there is more. In this book is a new hypothesis, which if correct will completely change our thinking about the measure of time. If I reveal more I will spoil it so I will simply give it the warmest of "must read" recommendations.

Jonathan Aitken

Former British Cabinet Minister and author of six books including: 'Officially Secret', 'Nixon: a life' and, 'Pride and Perjury'.

ACKNOWLEDGEMENTS

There are three people especially, whom I would like to acknowledge

- I had accepted that what I had been taught about evolution was probably correct, until I met Professor Vernon Wright who had the chair of Rheumatology at Leeds University. He was the most productive researcher I have known, and I was surprised to find that such a respected academic would take a minority position and believe in a special six-day creation. He thought that the conclusions about evolution and the dating of the age of the earth were based on unproved assumptions, and he thought that an acceptable scientific option was to take Genesis at face value.

- I met the theologian Nigel M.de S. Cameron, and learnt from him that a literal reading of Genesis made more sense of the Bible, than by treating it as poetry. I am indebted to him for some of the thoughts expressed in chapters 88 and 90 of this book.

- I was also greatly privileged in my friendship with Dennis Burkitt. He was probably the most original medical thinker of the twentieth century. He taught me two things - the importance of asking the big question, and how to think laterally.

So I have been asking a big question - "what is the meaning of time?" - and I have been trying to test a hypothesis that might bring science into line with Genesis - that time is slowing down and we don't recognise it. There is a way it might be apparent, if we were to look laterally and see the biological clock marching at a different step. And there are just some hints that it is doing that.

I am reading as many books as I can find on the subject of 'time', and I owe a thousand thanks to all the authors cited as references. These people have come from different disciplines. They are physicists, geologists, cosmologists, biologists, surgeons and theologians. They admit to holding very different philosophies. Some are atheists, others agnostics, some are theist evolutionists and others are creationists. Their literature has been a delight to read, and it has given me much to think about, especially when they reach different conclusions about whether the earth is old or young.

I owe a very big debt to my good friend Jonathan Aitken who has written a generous foreword. And to Jim Gordon for the illustrations. He is a long-standing friend from student days, and is now an acclaimed Scottish artist. I want to thank many people who have made suggestions and who have helped with proof reading, especially Jon Bellfield, Monty White, Philip Bell, David Wilkinson, Rob Frost, Enid Quenault and Richard Aspden.

Finally and most importantly I thank my wife Christine, and our four sons and their wives - Daniel and Barbara, William and Karen, Matthew and Sam and James and Katie - who have encouraged me to put something into print.

THE MAIN CHARACTERS

Jon Le Var is a 22 year old geology student from the island of Jersey.

Sophie his girl friend, is an Edinburgh medical student.

Mohammed Al Harty is a researcher in optics from Baghdad.

Phil, Jon's best friend.

Li Zhou is the governor of the Xinjang province of China.

General Kapta is director of the Military Hospital in Damascus.

Ania is his daughter.

Brother Joe is a Jesuit priest in Damascus.

Pastor Ibraim is the leader of a Protestant church in Damascus.

Frank lives in Jersey, and is a retired mariner and amateur astronomer.

Captain Kulikov is a Russian secret agent and an assassin.

Max Bellman is recruited by the CIA.

Steve and Danny are young members of the British Special Branch.

Marcus is the Special branch IT wizard.

Gorgin is the pastor of the Evangelical Church in Baghdad.

LIST OF ILLUSTRATIONS

GRAPHS

INTRODUCTION

This book is a story about two young people who unexpectedly discover a time-probe and develop a new theory about 'time'. It is politically dangerous because it has the potential to re-write history. They are pursued by ruthless assassins across Britain and into Iraq. They also take a spiritual journey.

It is a novel with a difference, because it allows us to explore seriously the subject of time. This has captured my imagination for many years. Like most people, I used to think of time as an invariable fixed process of years, hours, minutes and seconds. But I have come to agree with those who think that what we call 'time' does not exist apart from being an imaginary concept to explain movement and decay.

What we call 'time' is relative. A hundred years ago Einstein recognised that 'time' changes in relation to acceleration and gravity. Time slows down the faster we go and the greater the gravitational field. It runs at a different rate depending on our situation. In this book we are going further, suggesting that what we call 'time', can change from one epoch to another. If that is correct, then our particular time-frame, and *when* we are in time, will give us different views about the duration of time. I have tried to identify areas where I think science is providing a few hints that 'time' might be changing not only depending on *where* we are in space but also *when* we are within time. In other words, our frame of reference may be changing with the passing of time.

As an academic orthopaedic surgeon with a fairly narrow interest in a small area of physiology and pathology - the human spine - I am no more knowledgeable than any other layman when it comes to understanding some of the other scientific disciplines. Neither am I a theologian. However I recognise that almost everyone who attempts to write about time and origins has specialised in only one or two relevant subjects, and in this multi-disciplinary area, I am not alone in my ignorance.

I may have introduced errors, which if presented in a scientific treatise would attract justified criticism. I have therefore written this book in the form of a novel and I hope that mistakes will be forgiven. It is a hypothesis to be tested by those whose knowledge is greater than mine.

It is also written as a novel in the hope of capturing the interest of readers who though not inclined to read about science, may want to give their mind an opportunity to savour the subject of 'time'. It should also encourage readers to keep an open and questioning mind about those origins and processes which are currently being proposed perhaps with too much vigour, in cosmic and biological science. Science is only an approximation to the truth. Sometimes it goes down a blind-alley, and has to back-track. It is constantly under revision.

As a surgeon, I know that observations made in a clinical study have to be kept in context. The conclusions are relevant only for that particular group of patients at that specific time. An other group of patients at an other time may behave quite differently. It is not permissible to extrapolate outside the context of the study. That is conjecture. In a similarly way, observations made in the earth sciences should be kept in context. They are accurate only within the relatively short time of the study, but this does not provide a licence for scientists to make firm conclusions outside that context. We were not present in antiquity, and we can not be confident that this is a world of uniformitarianism - where everything is always the same. Processes and speeds of processes may be very different in other contexts. I therefore make a plea for more scientific humility, before present data is used to extrapolate backwards in time.

The book is written in everyday language, but if any sections seem heavy and cause the mind to 'boggle', they can be skipped without loosing the flavour of the ideas. For the more curious, some aspects of the scientific arguments are dealt with at a deeper level in the references and notes.

The new hypothesis which is proposed in this book - that time is changing and we are not aware of it - has some important implications, not least because of what we think about the Bible and our early history. It is important also because Genesis is 'scripture' to Christian, Jews and Muslims - 60% of the world's population.

If time is relative, our statements about days, millennia and billions of years, are dependant on *where* we are and *when* we live. Some observers could reasonably think that we are living in a young earth which would still be compatible with the main-line scientific view about a very old universe, if there is more than one time-frame.

Such ideas about a young cosmos are not new, although during the last two hundred years, the vast majority of contemporary scientists have come to accept the great antiquity of the universe, in spite of the imprecision and uncertainty of the methodologies and the inability to repeat the experiments. We are however, at the beginning phase of a new serious challenge to this paradigm, which involves the nature of time.

The community which is interested in asking questions about theories outside the ideological mainstream is small and it has a difficult life. However, the point of a paradigm shift is that it challenges the older, established model. A minority begins to raise the preliminary challenge, even if it is unwelcome by the majority at the time. Then if truth is on their side, the explanation will eventually supplant the older, majority paradigm. So it is an exciting and exhilarating time to be alive.

I write for several groups of people, particularly for the many who over the last 150 years have been persuaded that a biblical view of creation is not compatible with science. It is a most difficult subject, but I suggest that they take another critical look. It is possible to maintain scientific integrity and believe in a young earth, even if much is still wrapped in mystery. I would argue that it's not the best time to reach firm conclusions about what's out there, no matter what 'pop scientists' tell us on the television.

And also it is written for honest atheists who have discarded the old religion on intellectual grounds, that they may yet find it is a better option to have faith in a Creator whose knowledge is infinitely greater than our own [1].

PART ONE

A CHANCE MEETING?

1

THE 727 LIFTED effortlessly into the sky and Jon Le Var's small island home receded into the blue haze. After the vacation, he was leaving his idyllic Jersey, that British paradise island off the coast of Normandy, and was returning to his university in Scotland. It was an unexpected bonus to have such a companion beside him. He first met Sophie only a few days before and it seemed a remarkable stroke of good fortune that this lovely girl was travelling with him to Edinburgh to complete her final year of medical studies.

"How do you like Jersey? " he asked.

"The hospital work has been fascinating - so many chances to operate - I've never done so much cutting before."

"And the island?"

"Great" she said.

"I wish I could have seen more."

Jon smiled. "You must come back again. I'll show you around."

There was an awkward silence as Sophie flipped through the pages of the in-flight magazine. He had met Sophie at the Accident and

Emergency department after spraining his ankle. She was tall, blue-eyed, with fair hair and had a gentle smile. He knew it was her, even from a distance across the airport hall. When he realised they were both on the same flight back to Scotland, it took only a little persuasion at the desk to secure the seat next to her.

The Jersey sunshine had given his strong face a weather-beaten appearance. He was twenty two and at ease with himself.

"What course are you doing?" she asked.

"Geology. Not sure what I'll do with it, but it's a great subject."

She was a good listener and Jon thought she was really interested. He needed no encouragement to explain how this earth science was his first-love. His interest had started because of his island home, with its little valleys, outcrops of granite, sandy beaches and mysterious caves. He spoke of the island's history, its archaeology, and how he had become fascinated by this ancient legacy left by the flow of the long ages of time. He cast a sideways glance to see if he had lost her.

"How come we never met in Edinburgh?"

"I guess we move in different circles."

"Mine's geology and rugby. Yours?"

"Medicine and more medicine."

Twenty minutes into the flight they had crossed the south coast of England and Sophie shared her story. She had spent a few weeks getting some surgical experience in Jersey's busy hospital. The local over-worked medics were pleased to have an extra pair of hands in those early summer months when the island's population was beginning to explode with holidaymakers.

"All that theory of medicine I've been cramming into my head in Edinburgh is at last beginning to make sense - I just want to pass the finals and be a real doctor."

They fastened their seat belts for touch-down, shared addresses and Jon smiled.

THE SYRIAN DESERT

2

THE SUN HAD SET two hours ago, and the Syrian desert was still radiating the heat of the day as Mohammed Al-Harty left his Land Rover and walked bare foot into the dunes. The moon was yet to rise. The sky was full of stars with the constellations sparkling brightly in the pitch black. Way beyond were galaxies sending light from the far distant past. He lay on the sand gazing into the heavens. It was so quiet, so dark and majestic. Who had planned, designed and created all that? Or was it an accident of time and chance?

Mohammed was alone with his thoughts. There was Orion, described by the ancients more than three thousand years ago. And somewhere in that constellation another man-made star was sweeping across the sky. It was so small that it was invisible to his naked eye, but it was up there, and he - Mohammed and his team - was responsible. It was only a speck of dust in the infinite cosmos, but significant for all that.

Mohammed was exhausted. Two decades of research was taking its toll. He had been working hours that no one else knew existed. Day and night, seven days a week with no holidays. He had sacrificed so much - his energy, his career and even taking a wife - and now you'd expect that this satellite in space would have made him the happiest man on earth. Why did he have such a sense of foreboding?

Was it his imagination, was he being watched - followed ? Perhaps this was the burn-out his friends had predicted. He was cracking under the strain of too much work. Why should anyone follow him? Out here in the desert he could usually unwind. His grandfather had slept on these sands, and here too he would spend the night.

It might have been an hour that Mohammed lay half asleep on the sand, his troubled thoughts returning like a bad dream. It might only have been for a few minutes, but when a silent shadow crossed his face he jerked violently to his senses. The three men bundled him roughly into their four wheel drive, ignoring his questions.

REVISION

3

JON LIVED in the Old Town, the haunt of druggies and kids with pink hair and spikes through their nose. Sometimes he returned to Edinburgh with a feeling of despair, trudging up the three flights of stairs to his place, feeling very much alone - no soul-mate, no dog, no cat, no goldfish.

But this time it was different. It was truly a festival city. There was a spring in his step and he was singing as he opened the door to his top floor flat. This time he had enjoyed his return to Edinburgh. Had he talked too much? At least Sophie had given him her address. That was worth a song. He reached for a beer, put on some jazz and heard the shrill phone.

"Oh Phil. Great to know you're back. I've just got in."

Phil was his best mate, a muscular highlander. They played rugby together, climbed in the Highlands, and had both received respectable grades throughout their three-year geology course. Now the finals were approaching.

" No Phil, I never do enough work at home. But I'll be ready by the big day."

" I know, it's next week. Can we get together to do some mock orals?"

EDINBURGH - A FESTIVAL CITY

"Right, Wednesday for revision."

"Phil - I've something to tell you. I met someone on the plane."

Phil and Jon's revision was unconventional. They liked to meet in the luxury of the Atholl Hotel on Princess Street. For the price of a large pot of coffee, they could spend two luxurious hours in a quiet corner of the lounge reclining in soft leather chairs. They had a theory that the mind works best when the body is comfortable. It was a better option than a cold bachelor flat.

It was Wednesday night. For the first hour they fired questions at each other, some that might come up in the final, and they both felt quietly confident about their subject. Phil knew that his friend was bright and he expected him to do well in the examination even without much revision.

"The trouble with you Jon is that you can remember everything you read. We lesser mortals have to work and you just sail through."

"You're OK Phil. You're focused enough. I know you'll do well."

They got to talking about Sophie. Jon had never had a serious girl friend - no steady item - so this was news.

"She's tremendous Phil. She'd turn the head of any man from seventeen to seventy. She has looks, and is a really nice person. And she's given me her number."

"What did you talk about on the flight over?"

Jon confessed he might have talked too much. Had he been carried away in his enthusiasm for rocks and archaeology?

"You'll have to get off that single track Jon. If geology doesn't put her off I guess you've made it."

He was not sure whether she would see him again. Should he test the water?

CHINA

4

BEIJING IS ALWAYS HOT and sticky in August. Li Zhou wiped two fat sweaty palms across his blue Mao jacket and looked into the faces of the Grand Committee of Public Affairs. He remembered the times when the roles were changed, when he had been confidently sitting on the other side of the table. But now he was in the wrong chair and he was terrified. Inquisitor turned defendant - victim would be more correct. They wanted to know how he the Governor, could have let the situation in Xinjang get so desperately out of hand.

They looked in disdain as Li Zhou shuffled in his chair. His pronounced stoutness was uncommon in China, suggesting a life of ease. It made sitting at the table particularly uncomfortable. He was flanked by two young guards standing impassively beside him. In front were the stony faces of fifteen party members. They demanded an explanation.

"Urumqi in turmoil. We had to send in the army and even some of the military have deserted. Five thousand dead in the streets. How could the governor of the province allow such unrest?"

"A disgrace to the nation, to the party and to the beloved memory of Mao."

He stumbled for words to confess that the separatists had surfaced unexpectedly into the public domain. His police and the security bureau knew of an underground ferment, but they had been unaware of the size of the rebellion. The complex network of informers had failed to identify the magnitude of the problem. He could only plead forgiveness for so disgracing the name of the party.

" I have no worthy explanation and humbly accept your verdict."

They quietly shuffled the papers around, until the muscle bound chairman suddenly startled the committee by thumping the polished table with his heavy fist. Li Zhou saw a flash of red in his angry eyes. Li Zhou pushed back his chair and stood to attention to hear his fate. His shirt was sweat drenched, and was sticking to his back, and he would have liked to wipe his brow, but he stood motionless.

"Comrades. Li Zhou has shamed our great movement. He has confessed to allowing unworthy elements and insurgents to disturb the security of this important province of the People's Republic."

He looked intently at the prisoner.

"There is no alternative. Li Zhou, you are discredited before your friends, your people and the Party."

He should have know that those with authority also carry great responsibility.

"You will be taken from this place to the penal reform institution at Shi He Ze to serve a minimum period of twenty years. May you learn from the error of your ways."

With bowed head and a pounding heart he meekly shuffled after the guards. He knew he was not to blame for the unrest, but someone had to pay the price and he was the wrong man, in the wrong place, at the wrong time. How could anyone have recognised the signs? Would it have been different if he had been more brutal with the minorities, restricted more of their freedoms and prohibited all public gatherings? He had no way of knowing, but his future was bleak. Five hours by plane, and then a long ride into the Gobi desert. His feet and hands were manacled, chaffing at his delicate skin as the prison van jerked and swayed over the rough road. Such conditions were humiliating for a leader softened by the luxury of previous days. What new terrors awaited him?

FIRST DATE

5

THEY MET FOR a pizza lunch at Di Marco, a little Italian Restaurant behind the medical school. It had the familiar hum of noisy students, heightened by the anxiety of many who were about to sit their finals. Jon rested on his elbows. He looked across the table and knew again that Sophie was some-one special.

"Busy morning?"

"The usual ward round on twenty three with Prof and his team. And you?"

Jon had been in the library preparing for the exams.

"Steady revision. But I've put away the books. I'm getting saturated. My head's so full of geology."

He was unusually nervous about the coming examination.

"I know what I'm expected to say in the orals Sophie, and hope it's enough to pass. But its not just being sure of the facts, its the opinions - the theories. There's so much I'm not sure about. The problem is that I don't know whether I believe all that the lecturers tell me. I hope I won't appear too uncertain and get pushed into a corner, talking about unorthodox views."

She didn't understand. She thought that Geology was an exact science.

Their conversation turned to the recent summer holidays - the places where Jon would have taken her if only they had met earlier. He told her that maybe one day he would write something about the geology of his island home - Jersey.

"A book or a thesis Jon?"

He looked at her to see if this was the time to expand. Perhaps not. She was glancing at her watch.

" Later" he said. "You'll have to get back to the Infirmary."

She wished him well for the big day, and promised to phone and see how he got on.

The next evening Sophie was relaxing after a busy day, and she was sitting in her flat listening to Beethoven's sixth and thinking about the big change in her life. She knew there was something going for her and Jon. There was a certain chemistry between them. The way he had looked at her, and walked her slowly back to the Infirmary. Clearly he liked her a lot, and it was mutual. She was an unusual girl, perhaps rather old-fashioned. She had avoided many previous relationships because she was confident that destiny would eventually introduce her to the right man. Was this the moment?

They were both skating over the surface. She had volunteered so little about herself. She had not told him that she had a bigger vision than practising medicine in the affluent west. That one day she would like to set up a hospital in Central Africa. This would affect any lasting relationship and it might be better not to start something that would become painful. But she had promised to phone him and she punched in the number.

"Jon. How did it go?"

"Hi Sophie. Thanks. Could have been worse, but I might have blown it. Can we talk?"

"We are talking Jon."

"No, somewhere in town for a coffee."

"I'm tied up for a couple of days."

Sophie knew he was a hill walker and suggested a climb over the Pentlands.

They made a date for the weekend.

It would be a long two days' wait for both of them.

THE CASUALTY

6

THE BORDER BETWEEN Iraq and Syria is only a thin line on the map. But the desert recognises no such boundary. Tracks east and west follow the fertile crescent, the historic route pounded by nomads and their camels from ancient time. Abraham and his sons had followed this route, and the Assyrian armies, Semitic captives, Cyrus, Alexander, and the Roman legions. Today sometimes on foot, often by camel train, and more frequently hanging precariously on to lumbering trucks, travellers still follow these desert roads - scorched by the beating sun. Flat sand stretches to the horizon and beyond. Only an occasional cluster of palm trees breaks the monotony. Sometimes the track is a straight tar road rutted with potholes, a glimmering mirage in the unbearable heat. Sometimes it is an uncharted path, half obliterated by shifting sand.

The small caravan was moving slowly towards Palmyra, men and camels plodding in single file. The leader stirred and raised his head to peer through the shimmering haze. Ahead was a bundle of rags - perhaps it was something of value dropped by a previous traveller. The caravan stopped - a few men dismounted - it was only a worthless corpse.

On this border road the previous night Mohammed Al Harty had been thrown from a fast moving car. The dirt had ripped his clothes and burnt into his skin when he rolled into the dry ditch. He had come to rest, literally biting the dust. Barely conscious he had heard the car reverse, and felt the searing pain of a heavy foot bursting into his abdomen. Another blow had wrenched his spine, and then - darkness.

Now in the heat of the midday sun his bloodied flesh was being eaten by flies. What was left would be for the carrion and the desert foxes. Should a border patrol pass and there were few, this would be recorded as another unfortunate hit-and-run incident, or perhaps a wayside robbery. Questions are not asked about casualties in this remote part of the Syrian desert.

The caravan was about to move on when the corpse stirred. There was just a suggestion of life and that could mean a reward. The bruised bundle was lifted onto the back of a camel, packed with the baggage and taken slowly and without ceremony into Palmyra.

PRISON IN SHI HE ZE

7

THE OUTSIDE WORLD has no idea what life is like in a Chinese jail. There are no visitors to describe the scene. And for many inmates it is a one way journey. A thousand prisoners are executed every month. Some hang themselves. Others have a fatal 'heart attack' with no explanation for the marks around the throat. Some sink into silent despair. Many succumb to infectious diseases. All are severely malnourished, and often physically crippled for life. Those who survive against the odds, find the experience too painful to share.

Li Zhou had no illusions about what was awaiting him. His fellow inmates would know that he had been responsible for incarcerating others in this very place of slow death. He had been an ascending star in the Party, a child of the cultural revolution and he was still only in his early 40's. But this could be the end of him. He would be a fortunate man to return to the outside world.

The metal gates of Wusu prison swung heavily behind him, and the van jolted to a halt in the prison courtyard. His grim-faced guards pushed him from the cramped van. Through the glare of the low afternoon sunshine he noted a group of sullen prisoners, their legs chained together for the hour of exercise. They gave him no second glance. Jailers and inmates would know his story soon enough, and it would not take long for prisoners and guards alike to take their revenge on this disgraced party leader. But for now he was thankful to stretch his limbs and breathe the cold fresh air sweeping across the high plateau of north-west China.

He stood briefly in the bright sunshine, shifting his weight from foot to foot, and it was equally uncomfortable on each. Then two guards gripped his arms tightly and hurried him indoors, down a dark concrete corridor where on each side, prisoners were caged like rats. He met a foul fetid stench and heard the curses of angry men, until he was rudely pushed into his cell 514 - his new home - six by four and shared with five others. No bed, not even enough room for them all to lie down at night - one dirty urinal bucket - how long could he live like this? For now he squatted in his small allotted space, trying to marshall his thoughts.. Survive he would. Li Zhou would fight the system and with half a chance he'd live.

For two days, he avoided eye contact with the other prisoners, but in this crowded cell tempers were volatile. Li Zhou had been snoring too loudly. It was time for his initiation into the fraternity. He endured a severe beating, and lost two teeth. His left eye was swollen shut, his jaw was badly bruised, for several days drinking was a great effort because of his swollen lips, and the crunching noise he could hear when he tried to open his mouth suggested that he'd broken some bones in his face. In any civilised place, he'd have been hospitalised, but this was a Chinese prison.

For twenty three hours a day he sat silently in the far corner of his cell. The brief daily round of exercise in the outside yard was small relief, but it loosened his stiff limbs, and as the days turned into weeks he slowly adapted to life in a Chinese jail. What if food was scarce - didn't he need to loose some weight? He endured the verbal and physical abuse, and he kept sane by quoting to himself the sayings of Mao. He lived in his own world and he made some plans. The schemer that he was, he of all people knew that any system could be used to advantage.

Li Zhou was slowly accepted. He was not without skills and cell 514 became the hub of a lucrative business, in spite of - or because of - the dreadful conditions. He was writing letters for his jailers and fellow inmates at a price, and he became the prison adviser on Chinese law.

During the long monotonous months, he developed a fermenting hatred for those who had put him in prison. Not the Party because they had been correct to punish him. But the separatists, the militant Muslims and those religious groups that were rising in Xinjang. It was always in his mind - this obsessional hatred for the people that he had not been able to control. They were responsible. For the good of China they should be ruthlessly suppressed. Resentment kept him alive.

OVER THE PENTLANDS

8

JON ALWAYS ENJOYED a trek over the Pentland hills, and it was great to have Sophie with him. They left the grassy fields, climbed into the heather and up the steep hill-path getting an ever widening view of Lothian. They stood for a moment looking back at the city, beyond to the waters of the Forth and across to the Kingdom of Fife. The sharp westerly wind put a glow into Sophie's cheeks.

"Jon it's magnificent."

The Castle was in the middle distance, crowning a city of ancient spires and buildings, enough to stir the heart of anyone with a feel for history. This had been the cradle of the Scottish Enlightenment, when two hundred years ago Edinburgh was the centre of a great intellectual movement. This was the city where Simpson discovered anaesthetics, where Lister opened the door for aseptic surgery. Here lived Robert Burns and Sir Walter Scott, Adam Smith and James Watt.

For Jon, this city was the womb of modern geology. He told Sophie about the farmer James Hutton, whose geological paper to the first meeting of the Royal Society of Edinburgh in 1783 gave a new understanding to earth science, and of the orator Charles Lyell who followed him some decades later.

"Hutton and Lyell totally changed the scene of geology."

"Okay. Tell me."

"They claimed that the mountains rise and fall with 'imperceptible slowness'. They said that the same forces at work today have always been the same, and so this planet must be very, very old. They called it 'uniformitarianism'."

Sophie pointed to the silhouetted castle that had stood for a thousand years on a piece of granite deposited from a previous Ice age. Jon said it was a relative newcomer to the scene when thinking of the 2,000 million year old Grampians over the northern horizon.

Uniformitarianism
Hutton and Lyell changed the science of geology,
with their views on pure 'uniformitarianism'
knocking the old establishment off its ecclesiastical perch [2].

He let her take the lead, stepping over boulders and squeezing through a gap in the wall, until they finally made the summit.

"Let's sit for a minute. What about the holy books, Jon?"

He laughed. "The old biblical ideas you mean? A young earth and 'catastrophism' - Noah's flood and all that? Celestial thunderbolts? That was once and for all settled by Hutton and Lyell. Lyell took on the religious establishment in the 19th century, and he won the day. He was so persuasive. He'd been a lawyer and was a great communicator."

He looked at Sophie's questioning expression. "You're not one of those are you? Okay Sophie, there have always been some wildcards who don't go with uniformitarianism, who say it's unlikely that the forces shaping the planet have always been the same. They look at the rocks and see signs of major catastrophes in earlier times. At the far end are those fundamentalists who think the planet is only a few thousand years old because the Bible say so."

"What about you?" she asked.

"Difficult question. It's not quite so straight forward. There are more of us now who stand somewhere on the middle ground. It's OK for geologists today to say that there have been slow steady changes, with sedimentary deposits and slow erosion, interrupted by the occasional catastrophe. I think you'll find me there". He smiled at her. "I'm still working on it. We still live in the powerful shadow of Hutton and Lyell."

"How old is the earth then"? she asked. "Doesn't radiometric dating say the earth is very old?"

"We say 4.5 billion years old, but that's based on assumptions, and it might be less than we think."

They walked down the south side of the mountain range towards Biggar, and Sophie wondered if there was something else Jon was trying to share.

"Why did you read Geology Jon?" and he hesitated.

"It's such a long story. Are you a good listener?"

"Try me."

"Let's get to the Inn down there at the Nine Mile Burn."

They sat toasting their feet by the fire in the village Inn and enjoyed a large plate of ham and eggs. He told her about his plans for a doctorate. He also told her about the beautiful Island of Jersey. And his home - the little white-washed house sheltered in the westerly bay of St Ouen's - how it surveyed that wonderful five mile sweep of sand, stretching from Corbiere in the south to the rocky Grosnez in the north west. He described the barren raised beach, with the ever changing Atlantic ocean spraying salt over their six acres, and for all that, the land still produced an excellent yearly crop of sprouts and potatoes. He loved his home and she was a good listener.

He showed her how the island sits squarely on an outcrop of granite - nine miles by five - a mass of rock heaved up from the depths of the earth. It had weathered the centuries, the foaming winter oceans and the scorching days of summer. He balanced the now empty oval plate in his hand.

"The whole island tilts gently to face the sun like this" he said. "The cliffs of the north lifting high from the surging English channel, whilst the southerly sandy bays slope gently into the southern sea."

He showed her how from north to south the land is ribbed by small river valleys, with a rich topsoil supporting lush vegetation and pleasing both the farmers and their lazy Jersey cows. He described the abundance of scented flowers, splashing brilliant colours across the heath, the busy insect life, the many varieties of birds and small hedgerow mammals which make Jersey a paradise.

"When you're at home you must just want to soak up the sun and dream" she said.

"I've done my dreaming Sophie. I'd love to share them with you."

She gave him a listening ear. "On you go."

"I'm asking a question that I don't know how to answer. I'm trying to understand the mystery of 'time' - how we measure it - the whole sweep of time - starting with the deep time of the early universe, to the time of the earth's beginning, then the fossil palaeontology time, and when man first stepped on to this planet, to the more recent and present time. The stars in the sky, the rocks under our feet, the busy creatures swarming over the earth are begging us to ask questions about time. And they are not unwilling to share their secrets. The world of science claims to knows the answer - got it sussed - but I'm not so sure".

"Tell me more Jon."

Instead he asked Sophie about her family on the Pennines, and her brother Andrew reading theology in Aberdeen and they took the bus back to town.

"I've a confession to make" she said.

"Next week I go to Damascus."

THE RUINS OF PALMYRA

9

PALMYRA IS A LONELY desert outpost, the ghostly ruins of a once famous Roman city, now standing silently in the Syrian wilderness. It lies on the ancient trade-route from Damascus to Iraq and is still a stopping place for caravans plying their way to the Euphrates River.

Ten square kilometres of stones are scorched white by the merciless heat of the burning sun, and are being slowly eroded by the blistering wind. There are temples dedicated to the pagan gods, including the great Temple of Bel (Baal), and others bear the marks of the Emperor Constantine who turned them into Christian churches. A long colonnaded paved street leads down to Tetrapylon, with idols waiting hopefully for oblations, and silent statues speaking of long forgotten heroes. Theatres, forums and ancient baths which were once thronged by massive crowds, still boast of the mighty Roman Empire - with their echoes of slavery, cruelty, resistance and blood.

Today a small Arab population lives humbly in the shadow of these ancient ruins, waiting only to serve the passing traveller, or the occasional lucrative car load of western tourists who come to admire this ancient city, to walk the stone streets, drink ice-cold fruit juice and sport their Soni camcorders.

Midsummer, and the earth was turning slowly on its diurnal course. This was an other good day for Palmyra. A load of French tourists had come to spend their dollars. They needed a guide. He'd keep the foreigners in the sun until they asked for lots of drinks to slake their thirst. And they'd buy books, cards and souvenirs to take home.

By early afternoon this weary and rather dusty group of tourists was ready to return to their air conditioned limousine. They sat in the shadow of the Temple of Baalshamin, and watched a camel train drifting along the main avenue into town. It was carrying a semi-conscious Mohammed Al Harty.

The Arab merchants had found nothing of value in the wounded man's pockets, but from the cut of his clothes they knew that he was not without means. Allah might yet reward them. So they approached the curious French party and deposited their burden.

"Please take it to hospital in Damascus. If it lives we come in some days."

They might all have wished him dead - French and Arab alike - but when there was some life - what could they do but accept this unwelcome burden.

CELL MATE

10

LI ZHOU CHALKED UP his first six months in jail, and began to notice an unusual cell mate who came from his own home-city of Urumqi. This young man - Fang - had been a ring-leader of a minority group trying to overthrow the government. A capital offence, and he would be invited to the execution yard any day. He deserved it.

Li Zhou despised this emaciated weak-minded youth, not only because of his offence, but also because he chose to share his scarce food with an sick man.

"Let him die" said Li Zhou. "More room for the rest of us."

But he saw Fang enfolding this man in his arms, a man who was dying of dysentery - an unpleasant business! What madness to care for a complete stranger when Fang had no future of his own.

Although he had an intense hatred for Fang, he detected an opportunity. A feigned friendship might be useful.

"Tell me about your friends. It might get you a reprieve. Stop you being a kidney donor!"

But there was only silence. Fang seemed to prefer sitting with his eyes closed.

Then just before they came to prepare Fang for execution - before they could check his blood group for compatibility and for organ 'donation' - Fang caught the same bug and went steeply down-hill. He was going to cheat the executioner, and two poor guys needing kidneys would have to wait a bit longer. He died in a fevered sweat with his head on Li Zhou's knee, sharing in a wild delirium some very useful names and meeting places.

It was time to write to the Party in Beijing expressing his remorse, his plans for reform, and his new information and ideas which if adopted could hurt the enemies of the Party in Xinjang. He could still serve China. No one knew the underworld of north-west China better than he. Maybe his masters in Beijing could still find use for a disgraced party leader?

Perhaps they would listen to him. Such news in Beijing might yet restore the old Party leader.

UNREST IN URUMQI

11

URUMQI WAS COMING to the boil. The students were camping in People's Square and marching daily to the City Hall. They were throwing rocks and petrol bombs. Cars and buses were burning, covering the centre of the city in a dark cloud. The streets were barricaded, and the authorities were abused by uncouth shouting through loud hailers. The number of insurgents was increasing daily.

It was worse than Tianenman Square except that thankfully the world's press were not invited. Foreigners had been banned from Xinjang for months, and few Chinese were permitted to travel to this remote part of the north-west. Beijing was sullenly trying to contain the unrest, but locally they had lost face. It was totally out of hand, and the Leaders were in despair.

If the news were to spread across China, how would the other minorities respond? What about Tibet and the south-west and the hopes for Taiwan? If this rebellion was not handled correctly, all Mao's sacrificial work, the Party's progress over 80 years, the new economic revival and their own positions would be destroyed.

They feared three - Militant Muslims, Falun Gong and perhaps most sinister of all, the underground Church.

The Muslims had made their home in the Gobi desert for centuries, and now in Xinjang they demanded separatism. Hatred for the Han ran deep. Every Muslim knew of the ethnic cleansing of the 50's, with a mismanaged economy, famine and epidemics, and they remembered the million Chinese military and their families who had been relocated to this bleak outpost beyond the Great Wall. Enough was enough. Radicals from the Uygur ethnic minority had sophisticated weapons. They were carrying out terrorist bomb attacks and were murdering government officials in their beds. The Muslims of Xinjang clamoured for self-rule.

Falun Gong was a quasi-religious sect with a membership of 100 million across China. They railed against homosexuality, rock music, drugs and argued that science was responsible for much of the world's evils. The Party vowed to wipe them out but the more they were oppressed, the more they seemed to prosper. They were particularly powerful in the north-west with thousands of their members now joining the Muslims and meeting in Urumqi's People's Square where they practised their breathing exercises and protested about police brutality.

The Christian movement was the most dangerous of all, because it was underground. Throughout China, the Christians were closely regulated in the Three Self Church - a masterpiece of Mao's thinking. The Party controlled the pastors, and the quota of baptisms was limited by law.

But there was an underground movement that was growing exponentially, in spite of enforced closure of 10,000 unregistered churches and meeting halls. These 'believers' met illegally and they inflamed the passion for revolution. Their religion was not only capturing the minds of simple Chinese and Minority people, the old and the poor, but was deceiving a growing number of students and intelligentsia.

Perhaps across China there were over 100 million Christians. Although Communist dogma was taught every day in the schools, and the students learnt about Darwin and modern science - although religion was systematically ridiculed - increasing numbers of intelligent people were attracted to this old superstition. How could these people be so confident? Didn't they know the modern scientists said the whole universe was an accident. Where was their logic [3]?

In Xinjang these Christians ignored all authority. There was talk of thousands meeting secretly in schools, universities, hospitals and factories. This underground church could not be easily identified. It disappeared like the morning dew when they looked for it. Their followers had new, secret names. They for ever moved the place and the time of their meetings. They communicated with the West by fax and electronic-mail. And if any were caught, they only became martyrs and the movement thrived on persecution. The treacherous underground church was the biggest threat of all.

This triad made Xinjang a tinder bowl that could ignite the rest of China. With only 60 million members of the Chinese Communist Party trying to control the whole country, Beijing was understandably concerned. Here was a crisis that needed a cool head and a firm hand.

The leaders pondered Li Zhou's letter and decided to re-call the disgraced leader.

"A poor man gives thanks even for a grasshopper" said Confucius.

THE MILITARY HOSPITAL

12

THE FRENCH TOURISTS DEPOSITED Mohammed at the Damascus City Hospital, but when it was realised that this had been a bungled assassination - a victim thrown out of Iraq's back door and left for dead on the border - the Army was informed.

He was quickly taken to the Military Hospital, where the theatre lights burnt late into the night. Skilfully a nail was rodded through the middle of the broken femur with locking screws at either end. The tibia was a more difficult problem because the open wound had to be washed, cleaned and excised. It was left open to discharge its germs, and the bones were fixed together with pins and an external appliance. The spine had been badly bruised by savage kicks to his back, but the cord was intact. He was fortunate that the skull fracture was at the thickest part at the back of the cranium. If the blow had been to the side of the head, it would have scrambled his brain.

The general looked at him thoughtfully from the foot of the bed - stable condition, concussion and several broken bones.

"The body's a remarkable contraption" he said to no-one in particular. "It can die from a bee-sting or survive multiple trauma. This man is a survivor."

They filled him with antibiotics, and in the following days, gradually nursed him back towards health. Maybe he would have a useful story to tell.

Mohammed kept drifting in and out of consciousness, spending most of his time in a thick fog. He recovered his senses slowly and stared vacantly at the ceiling.

Why was he in a Military Hospital in Damascus? Who had tried to kill him in the Syrian Desert? Had his little secret been uncovered? Why were the Military asking such awkward questions? He feigned amnesia to gain more time.

"Where are you from? Who hit you?" they asked.

"I never saw it," he said rubbing his chin, and that was true. They made little sense of his rambling words, his false name and phoney Baghdad address, but his interrogators returned day after day. He could not deceive them for ever, and they would soon loose patience.

SOPHIE'S ELECTIVE

13

A COLD EAST WIND was blowing through Edinburgh Airport. It was the start of Sophie's journey to Damascus. The farewell was all too brief.

"Promise to write" Jon said.

"Course. There'll be lots to tell you. "

"Be good."

They laughed and then became quiet as the both realised how much they would miss each other. Their eyes locked and their fingers intertwined.

"I'll phone on Wednesday. Tell me the exam results."

There was a sudden passionate embrace that they both would remember through the long lonely weeks.

Four hours later it was twenty degrees warmer and she was guided through the chaotic "arrival hall" of the Damascus airport by a friendly Arab who couldn't speak a word of English. The Military had sent an official car and driver, and Sophie was clearly being treated as a VIP. At the hospital it was basic accommodation, but air-conditioned and clean and there were fresh flowers and a bowl of fruit in her room.

She was opening her luggage when General Kapta the Hospital Director swept through the door. He had a square smiling face, a small moustache, and his hair was half gone with the other half greying with age. He exuded authority. He promised her generous Arab hospitality.

"Welcome Dr Sophie. I have told your Prof - my very good friend - that we'll look after you well, and we'll not work you too hard!" His bushy eyebrows rose every time he completed a statement.

"There is much for you to see in our country. My daughter Anita will take you to the Old City tomorrow. Any problems you speak to me. Now you rest from your long journey." This man seemed too amiable a character to be a Syrian General.

She lay on the bed and reached to the bedside table. There was Jon's letter that she had read on the plane. She smiled. Three pages of tight script about how much he was going to miss her! It was reciprocal. When she was tucked up in bed, she opened the letter again and started to read. There were a lot of things a young man says to a girl he loves, and she would treasure this for a long time.

He was also envious of her opportunity to visit Damascus, one of the oldest cities in the world. He reminded her that it had been the hub of a vast commercial network with far-flung lines of caravan trade reaching into north Syria, Mesopotamia, Palestine, Persia and Arabia.

"The Greeks and Romans will have left their mark. Most people think that early civilisation is so far back in time that it's beyond their imagination - it's unreal. But be sure to see the Old City, and get a time perspective. Early Damascus - only a couple of thousand years ago - it's not really so distant."

Damascus would be fun. She turned over and dropped into a deep sleep.

THE OLD CITY

14

SOPHIE WAS AN HONOURED guest. Here she was on a six week elective placement sent by her Prof to learn some medicine and she was being treated like a member of the family. She sensed that because of her boss - a regular examiner at the Damascus medical school - she was receiving unaccustomed respect. She was still surprised that in this Arab country, a woman could be made so welcome.

The General's daughter Anita was slim and dark, with long waves of black hair. She was particularly open and friendly, and took Sophie into town. The colourful souk was bewildering with its mysterious labyrinth of dark alleyways and sweat shops. Merchants sold their spices, gold, leather, brass and wood carvings. Arab men eyed the two girls lazily as they gathered in drowsy groups to smoke their long pipes in the cool of the late afternoon.

"Do you still have the street called 'Straight'?" she said.

"It's only a stone throw away."

And there she was, on the very colonnaded street that Saint Paul walked 2000 years ago. The mile long bazaar, still cutting through the heart of old city of Damascus was every bit as busy and noisy as she imagined it to have been when Ananias was sent down it to find Paul who had been blinded by his vision of Christ. Here he restored Paul's sight. The ancient walls and the old gates were standing as she imagined them in New Testament times, and she took lots of photos.

Sophie thought about Jon's letter and the perspective of "time". Here was archaeology and artefacts going back two millennia - no more than 60 generations. And this was a blink of the eye, if Jon was right about the age of the planet.

"Come, I must show you something" said Anita.

She stooped low to step over the threshold into the shadows of a first century church of Ananias, and was met by a Franciscan friar named Brother Joe with liquorice gum lodged permanently in his mouth, who told her in a Chicago drawl -

"This is it lady. St Paul - great saint."

In spite of, or maybe because of his celibacy, Brother Joe liked the innocent company of pretty girls, and he offered to show them every corner of the ancient church. This genial priest readily responded to Sophie's questions.

"There's so much I could tell you Ma'am. This is where it all began."

They listened to his story, and he had the full attention of two wide-eyed girls.

"This place is a store house of antiquities. Where you from?"

No. He'd never been to UK.

They relaxed on low chairs, drank ice cold tea, and stabbed at a few sticky dates that Brother Joe had put on a crazy white plate, as he enthused about this important little place in Christendom. Anita had not met anyone like this brown robed priest before with his furry teeth. He looked at her and went straight for the jugular.

"You're a Moslem Anita. Forgive me - but the great thing about our faith is that the Christian God is a God of love. No word for love in the

Koran. The Lord Jesus told us to love God with all our hearts - then love one another, our Christian brothers and sisters - love our neighbours, that's my Muslim friends - and hardest of all He said we must love our enemies."

He carried on chewing his liquorice, and Anita was not slow to respond.

"How can anyone do that?"

"The Lord rose from the dead to make it possible."

Sophie wondered about his direct approach, but Anita was listening.

"Your faith agrees with ours about the virgin birth of Jesus, but Islam can't accept He died and rose again from the dead. Saint Paul had the same problem and that's the important message of this little chapel. The great apostle came to Damascus raging with fury that so many people were saying that Jesus had risen from the dead, and he was going to arrest believers like Ananias."

Brother Joe bent down and touched the dust on the floor. This priest believed what he said.

"What then Brother Joe?" But he didn't need encouragement.

"Saint Paul met the Lord on the road outside, and he was struck blind by a glorious, dazzling light. They led him in through these gates and Ananias found him, prayed with him, put his loving hands on him, and said 'Brother Saul, the Lord - Jesus, has sent me so that you can see again.' He got back his sight and became the greatest preacher of all time."

He got up from his seat.

"Come. Let me show you something."

He led them down a small flight of stairs, unlocked a heavy door which creaked on its old hinges, wiped away some fossilised cobwebs, and took them to a far corner where there was a large cabinet. He brought out a box wrapped in layers of cloth, and putting it on a table he lifted the lid. They gazed at the remnants of an old wooden basket.

He looked at them with bright eyes.

DAMASCUS CITY - Gateway to Straight Street

"When Paul met the Lord, and had his sight miraculously restored, he began to preach right away. It was mighty dangerous. The Jews here were furious and ...... he pulled a Bible out of his cassock pocket, and started to read aloud.

> 'In Damascus the governor under King Aretas had the
> city of the Damascenes guarded in order to arrest me.
> But I was lowered in a basket from a window in the wall
> and slipped through their hands.'

That's what Saint Paul says in second Corinthians chapter eleven and verses 32 and 33" and he shut his book.

The three of them looked again at the basket in Brother Joe's old box.

"How can you be so sure?" asked Sophie. She was sorry to be doubtful, because Anita seemed convinced that Brother Joe was telling the truth. Brother Joe certainly believed that this was the very basket. But with Sophie's medical training, she needed proof.

He carefully wrapped up his treasure, and took them back up the stone stairs.

"This basket was hidden for centuries until I found it in the cellars last fall. There it was - with a fragment of papyrus - and we could read the words 'basket' and 'Saul' and now I'm waiting for carbon dating from the States."

Sophie told him about Jon's interest in geology and measuring the age of rocks.

"Jon says there's a big margin of error on radiometric dating. The results aren't very reliable."

"I know Sophie, but it's the best we have."

He thought for a while and then asked.

"Can your boyfriend carbon test some of this basket for me. The more results we get, the better."

Sophie knew that Jon would want to help, and she agreed to take a small sample back to Scotland. She hoped this priest wouldn't be disappointed with the results.

Brother Joe looked at Anita.

"Do you know Anita, what was Paul's first job when he left Damascus?

He went first into Arabia - to the Arab people, and he was there for three years. This man was full of fire. The first people he preached to were Arabs. God loves the Arab people so much, and Paul preached to them first."

Anita's eyes were rather moist. She put some money in the gift box and they headed off into the busy street.

"What a fascinating man !"

She started to ply Sophie with questions.

They stopped, and Anita pointed above the city to the hills, where villages of Aramaic speaking people had been true to the Christian faith for two millennia.

Then looking at Sophie, "Can you get me a New Testament?"

MOHAMMED'S RECOVERY

15

MOHAMMED WAS AT LAST thinking clearly - enough to hate the boredom of his hospital bed, with the bedpans, the endless blood tests, relentless visits by the nurses at all hours and the serious chats with the doctors. They changed his dressings, and he could finally leave the constraints of his hospital bed. He stood up shakily, trying to balance on his crutches, and studied himself in the shaving mirror. He was not impressed. Bruises round his eyes, a long scar across his right cheek, healing abrasions, several days of stubble on his chin. It was not a pretty sight, but at least he was beginning to function again. Point the mirror to the ceiling and think again. Toothpaste on the brush - scrub.

The unravelling began. His research must be very important to the men who had tried to kill him, or to their masters. He had signed a secrecy agreement and honoured it. He had told no one the purpose of his work, not even his closest friends but his research must be dangerous material. Someone didn't trust him. They wanted him permanently silenced.

He thought about his recruitment by the Moscow Institute of

Physics in the 80's. He had been head-hunted because of his honours doctorate in optics, and they had promised him fifteen million dollars to create a research unit at the University of Baghdad. It was an offer no young scientist could refuse. The secrecy of the project presented no problem. Some of his best research had been plagiarised in the past, and he appreciated completing the project in private.

He had recruited a strong hand-picked team of electronic engineers, mathematicians and physicists to his department in Baghdad. And they worked in parallel with a team of space scientists in Moscow. His sponsors had insisted on being the bridge between Moscow and Baghdad, and he just got on with his job. It was a tremendous challenge to combine optics and electronics with the Russian Space Programme. Strange that his first brief meeting with the Russian team was at the satellite's launch.

The first prototype had been an immediate success. He monitored its orbit and picked up its reflected light perfectly. It was hailed as a triumph of Arab/Marxists co-operation - a new concept to convert reflected sunlight into night-time illumination for hundreds of cities. It had enormous economic potential. It was sustainable and could protect the earth's limited natural resources. This was the popular public message released to the world's press.

However there were more important objectives and he and his team had worked incessantly to produce the second satellite on time. The hardware on the ground had teething problems, but with a few modifications they soon had a perfect new satellite in orbit transmitting amazing signals. They could even see the number plates of the cars on the streets of London or New York, and there was much more - very much more.

Only a small group knew of their work, and this select team had been honoured by the Iraqi government and feasted in Moscow. It had been hailed as work that might cause a paradigm shift in science, and then when the research had so much promise, his masters fell out, the satellite was closed down and the data was impounded.

Working for government meant that he'd not been constrained by the academic's dictum 'publish or perish'. But now he had something good, it was irritating that he couldn't get it in print. Were these hopes and dreams the motive for eliminating him?

Then he thought of his small secret - the bank account in the Channel Islands and the software he had wisely deposited there, discs which summarised all the work he'd done in Baghdad, and a draft of the first two papers he would like to publish. True, it would be dangerous if his masters knew about it but they couldn't know. No one knew - but his lawyer.

Here in Damascus he was not sure if he was amongst friends or enemies. The military didn't know his identity. If they did, would they protect him or turn him over to the Iraqi authorities? It would be best not to wait for answers, but rather flee whilst he could. But without papers and money, where could he go?

He limped back to his bed taking care not to knock the external fixator, and there was a young English doctor waiting with a syringe.

"Mohammed."

"Ma'am" ?

"I'm Doctor Tristan - from the UK." She had an engaging smile.

"I'm not quite a doctor yet, but I hope to be in a few months. I'm a medical student on a work project here in Damascus."

"Good enough for me."

"Can you roll up your sleeve. I have to take some blood" She talked on to reassure him as she found the vein.

She could be his doctor any day.

"They say you had a serious accident, but are doing very well. This is to make sure the infection's cleared and that you've recovered from that loss of blood."

He looked intently at her young face, and wondered if he might ask her for help.

"Doctor Tristan. You are English. Could you do me a favour?"

FIRST CLASS DEGREE

16

JON JOINED A CROWD of anxious students gathering round the notice board to see the final ranking. At first he couldn't find his name, and when he did, he could hardly believe it. His was the first name - top in the graduating year. And Philip had done well with an upper second. They danced round the quadrangle with excitement.

"Unbelievable. We must celebrate Philip".

With high spirits they hurried to the tavern and found a quiet corner.

Philip took a long draught of his beer.

"I never thought I'd see this day Jon," he said with froth hanging on his upper lip. "I expected a 2.2. I knew you would do well. Congratulations Jon. First in the whole year and the gold medal to boot! What will your folks say? And Sophie ! Wait till she hears this".

Jon was really surprised because he had been rather argumentative in the oral. They must have been pushing him and no doubt they respected him for his views.

What he didn't know was that the professor had high hopes for Jon.

Here was a rare student who could look at things freshly and differently, someone with an unusual mind and 'a certain chutzpah'. He hoped he would go on for a PhD.

"It's too late to phone Sophie now."

He looked at his watch.

"It's midnight in Damascus. I'll try tomorrow."

"Where do you go from here Philip? BP will be offering you a job."

"You'll have to go for a doctorate Jon. Have you got the stomach for three more years?"

He wasn't sure, and he couldn't read the future.

LI ZHOU REINSTATED

17

THEY LISTENED to Li Zhou in silence and with some secret admiration. Was this the same man that sat before them a year ago, to whom they gave a one way ticket to prison? Then, he had been a failure - forty, fat and shabby. And now he was leaner and fitter, and telling Beijing how to solve their most difficult crisis since the unrest of '89. Some grasshopper! And so confident! He could have been a direct male-line descendent of Gengis Khan. And what he said made sense.

"I have vital information about the insurgents in Urumqi, and have a new plan to deal with them".

They drank tea and listened as he told them how he had tricked Fang.

"Fate plays strange games. I gained the confidence of my fellow inmates and learnt about many of their dangerous schemes. I've discovered a number of key meeting places, and the secret names of some of the leaders of this movement. If you would grant me the privilege of repaying the debt I owe to the People's Republic of China - I will certainly deal with those who are responsible for this unrest." He spread his hands in a meaningful gesture.

They studied this enthusiastic comrade. It might be a ruse to extricate himself from prison. But what other proposals were on the table? Not one.

They re-examined his personal file. Throughout his short career the record had been impeccable - a faultless meteoric rise until the recent troubles. His father had been on Mao's Long March. Surely that counted for something!

The chairman wiped his fat lips, and looked intently at Li Zhou. "Your wife is professor of Russian studies and Xi-xi your daughter is a faithful party member." They knew everything - his blood group and even his sexual perversions.

What was there to lose? Perhaps it would be good to show that the state could sometimes be lenient. And he might even be telling the truth!

They were pragmatists. "Li Zhou. The State is always benevolent to those who can reform - who can see the error of their ways. We value the service you and your family have given to the Party, and can overlook your recent mistakes. You will be reinstated to an important post - 'Deputy Mayor of Urumqi' with responsibility for Public Order and Religious Affairs. But we expect quick results from you that will justify our generous decision."

He walked from the room a free man - as free as any man can be in China.

PHONE CALL

18

THE SWITCHBOARD at the Military Hospital said they would give Sophie the message. And she returned Jon's call within the hour.

"Great to hear your voice. What news?"

"I'm through and so is Philip."

"What grade?"

"Guess."

"Wow. Tremendous Jon. Well done."

He asked about her.

"They're treating me like royalty. And the job's interesting."

"There's a guy recovering from multiple injuries asking if we can help him. It's a bit of a coincidence. He's from Iraq and now he can't get out of Syria. Says he's loads of money stashed away in Jersey."

"Wish I had."

"Put it there as a safe tax-haven, and wants us to withdraw some for him. He's got a problem Jon What do you think?"

Jon couldn't understand why the Arab couldn't remove the cash himself, but then he never understood international finance.

"Is it legal? Are there any risks Sophie?"

She told Jon that she'd be back in Scotland within the week and they'd discuss it then.

"Fancy a visit to Iraq?"

"What are you talking about Sophie? Has this guy offered you a holiday?"

"No Jon it's something else. Anita found me a church. She knew of one in the western suburbs and organised a driver."

Jon heard how she had gone to an old part of town with rather run-down Victorian-style houses. How she had been deposited on a leafy pavement outside a small traditional red-bricked church.

"I sat at the front with an old fellow who translated, because it was all in Arabic. I knew some of the hymns - at least their familiar tunes - and this guy kept whispering and explaining all through the sermon. It was really good Jon."

Jon understood that it meant a lot to her.

"The old pastor asked me back for a meal. They're collecting for a sister church in Baghdad - taking in a lorry load of supplies - food, clothes, medical supplies and a few luxuries."

"And they want you to go with them?"

"Jon, do you think we could? We could raise some support back home. I'd really like to go into Iraq with them"

He was bemused. "At a time like this? Not so fast Sophie. Sure, we could raise some cash for them, but you've got a job to do here."

"And one other thing Jon. I've got a job for you."

"Work or play?"

"You'll never guess. Can you do some carbon dating on a fragment of a basket?"

"Go on, what's it about?"

"It's said to be ...... a bit of the basket they used to lower Paul over the Damascus wall."

"You're joking!"

"No, really. I'll tell you about it when I get home."

"Don't be long my love. I'm missing you. Hurry home."

"Love you too."

REUNION

19

WITHIN A WEEK SOPHIE was back in Scotland, and she wasted no time to share with Jon. She parked her car in the street below, snapped on the car lock and cautiously looked to right and left. This part of the city was a cosmopolitan home for felons, women who plied the ancient trade and addicts who took everything that was legal and illegal. And here also a bunch of landlords exploited poor students.

She pushed open the tenement door and was met by the usual pungent smell in the stair-well. Then into the darkness and up three flights of stone steps. She rang the bell. There was no delay and he lifted her off her feet, spun her round and hugged her.

Jon's top-floor flat was as comfortable as any two-room student's bachelor-pad could be. He had been counting the days to her return, and anticipating this first meal they'd have together after so long apart. It had taken half the day to prepare, and he hoped she would be pleased with the result.

She flung her coat on the chair and offered to help.

"No need. It's ready."

She had been fêted in Damascus and enjoyed lots of new Arab delicacies, but Sophie was a traditionalist when it came to her palate. There was a solitary candle on the table.

"How romantic Jon!"

He smiled. Besides, Jon found candlelight was much kindlier on the dust. Sophie looked at the spaghetti Bolognese. If it wasn't her favourite dish, at least he'd tried.

"The joy of some good food again. Great Jon - full marks."

He really loved this girl. The memory of her warmth and gentleness had made their time apart an eternity. The way she laughed - a smile that made him smile however he was feeling. A mind that was always fascinating and fascinated by what was happening around her.

"Damascus?"

"Wonderful. In fact 'wonderful' can't describe these last few weeks."

She told him about the hospital, the souk, the archaeology of Bible days, Brother Joe and his ancient basket.

She opened her bag and put a small box on the table.

"Guard that with your life Jon. Brother Joe thinks it's a bit of the basket they used to lower Paul down the Damascus city wall."

Jon picked up the small box.

"He told me he'd used a spare container they'd sent him from the States, so it should be okay."

"It's a fascinating story," he said. "Nine times out of ten it's a mediaeval hoax. We've a PhD in the lab who'll test it for me. I'll not give him any clues, and see what happens."

Sophie told him about the farewell gifts they'd given her. And she also told him about Mohammed.

"He wants to get out of Damascus. He's got money in a Jersey bank and needs some of it for a one-way ticket to London. I said you might do this for him". She looked at him qizzingly.

"It sounds quite urgent. Can you help him Jon?"

It seemed harmless enough. Jon was planning to go home and see his parents anyway.

A tendril of fair hair fell over her face, and Jon had the sudden impulse to touch it and feel her soft cheek against his. He had always considered himself a 'loner', self sufficient and independent, but this remarkable young woman had stolen his heart in a way he had though impossible. He was beginning to realise that life without Sophie would be very bleak indeed.

"Sophie."

He hesitated.

"Er... will you come home with me. You can get this guy's cash and see my family at the same time."

She was not due on the wards for a few days. How could she refuse.

THE BAGHDAD LAWYER

20

MOHAMMED WAS on the mend and he was now thinking clearly. His plan might just work. Money talks, and if he could get cash out of Jersey, he might buy his way out of Syria. He had to speak to his lawyer in Baghdad first - one man he could trust, if you could be sure of anyone today in Iraq.

He needed money. If these thieves were after cash, his credit cards would already be milked dry, but it was not robbery. There must have been political motives behind his assault.

He borrowed a mobile, punched in the Baghdad number, and used only his first name.

"Mohammed ! Where are you? I've been waiting for you to call."

The line was poor, but he explained that he had had to leave the country at short notice - secret negotiations about research developments. If anyone asked, he had not heard from him. No one must know he had phoned. He might be away for a while. Yes he had lost his credit cards. They should cancel them if it was not too late. At least his Jersey account would be secure.

"Yes, I'll get the Jersey bank to release cash in the name of Doctor Tristan."

Mohammed didn't want to talk for long, in case the phone was tapped.

"Your mother's going crazy. She's asking about you. Lots of people are asking about you."

That wasn't good news.

"Tell Mama - not to worry. Everything's fine. I miss her. Now the cash."

There was a long pause, and he could sense the lawyer was nervous.

"That's a lot of money Mohammed. Are you sure?"

He was sure.

LONG DAYS IN JERSEY

21

IT WAS A GOOD time to accept Jon's offer, return to Jersey, meet his folks and see his old haunts. They stepped off the plane. The air was warm and summer had already arrived, and Jon's dad was waiting to drive them the short distance to the little white washed family home by the sea.

Mr Le Var was an outdoor man with a sunburnt face. Sophie looked at both men, and saw the uncanny family likeness. The older man was nearly as good looking as his son - the same open honest face, the same kindly manner, the same animation. He was not short of conversation, and as he drove down the narrow Jersey lanes he talked easily making Sophie feel comfortable.

"Over the hill and you'll see our little home."

Jon's rather plump mum was waiting at the door. She was jolly, and smaller than her husband.

"Let's help with your luggage."

She was given a tour of the house, and then back to the living room where Jon was relaxing in an easy chair. An old retriever waged its tail in welcome, and it soon attached itself to Jon by sitting on his feet. This was a home, and her shyness soon disappeared.

She settled herself beside the inglenook fireplace and looked around. It was rather old-fashioned. There was some polished mahogany furniture, a square central table covered with a red chenille cloth, and a large aspidistra in a green container at the centre. She stood to examine the faded family photographs. The Le Vars must have lived here for generations, and she noticed that several had been connétables of the parish in their time. There were two brown and white Staffordshire dogs on the mantelpiece and a photograph of an angelic little boy.

Jon caught her eye.

"We'll move that." he said breaking into a smile. "Sit you down in that rocking chair and Mum'll put the kettle on."

The window was open towards the sea, and she could hear the drone of a bee outside in the hot summer sunshine.

She reached for a book from the shelf, as Jon stood, bathed in sunlight, looking out to sea.

"Hear this Jon."

He turned and sat on the arm of her chair.

"All ears."

"It's William Wordsworth and just for you.

Books! 'tis a dull and endless strife: Come,
hear the woodland linnet,
How sweet his music! on my life,
There's more of wisdom in it.

Enough of Science and of Art;
Close up those barren leaves;
Come forth, and bring with you a heart
That watches and receives."

"I'll go with that!" And he kissed her briefly with a look of love.

• • •

ON THE FIRST DAY they meandered amongst the rocks of St Clement's Bay, following the retreating tide, sometimes walking along sandy gullies, splashing through the pools or scrambling over slippery seaweed covered rocks. They were a couple of miles out and still surrounded by rugged black rocks.

"It's magnificent" she said, the warm wind blowing through her hair.

"If we'd lived 11,000 years ago in the time of the last great Ice Age," said Jon pointing to the far horizon "we could have walked on dry land all the way to France. Then with warmer weather and melting ice the sea rose to fill the English Channel. We became an island people and here we are, with Jersey now separated from France by twenty two miles of shallow sea."

"Jon - what is there to see here that's older than the Ice age?"

Jon chose not to answer and changed the subject.

"We'll hit the town and sort out the money for your friend Mohammed first."

They walked through the pedestrian mall - a very pleasant street - French-style - with cafes, antique stores, book dealers and restaurants that had spread outdoors for long evening meals. Then across the historic Royal Square where the pavement was separated from old buildings by a strip of cobbles and into the States' Bank, were they were shown into the comfort of the Manager's office.

They were invited to take a seat in this inner sanctum, and Sophie explained Mohammed's problem.

The manager examined Mohammed's file carefully, and then scrutinised the letter of instruction. He removed his glasses and carefully cleaned them with his white handkerchief.

"This is a lot of money Miss Tristan, to be handing over to a third party, but the letters of authority I have from Iraq are in order. And Jon here is vouching for you, and er.." - he smiled - "....I knew his grandfather."

He leaned back in his chair, clasped his hands and started to reminisce.

"I've known Jon's family most of my life - went to school with his dad."

After ten minutes, they were given a money order in the name of General Kapta and US dollars for Mohammed. Then they walked down to British Airways and purchased an open first class ticket from Damascus to Heathrow, and sent them all by registered mail to Damascus.

"Duty done for that poor guy" she said, skipping along the pavement. "Thanks for helping Jon."

They mingled with holiday makers and he bought her a floppy tourist hat at the corner shop. She always looked stunning whatever she wore.

• • •

NEXT DAY THEY TOOK the old retriever on to the beach at St Ouen's, and helped Jon's father collect loads of strong smelling seaweed. The wind was blowing in their faces and they inhaled the heady sea vapours. And looking back, Jon's white-washed house stood proudly on its own, looking over the broad spread of St Ouen's Bay. From the sentinel lighthouse in the south standing in the foaming waves, to the northern headland which rose precipitously from the sea - this was his bay, his heritage.

"We've gathered seaweed like this for generations. When there's a full moon and a heavy sea, the ocean can drop 40 feet. It's the largest tide in the world."

He kicked some loose sea-weed, and a crab scurried across the wet sand to be chased by the inquisitive retriever.

JERSEY - La Corbiere Lighthouse

"The storms leave this seaweed - torn up from the deep - and it covers the shore line. It's great fertiliser and it is free. We'll help Dad fill his trailer."

After the first load, whilst Jon's father took the tractor back home, he and Sophie walked arm in arm along the wide open beach. They faced the breeze and looked out to sea. A few massed clouds moved deliberately across the blue and the sea itself.

Jon pointed beyond the shallows. "Submerged under the sea is a piece of history - the remains of a whole village. I sometimes think of all the people who have lived and died on this coast, and their bones lying a mile out under the waves in the old churchyard." He looked wistfully out to sea. "There are times when I lie in bed at night, that I can hear beyond the rhythmic murmur of the waves the faint tolling of a bell from the buried tower!"

"Don't scare me Jon!"

He laughed and pulled her to him.

"C'mon then - let me show you."

He raced her down to the shore line. The water was really low and at the north end of the bay, the receding tide had left a most curious picture. Rising from the low water were not buildings, but a legion of black fossilised tree stumps, standing silently like a long forgotten army.

"Those tree stumps are really ancient - they're sentinels of an earlier time - 12,000 years ago at the close of the ice age - when the water was much lower than today. These old trees were part of a greater forest. It's the submerged forest of La Brecquette - home of the Hairy Mammoth and the Woolly Rhinoceros. Deer and bear used to shelter under these trees - food for our hunting stone age ancestors [4]."

"Tomorrow Sophie you must see La Cotte."

LA COTTE

22

ALL BOYS LOVE a cave, and Jon had been no exception. He had spent many long hours on the far side of Ouaisné Bay where the rocky headland drops precipitously two hundred feet into the sea. Cleft into this rock is an ancient cave - La Cotte. How often he had scrambled over the rocks and climbed up to the cave's mouth to gaze in awesome wonder, and imagine its history.

"Come on Sophie. You must see La Cotte. The experts say it's one of the most interesting caves in Europe." They walked down the long beach to the sea, and then he helped her over the rocks and round the headland. They were quite alone, and could hear nothing but the surge of the sea and the lonely cry of nesting gulls.

"Teams of archaeologists have spent their summers digging here - even Prince Charles' royal fingers sifted through this rubble. And there have been a number of remarkable finds. Bones of Mammoth and Rhinoceros were laid out in such a formal manner that it must be the mark of early humans. The floor's covered with flint scrapers. We might find some today."

They stood at the entrance of this cathedral-like cave, looked up into the vault several hundred feet high, and then deep into its dark interior.

"We think it was a flint-making factory to make scrapers and cutters for the Mouserian tribes. Or it might have been an early abattoir where flints were used for skinning the Mammoth that had been stampeded over the cliff edge."

They stood in silence listening to the steady drip of water somewhere in the distant darkness. Whatever the secrets of the cave, La Cotte was quite breathtaking.

"Think of it Sophie. This remarkable place has the 35,000 year old fingerprints of my ancestors."

They moved a few stones and found a flint.

"It could even go back to much earlier times - 100,000 years ago to Neanderthal man."

"Who were they - also your ancestors?"

"Near relatives if you believe the telly, but it's anyone's guess [5] [6] [7] [8]. Some guy claims they also enjoyed very long lives !"

Jon had been reading about a scientist who'd examined the teeth of Neanderthals, and thought they'd lived much longer than people do today [9].

"Claimed some Neanderthals lived for up to 300 years - and that their children matured much later than our modern kids. That's hard to believe ! I think whoever Mr and Mrs Neanderthal were - maybe my early forebears - they must have been very like us. They laughed and loved and cried."

"But how could they have lived that long?" asked Sophie - almost to herself - as she tucked this small seed of knowledge into her mind. It might germinate one day!

Jon pointed out to sea.

"Those ancient people would have stood here and seen a breath-taking forest of tall aspiring trees, stretching right to the horizon."

Sophie was beginning to realise why Jon was interested in 'time'. The coast of Jersey was speaking to her of the changing centuries. Raised beaches on three sides of the island witnessed to an ancient past - from a hundred millennia ago. A spectacular cave had hints of very early human industry. Low tides now exposed fossilised trees of more recent times - perhaps twelve millennia ago - when Jersey was part of France. Now it was an island again. She saw how change was part of the island scene, and that to understand Jersey she needed a perspective of time. Nature was more important than books !

"Jon. You'll have to share this with Mohammed. He told me that his research had something to do with Earth Science."

THE BRIBE

23

MOHAMMED SAT BY HIS bed and slowly opened the registered envelope from Sophie. He then tucked the tickets away safely into his pocket, noted the money order, picked up his crutches, and walked carefully towards General Kapta's office.

"C'm in."

The General was hidden in a haze of cigar smoke, relaxing with his two arms spread lazily along the back of the wide semi-circular sofa upholstered in glorious red leather.

When he saw Mohammed, he stiffened slightly.

"Welcome my friend." He rose to his feet and moved over to his desk. "Have some coffee."

The hospital had been unable to establish the identity of this man from Iraq, but here was the General's chance for a private conversation.

After the formalities, the General flicked open the file he'd removed from the top drawer of his desk, and he stared down at the notes. It was time to talk about costs of this man's treatment.

"How's the leg now we've removed your fixator? They tell me the fracture is knitting well, and you'll soon be ready to depart. My accountants are asking who will settle your bill."

The general wiped his moustache, and Mohammed chose his words carefully. This man's gentle grey eyes were deceptive.

"I owe your hospital a great debt General, and you too personally. Without you I wouldn't be alive today."

He looked up at the vast portrait of the President behind the General's desk and lowered his voice.

"You must allow me to pay for the trouble I have caused."

The General sat back in his chair and folded his arms. "But what are your means my friend? You came with nothing."

"You have been more than helpful General, and I can pay. However, I need one more favour, and the price is not important. My work is paramount and it demands secrecy."

He sat up. "But I thought our psychologist told me you're still amnesic."

Mohammed dismissed the remark.

"You are aware" he said, "that I have no papers and I have to be careful about security. I need a passport and exit visa. You are a man with friends in the right places."

"You ask the impossible my friend." He fingered his moustache again.

"That's more than my job is worth."

"Tell me the cost of the hospital care and I'll double it."

There was an awkward silence. Mohammed opened his wallet, and pushed a money order across the table. It was in the name of General Kapta and read - "30,000 US dollars." It lay there for a minute and slowly the general put it in his pocket.

"We have not had this conversation. I am not a man without influence."

CATASTROPHE AND THE CREATOR

24

LIFE WAS GOOD for Sophie and Jon. The sky was blue for them, walking, sharing and spending exhilarating hours on the beach. Sophie had borrowed a wet-suit, and they had fun as she learnt to ride the giant breakers on the long fetch.

Jon had discovered that this special girl was unutterably dear, and he was momentarily saddened to think how soon these few idyllic days in Jersey would come to an end. She'd have to leave the island and return to Edinburgh to graduate. Further ahead were her residencies, with hard work and long hours, but that was what her training was for. At least he'd been offered a chance to do a PhD in his Alma Mater. It would be a logical progression for him, the first step towards loftier ambitions. He had yet to chose his subject.

"Sophie's last day Mum. We're off to the north coast."

"Take good care of that girl."

He knew his mother's thoughts, that Sophie was an answer to her prayers. His mother just talked to God and He answered, even if took time !

After a morning of rain it was a fresh, lively afternoon, with clouds scudding across the sky. They walked for an hour and then sat in the bracken, high on the cliff top. Below was the slow movement of the green sea, and they watched the white gulls circling effortlessly on the up-currents. The wind was blowing through Sophie's fair hair and Jon chipped with his hammer at a piece of granite.

"We'll make a geologist of you yet Sophie. All you have to do is use your eyes".

The patterns made by the layers of Jersey granite were quite remarkable. In some places they were horizontal, layer placed on layer. In others they were upended vertically, reaching to the sky. Some were tremendously twisted and contorted, as if an enthusiastic baker had been stirring up his mixture.

"All I know about rocks is from the little I have read in books and from the displays in our museums Jon."

"I've got a problem with geology Sophie. I gave the right answers in my finals and I got a good result, but I'm not really sure if I believe it all - particularly what we're told about the age of the earth. That's got to be the focus of my PhD, and it might be controversial."

She let him talk on. "If uniformitarianism is right, then the earth must be very old - four and a half a billion years or so. But there are many assumptions. How can we insist that we've been observers long enough to say that the same forces of today must also have been present throughout immeasurable time?

Catastrophe ?
How brief is our recorded history - 3, 4 or 5 thousand years?
Just because things have been fairly uniform
for that length of time,
can we assume that it has always been so?

I suppose that even with the occasional catastrophe the earth must be quite ancient. But how ancient?"

"I'll be stepping outside mainstream geology, but I don't think pure uniformitarianism is correct. Look at this coastline. Are these angled strata a sign of steady processes and very gradual change, or of catastrophe?"

He pulled out some pebbles and soft clay that was wedged between two layers of thick granite. Were these washed into the clefts by a turbulent earth? This is more like catastrophe" [10 11 12 13 14 15].

"Are you talking about Noah's flood 4000 years ago?"

"Course not." He looked at Sophie. "But I guess this is where science meets the religious texts - like the nineteenth century - so today."

"My family brought me up with the Bible" he said pensively. "That describes catastrophe, with the story of the deluge, and there are similar stories from so many other disparate cultures about major catastrophe. Perhaps that's telling us something. I don't believe the story of Noah's flood, but there is more catastrophe written into the rocks than we give credit for."

Sophie responded "The age of the earth has implications Jon. If you decide the earth is young, what about the sacred cow of Darwinism? And you can't sacrifice that!" She was winding him up.

His mind raced back to boyhood days. 'All things bright and beautiful' they sang at his little Methodist Sunday School, 'The Lord God made them all' and he believed it then. Some of the preachers thundered from the pulpit against evolution. Henry de Faye the old fisherman and Eli Le Maistre granddad's cousin were passionate lay preachers who always took a swipe at Darwin. They said it had to be special creation - because God and Genesis said so.

But then some of the clever lay-preachers gave other signals - the solicitors, doctors and teachers - that Darwinism could be accommodated with the gospel. The ordained ministers thought the subject was 'taboo' and avoided it altogether, perhaps on the advice of their colleges. But he noticed that they still lifted the roof at harvest time singing 'All good gifts around us are sent from heaven above.' What was a growing boy to believe?

At school he knew evolution was more than an idea. It was taught as a fact, and he had to say so in the examination papers. And at university he was assured that no respectable scientist could doubt the truth of Darwinism. So now in his early twenties, he didn't know how to answer Sophie's question without hurting her.

Jon knew there was a warm spiritual side to Sophie and she didn't go for Darwin's evolution. She believed that living organisms are far too intricate to be the product of random mutations and selection. There had to be a non-natural process for the wonders of living things [16].

"Darwinism? We'll put that on the back burner."

He looked at this lovely girl lying back in the grass, and he admired her simple faith. God's word worked successfully for her in everyday life, and she wasn't prepared to swap a working certainty for a questionable theory.

"I don't have your kind of faith" he said "but I am certainly asking questions about science. Believing in God seems to me much easier than the blind faith of an atheist."

He looked at a bumble bee exploring the heads of the purple foxgloves.

"I can go for 'Intelligent Design' - but I think God must have taken His time".

He thought about the academics he knew.

"Some of my teachers say they're atheists. But I guess deep down they've some sort of faith in a Creator God - some Supreme Being. In earlier days, most of the great scientists had a strong personal Christian faith, and they said so. You should read about them Sophie. Their stories read like whodunits [17]. These people had sharp minds and were probing into nature. They took big risks, wasted time, got burnt and often failed [18]."

> ### The faith of Scientists
> If we are standing on the shoulders of these people
> who had a deep faith, how can we take their results and
> ignore what motivated them to do that research?

Sophie didn't need convincing. They walked home across the headland admiring the view as the sun dipped into the sea. The sky was an artist's palate.

"I guess my ideas are fairly simple Jon. I take the Bible at face value because it's made such a difference in my life. I don't pick out the comfortable bits here and there, and discard those that conflict with science. I take on board that God breaks through in miracles. If He's the creator God, He can do anything, and I've come to accept the Bible stories and wait for science to catch up in its own good time."

They walked slowly and thoughtfully. Sophie knew that soon she'd return to Edinburgh. She'd fallen in love with this Jerseyman sharing with her long evening walks. But there was a big question - was this to be her truly romantic journey to Eden?

"Can two people ever find paradise, Jon?"

He turned and gently kissed her.

"Maybe" he said, as her beauty and fragrance delighted him.

But Sophie needed to know much more about Jon's ambitions. They were not too far apart, but that was not enough. If they were to have a future, they had to share a common living faith. That would be the only way for Sophie. Could Jon ever share in her plans to work in the poor villages of Central Africa? She really wanted him on board, and she could see that the Maker of this Universe was nudging Jon through science.

25

CLAMPDOWN IN URUMQI

RUSSIA AND CHINA FORGED a new regional alliance to combat rising fears that Islamic fundamentalism was poised to spread across the nations of central Asia. The Shanghai Five had made a modest start, as a body to broker border disputes - China, Russia, Kazakhstan, Kyrgystan and Tajikstan, and they were now joined by Uzbekistan, another former Soviet republic. These six good neighbours had signed an agreement to fight ethnic and religious militancy which threatened to affect the stability of the region.

President Jiang Zemin said "The importance of the region has grown in recent years with the development of oil reserves. This area will soon join the top five oil producing regions. It is essential to jointly crack down on terrorism, separatism and extremism to safeguard the region's security [19]."

The situation became more complex when the United States offered Kazakhstan several million dollars to fund a study for an oil pipeline that would bypass Russia and run to Turkey. President Putin intervened. "China and Russia must have a common policy and stand together to protect our interests." Their chief concern was for co-operation between intelligence agencies to prevent armed incursions over the borders.

Against this background and in a tense atmosphere, Li Zhou set to work immediately. The Urumqi daily newspaper editorials and the wall-posters warned against 'superstition', and insurgents were threatened with severe penalties for any illegal gatherings. Hundreds of plain clothes police-men mingled on the streets with the demonstrators. More than a thousand young people were rounded up, forced onto mini-buses and driven to stadiums which had been improvised as detention camps. Army deserters - and there were some of them - were summarily executed as an example. Fear stalked the city.

In addition Li Zhou organised nightly raids.

"They meet in the evenings. These are the addresses to be raided tonight" he said. "We can afford no mercy."

Over seventy students, nurses and academics were crowded into the first-floor flat. A young man read from the Bible, and talked at length whilst his rapt audience murmured approval. There was unaccompanied singing, and times of fervent praying. Then the sounds of heavy feet pound-ing up the stairs. It was frightening, but caused little surprise. There was no escape. They were all unceremoniously driven to the Police head-quarters.

In the early hours of the morning anxious relatives paced outside the building. There were cries from within, but barred windows and bolted doors prevented access. The interrogation was brutal. More information was gathered, and the seventy were never seen again.

The scene was repeated nightly at other addresses that Li Zhou had extracted from his cell mate, until several hundred underground believers were eliminated.

Li Zhou could not understand these people. Some were scared, trembling and broken. Others were defiant and almost arrogant in their rebellion. On one particular occasion he was touched by the beauty of a young woman. He would never forget the radiance in her face as she looked at him sorrowfully. She told him that her leader said, "Love your enemies, and anyone who loses their life for me and the good news will save it". What good news?

Hundreds of holy books were burnt, but not before Li Zhou rescued a Bible for himself and quietly placed it in his inside pocket. If this dangerous material could so affect people's minds, he would have to read some of the fables for himself.

He remembered his prison mate - that weakling Fang. He had known plenty of people prepared to die for hate, but what was this love?

"Curse you" he said to his own daughter, when he found her reading this same pernicious literature. Hadn't she been well educated? What if she joined the cult!

MOHAMMED FLEES

26

MOHAMMED WAS SWEATING as he slipped through passport control at Heathrow but he needn't have worried. The general's people had done a professional job, and his documents were in order. He left Victoria station in central London wondering how long he could hide in the West.

Sophie had given him Jon's contact number in Jersey. He found a phone.

"Jon. This is Mohammed. I'm in London. Your friend Sophie has been a great help."

"A friend of Sophie is a friend of mine. What can I do for you."

"Is Sophie there?"

"She flew back yesterday."

"Can I come over and see you?"

He was on the first flight the next day.

Jon was at the airport to meet him. This man from Iraq was rather small, with olive coloured skin. He was clean shaven and smartly dressed in his new clothes and he looked out of place in the more relaxed atmosphere of the Channel Islands. Jon guessed he was in early forties.

He wouldn't hear of Mohammed staying in a hotel. Anyway he wanted to talk to this man.

Mohammed was fussed over by Jon's Mum. "We've never met anyone from Iraq before. Do you like tea.....with milk?"

"I've heard about your Jersey milk."

Jon's Dad asked about his work.

"Physics sir. Research in optics. But I'm on sabbatical. I have an account in Jersey and I have to see my banker tomorrow. Sophie told me about you, and your welcome is wonderful. I shall repay you one day, but at the moment our political situation is ...er...difficult."

Without being too specific he talked of the Middle East, of political and religious strife and of life in Baghdad since the war.

THE BEGINNING OF TIME

27

ON RARE OCCASIONS two people find a natural affinity. It cuts across race and religion. Jon and Mohammed sensed this bond. It was more than just a shared interest in cosmic science. They drove along St Aubin's Bay into St Helier and Mohammed shared part of his story. He explained how he had been recruited by Moscow, given a generous grant to work in Baghdad which he couldn't refuse, how he had developed a team to build an optical satellite and which was now orbiting the earth every three hours.

"What's it for Mohammed? Is it for communications, or surveillance or is it part of a space laboratory?"

"None of these things Jon. The world's media know that we have placed mirrors in space to illuminate Russia's cities. But there is much more to it than that. It was a top secret space probe project. I would like to tell you, but I'm tied to a secrecy agreement. At the moment I can't share the whole story."

Jon didn't press him further but he was naturally curious.

"Mohammed. I have a friend in Jersey - an amateur astronomer. Who knows, with his telescope we might see your satellite?"

"It'll be too small and the mirrors won't be open, but let's see him."

Jon browsed around a second-hand book shop and purchased another volume on cosmology, while Mohammed spent a long time with his banker. Returning home through the evening traffic, they discussed the cosmos.

"Most of what I know comes from my friend Frank Johnson. He's an amateur astronomer at Grosnez - rather eccentric like the best cosmologists [20]. Tonight'll be a good night to see the stars. We can use his scope."

● ● ●

FRANK LIVED in a single story cottage on the cliff edge at Grosnez. He was a retired Marine pilot drawing a nice pension - enough to live comfortably and indulge himself with his hobby, searching the heavens every night with his new telescope. Frank knew everything about the skies.

He was more than pleased to meet a man who had put a satellite into orbit.

They stood outside and admired the magnificent sky. Orion was rising in the south-east, Cassiopeia hung on its side, and a hundred billion stars in the Milky Way stretched from one horizon to the other.

"It circles the earth every three hours" Mohammed was saying.

"If I was at home, I could show you its orbit."

They couldn't see Mohammed's satellite but over mugs of steaming coffee this strange trio - Jon the geologist, Frank the astronomer and Mohammed the researcher - talked long into the night about the farthest reaches of space, the expanding universe and the beginning of time. There was that singularity, the Big Bang in a blaze of light perhaps a White Hole - a shrinking event horizon with galaxies and stars flung into space, and now those distant galaxies were still speeding away from planet earth [21] [22].

Jon took up the discussion, and it became philosophical. "If cosmology is right, the Universe can only have been going for a finite amount of time."

> ### A beginning
> Most cosmologists say that any reasonable model of the Universe must start with a singularity.
> That means there must have been a beginning.

"Go on Jon" said the astronomer.

"But science can't predict *why* it began. For that, we have to appeal to God - right Frank?" [23].

Jon was winding him up.

Frank grunted and Jon continued.

They discussed the Second Law of Thermodynamics which says there is increasing entropy in the Universe - increasing disorder - and Jon argued that extrapolating backwards, there must have been a remarkable degree of precision right at the start [24].

"That means a Creator - right Frank?"

> ### A beginning and a Creator
> For such a wonderful Universe to exist,
> there must have been incredible initial fine-tuning
> suggesting an Intelligent Designer.

Frank wasn't so sure [25]. He leaned across to Mohammed and winked.

"Jon and I have this discussion every time. He thinks I'm an atheist. But he knows I half believe in his Creator because I can't explain the beginning any other way."

He looked at Jon. "I think - maybe - there was a God who started it all off billions of years ago, and then He just retired for an early Sabbath rest. No personal interaction after that. That's where I part company with you Jon. The Almighty left the Universe to run 'under its own steam'. It lets me off the hook from trying to be good - eh Jon?"

Mohammed had his turn.

"I'm an optical scientist and I have to work with precise laws. The Universe has one unique set of possible laws, but that is only a conceptual set of equations. What is it Frank, that breathes fire into the equations, and makes a Universe for the laws to govern? Although science may solve the problem of how the Universe works, it can't answer the question 'why does the Universe bother to exist'? What is the purpose of it all? Who knows the answer to that?"

Frank stirred his coffee. "I'm not totally irreligious Mohammed. I believe the first three verses in the Bible, but no more - 'In the beginning God created the heavens and the earth'. It says 'the earth was formless and empty' - and 'let there be light and there was light'. That's fine. There was a great Big Bang and a flash of brilliant light. But I can't believe that the God who created it all, has intervened any more. It's just a clockwork machine that will continue until it winds itself down. And it makes no sense."

"But what a machine!" said Mohammed looking up at the stars.

"Frank's God, if He exists is impersonal" said Jon. "He doesn't intervene in the brilliant system but lets it run."

"Correct Jon. As a scientist I believe the Universe evolves with well-defined laws. The laws may have been given by God, but it seems that He doesn't intervene in the Universe to break those laws. He wound up the clockwork and set the Universe going in the way He wanted. I can accept that the present Universe is the result of God's original choice about the initial conditions, but I can't see any sign that He's intervened since then. You can explain miracles and answers to prayer in other ways. I just don't know, but I gave up on praying years ago, when I got no answers."

Jon saw it differently. When he looked at the cosmos, he saw the hand of a personal God everywhere. He thought for a while.

"Don't give up on prayer, Frank. It's only a request to the Almighty. It's not a compulsion and of course it may not be granted. If an infinitely wise Being - the One who made all these stars - listens to the prayers of finite and foolish creatures like us, I'm sure that He will sometimes grant and sometimes have to refuse our requests."

Jon continued. "It doesn't mean He's powerless or not interested."

Frank then looked across at Mohammed and Jon.

"I don't mean to be disrespectful, but look at you two - a Muslim and a Christian. Your religions have been responsible for so many wars. Saladin and the Crusades. Jews fighting Arabs. You war amongst yourselves in Northern Ireland and in Iraq and Iran, then comes September 11th and the Iraqi conflict. You're still at it. The Muslim world is involved in this jihad - a Holy war against Christians. I'm better off as an agnostic."

"Half a minute Frank," interrupted Jon. "You're not being consistent. First you say that we're living in a morally indifferent self evolving Universe, and in the next breath you're making value judgements."

Jon knew he couldn't convince his astronomer friend. They talked of different models of the Universe - the preferred Big Bang that expanded for ever - or a collapsing Universe that would end in a Big Crunch [26]. They discussed ways in which cosmologists have tried to dispense with a beginning - the oscillating universe that keeps expanding and collapsing like a bouncing ball - Hoyle's idea of continuous creation of matter [27] - and an infinite number of parallel universes with strings and undulating membranes, and this one just happening to be the jackpot.

Jon turned to the work of Edwin Hubble who in 1929 discovered that distant galaxies are moving away from us, and that the age of the universe and its rate of expansion depended on an accurate interpretation of the meaning of the 'red shift' [28].

They talked about the new evidence of a universe that is expanding at an ever increasing rate, and if it's right, how one day we shall be left behind all alone in empty space [23] [29].

"What do you make of that Mohammed?"

They didn't get an answer, and Jon thought he detected a knowing smile on Mohammed's face.

SUMMONS TO BEIJING

28

FEAR GRIPPED THE PROVINCE of Xinjang. Those with long memories were re-living the days of the cultural revolution. Any who ventured out into the city streets and alleys had solemn faces and bowed shoulders. Even the birds had forgotten how to sing. The hopes of freedom had been replaced again by the strong arm of the Party. People spoke in whispers and no one had an opinion about anything.

Li Zhou had won, temporarily at least. He had regained the respect of Beijing by dealing a swift and heavy blow to all dissenters. Muslims and Christians were equally suspected of subversion, and were forbidden to meet on pain of death. The Falun Gong kept indoors. Foreigners were totally excluded from the province - teachers, businessmen and tourists were unwelcome. The north-west border of China was secure.

Li Zhou gathered his henchmen into his office to thank them, and he would have smiled if only he could have remembered the sequence of muscle movements. Instead he spat across the room into a colourful tin spittoon, and they drank white fire and shouted obscenities.

Li Zhou was not surprised to receive an urgent summons to the capital - perhaps to receive an honour? He was met at the airport and taken a little too fast, to the Party HQ in a large black Chaika limousine with lights on. Every time he visited Beijing there were more motor vehicles and less cycles on the road. The new economic revival was a triumph for communism!

He was feeling optimistic. Two guards sprang to attention as he passed through the doors into the spacious committee room of the Central Office. How different to his last visit! A delegation of expressionless men from Moscow were seated at a large oval table, muttering in low voices and he was invited to a place at the far end. There was a hush of expectancy and the Minister for Internal Affairs was ushered in. They scrambled to their feet, until he raised the palm of his right hand and they were invited to sit.

There was a preamble, lengthy introductions, bowls of tea to drink and the Minister's eyes rested on Li Zhou.

"Li Zhou. The situation is complex and I want you to listen carefully. We have a new crisis and your recent success in Urumqi makes us think you are the man to help us."

He maintained a respectful silence.

"Like you in Xinjang, our Russian friends have problems with their quasi-religious groups just across your border. In addition they have uncovered some pseudo research that, if it became public knowledge, would provide fuel for these ignorant people who are causing us all great trouble right across Central Asia. You need to understand the background of this research because it affects you personally, and it has implications for your own religious extremists."

He was listening with interest.

"We also need someone to visit the West, find the source of the problem and root it our before it becomes public knowledge. You have earned a break from your arduous duties at home. You have distinguished yourself, and we think you are the man."

Li Zhou was mystified. They must have had some ulterior motive to call him from Xinjang, but he gave his full attention to the news that was being shared by the Russian delegation.

"This must be kept in strictest confidence." Confidentiality was a problem for Li Zhou and he listened with interest.

"There is a top secret space probe project that our Russian friends have been supporting in Iraq, and unfortunately it has gone dangerously wrong."

"An understatement" murmured the Russian leader leaping to his feet. The Minister gave him the floor.

"We funded a joint project with the Iraqis to illuminate our cities at night" he said. "We put a satellite into space to reflect light from the sun. It was a success, but not really economically viable."

He continued in a more anxious voice. "In addition we agreed to help them add on a further project - a 'time-probe'. It was novel idea - designed to bounce light back and forwards from Baghdad to the satellite, and in simple terms it was an attempt to use the satellite mirrors to look back in time !"

The men round the table stopped drinking their tea. Li Zhou grew more curious and he dared to speak.

"I'm no scientist" he said "But I thought that was impossible."

"So did we" growled the Russian "but we let these people have their heads and they produced unexpected results. They are clever devils. This thing really works, and it's terrifying."

Li Zhou could not understand why both the Russians and Chinese governments were so concerned until the Russian barked.

"This is dynamite in the wrong hands."

Li Zhou's eyes were getting wider.

"They can look back in time and it reveals the past, at least for a few years and" - he lowered his voice - " the record of our history and yours is very embarrassing if it gets into the wrong hands. I am thinking of our troubled places in Europe, Siberia, Afghanistan, the Middle East - and your Tianenman Square."

Then he looked at Li Zhou. "Your activities on the streets of Urumchi are also revealed."

Li Zhou's heart missed a beat.

"It's the most terrifying invention you can think of - total transparency. I doubt if civilisation will survive such a thing [30]."

It was obvious to Li Zhou that this was indeed the seed of political mischief. It was devastating. He thought of the International Court of Human Rights. This space satellite would affect his future.

"It will also fuel dissent if it should reach the public domain," the Russian said .

The Minister agreed. "The idea of a 'time viewer' - a re-write of history - will inflame the fanatics who need no encouragement to believe they know how to run our country."

Now he knew why he had been called from Xinjang. It was personal. He was ready to help.

ON THE TRAIL

29

AFTER RECOVERING from the initial shock, Li Zhou began to relax. It wasn't all bad news. A trip to the West would be novel, and they promised to pay him handsomely, ten percent in advance and the remainder to be paid into any bank of his choice in any country of his choosing when the contract was completed.

He spent the next day in Beijing and purchased some crisp new clothes anticipating his first overseas visit, and then tasted some aspects of night-life that he would never find in Urumqi. In the process he drank too much white fire, pure Chinese alcohol that burnt all the way down to his toes.

Li Zhou studied the dossier on his brief, and the profile of the Russian who was to be his colleague. He needed to study this man carefully. The Russian was certainly unusual. He was neither conspicuously tall, nor conspicuously handsome. His hair was brushed backwards at the temples, and his skin seemed to be pulled backwards from the nose. He seemed to be constantly irritable. Li Zhou had the unnerving impression that he was about to go for his neck. He would have to watch this man.

He learnt that the Russian was a man of action - he certainly was not a man of words. He'd escaped bullets, hidden in forests, negotiated rapids, murdered three men at prayer, poisoned a spy in Constantinople, he understood many languages, he'd fought in three wars and was going to prevent the next one. What a CV !

In spite of his distinguished record, and his important assignment, the Russian was not a happy man. He was embarrassed to tell Li Zhou that he had failed in the first attempt to assassinate Mohammed the researcher, and that this key man was still missing and unless they found him, he would soon publish this unusual research.

Li Zhou might have wished to remain in Beijing and savour its pleasures, but the urgency of the task left him no such freedom. Speed was essential.

• • •

WITHIN TWO DAYS THEY were at the Military Hospital in Damascus, a city where life crawled at a slow pace. Although their mission was urgent, they depended on Arab hospitality and could move only at camel speed.

They sat tapping their fingers in the General's plush office, the same one that Mohammed had occupied only a short time before, and they waited for the right moment. Anyone could be bought if the price was right. They drank the General's strong coffee and both sides parried, each wondering how much the information would cost. Patience was not a virtue, it was nine tenths of their job.

General Kapta was secretly delighted. He watched them carefully, like a desert fox with a snake. These men wanted information.

"Mohammed you say. Mohammed Al Harty?"

The stakes were high. If the truth about Mohammed's unofficial departure was known it would be more than an embarrassment for him. He would cost him his job. He touched his moustache nervously. But these men also needed secrecy. Perhaps there was room for negotiation. There would be a price, and there was money on the table for the General if he played his cards right. He tented his fingers appraising them in an attitude of prayer.

"I may be able to help you" he said, "but in this hospital we have to observe both medical confidentiality and maintain military security."

The Russian parried in a monotone. "This man needs our help, General. We've traced a phone call he made from your hospital, and there are people seeking his life. You will be doing him a favour if you can tell us where he is."

There was no need to bargain when they proposed a much higher price than he was going to suggest. The dollars exchanged hands and the two men had their information. Mohammed was indeed their man. Picked up on the desert road - this was the researcher from Baghdad - he was now somewhere in UK through the good offices of a Doctor Sophie. That was their contact. Find her and they'd find Mohammed.

"One more request. We must meet this doctor. Our masters in Moscow and Beijing do not forget favours." As the Russian looked the general straight in the eye he said very slowly "Our people have long memories. Total secrecy is paramount."

He gently ran his index finger across his throat to emphasise the point .

VISITORS

30

WHEN SOPHIE RETURNED to her flat, the letter from Damascus lay on the door mat. "Greetings dear Sophie, from General Kapta." He was asking her to reciprocate a favour in return for his generous hospitality in Damascus. Could she obtain an official invitation for two of his friends to visit Scotland?

Sophie's life had been hectic, first with her graduation and now she had started her residency. She could do without these two visitors. But with good grace, she collected them from the airport on Tuesday after-noon.

She instantly disliked the little Russian, and could not understand his Chinese friend with a briefcase who claimed to be a hospital doctor from Xian wanting to foster medical relationships with a UK orthopaedic rehab unit. The Chinaman claimed to be the big guy - the leader - and the Russian who could speak fluent Mandarin was his interpreter. Strange bedfellows, but for the sake of General Kapta, she had to be hospitable. Anyway, you never knew the outcome of these contacts, and she would try to help them. They would visit the Orthopaedic Hospital tomorrow.

" You've been to Scotland before?"

The Russian's face cracked painfully into a dry smile, and the Chinaman didn't move.

"Came to your festival in '93" he said dryly. "Toured the north-west. This time it's business. Dr Zhang is building professional bridges with your famous hospitals. General Kapta told us you'd be most helpful."

As Sophie took them into the city it was already getting dark and the lights along Princes Street were flickering. Her visitors looked out of the window at the luxury goods, but were silent - perhaps tired from their flight. They were not given to small talk and she was pleased to deposit them on the wet cobbles of Hill Square. University lodgings would be in their price range, and it was convenient for Sophie.

"See you at 10 o'clock tomorrow" she shouted. She crossed the city and ten minutes later turned into Queens Street and found the last vacant space to park her old Vauxhall.

The Russian had wasted no time. Sophie didn't see the taxi pull up behind her, nor the little man under the umbrella get out and walk twenty paces behind her. She didn't see him pause and light a cigarette as she greeted Mohammed nor when they walked together into Jenkinson's the outfitter. She had no idea that they were under video surveillance as she helped Mohammed buy a dark blue Cashmere overcoat, nor that her plans to meet up with Mohammed for dinner that night had been overheard.

THE TIME PROBE

31

MOHAMMED HAD FOUND LODGINGS in the Old Town, and he had been spending much of his time closeted in the library. Edinburgh in December, gripped by a freezing east wind, is no place for an Arab.

This evening, he met Jon at the Greyfriar's Inn.

"May I take your coat, sir?"

The waiter led them to a table by the log fire, and they waited for Sophie to join them for a meal. Mohammed felt secure with his friends. They were his new family - people he could confide in.

They ordered a drink. Mohammed was deep in thought, and then put his hand to his face. Jon thought that his red scar was more noticeable tonight.

"My accident in Syria was no accident Jon."

"Why, Mohammed?"

"I'll share the whole story when Sophie comes."

A cold blast of air and a flurry of snow announced Sophie's arrival, and they moved up to give her a place by the fire. She sat down quickly beside Jon, as they ordered some broth and then haggis and neeps.

Her cheeks were flushed from the cold night air and also from the excitement of being with Jon again. He turned to her. "Mohammed's has something to tell us, Sophie. You might need a very stiff drink."

She asked for an orange juice !

In a low voice, Mohammed began his story.

"My accident in Syria - someone tried to kill me - left me for dead on the border. It wasn't robbery. I was caught up in some political intrigue."

"Is it your research Mohammed?" Jon asked. "You haven't told us about it."

He looked up at his friend, hesitated and then came to a decision.

"I'm going to tell you the most important thing you've ever heard. I'm going to tell you now. You'll find it mind-blowing. It changes the foundation of science. I know I can share it with you and Sophie, but I need total confidentiality."

They leaned over the table - heads together. He explained how he had started his career in mathematics and physics. A doctorate in optics was followed by a fellowship at Harvard. The Russians then recruited him in the early 1980's for a joint project with the Iraqis in Baghdad. They had offered a salary he could not refuse. He had agreed to confidentiality and no one knew of his results beyond the immediate team.

He glanced around the room, lowered his voice and then looked at Sophie.

"My accident in Syria was not an accident Sophie. It was a bungled assassination. They'll try again, and I must share this with someone I can trust."

Jon was trying to understand why Mohammed was looking so anxious.

"But who'd want to kill you Mohammed?" asked Jon incredulously. "You're the man who put mirrors into space to save on electricity. Our western press said it was a new source of energy, a triumph for the Greens, good use of natural resources, a tremendous breakthrough. It was going to be so successful that electrical illumination will soon be obsolete. Or was it a hoax?"

"Jon, you don't understand. Yes - the official communication about the work described the way we can illuminate cities from reflected rays of the sun. That was the first satellite. That's partially successful but it won't be economically viable for a long time. But there was something else. Piggyback onto this research we've been doing some basic science to look back into the past."

He paused.

"We've invented a 'time-probe'."

Jon and Sophie were silent. They looked at each other and then exploded in laughter.

"It can't be done Mohammed. It's not pure science. It's science fiction."

Sophie had a little more respect than Jon. "Tell us about it Mohammed."

"We put another great satellite into space" he said " in a different orbit. The Russians built that. It's sixty metres long, the size of an articulated lorry and perfectly white, packed full of electronics and covered in mirrors and radio transmitters. It's probably the most sophisticated, innovative laboratory ever put into space. I was there at its launch. The greatest day of my life. It was rolled back to its pad and under a full moon, and with a rumble that echoed for miles it powered off into space. It stretched out its antennae without a hitch, and it now crosses both poles and sweeps the entire earth every three days."

"And how does it work Mohammed?" said Sophie full of expectation.

He lowered his voice again.

"Every time you look into a mirror, you are seeing the past, Sophie. Light is a mystery, but it's speed is finite [31]. Have you stood in a lift with mirrors on either side of you, and looked down the long corridor of mirrors until your image disappears into the distance? The small image you see in the far distance comes to you from the past. With the speed of light at about 186,000 miles per second and one or two transmissions, we are only talking about milliseconds. We have been working on this simple principle that light has a finite speed, and by reflecting the light we can look back in time and see when the light was first transmitted. Even with our reflectors in space, each transit of light takes only fractions of a second. But with repeated transmissions it accumulates."

Jon looked disbelievingly at his friend.

"Mohammed - I'm no physicist but I've two problems. First you've already said you can't look very far back in time, and secondly as images lose definition, eventually you'll see nothing."

"Second question first Jon. We found a way to enhance the image from the mirrors. We blow it up in size and get rid of the noise. We've worked on the probability theory, reinforcing the fuzzy photons to the probable image. We convert in to a digitised radio signal, send it back to the satellite and the images go back and forth many times, being cleaned up each time they hit our receiver in Baghdad and then they are re-transmitted again."

"For your first question - we can actually go back quite a long way, because there is no limit to the number of times we bounce the images off our reflectors. It means we can now reconstitute from our reflectors the same light that left the earth many years ago."

"So you are saying that you have found a way to look back in time. Come off it Mohammed. There's another problem that's much bigger. Surely even if you are right, you can only see the light that was transmitted when you first started the research. The photons that left the earth before your satellite went up into space, have long since gone off to some distant star. Some creatures out there might be able to see what we did in the distant past, but we can never catch up with those images. The train has already left the station."

Sophie was more defensive, "Well if he can look back to the launch of his satellite, that's something Jon. When did you put your first mirrors into space Mohammed? Two or three years ago?"

"It's better than that Sophie. We first positioned out mirrors in 1986 and refined them two years later. But you're right. We can only look back to the late 80's."

"Our satellite is 600 miles up in space. It takes 150 transmissions to look back one second. But multiply that by infinitely large numbers and we can see events that happened on the earth right back to the start of our project."

They'd managed to work their way through half the meal without tasting anything.

RE-WRITING HISTORY

32

IT TOOK JON AND SOPHIE some time to understand what Mohammed was saying. They could do no other than believe him. He certainly believed himself. And if he was right what did the pictures show? What made it such a dangerous piece of work for someone to want to kill him?

Mohammed continued. "From the start the mirrors were focused on the trouble spots of the world - Moscow, Beijing, Yugoslavia, the Gulf, Israel and Central Asia. In our own country, Iraq, we were watching the Kurds, the Shiites and the Marsh Arabs. As long as the mirrors were directed at places of interest, we didn't have to process them until we wanted information. We didn't even have to store the images like video pictures, but the light could be retrieved any time at a later date whenever it was needed."

They had stopped eating and were listening in silence.

"The Russians wanted us to process some of the important events like Tienenman Square. The definition was remarkable. You can go back time and again and get the same views, and I can tell you, the official Chinese explanation of 1989 is a fabrication. The students had no chance.

Hundreds of them were killed. I can show you history without censorship. And that must be dangerous."

Jon and Sophie were beginning to understand.

"We were not permitted to process the pictures of Iraq - the chemical and biological weapon systems, nor the mass murders! They are stored up there on the satellite, but our government wouldn't let us down load them. It was too risky."

"Say that again!" said Jon.

"If the UN knew about our 'time probe' it would alter the politics of the whole of the Middle East. It would show who are the people with blood on their hands. Some of them are still in power. The Israelis wouldn't be able to hide their war efforts. Russia too would have to re-write the history of Chechnia. It's a secret nobody knows but my bosses in Iraq and Russia."

"And you !" said Sophie and Jon together.

Now they knew why Mohammed had a price on his head.

"There's more my friends, but that must wait for another time."

"Where do you keep your data Mohammed?"

Jon had identified the important question. If others could get the data, Mohammed was lost.

" I'll tell you one day Jon."

MURDER

33

THEY PAID THE BILL, and were about the leave the comfort and security of the inn with its warm log fire and friendly atmosphere. It was snowing heavily outside, and was bitterly cold. Mohammed was thankful for the new woollen overcoat he bought earlier in the day, but when he reached up to the coat stand it was missing.

"Oh no!" said Sophie. "We were so engrossed in what you were saying, we didn't see your coat had gone. And three hundred pounds!"

"No worry. Better mine than yours." He was not distressed. He was not a penniless student.

"A new coat isn't a big deal for me. Some poor guy's got a greater need than me."

It occurred to Jon that Mohammed might have a lot more money in the Jersey bank. But about the coat - they could do nothing.

"It's probably drugs Mohammed" said Sophie. "We've such a big junkie problem here. They steal anything to feed the habit."

"Let's get you a taxi and at least you'll get home without freezing to death."

They left the Inn and were about to pile into the taxi when Mohammed was relieved to see his coat a only a few yards away. It was in a bundle at the corner of the street.

"Wait a minute" he said and stepped cautiously through the snow towards it. He then turned to his friends urgently.

"Sophie - Jon - over here."

Looking closer, Mohammed's coat was covering a sleeping addict. Or was he sleeping? Mohammed touched him with his foot and there was a trickle of fresh blood, scarlet on the snow. The wearer of the coat had been shot through the neck. It was precise - one clean shot by a disciplined professional. And Mohammed knew immediately that the bullet was meant for him!

Mohammed glanced right and left. There were assassins out there, who'd followed him from the Syrian desert. Were they watching even now from the shadows?

A few curious on-lookers gathered round. At this time of night, the city was over-run with boozers, ruffians and hell-raisers in general, but Sophie had not seen death on the streets before. This really hit her in the pit of the stomach. She thought she was a tough member of the hospital crash team who could be at the scene of arrests within two minutes. She had a diploma in Advanced Trauma Life Support and had seen the more gruesome side of medicine. She was no stranger to sudden death, but this was personal. This was intended for her friend. She used her mobile to call the emergency services, and left no name. They piled into the taxi, to hurry home with Mohammed through the driving snow.

TIME IS SLOWING DOWN

34

THEY TALKED NERVOUSLY long into the night, and decided that Edinburgh was no longer a safe haven. Mohammed was also troubled that he was putting his two friends at risk and he would need to find a secure place for their sakes.

"Mohammed, if there's more, you'll have to tell us. Was your research more than surveillance and intelligence?"

"That's probably why some politicians want me out of the way. They want to keep their real history hidden. The data's in the satellite, and I know how to process it. They must know I've kept records. If I was dead, the data would probably never see the light of day. It would burn up one day, when the satellite re-enters the atmosphere."

Sophie looked at him. "Shouldn't you tell us about this Mohammed - in case these guys win - where've you stored it and how to access it? It sounds awful, but at least if we knew, you'd know that your work wasn't in vain."

"If I told you, then you'd be the next target Sophie."

Jon was looking worried. "I agree with Sophie. But what's this about 'more'? You said there was more to your research than surveillance and intelligence. Tell us everything Mohammed."

They settled down with hot drinks hoping to hear the rest of the story.

"Well my friends - yes - there is a lot more. It is to do with cosmic science. It's what we were discussing with your astronomer friend Frank. It's a scientific breakthrough, but not really politically dangerous. The data shows some dramatic changes to the earth in the past fifteen years. You'll appreciate it Jon."

"You are saying that the earth is changing !"

"The satellite shows that the days are getting longer. The 24 hour day when we first put the mirrors into space is now a longer day."

They just listened.

"It's not much, but there is a 0.7% increase in the length of the day over a fifteen year period - it's a real change."

Jon and Sophie still said nothing. They looked incredulous and then spoke together.

"Can you be sure it's not an error in the system?".

"What do you think it means?"

"Not only has time changed, but the size of the earth has changed. It is definitely bigger than it was fifteen years ago. The satellite is so sophisticated that it can detect one millimetre disturbances in the ground over a year. It's not a big increase - only about 0.4% - but it's genuine. If that has been going on for a few hundred years it means that the earth is expanding at some rate."

Jon was now speaking to himself.

"You say there's more time in the day - 'time' is getting slower - and the earth is getting bigger - expanding continents - that means lower gravity. It has been suggested before, but not as rapidly as this. And you've published nothing Mohammed?"

He realised as he asked the question that there was nothing in the literature or he would have heard about it.

"Are you confident of your data Mohammed?"

Not only was Mohammed sure of his facts, he was sure they would impact on all the earth's sciences.

"This affects what we think about the meaning of time. We're on the brink of testing a revolutionary new hypothesis on time and the universe."

"You're right." Jon realised the implications immediately.

"It means the earth is younger than we think !"

"There in one, Jon."

Mohammed could see that Sophie didn't understand so he turned to her.

"It's as though you watched a high-speed power boat crawl into the harbour at 4 miles an hour after a journey of a hundred miles. If you assumed it had been doing the same slow speed all the way across the ocean, you'd guess it had been travelling for 25 hours. In fact you didn't know it had been doing most of the journey at 50 miles an hour and the travelling time was really only two hours."

"So a slow pace of time now," said Jon "might hide a much faster pace in the past, and the real age of the earth could be young."

Mohammed draw a graph (Fig 1).

"If it's true, it's fantastic," said Jon thoughtfully.

Mohammed agreed. "I guess the main people out there who want me silenced are the politicians - they want to hide their history. But I won't make many friends in the scientific establishment either. There are interested parties who don't want any change in the status quo. They have vested interests.[32] "

Sophie now took charge.

"And do you have records of this Mohammed?"

He nodded. He had to trust these two young people. "Computer discs. And in the safest place - Jersey."

"Mohammed, if what you're saying is right, you're onto something unique. The men who are after you are not playing games. I suggest we all get some sleep, and tomorrow we'll get you away to the north."

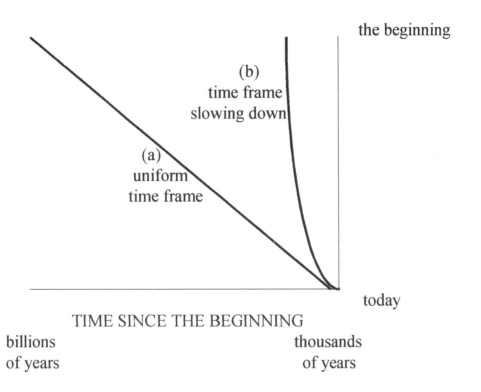

the beginning

(b)
time frame
slowing down

(a)
uniform
time frame

today

TIME SINCE THE BEGINNING

billions
of years

thousands
of years

FIG ONE. Diagram showing a different estimate of the age of the cosmos if time in the physical time frame has (a) always been uniform and if (b) it was faster in the past than it is today.

FIG 1

The estimated age of the cosmos depends on the speed of time

They decided to stay in the flat together. Sophie had the bed. Jon found a sleeping bag and Mohammed bedded down on the couch. Sleep came in short naps.

THE TRAIN NORTH

35

JON HAD NO IMMEDIATE commitments beyond gathering material and reading to prepare for his PhD degree, but Sophie was in the middle of her first residency. She had no alternative but to stay in Edinburgh. Jon could take Mohammed to Aberdeen in the north where Sophie's brother Andrew had a student's flat.

Heavy snow had fallen all night, and the sky was grey on that Wednesday morning. They peeked through the blinds and scanned the street.

Mohammed gave Sophie a white envelope. "Open this Sophie if I don't come back."

"Never" she said. "You'll be okay. Know you will" and she hugged him.

An embrace with Jon. She hated the thought of him leaving her - every farewell was now painful. He'd become the love of her life.

"All clear."

The two men stepped carefully through the uncleared snow, and along the slippery pavements to Waverley railway station, glancing anxiously around to be sure they were not being followed. Maybe the assassins, whoever they were, thought they had silenced the right man.

"Two singles to Aberdeen."

They found corner seats where they could talk and the 10.18 train lumbered slowly towards Haymarket and then over the Forth bridge. The forecast was ominous. Snow covered the hills, and there were heavy dark clouds ahead. They had warm clothes, a back pack and heavy boots, and for all the world looked like two men about to start a winter holiday.

Jon was the first to speak. "I phoned Andrew and he'll give us a bed for tonight, and then help us get up to Nairn on the Moray Firth. Will that leg stand up to a bit of skiing Mohammed?"

He had recovered well enough from his injuries and had lost his limp, but skiing was an other matter.

"I'll give it a try, but it's some years since I was on snow." He was not as fit as Jon, but he was looking forward to a mountain retreat and the chance to bounce ideas off his friend.

"I've been thinking Mohammed. There are only two options. Either your research is flawed, or you are right and time is slowing down. And I'm sorry to say so, but I think it is more likely that your work is flawed."

"That's what I thought, but I've gone over the data again and again. I don't think there is any way that the optical system could make the days seem longer nor change the size of the earth. Take it from me Jon, I sincerely think that time is slowing down, and the earth is getting bigger."

Jon looked disbelievingly, so Mohammed continued.

"Part of the slowing down of time is linked with the expanding earth. It's like the ice skater curled up into a small ball spinning very fast, and then they decelerate by stretching out their arms. If the earth is expanding, its spin will slow down. [33] [34]"

" Are you saying that's the reason for the longer days?"

"Not sure, but it might be important."

He looked up at Mohammed.

"We know the continents are slowly moving about [35] and you're not the first to say that the earth's expanding [35] [36] [37] [38]. It reminds me of the 'shrinking Sun' [39]. It's debatable, but if the Sun can have a cyclical change in size why not the earth? And nuclear fission within the earth could heat up the planet and make it expand."

He started to draw. "So what does it mean if the earth's getting bigger?

There are three implications - a longer day - a longer year - and with a smaller gravity on the earth's surface, a slower pendulum for Big Ben! An expanding earth would make these three clocks all slow down together "

The earth gets bigger

it rotates more slowly - *a longer day*
the earth's circuit round the sun takes longer - *a longer year* [33] [34]
gravity on the surface gets less - *a slower pendulum* [40] [41] [42]

The train rattled round the bends and into the Fife countryside.

Jon thought some more. "The pendulum would swing more slowly, but what about atomic clocks and the quartz crystal. Don't they keep perfect time. If the earth is revolving more slowly, why aren't the atomic clocks running faster? There'd be more time in the day for molecular vibrations."

"Jon, you are asking the same questions that I've been struggling with for months. It can't be only the cosmos - the macroworld - that's moving more slowly, but the microworld of the quantum must also slowing down. If it's all slowing down together, then I think we're living in a time frame that's slowing down, and we don't know it."

> **We would not know**
> that time was slowing down if both the *cosmos*
> and *molecular activity* was slowing down together

"Is it possible Mohammed?" asked Jon, almost as if he were asking himself.

"There's nothing in physics to deny it. Einstein said that there's no such thing as universal time. Time is not absolute - it can change in relation to gravity and to acceleration - so it can clearly change from place to place [43] [44] [45] [46] [47]."

> **Two simultaneous time frames in different places**
> Time frame in place (a) is different to time frame in place (b)

"Slow down Mohammed. Let's go a step at a time. We agree that time is affected by gravity and by acceleration. So there's a different time frame from place to place. If we experience a major gravitational force like being close to a black hole, time will slow down - and with infinite gravity time will eventually stop. Yes - we all know that the atomic clock at sea level, runs slower than the same clock at the top of the mountain where gravity is less. I accept that. And acceleration also makes time slow down. A twin who leaves the earth in a space craft returns younger than the brother he leaves behind. I accept that too.

But you're also saying that time can change in one place, over a period of time - it can change sequentially - from time to time."

> **Two sequential time frames in the same place**
> Time frame at time (a) is different to time frame at time (b)

"Sure. I'm suggesting that time changes from one epoch to another. I'm saying that the time today is no longer the same as time was a decade ago, if the whole cosmos is slowing down. Today's atomic clock is running slower than the atomic clock fifteen years ago when we sent our satellite into space. I don't know why it is running slower. It's not *local* gravitational change because I think the earth's gravity is getting less not more. It maybe the whole of motion of the cosmos in space, or just our swirling galaxy that is slowing down relative to yesterday, but in the process, time is slowing down. We might be approaching a black hole!"

Jon thought there must be a flaw in the argument.

"Even when approaching a Black Hole the astronaut wouldn't know that time was slowing down."

"Exactly" said Mohammed. "He'd only know if he had an independent clock in a different time-frame, and that's what our 'time-probe' has discovered - the chance to look back fifteen years into a previous time-frame."

Jon was deep in thought.

> **We'd know if our time frame was slowing down**
> if we could get records from a *previous time* frame or
> if we could see a *parallel* time frame somewhere else

The food trolley knocked against Jon's arm

"Sorry sir. Tea or coffee?"

"Thanks."

They warmed their hands on the hot paper cups, both of them deep in thought. Even though Jon was a geologist with some understanding of the concept of time, Mohammed was going too fast for him.

"If time is slowing down, and the earth is younger than we think - how young ?"

Mohammed had been there before.

"I can't speak for the events in deep time Jon [48] . We have to keep our research in context. But I can say that just now the earth's rotation is slowing down quite quickly. The scientific world doesn't know it, because everything else is slowing down as well."

The swaying train wound its way through the Fife countryside and Jon looked at the white landscape. Across the Tay bridge to Dundee, round the coast to Arbroath and then into Montrose. They kept talking, and the snow was getting deeper as they travelled further north.

"Mohammed. Never mind the politicians. You're also taking on a powerful scientific establishment. They'll drive a coach and horses through your arguments. There's always the odd ball who'll go along with you - who likes to be different and will latch on to anything novel - but there are powerful guys out there with all sorts of interests who will slay you. Scientists with their own lifetime of precious research don't want to see their work toppled. Philosophers and humanists, media giants and educationalists - all of these will be out for your blood. They'll discredit your work, call you dishonest or even crazy. Never mind the politicians who don't want to know the truth about Tianenman Square or Kosovo. They're small fry. If you start talking about the slowing down of time, the implications are tremendous. You'll be a martyr."

THE WRONG IDENTITY

36

THE RUSSIAN LOOKED in amazement at the front page of Wednesday's *Scotsman*. He translated for Li Zhou. Something had gone seriously wrong with the job. They'd iced the wrong man, and they were both angry! There was half a column about a new twist in the drug war with a dealer shot dead in Old Town and they cursed in several tongues.

In spite of their irritation they waited for Sophie to take them to the rehab unit.

"Had a good night?" asked Sophie in her ignorance, as she drove them through the city.

They exchanged a few pleasantries and asked how often Sophie received visitors from overseas.

"You're the first" she said as she left them with the assistant hospital manager.

They maintained their cover and stayed at the hospital asking all the right questions. They distributed gifts of oriental silk and worry balls, and invited several physiotherapists to China.

Sophie collected her guests at the end of the morning, and drove them into town. As she edged her way through the city traffic, her mobile bleeped.

"Hello Jon." She lowered her voice but they heard her. "Where are you? Love you too. Yes, I'll ring you at Andrew's tonight."

They were professionals. They'd done their homework and knew Sophie had a brother in Aberdeen.

"Thank you Dr Tristan."

They packed their belongings and made a hurried departure, taking the last train north.

PART TWO

USA

37

THE LONG ARM of the USA reached to Baghdad. The mighty dollar works wonders and it had not been difficult to put Mohammed's lawyer onto the American pay-role. When they were using mirrors to illuminate Russian cities, Uncle Sam maintained only a passing interest. But once Mohammed's lawyer said that that this was a screen for a 'time probe', it had international significance, and the President was informed.

The White House aids were in a flurry of activity with a series of top level discussions. If the work was genuine and it was really possible to see into the recent past, it could cause enormous mischief, especially if someone else was in control. The propaganda potential was enormous and the US was understandably jealous. The President could not sleep easy.

Espionage and counter-espionage meant that the three great powers - USA, Russia and China - all knew that they each had a common interest in Mohammed. Their leaders conferred, albeit with their own agendas. First the Russians had promised to remove Mohammed. But they had bungled it. Mohammed was on the run and had disappeared. The Iraqi laboratory had been sealed and the equipment was under wraps, but the key research worker was not yet buried. He had the essential knowledge and perhaps some important data which could bring some criminals to trial.

At least Mohammed's trail was not cold. Two wolf hounds had picked up the scent. It led to a bank account in Jersey and to an English doctor.

The President thought this one was important. He scanned the dossier and reached a quick decision. He wanted his own man over there, to find Mohammed quickly and bring him over to the States, because he was the one man who knew the whole project. There was a fall back position to keep this work out of the public domain - retrieve the data and silence the man permanently.

However, the Scientific Division had been called in, because there was an unbelievable twist in the story. It was an new complication. The lawyer's last message said that Mohammed had evidence that 'time' itself was changing. And he believed that the earth was expanding. It sounded like one of the Baghdad bluffs, but they could take no chances. It was even more essential to find Mohammed, and get this piece of work onto the right side of the Atlantic. The big problem was that the Russian and the Chinaman were hot on Mohammed's trail, and they had left the world's super-power out of the race.

The emergency meeting of the President's advisers lasted into the dark hours. How could a little Arab with a box of tricks threaten the global security? A time probe that could re-write history was dangerous. That was bad enough. But there was this business about the concept of 'time'.

The head of the National Scientific Division began to speak in his Boston accent.

"If there's evidence - false evidence of course - that time is slowing down, it will be a problem for our scientists" and he mustered a faint smile. "It has serious implications because this is the cross roads between science and fundamental religion. If it were true, it would mean that the world is young - interesting but dangerous and inflammatory. It affects what we teach in our schools about evolution. The religious right will not leave us in peace".

It was bad news for this administration because the main constituent group of the opposition party was the Christian conservatives.

"It's not just propaganda for the religious right, but it will fan the flames of fanatical Islam across the Middle East. Any ideas that undermine the science on which the West is built, will bring more volunteers to the Taliban, help al Qa'eda, and recruit more suicide bombers to attack our cities. It will encourage the Muslim religious revival in Central Asia, and destabilise China."

The President looked at his CIA Chief.

"These little ideas can become mountains. Use one of your best men" he said and he swept out of the room.

• • •

SINCE THAT FATEFUL DAY of September 11th 2001, the rules governing the CIA had been relaxed. The system was now free from constraints. The gloves were off. It meant they could employ their new man - Max Bellman.

"He's waiting outside," said one of the aids, looking at the Chief.

"The big guy. Tex—"

"Get'm in here!"

Max stood before an impressive array of seniors. They looked at his record. It was dodgey, but he was cunning and efficient. His criminal background mattered no more. He had once been a professional confidence trickster, but now he was on their side, having exchanged a long jail sentence to work for the CIA.

Max liked his new fictitious name - Max Bellman. Here he was, called to the White House for the biggest job of his life. He was told enough to understand the importance of his mission. Find Mohammed and retrieve the data.

The chairman of the influential House Intelligence Committee looked across at Max.

"The President needs all the data" he said. "Some of it is pseudo-research, but it has potential to rock the foundations of science. There is enough fringe science - belief in the occult, mysticism, spiritism and fundamentalist religion. If this gets into the wrong hands ...... get his data for us whether Mohammed is dead or alive."

Max was the man for the job. He was an impressive six foot three and nearly 100 kilograms. He was as fit as any quarterback in America. He did a work-out in the gym every day, climbed ropes, pumped iron and practised karate exercises.

This man looked startlingly young. His healthy appearance belied his 36 years. His tight T-shirt stuck to his chest and arms. He was a serious weight lifter and he wanted folks to know it. Max exuded confidence, having long decided that his previous problems were not of his own making. They were the result of genes; his alleged father was an alcoholic and had died in jail and his mother a manic depressive. And they were the result of his environment; wouldn't any sensible man, brought up in the Bible Belt, be the same?

"I'll be honoured to help, by God!"

Who was God anyway? Hank had done so many evil things that if God existed he knew he would have a bad time on judgement day. Best not to think about it. It had been a hard road, but life's experiences had combined to make a man of him. Here he was in the White House to prove it, and there were 'big bucks' if he got it right.

Max was fully briefed and was on the first plane to Scotland. He had to find Sophie. That was the start of his trail.

A WARNING

38

IT WAS A BUSY DAY for Sophie. She'd deposited her two guests in at their lodgings in Hill Square, and now Max Bellman stopped her in the hospital car park. He touched his fur hat - had a predilection for fur hats and he knew how to treat a lady.

"Ma'am - you must be Dr Tristan - Max Bellman."

He showed her his identity, and decided to be direct. He was from the US government seeking Mohammed Al Harty. He had good news for him, but he knew of a bogus medical delegation from Russia and China who were agents intent on doing him harm. He wanted to know it she had any clue to Mohammed's whereabouts.

She froze at the news - that she knew the assassins, those who had shot a man on the pavement only the previous night, and even now must be trailing Mohammed. Were they the very people she had been entertaining? She may have actually helped them find Mohammed.

She glanced warily at this smooth-talking Max. "Let me make a call."

"The university residency?"

"Yes - they checked out a few minutes ago with their luggage."

Max was right. It must mean they were going north.

"Why is Mohammed so dangerous?" she asked. "And how come the States are involved?"

Max took in a deep breath. He wanted to know if Mohammed was in safe hiding and how he could find him before the others.

"This is confidential stuff ma'am. C'mon. We need a place to talk." They crossed the street, found a quiet cafe and Max bought her a cappuccino.

He spilled half of his coffee in the saucer. This strong man was nervous, or was he an actor? He pulled his fingers through a mass of thick hair, looked around and continued in a southern drawl. "Mohammed's work interests certain political groups. It's to do with surveillance, and some governments would rather forget their history. They'd rather re-write it, and Mohammed's work won't let them. We have an interest because it affects our international relations - and world peace. We can offer him work in USA. We'll pay for his knowledge but just now he is in more need of protection than we are in need of him. And so are you ma'am. Anyone who knows Mohammed's whereabouts is in the shooting line".

This American knew his facts. He seemed genuine, but she was wise enough to just listen and let him talk.

She could honestly say - "I'm not sure where he is just now" but she had difficulty hiding the truth.

"Yea. But Sophie, I need to know how to warn him. This is serious ma'am. It is a matter of life and death."

She sat for a while before making a decision. She had to trust him.

She told him about Andrew in Aberdeen and the contact number, and as soon as Max left she picked up her cell-phone and was through to Jon again.

This time her voice was trembling. Jon knew there was something wrong.

"Jon, you're being followed. The two 'doctors' I've been entertaining in Edinburgh are the assassins, and they've checked out. They must be on their way to Aberdeen."

There was pause as Jon took this in.

"How do you know Sophie?"

"I've met an American. He wants to offer Mohammed a job in the States, and he says this Russian and Chinaman are in hot pursuit. It makes sense. Oh Jon, take care!"

"We'll talk about it tonight Sophie. What about this God of ours? He knows all about it. Love you."

ANDREW'S LIBERAL THEOLOGY

39

ANDREW WAS WAITING for Jon and Mohammed at the station. He was so unlike Sophie - tall, lanky and deliberate in speech. His sallow complexion and solemn features suggested that he could do with some fresh air. The city too, was more grey than usual on this early Wednesday afternoon when it was already getting dark.

"We're almost inside the Arctic Circle up here."

Andrew took them to his lodgings where they phoned Sophie. She was full of remorse. It was not good news. She was sure they were being pursued by two ruthless killers, and she didn't even know if they could trust this American. If the Edinburgh train got through the blizzard tonight, they would be in trouble. The best thing was to bed down, and head further north in the morning.

"Take care Jon. Love you."

"Love you too."

Andrew agreed to loan them his car for the journey north the next day - if the roads remained passable.

For now he raided the freezer to feed his unexpected guests.

"You can't leave Aberdeen without tasting kippers!"

He had a palate for Arbroath kippers - smoked herring. He bought them by the kilo on the quay side, and they kept for months in the freezer. Jon smiled to himself. If Aberdonians are not mean, they are thrifty. Dissecting kippers was a new experience for Mohammed and he struggled valiantly with a couple of fish. He responded with some hilarity.

"You come to my home Andrew and you'll have curry! More seriously - I've got a hot subject for you tonight."

He put his plate of herring bones to one side.

"Andrew. I need your views."

Mohammed wanted to know what Christian theologians thought about the book of Genesis. If Andrew was training to be a church minister, he should have the answer.

"We Muslims have a spectrum of different views - from the strict fundamentalists to the more liberal academics. What about Christians?"

Andrew relaxed. He leaned back in his chair and clasped his hands on the top of his head. This was his subject.

"Sophie will tell you that Genesis is verbally correct [49]. She's one of these evangelicals - and there are more around than you'd think. Without any logic, they hold to the literal accuracy of the Bible whatever science may say. She thinks the earth is young - Genesis is right - and that Methuselah lived for 900 years. Never mind what Jon here says about a fifteen billion year old universe and Darwin telling us about slow evolution - Sophie will have none of it."

"I should take you to see Job's tomb" said Mohammed. "Job of the Bible is buried in Oman and the inscription on is tomb says he lived 287 years! [50] "

Andrew thought that was ridiculous. He didn't take the bait, but instead looked apologetically towards Jon.

"Sorry Jon, but my sister really irritates me on this! She doesn't read fourteenth century medical text books to understand medicine, so why does she believe in a literal Genesis? We've arrived at the 21st century.

When she comes to Genesis, she rejects all the major scholarship in biology, geology, physics, chemistry and palaeontology. She ignores what countless scientists have said - Christians included - over the last two hundred of years."

Mohammed looked at him. "Then what do you think Andrew? What do they tell you at the University?"

Andrew grinned. He was riding his hobby-horse.

"Central to the whole subject is the hermeneutical question."

"Andrew ! Make it simple. Even I don't understand you."

"Okay." He went on slowly. "It's about hermeneutics - the science of interpretation. You have to think about the contemporary culture - when it was written. And to understand the ancient text, you need twenty-first century spectacles."

"So what's it saying to us now Andrew?"

"It was written for the pre-scientific people of earlier days. It's obvious that God took His time - lots of it - and the 'days' of Genesis are only 'epochs'. We've got to be fairly liberal with the interpretation of Genesis."

He continued, "Old Galileo said that the Bible was written 'not to show how the heavens go, but to show us how to go to heaven'. He was right. There's more to the Bible than Genesis. It has an important message - but frankly we think lots of the Old Testament is myth."

He looked at Jon for support.

"So you don't read it literally?"

Andrew shook his head. "There was probably no real Adam and Eve. When the first man and woman developed in the long evolutionary line, it was not a sudden change but a gradual process. Presumably the unique features of humans - the ability to worship, and to hope for immortality - are the features which our Bible talks about when it says that mankind was made in the image of God, but we can't hold to a six day, unique creation of different kinds of living things any more."

They were listening.

"Yes God was there in the beginning. He controlled it all, and evolution was not just chance, but He worked out his design very, very slowly. We have no difficulty agreeing with the views of science and giving free interpretation to Genesis [51]."

Andrew was somewhat surprised when Jon didn't back him up. Perhaps Jon was so besotted with love for his sister that he'd lost his judgement. He'd expected Jon to be saying that the evidence from geology made any view about a young earth look absurd. But Jon didn't respond.

Jon just looked thoughtful. This was not the time to challenge Andrew, but he thought Sophie's brother was not being consistent. If he blamed Sophie for being ignorant about the patient work of scientists when she preferred the Bible's account of events, wasn't Andrew doing the same in his own discipline? As a theologian he was forgetting something.

> **A succession of scholarly Christians over twenty centuries**
> have stood firmly on scripture in spite of living in a world of disbelief,
> and have not been afraid of being
> at odds with the world.

Jon was becoming suspicious of a liberal Christian theology, which seemed to reject, or at least re-interpret the kind of God described in the Christian scriptures. It didn't match with the Bible he was reading. But he reserved his counsel.

• • •

WHILE JON AND MOHAMMED enjoyed their smoked kippers, the train carrying the Russian and the Chinaman was fortunately making very slow progress through the ever falling snow. It was unusual for the last train of the day not to make Aberdeen, but then it was very unusual weather, even for Scotland.

Once north of Dundee the train crawled. The driver couldn't see more than a few yards into the night because of a blanket of heavily falling snow. The train stopped several times in mid-country and finally the guard announced that they would not get beyond Montrose that night. They pulled into the station where there was hot soup waiting for them, and camp beds were laid out in a dank waiting-room. The night closed in, and they bedded down on pillows that smelled of mildew, and under blankets that smelled of mould, vainly trying to sleep.

Li Zhou thoughts returned to his prison cell in Shi He Ze.

FURTHER NORTH

40

AT FIRST LIGHT Jon and Mohammed were in a small VW with skis strapped to the roof. Jon glanced several times in his mirrors and watched his tail.

He laughed with relief. "Never done this before ! We're in the clear - up the coast - and then inland to Elgin."

The deep snow meant that it was single track by the time they got to Nairn.

"Once at Kilranan Castle we'll be lost to the world" Jon said. "It was good enough for Bonnie Prince Charlie when he fled from the English red-coats in 1746, and it should do for us." Jon had stayed at the castle with the University Mountaineering Club, and he knew that the head of the Clan kept an open door.

It was a white-out, and when they took to the small secondary roads they had to abandon the VW and take to their skis, covering the last couple of miles over deep powdered snow to reach the castle entrance.

They looked up at the turrets of the imposing castle, and Jon turned to his less fit friend. "The corridors will be cold and windswept, the ball cocks in the loo frozen, the hot water will come fitfully in small peaty trickles, but I promise you the welcome will be warm enough!" And he was right.

"C'mon in. Where have you two strangers come from on a night like this?"

They were welcomed with a large bowl of steaming Scotch broth. There was no problem with accommodation for a few days, because they were the only guests.

• • •

LATE INTO THE EVENING, they sat alone in the mahogany-panelled lounge with a jug of coffee, and talked by the flickering firelight. Around them were pieces of shining armour glinting in the shadows, and the finest collection of antique muskets in Scotland. A gallery of proud family portraits from many generations, seemed to eye them with curiosity.

They continued talking into the wee hours.

"It's strange Jon, that Andrew who's reading theology doesn't believe the Bible is accurate, and yet Sophie a medic has no problem. She thinks that the earth is young - she's no confidence in evolution and says that each of the different kinds of life was a special creation. She's had a science background and she has no problem with a six day creation and the long ages of the patriarchs."

He looked across at Jon. "Where are you Jon? Do you agree with Sophie, or go along with Andrew who thinks that the Bible is a book of fables useful for people in a previous age, but it needs re-interpreting today?"

Jon had been deep in thought for much of he day. He put more wood on the fire and watched it blaze.

"I'm on a journey Mohammed, and if you're asking about my theology, lets take it slowly. We've got three friends with widely different views - there's Frank the astronomer, Andrew the theologian, and Sophie the doctor.

Frank with his astronomy used to influence me a lot. He believes in a God who was there at the beginning and created everything, a universe that was finely tuned, and then he says the Almighty just stepped back and let it run its course. God is the 'absentee landlord'. No more miracles. We're on our own. Frank only accepts the first three verses of Genesis and - finish.

Frank's a great astronomer but I think he's missing the point. God's spoken in nature and He must be a great God. He can't be less than his creation. That was my motive for doing geology. God's fingerprints are in His creation and I am trying to think His thoughts after Him.

Science - natural theology - reinforces my belief in a God who cares enough to make such an amazing world. If an infinitely wise God spent so much effort to create this Universe, it's logical to me that He'd want to say something to His creatures about 'why' He bothered to create it. Surely the Creator wouldn't leave us totally in the dark, but reveal some of the reasons for our existence.

So I take on board that the Author of the Universe has spoken not only in nature and also by special revelation - miracles, answered prayer. And if we human beings, with that unique bit of our brains called Broca's area, can communicate by speaking, talking and reasoning like we're doing now, then I think it's reasonable that the Almighty has spoken particularly in words, by inspiring holy men to write Scripture."

He remembered his childhood days at church.

"He's spoken to me and thousands more, through reading the Bible."

Mohammed seemed to understand.

"So you think the Almighty made it all, He's a great God and He cares enough to reveal things about Himself to anyone who will listen."

Jon nodded, and he had the uncanny feeling that one of the oil painted portraits hanging on the wall, was smiling at him!

"Then there's Andrew the theologian. He says that although God has revealed some things about Himself through nature and the Bible, a lot of the Bible stories are myth and poetry. He says that it's not to be taken literally, and we have to interpret it in the light of modern culture. He believes in some of the New Testament but not in miracles, and certainly not in a six day creation. He thinks the Old Testament is a book of fables.

I can sympathise with that because I used to be there myself, having problems taking the whole Bible as gospel. Andrew says he tries to decide what is *literary* and what is *literal*. But that's not the point. The real question is not about style. It's not about what is literary interpretation as opposed to literal interpretation. The big question is whether it's saying things that are true or false[52]. A beautiful poem is okay, but if it is not about true facts, it'll only mislead.

> **The One who made the Universe**
> would have no difficulty in making any literary form match
> exactly with the very way He had created everything -
> as it says - in six days.

Should I agree with Andrew and discard the difficult parts that don't seem to agree with science? But then where do you stop? If God has revealed true things about Himself and about the reasons for our being here, if He's shared this revelation in a holy book, why shouldn't the important facts like the creation story be right?"

"I guess Jon, that lots of theologians shifted their position when Lyell and Darwin came along!"

"You're right. One hundred and fifty years ago, science made them re-examine the Bible. For me too, geology seemed to contradict what I was taught at Sunday School and the early chapters of Genesis. Cosmologists say that the Universe is 15 billion years old, and we geologists claim that the earth is 4 billion years old. And Darwin needed that sort of time scale or even more. I used to say, 'surely these giants of science can't be wrong !'

I'm no biologist, but Sophie thinks Darwin is wrong. She thinks Darwin's had his day. She asks what's the difference between a slow miracle and a quick one? She quotes Chesterton who said about Darwin that 'an event is not any more intrinsically intelligible or unintelligible because of the pace at which it moves [53].'"

"So you think we should read the Bible literally and wait for science to catch up."

Mohammed put some more logs on the fire. He thought about Sophie who'd got him out of Syria, and who obviously loved Jon.

"You're a fortunate young man Jon. I think you've won the heart of a beautiful girl. She's a wonderful person. What does she really think about this?"

Jon was pensive.

"Sophie?" He smiled to himself. The love of his life. She'd swept him off his feet. He never thought he'd miss her so much. Only two days apart had seemed like an eternity. Jon sat back in the chair and looked across at his friend through the flickering firelight.

"Then comes Sophie the doctor," he said. "She's made me think a lot. She's confident that God has inspired the whole Bible. She says we should try to understand what the writers were trying to say when they wrote it, and then take it on board at face value. If God's two books - His book of words and His book of works - seem to be in conflict, it'll always be the reader who's dyslexic."

> **The dyslexic (word-blind) reader**
> If there's a conflict with science, then either science is mistaken or we are mis-interpreting what the Bible really says.

"I'm coming to think that Sophie could be right. You must tell me what you think Mohammed - but wait a minute." He went into the kitchen and returned with some more hot coffee.

Mohammed had been a good listener. Now it was his turn.

"I asked the same questions from the Koran. It was written several hundred years after the New Testament. There are small passages about creation scattered about its chapters, and some of its early stories are similar to yours. I guess it picks them up from Genesis, and the Koran also says creation took six days. The orthodox Muslim can't take evolution. Of course some Muslims accept Darwin [54] and try to come to terms with the conflict."

They watched the log fire, poured more coffee and Mohammed looked up.

"If science has got it wrong about 'time', maybe there's no more conflict [55]. We talk of the billions of light years it takes the light from the most distant galaxies to reach the earth, but I wonder if we've found the answer. If you were travelling on one of those photons from that far distant galaxy, time would not be moving at all. Time stops when you travel at the speed of light. It seems to us on earth that the light left billions of years ago, but to the traveller who is riding on the photon, the light just left 'now' [56]. There is no universal 'now' in the cosmos."

Mohammed stood up. "It's been a long day" - and put his hand on Jon's shoulder.

"You've got all the necessary facts Jon. Put them together, wait a bit and I know you'll see."

They climbed the turret stairs, Jon to his four-poster bed and Mohammed to the tower where Bonny Prince Charlie spent his last night before the Battle of Culloden.

Mohammed lay awake, watching the large flakes of snow fall silently outside his window. He picked up the bed-side New Testament, and for some unexplained reason he thought about his mother. She was the only person who'd ever loved him - until he'd met Sophie and Jon.

He read a few verses about Jesus, and in spite of the danger he was in, he drifted into the most peaceful sleep he'd known for years.

THE CHINESE TAKEAWAY

41

AT SEVEN O'CLOCK on Thursday morning the two pursuers awoke in Montrose station. They were both painfully stiff. When they opened the waiting room window there was nothing to see but white. They quickly shut the window again, ignoring the fug of sweaty bodies - it was better than the blast of cold air - and they retreated again under the blankets. It was fortunate that the cheery Scotsman who brought them steaming tea could not understand their angry expletives.

The railway line was eventually cleared by midday and the train continued slowly on its journey north, and crossed the iced river into Aberdeen. The irritable and worried looking Russian walked out of the station ahead of Li Zhou, whose collar was up and his hands were shoved into deep pockets. It was cold.

An obliging taxi man took them to a boarding house above the harbour. It was basic but adequate. The frugal Aberdeen landlady demanded advance payment from her two unusual guests, but it reminded Li Zhou of China, and he paid without complaint. He was first up the stairs, and he claimed the comfortable bed by the lukewarm radiator -

and he lay down fully dressed for his midday nap. The Russian was left with the smaller bed by the draughty window. He sat beside it on a wooden chair and looked out of the window at the busy harbour below. It was time to think.

Li Zhou opened one eye. "Keep thinking comrade. Find the doctor's brother" he murmured "Andrew - that's the lead we need."

The Russian thought that this was too obvious a statement to be worthy of a reply. He got up, left Li Zhou to his slumbers, and slipped quietly out of the room. In the town, after a few enquiries, he had the address of the student's Union. That would be the start of his search in the morning.

Next day Li Zhou enjoyed his breakfast of porridge, two fried eggs, hash Browns and black pudding. The Russian endured a bowl of prunes and some rye bread. Small talk was not one of his assets and there was no conversation.

Li Zhou decided it was time to write a letter to his daughter Xi-xi. He'd been thinking about her a lot. By contrast, the Russian was totally focused and he walked purposefully up Union Street and then a few blocks north to the Student's Union.

"Andrew Tristan," he said to the unsuspecting gatekeeper. "Do you have a theology student - Andrew Tristan?"

The doorman looked obligingly at a well thumbed dossier in his top drawer.

"Andrew Tristan? D' ye ken t' laddie?"

Although the Russian boasted that he could understand every language from the Atlantic to the Urals, he was totally mystified by this broad north-eastern accent in Aberdeen. The doorman saw the confusion and tried again in English.

"Do - you - know - the - boy?"

The Russian nodded.

A fellow student was leaving the Union, heard the conversation and asked if he could help.

"Andrew? Sure. We all know Andrew. He's got a half day today. He'll be in his digs. Elgin Street - number 83 - top floor. He'll have his head in a book."

"Thanks," muttered the Russian. He was not used to saying much, and 'thanks' was especially painful.

When the Russian returned to the little room above the harbour, Li Zhou was reading a small book. He quickly concealed it in his pocket, but the Russian noticed. He saw everything.

"A job for you Li Zhou" growled the Russian - "time to earn your keep. Ever worked in a Chinese take-away?"

The two men purchased several cartons of food from a nearby Chinese Restaurant, and walked steadily to 83 Elgin Street.

"Here's the bug," said the Russian, putting it into Li Zhou pocket. "You know what to do! Up you go. Top floor. No mistakes."

• • •

ANDREW WAS WONDERING WHETHER to have kippers for his supper again, when there was a knock at his door. He was surprised to find a Chinaman offering him unsolicited boxes of savoury food.

"You ordered take-away sir?" he said, looking at his white square box and his note book.

"Not me - but wait" Andrew suggested. This was a godsend.

"Leave it anyway. It will solve my problem."

Li Zhou handed over the food and asked "Telephone sir - may I phone boss? Must explain mistake. "

"Course. C'm in."

While unpacking the food, Li Zhou picked up the phone and placed his bug.

Andrew enjoyed his 'Sweet and sour pork', and the two men sat in their little room above the harbour and waited.

It was rather boring because Andrew didn't use his phone very much. But after two days they struck gold.

It was a call from the Nairn Police asking why Andrew's VW had been abandoned on a snow bound road two miles from Kilranan Castle.

The Russian made the plans, and Li Zhou followed. It was to be a journey further north in very harsh wintry conditions. But this was no worse than north-west China, or the Russian plains. They purchased cross country skis, appropriate clothes and set off in a hired Toyota 4 x 4 to pursue their quarry.

The noose was beginning to tighten.

TO CULLODEN

42

ANDREW'S GREY CELLS were working silently though the night, and he woke up abruptly and looked at the clock. It was 2am. Why was he thinking about the mistaken Chinese takeaway? He remembered what Sophie had said - that one of the pursuers was a Chinaman - and he sat up in bed. Was it coincidence that an uninvited Chinaman had entered his flat?

Before the sun rose over a frosty Aberdeen, Andrew made contact with Kilranan Castle and shared his concerns with Jon.

"I don't like it Jon. It may be innocent." He had not given the Chinaman any information, but it was possible that the trail was still warm.

Jon was apprehensive and agreed that Kilranan was no longer the safest haven. He woke Mohammed from his slumbers.

"Mohammed - sorry but I think we should move on. It means crossing open country - heading for Inverness over the moors, and in this weather it has to be on skis."

Wrapped in warm clothes, and carrying a generous packed meal, a map and a compass, they left Kilranan in the crisp early morning for a day of cross-country skiing. The air was sharp and the snow sparkling, clean and dry.

"Only twelve miles across Culloden Moor. It shouldn't take us long Mohammed." They were in high spirits, keeping to the back roads and skiing over virgin snow. The woods were silent and the only tracks were of deer and pheasant. They felt secure.

Little did they know how close behind were the two pursuing foreigners. They'd also taken to their skis, and had stopped at the Castle gates to question old George the gardener. He was chopping logs and was pleased to rest for a few minutes, leaning on the long handle of his axe.

"Gone skiing for t' de - left an hour ago - yonder." He pointed in a westerly direction and his hot breath hung momentarily in the air, before it froze on his red whiskers. "You'll be welcome at the Castle. They'll be back t'nite."

But they didn't want to wait.

Li Zhou nodded to the Russian. They had to dispose of this witness. Old George had no time to defend himself. It was done quickly and cleanly.

And now Li Zhou and the Russian followed the fresh tracks of two pairs of skis.

Old George was discovered at midday. There was no reason to suspect foul play. He'd not been in the best of health. It seemed that the exertion in such cold conditions had given old George a heart attack.

MOHAMMED'S RE-FRACTURE

43

JON EXPECTED TOO MUCH of Mohammed. It was only six months since he had fractured his tibia and skiing over the snow was causing a lot of pain.

"We'll shelter in that bothey to give the leg a rest, and have some food".

"Bothey?"

"They're little huts. They're dotted all over the highlands. Protection for walkers and climbers when the weather's bad."

It seemed a good idea.

They sat in the doorway munching sandwiches and they looked out across the bleak moor, as Jon explained its history.

"This is the place where Cumberland's ruthless soldiers came over the hill to slaughter the courageous but less disciplined Highlanders in 1746."

They could imagine the skirl of the pipes, the shouts and the shots, the whistling musket balls, the clash of swords and the cries of the dying, as wild English redcoats and fierce Highlanders in kilts were locked in mortal combat. But now there was just an eerie silence as the wind blew across that bleak Scottish moor.

"Let's go" said Mohammed. The thought of ghosts made him uneasy, and his leg was feeling better. It was all downhill to Inverness and he'd now be able to keep up with Jon.

They had only just started when there was an audible "crack" and Mohammed was a heap in the snow. His leg was flail, obviously broken in the shaft of the tibia.

Jon carried him carefully back to the bothey, applied a temporary splint, and gave him his own greatcoat for extra warmth. It was obvious to Jon that he had to get to Inverness as quickly as possible and return with paramedics. Mohammed needed hospital care.   Confident that he had done everything possible for his friend, he set off at speed. At least it had stopped snowing, and he might cover the remaining ten miles to the city in short time.

PRESUMED DEAD

44

THE TWO FRIENDS were being stalked not only by the Russian and Chinaman who were close to their quarry, but also by Max who was not far behind. These three men shared the same evil objective, even if they were driven by very different motives.

The Russian was a sadist who enjoyed the chase.

The bottom line for the Chinaman was self-preservation. He had to make sure the time-probe didn't expose his dirty tricks in Urumqi.

Max on the other hand saw his mission as a chance to do something for his President.

This trio of vengeance was a powerful combination.

Max raced up to Aberdeen to find Andrew, and was angry to find the young theologian so evasive - uncooperative. He needed persuading.

With one hand he gripped Andrew's arm.

"If I don't reach Mohammed soon, it'll be too late."

And with the forefinger of the other, he pointed meaningfully to the side of his head.

"He'll get the ole bullet in the ear"

Andrew got the message.

"They're at Kilranan Castle."

"Where on earth is that?"

"It's the back of beyond. We thought they'd be safe there, and doubly covered by this blanket of snow. But........" And then he shared his troubled conscience with Max.

"I did get an unexpected Chinese takeaway - and I've warned them."

"A Chinese takeaway !"

His eyes widened. It was all in a day's work for Max. He took two paces across the room, but he knew before he reached the phone he'd find the bug. He held it in his palm.

"All the proof you need Andrew. They're on the trail, okay?"

He pulled his hand through his hair in frustration and spelled it out angrily.

"These men are already at Kilranan."

Max knew in his guts that he'd never catch up with Mohammed and Jon, at least he'd not find them alive. He'd failed, and he would never get Mohammed to the States. It was now 'plan B'. That would involve young Doctor Sophie.

IN FOR THE KILL

45

MOHAMMED RESTED in a corner of the bothey, and he pulled Jon's greatcoat tightly round his shoulders.

He made himself as comfortable as possible whilst waiting for his friend to return, but it was difficult. The wooden floor was harder and somewhat colder than the desert sands of Iraq. He shuffled and grimaced because of the sharp pain in his leg.

He surveyed the ten square metres inside the bothey. There was a pinewood table in the corner, with two chairs and a small bench. His skis stood by the door in a pool of wet melted snow which added to the dampness of the place. He shivered. Not only was it cold, but he was in a degree of shock from the new fracture. In addition, the peace of the previous night had left him. He was alone with his thoughts, and he had a fearful foreboding.

Mohammed knew that the two assassins were on his trail. These men had bungled their first attempt in the desert, but they had not given up. They were persistent, and they were professionals. They'd followed him to Edinburgh, and then ruthlessly killed an innocent man at Greyfriars. They'd discovered Andrew in Aberdeen, and they knew he was at Kilranon

Castle. They were somewhere out there in the snow, getting ready for the kill.

Mohammed lifted himself on his elbows and peered through the small window at the snow covered moor. The sun was breaking through the clouds. If only it would start to snow again and then his tracks would be covered. With this temporary lull in the storm, his path to the bothey was plain to see. Somewhere out in that wild wilderness, some determined men were making their way towards him, and the trail would be obvious.

He looked again. If things had been different, he would have said it was truly beautiful. It had stopped snowing and all was still. The afternoon sun was shining brightly, throwing long undulating shadows on the expanse of white moor. It contrasted with the distant dark pine forest half a mile away - mysterious and threatening. For now all was still and silent, and nothing moved in all this wide open space.

Mohammed was only half awake, and his chin dropped incrementally onto his chest. Jon would soon be back with the paramedics. They'd find him a hospital bed, and if he needed surgery, so be it. His breathing became heavier, and his eyes closed as he drifted into sleep.

Ten minutes later he jerked into consciousness again, aware of pain in his leg. He moved his position carefully. It was snowing again with large flakes drifting lazily past the small window. He looked again at the moor in its hazy whiteness and at the forest beyond. All was well - he would be safely hidden by this fresh fall of snow.

Then Mohammed's eyes opened wider. Had he imagined a movement amongst the distant trees? Perhaps a deer had broken cover. It was difficult to be sure with the newly falling snow. What was that? Something stirred. This was no deer. He could see a black figure - and an other one - moving purposefully. Was this his rescue party? He forgot the pain and sat up for a better view.

The two figures had now left the forest and were crossing the open ground towards the bothey. They were making good progress with their

BOTHEY ON CULLODEN MOOR

cross country skis. The leader was a diminutive figure striding out in front, and a heavier built man followed behind.

Mohammed's heart began to pound. These were the two men he most feared. He'd made a provisional plan and he had four minutes - maybe five.

He felt in his pocket for a pen and paper, and quickly scribbled a note. It was permission for the bearers to retrieve the precious data on disc from the Jersey Bank. If he gave this to the assassins, they might spare his life - but he guessed they would not be so easily duped. He continued to write quickly in Arabic - a language the assassins would not understand. If the Bank manager was astute, maybe one day this letter would fall into the hands of Jon and Sophie.

He glanced again through the window. The two men were now only yards away. He said a prayer and watched the door burst open. Although he'd not seen these two men before, he knew from Sophie's description that he was confronted by the Russian and Chinaman. He held out his recently written letter, but no words were spoken. They made a few paces across the room, cast the letter aside and grabbed his arms. He was hauled to his feet and unceremoniously bundled out of the door. No time to talk. He felt no pain from the violent blow crushing the side of the head. Mohammed who had made such a remarkable discovery about time - had no more time.

A VAIN SEARCH

46

JON RETURNED to the moor, guiding the paramedics' rescue helicopter. The snow was falling heavily again, and visibility was poor, but the pilot knew his job and landed close to the bothey. Jon leaped out, dipped under the rotating blades and hurried through the snow to the bothey. It was empty with not a sign of Mohammed ! No evidence that he had ever been there. He'd left his friend wrapped up in the corner, but now there was nothing. He looked around, and was sure this was the right place. Someone had left their calling card - an oriental trade mark - recent spittle on the floor.

Outside, new snow had covered every track. He could see that the paramedics were bewildered.

"Perhaps he tried to follow me" said Jon.

But as soon as he made the suggestion, he knew it would have been impossible for Mohammed to move on the fractured leg. It was foul play.

The police arrived with Mountain Rescue and their tracker dogs, and they spent a couple of hours before dusk searching the moor in ever widening circles, but there was no sign of Mohammed. They systematically prodded the snow-filled gullies, but it was late. Night closed in and the search was reluctantly abandoned.

A sympathetic constable could see Jon's distress. He put his hand on Jon's shoulder.

"I'm sorry laddie. He must have left the bothey for some reason. Got lost in the blizzard. When the snows melt, we'll find him in a drift".

Jon knew that it wasn't going to be death from natural causes.

GRIEF

47

JON HAD NEVER SEEN Sophie so upset. Her eyes were red with much crying.

He held her in his arms. "It's all right, precious."

"But Jon, I just can't believe he's dead."

They sat together in the Edinburgh Hospital residency, and Jon tried to console her.

They rehearsed the story, and there were lots of unanswered questions. Should they have acted differently? If they had involved the police, would they have been believed and would they have given Mohammed protection? Would it have saved him? Was this now the time to publish? But how, if they didn't have Mohammed's data? Even now should they share what they knew with the authorities? There were no simple answers.

The decision was not made easier when Max Bellman arrived. Max was meeting Jon for the first time. He stepped across and pumped his hand.

"A real pleasure Jon. How ya holdin' up?"

And when he saw their anxious faces,

"What a mess !"

There was nothing to add.

"Dumb-ass to get himself iced. Those two rats were professionals - sole purpose to kill him. They got him all right - in the bothey. The only blessing's that you weren't there Jon, or there'd be two men in boxes."

That was little consolation. Sophie wiped here eyes and grasped Jon's hand.

"Nothing must happen to you Jon."

She thought for a while.

"But for Mohammed's sake we have to continue."

Max nodded. This master of deception was not sure how much these young people really knew.

"He'd such a bright future if he'd only come to our side of the Atlantic."

He looked up and pulled his hand through his hair. "At least his work'll survive if can access his data. The three of us owe it to him to take this work forward."

"Mohammed had it all on computer discs. They're in a safe place" said Jon.

Max's heart missed a beat. He told them not to involve the police.

"Hang in there Jon. If they get his work, they'll only impound it, return it to Baghdad or Moscow and then it'll be gone forever."

Max paused and looked again at Jon. "Where are these discs Jon? We must get them, and have them in the States for safe keeping - and see that the work's not lost. And if things go south for you two guys, there's a job for you back home."

Sophie and Jon were silent. Sophie didn't trust this smooth talker, this man who liked his hair so much he couldn't keep his hands out if it. Whenever he flexed his elbow, his biceps bulged and he knew it. Jon hadn't yet picked up the vibes, but neither of them wanted to talk about the future.

"An other time Max."

CRAMOND TO THE BRIDGE

48

SOPHIE HAD A COUPLE of days 'on-call' for emergencies, and then she met up with Jon again.

"I can't stop thinking about Mohammed. Let's get some fresh air." She was more composed, but she needed a break. "Let's take a walk by the Forth? We can get a bus to Cramond, walk to the Bridge and pick up the '43' back to town."

Jon reached for his walking boots. "Okay. A five mile walk'll be good - help clear the brain."

They took the small ferry boat across the small muddy estuary and set out into the woods and along the coastal path, arm in arm and faces into the wind. There were no yachts on the choppy waters of the Firth of Forth today.

"Oh, Sophie. Some news. I was in the lab this morning and have the radiocarbon analysis of Brother Joe's basket."

She stopped and looked up at him. "Jon - tell me. What's the result?"

"Guess."

"Eight hundred years ?"

"No. Much better than that.

He took a print-out from his pocket and showed her.

She read '^{14}C years BP - 2,100 +/- 160'

"What does it mean Jon?"

"The wood that the basket was made from, is dated 100 BC give or take a few years."

"Brother Joe will be thrilled. Could it be the real basket?"

Jon was sceptical. "These dates aren't precise. There's always a big margin of error.   I'll write to him, and see if he's got the results from the States. That'll be interesting."

They talked for some time about Brother Joe and his basket, and then turned to discussing Mohammed. They had to decide what to do with Mohammed's work.

"Jon. It's decision time. Do we get Mohammed's discs from the Bank in Jersey? Do we give them to Max and his people in the States? Or shall we offer them to a journal?"

Jon was quiet for a while. "I think Mohammed deserves to have his work published."

"Me too. We can try - and let the competitors in the States and Russia live with the consequences."

"But then we'll be on the hit list too."

"And it'll mean there's no job in the States for you Jon."

"That's not for me at the moment."

"Then we've no choice but to get those discs?"

"I could go home next weekend and get them from the Bank, before someone else discovers them."

"Sensible - and keep Max and his American friends in the dark for now."

They followed the winding path through the woods, and from time to time came close to the water's edge. They were on their own, secure for now even if there were uncertainties ahead, and Sophie felt protected with Jon's strong arm round her slender waist.

"The good Lord knows about it Jon," and he held her tighter.

They stopped and Jon skimmed a few flat pebbles across the water.

"Can I give you something to read while I'm away Sophie?"

For some weeks, Jon had been reading everything he could find on the subject of 'time' and he'd discovered Ernst Mach's book.

"This man says he doesn't believe in 'time' at all. He thinks it's quite beyond our powers to measure the change of things by means of 'time'. It's just the opposite. We measure 'time' by a change of things. Afraid it's a thick volume."

"Some bedside reading whilst you're away Jon!"

"Let me know what you think - whether 'time' exists at all. I think he's right [57]. He says you can't measure 'time' like you can measure distance or measure a force. If you can imagine a closed box and inside it nothing moved, would there be any time? It's an abstraction."

> **What is time?**
> Time is only an imaginary concept to describe
> the change of things. To say time has passed,
> something must move or decay.

Jon reasoned that movement of the earth, of a pendulum, of a quartz crystal gives us a measure of what we call 'time', but it's an abstract artificial concept that can change as movement changes.

"I'm sure he's right Sophie. Duration is only a measure of something moving. We use 'time' to describe the interval between some point moving a certain distance in space. It can be the interval between the earth returning to the same position again, after a circuit round the sun - a year - or the interval between the earth rotating once on its axis - a day."

He lifted her off her feet and spun her round.

"Like this."

Then Jon stepped out quickly, pulling Sophie after him.

"Or the duration it takes us to walk 100 paces."

"Tell me again Jon."

He stopped for a moment. "It's fundamental to everything we have to say about 'time' Sophie. Movement records time. It's not time that measures movement. And if Mohammed's right that 'time' is slowing down, it's really movement that's getting slower. If he's correct, the solar system is slowing down, even the caesium atom, and we only know about it because of Mohammed's 'time-probe'."

They rounded a headland into a more sheltered bay, warmed by the late afternoon sunshine, and passed a budding chestnut and beech, full of promise of springtime. Sophie stopped to admire some lively new born lambs in the field. The world seemed at peace.

Jon wanted to talk more about Mohammed's ideas, and he looked at her.

"I wonder if there is a clue about another time frame - a hint that Mohammed's right. Do you know anything about the red shift of light?"

"Tell me about it Jon, but we'll have to press on, or we'll not make the Bridge tonight."

"Well it's possible that hidden in the properties of light - in the red shift - is a record of a previous time frame, and a clue that time was faster in the past - faster when that light left the stars."

"Red shift - isn't that to do with the Doppler effect?"

"Sure."

They rounded a headland and caught a view of the Forth Bridge, with a passenger train lumbering across to Fife. They talked as they walked, with his arm still wrapped around her waist.

"Tell me about the Doppler effect."

"If you hear that train coming towards you Sophie, it'll have a high pitch siren. The sound waves are short because they are pushed closely together. Then as the train passes you and goes off into the distance, the sound waves are stretched out and the sound is lower."

> **Doppler effect**
> The wave lengths of the sound of an
> approaching train are compressed - *a high pitched sound*
> The wave lengths of the sound of a
> receding train are stretched out- *a low pitch sound*

"And the red shift Jon - is it like that? If a star is speeding away from us, its waves are stretched out and the light is shifted towards the red end of the spectrum?"

"Almost, Sophie. But the speed of light is the same whether the star is speeding away from us or racing towards us. Most cosmologists think the red shift occurs not because of speed, but because of time. When a light source is moving quickly away from us, time itself is slowing down due to star's velocity. It's the slowing down of time - time dilation, that causes the red shift."

> **Red shift of light**
> The spectrum of light is shifted
> to the (longer wave) red end of the spectrum when light
> comes to us from a star that is receding
> because at high speeds, *time slows down*
> and the waves are stretched out

"Is that how they decided on the Big Bang?"

"Sure - until recently everyone agreed that distant galaxies have a greater red shift than galaxies near to us. The light from those far away galaxies left when the universe was young. They said that a big red shift meant that in the beginning, the expansion of the universe must have been very great. They said that the expansion must now be slowing down - and looking backwards, in the beginning there must have been the 'Big Bang'."

Sophie thought she understood.

"So because the nearby stars don't have such a big red shift, the expansion of the Universe must be now slowing down. [23] [28] [29] "

And then she asked "What's that got to do with our ideas about time slowing down?"

"Right. There's a spanner in the works for the red shift. There's new evidence that the opposite is true. Some of the nearer galaxies have a greater red shift than those further away! [23] [29]   They now talk about Einstein's cosmological constant, a force that might be pushing the Universe apart at an ever increasing rate. They say that everything must now be receding from earth - faster and faster. If that's right, one day our little solar system will be left all alone in the vast emptiness of space."

She stopped.

"So I think I'm beginning to understand what you mean. You think that's the wrong conclusion. It's not expansion. You think that the new evidence that there is an increased red shift of light from nearby galaxies, is a clue to an other time frame. If we're now living when all the cosmos is slowing down - time is slowing down - there's a time dilatation right here and now, and that explains why nearby galaxies have a greater red shift."

> **Is the red shift a clue to a previous time frame?**
> The light from *nearby stars* may be red shifted,
> because light from these nearby stars is travelling
> through proportionally *more space with slow time,*
> than is the light from faraway stars whose light left
> when time was faster.

"It's possible Sophie. The red shift may be time dilatation - here and now - time slowing down - and not recession."

It was now dusk, and the evening star was twinkling in the dark blue as they boarded the Edinburgh bus.

MISSING DATA

49

THE BANK MANAGER was puzzled, and he was rather embarrassed. He looked at Jon over his half moon spectacles.

"Cup of tea Jon?" He poured it slowly and then cleared his throat. "I can't give you access to Mohammed's safe deposit without his consent, even to you Jon. I hear what you say about his death in Scotland, but is there a will? Who are his executors?"

Jon explained that the Procurator Fiscal was delaying the inquest until they recovered the body. In the meantime he had Mohammed's written permission to publish his data posthumously, in the event of his demise. He showed the bank manager Mohammed's note, which gave Jon and Sophie authority to take Mohammed's computer discs from a safe deposit in Jersey, and permission to publish his data.

"How did you get this?"

"Mohammed gave it to Sophie some weeks ago - in case something happened."

"Well that's good enough Jon."

Then came the bombshell.

"We have a problem. Mohammed did keep some discs here. They were originally lodged in our basement safe, but they've gone. Last week I had two visitors in this office with the same request. They also had Mohammed's written permission to collect the discs."

He unlocked the top drawer of his large desk and produced a note allegedly scribbled by Mohammed.

"Here it is. I thought you might come, and I took the liberty of photocopying Mohammed's letter of authority."

Jon thanked him and studied the note. It was written in English - a second note - giving the bearer permission to receive all the computer discs stored in the Jersey Bank in Mohammed's name. But in addition there were several lines in Arabic which Jon didn't understand. It was written in tight script, as though the writer thought paper was an expensive commodity. Jon looked at the date and knew why. It was written on the day of Mohammed's death.

"So that's it."

He looked at the floor in despondency.

The bank manager continued.

"I had to tell them the discs were no longer in the bank. Mohammed removed them from safe deposit when he was here with you last time."

Jon raised his eyes. So it was both good news and bad. A relief that at least the discs were not yet in alien hands, but bad enough that Jon had no idea where they were.

"May I keep this letter?"

"No problem, Jon."

THE POLICE

50

BACK IN EDINBURGH he shared his disappointment with Sophie.

"I couldn't get the computer discs. They're not in the bank. I don't know where they are. Mohammed took them out when he was over there, and he must have found an other safe place. Why didn't he tell us? And what's more, the Russian and Chinaman have been to Jersey but neither could they get the discs. So we're all looking for them."

"Jon - if this material is lost for ever, presumably our enemies have won. The research will never see the light of day and that's what they want. But if they know we are looking for the discs and could publish for Mohammed, then we are now their legitimate targets."

"It's time Sophie - that we went to the police. We can honestly say that Mohammed had fallen foul of his employers in Baghdad, and he believed they had political reasons for eliminating him. We must tell them how you got involved in Damascus and how we helped him get money from his bank in Jersey. We can say we suspect that the two men sent over by General Kapta in Damascus were probably trying to finish the job off with a second attempt on Mohammed's life. There was that bug in Andrew's flat. And now these two guys have vanished."

"It sounds a bit thin, but it might get us some protection".

That night they were in the police station giving long statements to two incredulous and unfriendly detectives.

"We were intending to get a statement from you anyway Mr Le Var, about Mohammed's disappearance" said one of them, sipping steaming coffee from a tall plastic cup, and watching their every move.

"We hear what you say about your relationship with Mohammed. First meeting him in Damascus, and getting money for him from the bank in Jersey. These two foreigners - a Russian and a Chinaman - who visited Edinburgh. And you're saying there was a bug in your brother's flat. Where is that bug? And who is this man Max?"

They explained that Max wanted to recruit Mohammed to work in the States but they had no way of making contact. They had not seen Max in days.

"We'll have to get Home Office on to this, and perhaps Special Branch. We'll keep you informed."

"But do you think Sophie is at risk?"

"You may both be at risk my friend. Not enough to get protection, but enough for you to take care. Keep your heads down. Get on with your lives. Leave all this to us, and I'm sure you'll be all right. If these two are professional assassins, and unfortunately such people exist, they'll leave you alone."

He looked up. "You young people are not politically involved are you?"

BIOLOGICAL TIME

51

SOPHIE BOUGHT SOME fish and chips at the corner shop, and took it up to Jon's flat where they were planning to spend the evening. Jon looked glum as he emptied the fish from their newspaper wrapping, onto two hot plates.

"Perhaps going to the police was not our smartest move," he said licking his fingers. "They're asking us to get on with our lives as though none of this has happened. But Mohammed's hit on a great idea. He's shared it with us, and we owe it to him to follow it through, never mind the risk."

Sophie was humming to herself.

"Why are you so cheerful Sophie?"

He pulled her onto his knee. She had something to tell him.

"Let's sit down Jon - ask a blessing on the food."

They held hands. It was a long grace, and then Sophie looked up, smiling.

"I've been reading your book Jon - Ernst Mach says that 'time' is only an artificial concept. He must be right, but we still can't live in world without using 'time'. I still have to measure the number of my patient's heart beats in a minute, even if I can't describe 'time'.

He's right that what we call 'time' depends on motion and particularly on cosmic motion. There's no reason why all the clocks should have to keep in pace with each other. The earth's rotation doesn't have to keep in pace with its circuit round the Sun, and the pendulum can change its rhythm whenever gravity changes, and there is no reason why the electrons can't do their own thing. Thankfully all the clocks seem to agree with each other, even though every one is independent. So if it's true that 'time' is slowing down, it's the whole cosmos that's slowing down in unison. And we have no absolute time-keeping mechanism outside the cosmos in order to check the progress of this motion."

Jon interrupted.

"That's until Mohammed invented his 'time-probe'. He found a measure outside these systems."

"Mohammed might be right. And your idea Jon, about the red shift, may also give a clue that time today is slowing down. But clues aren't facts. They just point in one direction."

Sophie passed Jon the bowl of chips. She was still smiling, and for sure there must be something she wanted to tell him.

"There might still be another clue."

He was waiting - "I'm all ears, my beautiful."

"I'm serious Jon. What about biological time?"

"I know nothing about it."

"Right. Think of biological time as a clock inside every living cell. It's beating away at a regular rhythm, day after day, year after year. What if it's an independent external measure - steady as a rock - and it's running at a different rate to physical time?

Is Biological time in a different time frame?
There could be two distinct and independent time frames [58],
physical time and biological time."

"Why do you say that Sophie"?

"Because if Mohammed's right about physical time slowing down - and if biological time is not like physical time, but it's stable - we'd have two parallel time frames running at different rates, and there'd be a few predictions - I've thought of several."

"Go on."

• • •

"FIRST - PEOPLE IN ANTIQUITY WOULD HAVE LIVED MUCH LONGER THAN THEY DO TODAY, AND THEIR CHILDREN WOULD HAVE REACHED MATURITY LATER

These people in antiquity would have had many more years before they got old. Remember telling me that Neanderthals lived to a great old age ? Some of them lived for 250 to 300 years and their children weren't mature until much later than kids today?"

Jon tilted his head to one side and smiled. "That was an ortho-dontist - Cuozzo I think he was called - he was looking at Neanderthal teeth in Berlin. The establishment thought he'd got it wrong." Jon knew what was coming.

"Well, I've been reading his book [59], and he's found lots of evidence not only about Neanderthals, but that children in the past took a lot longer to reach maturity than they do today. It's been well recorded over the last 200 years. Puberty was at 17 years in 1800 and its now at 13 years. The first baby tooth used to erupt at 12 months in 1800, and now it's 6-8 months."

"So ? That's because our nutrition is much better today."

She smiled. "Maybe - I thought you'd say that. But Mohammed was saying the cosmos was moving much faster in the past. Now - what if biological time was stable? The first tooth used to erupt a year after birth, when the earth had done one complete circuit round the sun. Now that the circuit of the earth is taking longer, the first tooth is erupting when the earth's gone only half way round - at six months."

She continued. "And it fits in with the Old Testament Jon. The patriarchs in Genesis were said to have lived to such a great age. All these guys before Noah lived for hundreds of years, and they were getting old when they had their first sons. If their nutrition was so poor that they reached maturity late, why did they live so long?"

Patriarch	Age when first son was born	Age at death
Adam	130	930
Seth	105	912
Enosh	90	905
Kenan	70	910
Mahalalel	65	895
Jared	162	962
Enoch	*65*	*365*
Methuselah	187	969
Lamech	182	777
Noah	500	950
Shem	100	600
Arpachsad	35	438
Shelah	30	433
Eber	34	464
Peleg	30	239
Reu	32	239
Serug	30	230
Nahor	29	148
Terah	70	205
Abraham	86	175
Isaac	60	180
Jacob		147
Moses		120

They looked together at the fifth chapter of Genesis. It said that Adam lived 930 years, and the many generations after him up to the time of Noah lived between 700 and 900 years. They were even getting on for 100 years old before they had any children. They were long in the tooth before they reached puberty! They tabulated the ages of these men. It looked impressive.

"Do you really think it's true Sophie? Did they really live that long?"

"I've been thinking of all the explanations. Some say the writer got it wrong and he was only trying to say that these men of antiquity were worthy of respect, so he invented a story that they lived a long time. But, that's not really true to the text, and many of them were thoroughly wicked and did not deserve much respect anyway."

Jon interrupted.

"Maybe they measured years as lunar years, but that wouldn't be consistent with the rest of the book."

Sophie continued.

"They might have been very healthy people, free from pollution and eating organic food. They might have had a better set of unmutated genes. But why like the Neanderthals, did they only start having children after they were so old?"

"What does Andrew say?"

"He thinks that the long years of the patriarchs are mythological and have some odd mathematical significance. Enoch lived 365 years - the number of days in a year. Adam lived 930 years - 30 squared plus 30 - the basis of calculation in ancient Mesopotamia."

"Ingenious!" murmured Jon. He remembered what Mohammed had told Andrew about Job of the Bible.

"Mohammed said that Job's buried near Salalah in the south west of Oman - the Muslims go there on pilgrimage [50]. They think he lived in about 2000 BC, and it says on his tomb that he lived for 287 years !"

Jon remembered the Pharaohs who were ancient according to the Egyptian records, and yet their mummies looked biologically young.

"But Jon" - her eyes brightened - "these old records could be true. If Mohammed was right and physical time is slowing down, solar time three to four thousand years ago might have been moving six to ten times faster that it is now. But if biological time - the rate of biological processes - was just the same as it is today, then these patriarchs would have more days to reach puberty. They'd have had more time to grow old - along with poor Job and the Neanderthals and the Pharaohs - and there'd have been more time for their kids to reach maturity than there is today."

"I'm with you Sophie."

He looked again at the Bible. "There seems quite a sudden change in life-span after Noah. How's that?"

"Well wasn't the flood unique. It's a catastrophe that's recorded in practically all the legends of the different races. If there are two time frames, the changes may not have been linear changes. Perhaps a big hiccup at the flood?"

He gave out a low whistle and there was a long silence. He thought about geology and sediments.

"There's more Jon. And you're not eating !"

• • •

"SECOND PREDICTION - TRACK RECORDS WOULD BE BROKEN WITH PEOPLE SEEMINGLY RUNNING FASTER THAN THEY DID IN THE PAST."

This girl had been busy whilst he was away!

"In 1954 Roger Bannister shook the world when he ran a mile in an unbelievable 'less than four minutes'. It was 3 minutes 59.4 seconds to be exact. Today the record is 3 minutes 43 seconds, and there are over a thousand men who can run a mile under four minutes ! Every year the world track records are broken. We say that's because physiology has improved with better training, and that social change has opened up athletic opportunities to lots more people. There are more fish in the pool."

"Sure - and the shoes and the tracks are a lot better."

"Some of these things are true, but is there a possibility that if time is slowing down, we now have a more time in those four minutes to run the mile? If Mohammed is right, and time has slowed by a half percent in a decade, that will give several more seconds in the four minutes than Roger Bannister had fifty years ago."

"What about the field events Sophie. They are improving as well."

"But Mohammed said he had evidence for an expanding earth. If the planet is really getting bigger, gravity is getting less, and it's easier to throw weights and jump higher."

"Gosh, you'll have no friends at the Olympics. The major players think their athletes are examples of an evolving super-race, fitter and faster than ever before in the history of mankind. Russia, China and the States will be fighting over the medals in the Beijing Olympics in 2008. Don't tell them that they are not doing any better than the competitors a hundred years ago. That'll go down like a damp squib."

They smiled and wondered if this had occurred to the opposition.

"You were going to tell me about the biological clock Sophie."

• • •

"NUMBER THREE - THE 24 HOUR CYCLE OF THE BIOLOGICAL CLOCK WOULD BE FASTER THAN THE PHYSICAL CLOCK."

She reached for her text book on 'Endocrinology' - the study of hormones.

"Look at this on melatonin. It is a hormone secreted from the pineal gland and it regulates the daily rhythm. It's responsible for the 24 hour cycle of sleep and wakefulness, changes in body temperature, water retention and body weight. Throughout the day our physiology has a diurnal cycle of activity. I'm at my lowest at 2am in the morning."

"When they call you to A and E" he grinned. But he wasn't sure where she was heading.

"Be patient Jon. Hear me out. Melatonin resets the clock when you get jet lag. And its not just for humans. Every living creature has an in-built clock [60] [61] [62]. In fact this timepiece is present in every living cell, and it's a function of DNA itself [63][64]. There's a spectrum of rhythm, from the nerve impulses in microseconds, to the heart-beat, the hormonal and metabolic oscillations, the 24 hour diurnal changes and the woman's monthly cycle.

The odd thing Jon is that it is more than a just a response to the rising and the setting of the sun or the waxing and waning of the moon. It is far more subtle. If you take a creature to the south pole and place it on a turntable so that it keeps pace with the rotation of the earth, it's moving in step with the sun - no sunset and no sunrise. What happens to this clock? It still keeps the same daily rhythm. The free running oscillations just continue. The driving force is from within not without. Put living creatures in a dark cave and they behave in the same way. The leaves of plants, open and close just the same, and cockroaches and mice kept out of the sunshine still keep their same periods of activity and sleep."

"That's fine Sophie, but what's it to do with slowing down of time?"

"Here's the rub. The cycle of activity is not strictly 24 hours. Take away the influence of the sun, and it's more like 25 hours [65]. If a creature is kept in the dark for several days, it adds about an hour each day as the physiological circadian cycle is repeated. Unless it's constantly being adjusted by the sun, the living clock is not quite synchronous with solar time."

Jon was beginning to understand what Sophie was saying.

"So an independent biological clock is running at a slightly different rate to the solar clock."

"Right. Maybe living cells remember earlier days when time was faster. They were programmed at an earlier time when one rotation of the earth - 24 hours of solar time then - is now 25 hours."

"But that wouldn't be the right scale factor - 25/24 - to explain people living 10 times as long in antiquity."

"True Jon, but if cells have to be constantly reset again generation after generation, to try to keep up with changing solar time, you would expect - if the earth's rotation was quicker in the past - that the biological circadian cycle would be slightly longer than the current 24 hours. Well isn't that possible Jon?"

"Could that affect jet lag?"

"Slowing down of time, will predict that jet lag is less of a problem travelling East to West, say to the States, than returning home. If the earth's rotation is slowing down, you'd feel better with a current 25 hour day - that is, if we were programmed to a circadian rhythm of more than one current rotation. You'd feel better with a longer day than with a shorter day, and feel much worse coming back from the States."

Jon got to his feet, and walked to the window deep in thought.

"There's more Jon."

He sat down again. The chips were cold - most of the meal was untouched - but who cared. Time had been suspended.

• • •

"FOUR - YOUNG DNA WOULD BE FOUND IN MILLION YEAR OLD DEPOSITS."

"Not possible."

"Well someone's already found DNA in rocks that are said to be 425 million years old - older than the Dinosaurs. Some guy's written in "Nature" that he's found fragments of fossil bacteria DNA inside salt crystals from sediments thought to be 11 to 425 million years old [66]."

"I'd say that's pretty spooky Sophie. Even in the best storage conditions DNA's not meant to last for more than 50,000 years. Water breaks it down, and even without water and oxygen, the background radiation alone will eventually wipe out all DNA information [67]. Either the rocks are not that old, or the bacteria are recent contaminants."

"Critics said the DNA might have been a contaminant that's found its way into the salt, but the sequences are unlike any bacterium today with a 2% genetic difference, so that's ruled out. And they don't doubt the million year old age of the salt, so they think that against the odds, somehow salt has a preservative property for these ancient bacteria."

"But Sophie, they have another problem. Two percent difference from today's bacteria doesn't match up with what the evolutionary biologists think about the molecular clock. There's a recognised speed of mutation, and over 425 million years bacteria should have changed much more than 2%. And worse than that, bacteria have such a short generation time. They multiply at a tremendous rate - 400,000 times faster than humans."

"They've thought of that Jon, and say that the molecular clock must have run slowly for these types of organism."

Jon nodded, and his eyes widened. "And that's exactly what you're saying. The biological and the physical clocks are running at different rates. I see.........."

She passed him the salt for his fish and chips.

"Who knows what I'm eating Sophie?"

"But what do you think Jon? Is this another illustration of the uncoupling of biological and physical time? The bacteria are genuine inclusions. They are young according to biological time and their DNA would not last more than a few thousand years. The rocks on the other hand are millions of years old if you measure by today's physical time."

Jon remembered something.

"Wait a minute. Have you heard that red blood cells and haemoglobin have been found in dinosaur bones?"

"Where did you read that?"

"Some geology book. Everyone said it wasn't possible. Broken down blood cells might last for a few thousand years, but how could they be preserved in the bones of dinosaurs that lived 65 million years ago [68][69]?"

"Not unless there are two time frames."

Jon had been scribbling a few notes, and he displayed them in a Table.

Changing relationship between physical and biological time

(1) Fossil DNA probably less than 50,000 years old is included in salt crystals estimated at 11 to 425 million years old [66]

= **220 to 9,500 times difference.**

(2) Haemoglobin probably less than 50,000 years old found in dinosaur bones of 65 million years old [68] [69]

= **1,300 times difference.**

(3) Around 3rd millennium BC, Patriarchs in the Bible had a life-span of 900 years, compared with today's life-span of 70-90 years

= **10-13 times difference.**

(4) Job lived around 2000 BC. Muslims claim he lived for 287 years[50]

= **4 times difference.**

(5) Neanderthals said to have lived for up to 250-300 years [59]

= **4 times difference.**

(6) Egyptian pharaohs were chronologically old but looked young [59]

(7) Children in 1800 in London first erupted their teeth at 11 months; today first eruptions are at 6-8 months [59]

= **1.57 times difference.**

(8) Menarche in 1800 was 17.5 years; today it is 13.0 years [59]

= **1.36 times difference**

(9) Boys voice change in 1800 was at 17 years; today it is 13.5 years [59]

= **1.27 times difference**

(10) Mile record in 1954 was 4 minutes, and is now 3 minutes 43 seconds

= **1.08 times difference.**

(11) Biological circadian clock is 25 hours, compared with the 24 hour day

= **1.04 times difference.**

Jon looked up at Sophie. "There are some uncertainties, a big margin of error, and lots of possible explanations, but you're right it doesn't deny the possibility of two un-coupled time frames. Put that onto a graph and you get the idea of an exponential divergence between physical and biological time."

And he drew two graphs (Figs 2 and Fig 3).

"So maybe biological time is a parallel time frame here and now. Biological time is running in a separate time frame that's uncoupled from physical time."

Sophie liked to make mind-pictures. "Think of physical time like a wagon uncoupled from the back of a train - it's going slower and slower," she said. "But the train at the front - biological time - keeps going at the same old pace."

> **Evidence that physical time might be slowing down**
> *Sequential* change in time -
> Mohammed's time probe and red shift of nearby stars
> *Parallel* change in time -
> uncoupled physical and biological time

This was mind blowing. Jon got up and took Sophie's hand. "Let's go for a walk."

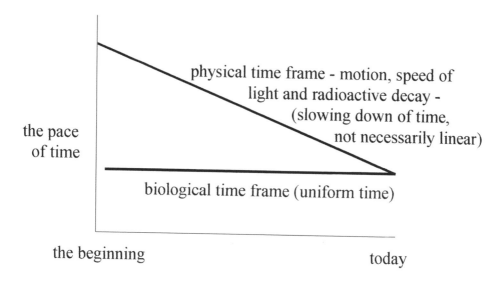

FIG TWO. Diagram to illustrate the hypothesis that there is a slowing down of time in the physical time frame - (motion, speed of light and radioactive decay) - whilst in the biological time frame, time is uniform.

FIG 2

Two time frames - physical time and biological time

the beginning

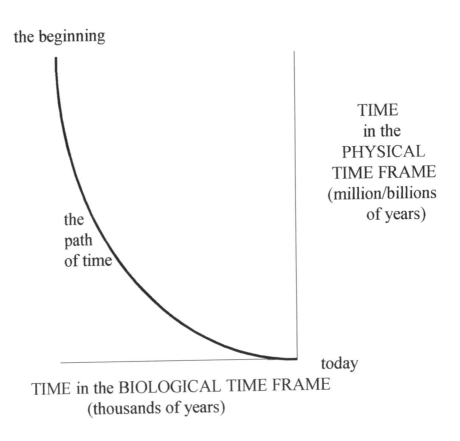

TIME
in the
PHYSICAL
TIME FRAME
(million/billions
of years)

the
path
of time

today

TIME in the BIOLOGICAL TIME FRAME
(thousands of years)

FIG THREE. Diagram to show that if physical time frame - motion, the speed of light and radioactive decay - were slowing down, whilst the biological time frame remained uniform, we would expect to observe a changing relationship between biorhythms and physical time.

FIG 3

A changing relationship between physical and biological time

CHANGE IN LI ZHOU

52

THE RUSSIAN WAS VERY concerned about Li Zhou. Their experience in Scotland had unsettled him. Not the business of dealing with Mohammed; that was all in a day's work for a man like Li Zhou. No - he wasn't communicating any more. He spent so much time reading. He was not exactly depressed, but he wasn't himself.

Li Zhou slept with a book under his pillow at night, and kept bringing it out of his breast pocket at odd times during the day. He had rescued this book from the people in Urumqi. It was their text book - the Bible. He had started to read it in anger, but slowly the mysterious power of its words cut deep into his mind. It was the stories about the man Jesus that really gripped him. It turned Li Zhou's agenda upside down.

Here was someone who championed the cause of the weak and the poor, who said the peace-makers were the happiest people. And He not only said it but he lived it. He lived a life of pure goodness. This man owned nothing, never travelled very far, lived with a few simple people and He wrote no book. It was perhaps not surprising that His teachings so goaded the authorities that they killed Him. Li Zhou had done exactly the same to those insurgents in China. And Jesus, like the believers in Urumqi, and like his cell mate Fang, went to his death with forgiveness on his lips.

"Father forgive them, they don't know what they are doing."

He had many questions. Was Li Zhou in need of forgiveness? He'd ask his daughter Xi-xi to forgive him. But what about all those people he'd murdered? Could God forgive him? His hands were blood stained. And this Jesus claimed to be the Son of God. Li Zhou had been taught that Jesus was a wicked man, a deceiver trying to make political capital, but the more he read the more he was sure that this man was not wicked but good. He had lived with the idea that Jesus was mad, deluded in his thinking, but there was never a more rational person than this man he was reading about. He was left with the only possibility that Jesus was the perfect person He said he was - God in the flesh.

He was beginning to look at himself and wonder if he was more than just physical substances - spongy lungs, cartilagenous windpipes, chemical compounds and so on. He might be more than a carbon-based bipedal life-form descended from an ape. What if something transcended matter, a supernatural? There might be a God up there after all, and a God who was still trying to speak to him in the person of his Son Jesus. He began to think that there was such a thing as wickedness, and a possibility of offending this God. And if anyone had caused offence it was surely Li Zhou. No one knew all the wicked things he had done. And here was this book saying it was all right - Jesus himself had taken the offence - if he believed. He could be forgiven and he could start again as if it had never happened.

The Russian noticed that Li Zhou was weeping.

He was reading about a father who had lost his son. The boy that had gone to a foreign land, spent all his father's money, wasted his life and was desperately unhappy. He had decided to return home, and accept his father's anger. But as he came over the hill, there was the father looking for him, ever hoping that one day his lost son would come home.

He saw his boy, ran to him, kissed him, put a ring on his finger and a shirt on his back and returned to the house to throw a party for this lost son who had come home.

"How he must have loved that son," he sobbed.

Grown men don't cry, but for the first time since childhood, Li Zhou was weeping.

The Russian was seriously troubled. They had a job to do - to find and destroy Mohammed's work - but this Chinese henchman was a liability. What if he decided to seek political asylum and defect? The materialistic West had enticed better men than Li Zhou. And what secrets he might take with him! He could never condone such betrayal. The thought of it set his teeth on edge.

He slightly raised one eyebrow. "Tea my friend?"

Li Zhou drank his tea. "Why can't Russians make real tea?" he asked.

The Russian turned away as Li Zhou spoke to himself. "It's always too strong."

This time it seemed stronger than usual, and he began to sweat. He stood up - took two paces across the room - grasped his abdomen and murmured a few desperate words.

"Remember me when You come into your kingdom."

He fell heavily to the floor and expired.

WHERE IS THE DATA?

53

SOPHIE AND JON had reached a decision

"We owe it to Mohammed to find his data and publish it, cost what it may."

"Agreed Jon, but where do we begin?"

They tried to remember again what Mohammed had said to them.

"What was it? 'The data's on disc in a safe deposit in Jersey'. But if it's not the bank, where can it be?"

They checked with Frank Johnson at Grosnez, but it was not with him. John's mother spent a day digging through drawers and cupboards but found nothing. Perhaps Mohammed had opened a safe deposit in another bank, but he had hardly had time for that. They'd reached a dead end.

He walked Sophie to her flat watching his back all the time.

"We'll have to be careful Sophie, because whoever killed Mohammed knows our every move."

The night was dark and silent and only their footsteps echoed on the pavement. He then stopped and held her close to him with the ardent intensity of young love.

Next morning Jon was his usual self - half asleep, kettle, plug, fridge, milk, coffee, yawn - until he suddenly woke up. This was the answer ! He pulled on his coat and raced round to Sophie's flat before she left for work.

"I know where they are," he said breathlessly. "It came to me in a flash. Can you get the weekend off and see if I'm right?"

She managed to swap her 'on call' with a colleague, and Jon booked two seats for the Friday night flight to Jersey - but this time under false names.

They met at the airport, checked in, passed 'security' and into 'departures', scanning their fellow passengers to be sure that they didn't have unwelcome company.

"None of our friends here," said Sophie as they boarded the plane. And then with some relief they snapped their belts and relaxed in their seats.

As the plane raced down the runway gathering speed, Jon closed his eyes and tilted his head upwards, thanking God. Such a change had come into his life !

"Sophie," he said turning to her, "do you believe in guidance?"

"Why Jon?"

"Our friendship for one. So much has happened since we first met - and it was on one of these flights. My life's been turned upside down. Not just these ideas of Mohammed's and the ideas about 'time'. I'm talk-ing about something else - something spiritual."

She took his arm.

"I'm sharing your faith," he said. "It used to be up here" - tapping the top of his head - "and now - it's inside here," and he thumped his chest. "And it's - erm - wonderful."

"I know" she said with tears. "God makes no mistakes Jon." And she grasped his hand as the flight soared into the air.

• • •

JON'S MOTHER WELCOMED THEM with her warm embrace, reserving a big hug for Sophie who was becoming one of the family. She showed her up the wooden stairs to the guest room. "This is where Mohammed stayed and I searched the room again. He left nothing here."

Jon looked in. "No Mum, but Sophie and I are going on a treasure hunt tomorrow !"

Next morning they stood in the entrance of La Cotte. "Back there" he said, "I saw Mohammed scratching about looking for flints. He could just have easily been burying something". It took Jon more than an hour probing through the rubble with a small trowel. Then about six inches down under some loose stone he struck a soft resistance. His heart was pounding. It was cloth, and there in his hand were four Compact Discs. The precious data that had cost Mohammed his life.

They scrambled over the rocks back to the beach and knew that they had to be vigilant.

"We need some back-ups Sophie - in case we loose these."

Nervously they opened the computer and zipped a new file.

They poured over the data throughout the afternoon, until they were interrupted by Jon's Mum late in the evening.

"There was a call for you while you were out Sophie" she said.

"Your friend from the hospital - a foreign sounding doctor - wanted to know when you'd be back. I said probably Monday. I hope that was right."

Jon was anxious. "Did he leave a name Mum?"

"No. Just thanked me."

Sophie also looked concerned.

"I hope I did the right thing."

"Course."

They looked at each other.

"Jon, they know we're here."

LOST AGAIN

54

THE RUSSIAN'S TRAP was set. He'd even bugged the bathroom, and if these two young people had found the discs he'd soon know.

"Patience. Just wait and listen" he said to his new American friend, who sat there slowly chewing gum.

It was Monday night. Jon had returned. Singing - draws opening and closing - dishes were clattering. Soon Sophie arrived. The Russian sat back and turned up the volume. He let his imagination ride - two young lovers - decadent Westerners.

And then his right eyebrow twitched. And Max also stopped chewing his gum. This was the news they had been waiting for. Jon and Sophie were talking about Mohammed's work and about publications.

"We can send both papers right away Sophie. They are already in the format for 'Nature'".

Jon hesitated, and he put his forefinger to his lips. He remembered Andrew's flat in Aberdeen.

They heard Jon say in a whisper, "We have to be......." and the rest of the conversation was lost in background music.

The Russian removed his earphone, thought about his employers in Moscow and spat on the floor. Max who was sitting beside him, remembering his painful experiences as a youth, clenched his fists until the knuckles were white and commented, "Now they're within our grasp. Nice kids - but dumb."

Jon and Sophie looked again at the papers. The first was - 'An optical study of the recent past'. It described the satellite mirrors, and the data processing that Mohammed had used to look back in time. It showed brilliant examples of recent events, and avoided anything that could be politically sensitive. There was an aerial picture of Princess Diane's funeral in 1997 with the royal Princes solemnly marching behind the cortege, the Olympic ceremonies of 1988 and there was a picture of Tiger Woods winning his first Open.

They looked at the screen with open mouths.

"This has to be available for the world scientific community - not buried in Moscow or the States."

Jon agreed. The implications were tremendous.

"If someone can repeat this, no government will ever again be able to doctor their history. 'Nature' should say it's the scoop of the year."

"What about the second paper - 'The relative change of time' - and subtitle 'How old is Father Time?' - it's more controversial?"

Mohammed's results showed that the rising and setting of the sun was 0.7% faster in 1988 than in 2003, and during the same period the diameter of the earth had increased by 0.4%. Neither Jon nor Sophie knew enough physics to offer any serious comment, but Mohammed had anticipated a critical review, and had discussed other explanations for his results. He had argued that any apparent slowing down of time was not an artefact of the method.

"Neither of us understand the physics" said Sophie "but Mohammed has made his case that time is slowing down. We'll send both papers, and see what the reviewers have to say."

Jon was cautious. "Expect some flak Sophie. Two time-scales means a young earth, and that will upset a lot of scientists."

"Especially those who have no alternative to evolution." said Sophie. "Only special creation or something like that, will do."

Sophie thought of her brother. "And some theologians'll have to think again if cosmology can stand alongside a literal Genesis [70] [71]."

They wrote to the journal and put two discs and hard copy in a large envelope.

"Truth is never decided by majority vote." said Sophie. "Let's go." And they danced all the way to the little red post-box at the corner of the street.

No terrorist organisation admitted responsibility for the bomb that destroyed that post-box half an hour later.

PART THREE

THE PROCURATOR FISCAL'S COURT

55

THE COURT CAME to order, and the Procurator Fiscal, resplendent in his scarlet gown and grey curled wig carefully took his seat. He glanced over his spectacles at the assembled rag bag of solicitors, police, and inquisitive members of the public and said in a soft Highland accent -

"This court seeks to identify the cause of death of an unidentified male, who was discovered at Culloden on March 10th last. This Fatal Accident Enquiry is examining a possibly suspicious, unexplained death. We shall hear first from the pathologist Dr McBride" he smiled at him, "then from Constables McGreggor and Duffy" he nodded in their direction, "from Miss McDonald"- he looked around the court for the elderly post-mistress.

"There you are Miss McDonald."

She lowered her head in nervous embarrassment as he caught her eye.

"And finally from a witness Jon Le Var."

He did not look up before he murmured - "Dr McBride please."

The small bespectacled Highland pathologist took the oath, promising to tell "the trrr..uth, the whole trrrrr..uth and nothing but the trrrrr...uth."

He paused. "The deceased was male m'Lord" - he looked closely at his notes - "approximately forty years of age, and had a five inch scar on the right cheek."

After describing in some detail the results of the post mortem he concluded - "I found the cause of death m' Lord to be (1) cardiac arrest (2) hypothermia and (3) fracture of the skull and re-fracture of the tibia. I believe that the fractured skull and tibia pre-dated death by a up to six hours. Whether there was a lucid interval between the skull fracture and the time of death I can not say." Without altering his expression the Procurator Fiscal scribbled in long-hand, then dismissed the pathologist and called for the police evidence.

"M'Lord" said PC McGreggor " We were called to Culloden we were, by Miss Isobel McDonald yes - the post-lady. She told me" - and he looked at his note book - "there's a body half-buried in the snow by the low road. PC Duffy and I attended the scene at 10.15 am on March 10th last. The photographs in m'Lord's file show the position of the body. It showed no evidence of having been disturbed. Ye ken there were signs of congealed blood on the ground m'Lord."

There was some delay as the Procurator Fiscal examined the photographs. Duffy then made a similar statement, and then Isobel McDonald was called.

"Miss MacDonald. You are the postie at Culloden?"

She confirmed her identity, and in a whisper that could hardly be heard.

"Yes, dearie."

The Procurator Fisal gave her a benevolent smile.

She tried to describe how she had discovered part of a human body protruding from the snow on her way to work. Sophie and Jon were amazed that such simple formalities could take so long.

Now it was Jon's turn. He had been formally summoned to attend the hearing or suffer imprisonment for contempt of Court. Sophie assured him that it would be a formality.

"They only want to know the 'who, where, when and how' of Mohammed's death" But he still felt threatened.

Sophie squeezed his hand as he left his seat and took his place in the witness box. He was aware that the temperature in court had suddenly turned icy. The Procurator Fiscal furrowed his brow and he gave Jon a suspicious stare as he took the oath.

He leant forward. "I must remind you Mr Le Var that you are now under oath, and that although this is not a criminal court - we are merely trying to determine the cause of death - any statement that you choose to make could be used in criminal proceedings and false statements are liable to the serious charge of perjury. Do you understand ?" He gave Jon a condescending smile.

All the eyes of the court were suspiciously fixed on Jon. "Yes sir, er ...my Lord." He was surprised to find his knees feeling rather weak.

"We have before the court your previous statement to the Edinburgh Police. Is that true and correct?"

"It is m'Lord."

"You say this man was a friend of yours and he was know as Mohammed."

"Indeed m'Lord."

"You have identified him as Mohammed, a skiing friend. Did he have distinguishing features?"

Jon described the scar across the right cheek.

"There were no papers on the body. Can ye tell this court how ye came to know him."

Jon explained that Mohammed was from Iraq. He believed he was fleeing for his life, and he was seeking asylum in Britain. He had helped him get money from his bank in Jersey. They had struck up a friendship, and had decided to spend a few days together in the Highlands. He could say little more to help the court. He had decided not to volunteer un-necessary information, unless he was asked, but it sounded rather thin.

He was then faced by a sour-faced advocate, who grasped the tapes of his black silk gown, and puffed out his chest. He ignored Jon's written statement to the police, but focused on the events at Culloden. He asked Jon to confirm that he had called the rescue service on the afternoon of January 14th, allegedly to bring Mohammed from Culloden into the hospital. But when they returned to the Bothey, no trace of Mohammed had been found.

"Is that correct Mr Le Var?"

"Yes it is."

The advocate hitched his gown onto his shoulders again, turned to Jon and startled him with an unexpected question.

"What had you and the deceased been quarrelling about on that day?"

Jon stuttered that there had been no quarrel and that he and Mohammed had been the best of friends.

The advocate paused. Time seemed to stop for him. It was a trick he'd learned when addressing a jury, and it served again.

"Friends! I thought you'd say that. How close was this friendship?"

Jon resented the sexual inference but remained composed.

"Just good friends."

The solicitor was not convinced. The next question stunned him when he thought of its implications. The solicitor was waving a Casualty card before the court and shouted "Good friendships can sometimes turn foul. How did you come by the bruise on your face and the laceration on your forehead that was treated in the Accident Department that day?" and rather than look at Jon he stared vacantly at the visitors' gallery where two young men in dark suits gazed at the dock impassively.

"I fell my Lord, when I was hurrying into Inverness. Mohammed was in need of urgent medical attention and I slipped on the frozen snow."

"Ah indeed, that is what you told the casualty officer" growled the solicitor, and he sat down.

The Procurator Fiscal thought for a while, scratched his chin and then leaned forward again.

"Mr Le Var - you cannot give us the full name of the deceased. You call this friend of yours only Mohammed. You can't help us with his address, nor can you tell us what he was doing in this country. Can ye give this court an explanation, why this man you were travelling with, fractured his skull and was buried in the snow? A curious incident wouldn't you say?"

Jon shook his head and was permitted to leave the box.

There was a buzz in the public gallery, and a bevy of reporters scratched in their note-books.

The hands of the court clock moved slowly, and there was some delay and shuffling of papers before the Procurator Fiscal said "This court believes that the deceased - a man known to Mr Le Var as Mohammed - approximately 40 years of age - died a violent death on January 14th from a blow to the head. It is not known whether such a blow rendered him unconscious. He was subsequently buried in the snow by the heavy blizzard of that day, and as a consequence of hypothermia, he died of a cardiac arrest. I have considered various options open to me, particularly accident-misadventure, but I am persuaded to issue an open-verdict" - he then looked at Jon before continuing - "depending on further invest-igation."

The Sheriff agreed to produce a detailed 'determination' within a few days.

As Jon and Sophie were about to leave the court a detective approached Jon. "Do we have your correct address sir? We shall need to interview you in a few days' time, so we would be grateful if you will not leave Scotland and will keep us informed of any of your movements outside Edinburgh."

"Of course" murmured Jon.

As they walked to the station, Jon was angry. He couldn't stop talking.

"Call that a judicial system. They inferred I could have murdered Mohammed!"

Sophie tried to be understanding. "Jon don't forget the police have no evidence that the Russian and Chinese were involved. We know that you were followed to Aberdeen and then to Kilranan, and they finally caught up with Mohammed at Culloden, but the police have no hard evidence to prove it. They only know that two foreigners I looked after in Edinburgh checked out on the day you went north, and they think they returned home to Russia and China."

That didn't satisfy Jon.

"They think I'm guilty Sophie" he said. "I suppose not mentioning Mohammed's research was no help, but I didn't like the pompous old Procurator Fiscal. I guess it's my English accent that upset him and he has nasty memories of Culloden."

He was seething all the way to Edinburgh.

THE ALLIANCE

56

IT WAS FRONT PAGE news in the *Scotsman* the next morning, with a photograph of Jon leaving the court. "Suspicious death at Culloden. Open verdict as Procurator Fiscal says Edinburgh Geology student failed to give a clear account of the accident".

He went into the department to do some reading but his friends eyed him suspiciously all day.

That night Jon and Sophie tried to take stock of the situation.

"We're getting out of our depth. Let's look at the facts Sophie". They discussed all they knew about Mohammed.

• • •

MOHAMMED'S EMPLOYERS - RUSSIA AND IRAQ

- Mohammed had been employed jointly by the governments of Iraq and Russia to illuminate Russian cities at night
- that was only a cover for the main purpose of the project, which was to conduct retrospective surveillance from a satellite in space, a 'time-probe'

- it had proved to be remarkably successful. It was a tremendous scoop for both countries, and while they remained allies, Russia and Iraq could have a propaganda edge over their enemies
- they could bury those parts of their own history that they would rather forget and embarrass their enemies with the truth about theirs - potential blackmail
- unless Mohammed defected, it would not make any sense for either of them to assassinate Mohammed

• • •

A YOUNG EARTH - A REVOLUTIONARY NEW HYPOTHESIS

But then there was the second unexpected discovery. Mohammed found that the world was now spinning more slowly and the earth was getting bigger.

- Mohammed had concluded that time was slowing down
- this in turn suggested that the age of the earth could be much younger than the 4.5 billion years claimed by geologists
- it would be fuel for the fundamentals who believed the creation stories in the Bible, Koran and Jewish Scriptures
- but was that worth killing Mohammed for?

• • •

OF GREAT INTEREST TO THE RUSSIAN AND CHINESE ALLIANCE

It seemed to Jon and Sophie that the assassins were agents of the Russian and Chinese intelligence service, and the Iraqis were not involved.

- perhaps Mohammed's Iraqi employers welcomed the research because it supported the Islamic view of a young earth, whilst the Russians wanted to bury it, because they had problems with Muslim extremism in the Central Republics.
- that would also make allies of Russia and China who were both trying to contain the same Islamic problem

"Makes sense" said Sophie "But where does the United States come in?"

Jon tried to summarise his thinking

• • •

INVOLVEMENT OF THE UNITED STATES OF AMERICA

- the world's most powerful nation would want to control a 'time-probe'
- if Mohammed was right, that the satellite of the 'time-probe' had evidence of historical atrocities - such as the Iraqi massacres of the Kurds and the Shiites - the US would want to know how to access that data
- the USA would be interested in the theory of a young earth. Their main foreign policy since 9.11 had been fighting Islamic terrorism, and any fuel to that fire, like this evidence for a young earth was dangerous
- it was compatible with the anti-terrorist alliance between USA, Russia and China
- these three strange allies would join forces to control Mohammed's work
- there were US civil liberty groups who would not want to see the Christian right prosper, and the right wing Christians were a thorn in the flesh to some of the American administration. They wouldn't want to give them any more support
- Max was probably in league with the Russian and Chinese assassins.

"No wonder we've lost Mohammed. He had so many enemies. No surprise either that the letter box exploded last week! They want to kill this research. They'll do whatever it takes to keep their secret. And Sophie, you and I are in the same firing line. They must know we have back-up discs."

"If the British Special branch are involved Jon, it would explain the Procurator Fiscal's Court in Inverness. Someone's twisting the arm of the law. If they can frame you for Mohammed's murder and put you away for a few years, you won't publish anything. Did you see those men in dark suits sitting at he back of the court?"

"I guess we're in much deeper than we thought". Do we give in and let them have the data, and get on with our lives? Or do we stand up and fight?"

DRUG INVESTIGATION

57

SOPHIE WAS EXHAUSTED. She had been working all night taking emergencies. There was not a spare bed in the place, and patients were still on trolleys in the corridor. She had been admitting and clerking, taking blood samples and setting up drips, with no time for the sleep of the righteous. She had helped in theatre and was exhausted even before she scrubbed up for the morning list. She had to assist her boss even though she had not stopped for twenty-four hours. She made polite conversation to the sister in charge, and towelled up looking enviously at the Prof who she suspected had slept like a baby.

It was a long morning. She held retractors like a robot for the four operations, before being invited to sew up the last case. The senior members of the team went for lunch. She didn't complain. This was a resident's life. It could only get better.

She walked through the anaesthetic room pulling off her sweaty mask and noticed that the drug cupboard door was ajar. Half empty boxes of narcotics and anaesthetic agents were scattered across the shelves, and the drug book was open on the bench below. Locking the cupboard door she threw the keys to the theatre assistant.

"Careful Mike - you never know."

There was a middle aged man sitting in the surgeon's room. He looked like a rep from one of the drug firms - smart suit, polished shoes, plain tie, short hair - but she didn't remember giving anyone an appointment. He stood up and extended his hand.

"Detective Roberts ma'am. I guess you are Dr Tristan."

She was not at her best, and wondered if he knew this, and had chosen his moment with care.

"What can I do for you" she said turning on the kettle and trying to look casual.

"I'm sorry if this is an inconvenient time, but I need to talk to you quite urgently."

She thought this was the time to listen rather than talk. "What's it about?"

"You might be able to help us with two problems ma'am which may or may not be connected. First we are investigating the death of a man at Grey Friars ten weeks ago. He was shot in the late evening and we have reason to believe you may be a material witness. Someone reported the incident by making a phone call to the ambulance service, but they left no name. We have been able to trace that call to your mobile. Can you please say whether you made that call?"

She guessed there was a recorder in his breast pocket, and she chose her words with care.

"Yes, I'd had a meal with some friends at Grey Friar's Inn. We came out - noticed someone lying on the pavement. I didn't know whether it was a drunk or a man who' been injured but - yes - I called the emergency service on my mobile."

"Forgive me, but was that ethical Dr Tristan? You're a doctor. Didn't you examine him to see whether some emergency resuscitation was necessary?"

Sophie realised that she had fallen into a trap. She should have told the whole truth - that she had made a quick assessment and yes she did know that the man had been shot and was dead.

"Well - I did look at the guy and it was obvious he'd been shot" she said shaking her head. "There was a bullet wound in his neck and he was decidedly... er... dead". The detective didn't look impressed.

"We also have reason to believe that you made a purchase of a man's Cashmere overcoat that same afternoon at".... he looked in his notebook.... "Jenkinson's in Rose Street." She knew she was not thinking straight.

"No, but a friend of mine did".

"Then why was it paid for on your credit card?"

She explained that it cost £300. Mohammed had no credit cards and his cash was in his flat. She used her card to loan him the money.

He looked puzzled. "You must tell me about Mohammed."

"I'd rather not" she said. "It's very complicated. I've had no sleep for a day and a half." She felt very tired and wished Jon was with her.

"Dr Tristan. Can you explain why this man who had been shot, was wearing the same coat that you purchased for this - Mohammed - only a few hours earlier? You must have noticed it - a very expensive coat - and yet you left it at the scene."

She had no answer. He paused and studied his note book.

"The second problem you might help us with Dr Tristan is related to drugs. This man who was shot at Grey Friars was a registered drug addict - heavy on pethidine. Did you know that we're investigating the theft of pethidine from these theatres."

She knew that there was an ongoing investigation into missing drugs throughout the hospital, but countered....

"I don't understand your train of thought. What could be the connection between this drug addict at Grey Friars and missing drugs from the hospital"?

She understood the connection in the detective's mind immediately.

"That drug cupboard you found open a minute ago," he pointed across the corridor to the anaesthetic room, "the cupboard was open and you threw the keys to the theatre assistant. Do all the medical staff have access to the drug cupboards?"

Before she could answer he continued.

"Edinburgh has as major drug problem, and I'm in the Drugs Squad. You must appreciate that we have to investigate every possible link between this man found dead at Grey Friars, who was a know addict, your link with him however tenuous, and any possible source of drugs."

"I don't like your inference mister detective." She drummed her fingers on the arm of the chair - "and I think it's better I don't answer any more of your questions."

He left promising to be back.

A WEB-SITE

58

SOPHIE WAS ASHEN WHEN she found Jon that afternoon.

"Come on Sophie. This is not the place to talk." He helped her on with her coat.

"Fresh air's what you need."

They'd learnt not to talk in the flat. Although Jon had climbed all over it - and discovered an arachnid eco-system that he didn't know existed - he'd found no secret cameras hidden in the air vents, and in the cramped attic he'd found no receivers or monitors hidden behind boxes. Yet he still suspected it was bugged from top to bottom.

The sun was shining as they walked together across the Meadows.

"Jon we're both in this up to our necks. They're framing you for Mohammed's death. They're trying to get me for stealing and pedalling drugs. It's only circumstantial at present, but when will they have enough to arrest us?"

He put his arm protectively around her.

"You're right Sophie. We are being deliberately fixed by someone at the top. The British establishment is a lackey to the United States. The

American CIA says jump, and they jump - right on top of us. They are determined to get Mohammed's work silenced at all costs. We've agreed to fight, so let's get our act together."

Mohammed's work had exited Jon and Sophie with spiritual and scientific curiously, and they were not going to let it rest. A plan had been forming in Jon's mind.

"We've got to get Mohammed's work published. Another paper to *Nature* won't do it. There must be a better way. Even if the letter box is not destroyed next time, they'll get to it somehow - through the editor, or through the peer review process - and make sure it never gets into print. They'll lean on the reviewers. Sending in a straight paper is no guarantee of success. I think the odds are stacked against us."

"But it's revolutionary Jon. Surely someone will see that."

"I know Sophie, but even if it gets to the review process, most of the elite scientists have closed minds to any work that contradicts their own. It's human nature. The editorial boards have a vested interest in excluding radical ideas, especially something like a young earth. These high priests of modern thought think they have so much to lose if their own 'explanations' are discredited. We've got to find another way."

"So what's on your mind Jon?"

"What about the net?" he said. "A secure web-site would be a good place to start, and we can describe all Mohammed's work stage by stage. We could open it up for a world-wide discussion on the subject of 'time' - multiple time-frames and evidence for a young earth. We could get lost somewhere, and open a cyber magazine. If we're smart, we could avoid detection for a long time - maybe change the web-site from time to time - and bury ourselves until the job's done."

Sophie nodded.

"It's an idea Jon. There might be a big audience out there who'd contribute."

It was a very ordinary spring-time afternoon as they walked hand in hand across the Meadows, young with fresh almond blossom and alive with the singing of birds. A couple of dogs chased each other. A mother pushed her infant. An old man stumbled past with his stick. Nothing exceptional as happening. Who could have guessed that these two young people held such a big secret ?

"Jon. If it means a cyber magazine, we'll have to include something about Darwinism."

He knew what she was thinking. "That's your field Sophie."

"If we're right and the earth's young," she said "there's no time for evolution."

> **A young earth,**
> puts *evolution* squarely on the agenda.

Jon nodded. "Lyell wrote about uniformitarianism and a very old earth, and that was Darwin's chance to write his *'On the Origin of Species'*. But if the earth's young - that would make Darwin turn in his grave."

"We'll have an uphill problem with evolution Jon. It's widely accepted by non-Christian and Christian alike, and it's based on so much data that they think is true - so they'll say the earth has to be very old. Lots of scientists will give us the thumbs down on that score alone."

"True. It's presented as a fact that tolerates no doubt - no competition. Ever seen it challenged on TV?"

She nodded agreement. "They claim the authority of 'science' as proof of what is largely speculation [72]. What does it say in Proverbs - 'Any story sounds true until someone tells the other side and sets the record straight'[73]."

Jon stepped back. His eyes rolled as the truth dawned on him. "So I've become a six-day creationist ! The scientific world call these people weirdoes, foolish, simple-minded. And I'm one of those!"

Jon knew it was okay to be a respectable scientist and still believe that God started it all off in the beginning. That's acceptable - a God who is an invisible imperious clock-winder, who set it in motion, and then leaves it to run on its own. A God who allows a slow and steady, evolving, linear progression towards *Homo sapiens.* That's okay.

"What some of these specialists in Geology and Biology will not permit," Jon said "is upstarts who believe in a young earth and the special creation of distinct kinds of life. They'll not permit a God who marks his existence and care by peppering the world with six day miracles and more. That's contrary to their perceived science - no personalised power permitted ! [74] [75] [76] [77]"

He laughed. "We're going to get tremendous flak Sophie. A secure web page must be the best place for us to start."

They also knew that if they stayed around long enough, the arm of the law would pull them in and they'd be silenced for a long time.

"Have you any ideas Jon - how we could go to ground for a while. My job finishes soon and I've been thinking about West Africa. Is that far enough?"

"Anywhere with you Sophie. Let's have a romantic meal Saturday night, and we'll make a plan."

Jon had a plan of his own, and when he left Sophie at the hospital residency, there was a spring in his step as he walked down to Princes Street and purchased a three cluster diamond ring.

59

XI-XI

THE DIMINUTAVE CHINESE GIRL sat in her small top-floor apartment in Urumqi and carefully opened her father's letter. The little characters in his distinctive hand-writing filled six sheets of semi-transparent paper. He described the grand city of Edinburgh, the Old Town and the Castle, and the bitter wind that blew down Princes Street which was even colder than the icy gales from the Gobi in mid-January. He described the granite city of Aberdeen and how he hoped that one day she would visit the West and see how these tall foreigners lived their lives. He didn't know why there were so few bicycles unless it was because some of the streets were cobbled, nor why when shops were full of luxury goods, some of these prosperous people looked so gaunt and miserable. She turned to the next page.

Xi-xi was leading a double life. Although a party member, she had changed course in recent months. She had secretly joined a group of believers in her university class. She had asked them to pray that her father would meet some people during his trip to Britain, who would share with him the good news. She read her father's letter and looked for a sign that her prayers were being answered.

He wrote about a young doctor - Sophie - who seemed to be remarkably kind. And then a few tears had smudged the letter. He was writing to a daughter he hardly knew and he became unusually personal.

"My dear child, I've been reading God's book, the Bible. It's been my companion ever since I left China. It is such a beautiful book. It gives me hope, that God is interested in someone like me who has done so many bad things. I should have been a better father to you my dear Xi-xi, and when I get home I will not be angry with you any more, and you will see I am a different man."

A remarkable letter, but then not totally unexpected. Hadn't they been praying, and there were stories like this right across China. That night, the believers gathered round this young Chinese girl laughing and clapping their hands as they heard her news. A Christian Deputy Mayor! He would have to walk carefully, but what a change he might bring to their city. They knew of many party members in high positions who were secret believers. This was the hope for new China. And they sang their songs, read the Bible and prayed for a long time. That night Xi-xi wrote a reply to her father hoping he would receive it before he left Edinburgh. How could she know that he would never read it?

• • •

ACROSS THE GLOBE it was Saturday 0800 GMT in the hospital residency, and the phone woke Sophie up. She had hoped to have a lie in. Where was she? Was she on-call? She fumbled for the phone, knocking a couple of books to the floor.

"Dr Tristan. You there?"

It was the landlady in Hill Square about a letter for the Chinese gentleman. He had left without any forwarding address. What should she do with it? Sophie yawned and said that she would be round later.

She hung up.

Over breakfast she wondered if the letter had some useful information about the Chinaman.

Jon was enjoying his second cup of coffee when the phone rang.

"Sure Sophie. How soon? An hour? That's fine."

Sophie hung up quickly, but for a moment Jon held onto the receiver. He glanced at the state of his flat, and his eyes focused on a pile of dirty dishes in the sink. A man can do a lot in half an hour.

Sophie was at Hill Square within the hour and then arrived breathless at Jon's place.

"Look at this Jon" she said, spreading the thin sheets of paper on the table

They couldn't read Chinese script, but it was clearly a letter from someone called Xi-xi in Urumqi.

Jon pulled up a chair close to her. "Sounds like a girl's name, but where on earth is Urumqi?"

They reached for a world atlas.

"There" she said as she put her finger on the top left side of the page. "Further up than Tibet in north-west China."

Sophie looked at the letter again. Would it help them nail one of the assassins? No doubt he had gone home long ago and it was too late. She tucked the letter away for safe-keeping. She knew of someone who could translate.

Sophie then looked around Jon's untidy room.

"Don't you ever clean up this place Jon!"

At midday she found the researcher working in the laboratory. He was doing a fellowship with the professor and he worked Saturdays.

"Lu, can you do me a favour? I need someone to read this Chinese script for me."

He stopped his titration and put the letter down on the bench, reading slowly and murmuring from time to time.

"How did you get this?"

She explained it was sent to the Chinese visitor who had now gone home. What did it say?

"Sounds like a letter from his daughter. She's not saying much, perhaps being careful in case of censorship. Lots of news about her student life and asking her father to come home soon. It gives an e-mail address, and it mentions you. 'I'd like to meet Sophie one day' ."

"Thanks Lu."

THE PROPOSAL

60

THE BLUE PARROT was the best restaurant in town. It was far out of Jon's and Sophie's price bracket, and they only knew of it by reputation. The waiter took their coats at the door and as he ushered them to a quiet corner, Sophie caught a few looks.

"Your table sir - madam."

Someone was playing Mozart's 23rd symphony. They looked at the menu, chose salmon for a starter and then venison. The conversation flowed from Sophie's day in the hospital to Jon's hopes for the rugby international, and from Sophie's new dress to his number two haircut. Jon shared three new jokes and got the punch lines right. It was good to see her laugh. Their troubles seemed miles away.

Through the candlelight he caught the flush on Sophie's cheeks and the deep blue of her shining eyes. He wanted this to be a special evening for her. She smiled at him. He loved her every expression and he reached out for her hand across the table.

"Sophie I love you so much."

There was an awkward silence and he chose his words carefully, because he knew this girl took her orders only from God.

"Sophie, will you marry me? I want to ask you to share the rest of my life, and I'll look after you - always. For richer for poorer, they say. But whatever - if we just have each other we'll be rich. I'll do my best for you and try to make you happy." He was feeling very protective and felt her gentle fingers squeeze into his.

She did not reply for a while and looked into his face. She had been anticipating this question for a while, but it still came as a surprise.

"Jon, there's no one else in all the world I'd want to marry but you. But I don't know if you'd want to follow me to Africa. What if God is calling me to work out there. If I said yes, you'd always be the most important person in my life, but you know I also have an other allegiance. I wonder if...."

Jon interrupted. "Sophie, you've shown me a new way - how to know Jesus personally. This stuff about 'time' and 'origins' - it's all very interesting but there's something much more important. It's been a faith journey, and I now understand why Jesus came. The old stories in the Bible have started to come alive. I've come alive. I really believe that the rotten things I've done have been forgiven - wiped clean. When you're on a journey, you're not looking behind you. I'm looking ahead Sophie, and I'm seeing things I've never seen before. I'd like you to come with me."

She listened as he shared his inmost feelings.

"Your faith journey - to Eden, Jon" she said smiling.

He nodded. "For the first time in my life I know that Jesus is who He said he was - I can feel His secret companionship - and you've made that possible"

There was much more he wanted to say, but he stumbled for the words.

"I think it says that in marriage, two people become one flesh. That must mean we do things together. And about Africa - I'll go with you anywhere."

There was another thoughtful moment before Sophie replied.

"Yes Jon. I'll love you for ever. You'll help me too, and we'll learn together."

He felt in his breast pocket for the diamond cluster ring, and put it gently onto her finger. It sparkled in the candle-light, and they were the happiest people in town.

VISIT TO THE ZOO

61

SOPHIE GLOWED WITH EXCITEMENT. For two days, her feet seemed hardly to touch the floor. To be loved by a man she adored, and to know they were spiritually at one. That had made all her dreams come true.

"Wednesday's my day off," she said. "Let's celebrate. Let's go to the zoo!"

"The zoo?"

" 'Course. We can be children again."

For a hundred years, Edinburgh Zoo has been home to a unique colony of Antarctic Emperor Penguins. These magnificent creatures stand proudly upright, perhaps the only truly upright creatures apart from humans. Jon and Sophie joined the spectators at three o'clock feeding time, and watched the slow procession of fifty birds, resplendent in their yellow, black and white oily plumage, waddling slowly down the rocky hillside. At the water's edge, one by one they dived into the water, waiting for their big moment. The keeper stood on his raised platform, and was about to feed them with buckets of herring, to the entertainment of an expectant and admiring crowd.

A teacher's shrill voice could be heard giving words of wisdom to her own little brood.

"These penguins are a perfect example of convergent evolution" she said.

Sophie nudged Jon and they edged towards the little class of young teenagers to listen.

"Primitive life started in the water many billions of years ago."

The children were not listening but she continued in an authoritative high pitched voice.

"Small creatures gradually became more complicated, and then amphibians moved onto the land." She told them that dinosaurs evolved into birds, and amphibians into mammals.

"Some mammals have gone back to the water again," she piped "like whales and dolphins. They've adapted again to a watery habitat."

Everyone was applauding the magnificent penguins.

"And these Emperor Penguins are really birds, and they have done the same."

No one was really listening. The children were more interested in the skill of these streamlined creatures, swimming and turning in the water, than they were in any lesson about evolution. But the indoctrination was probably reaching them at a subliminal level.

"You wonder how anyone can believe all this nonsense. Who will ever tell these kids that there's an alternative? " said Sophie.

"Convergent evolution!" She looked at Jon in despair. "What about the Platypus? It has fine fur like a mammal, a beaver-like tail, claws for burrowing, webbed feet for swimming, and a bill like a duck. It's such an amazing hotchpotch that no sensible person could really believe it has evolved. There is no imaginary tree to explain it. This so called 'convergent evolution' claims that these creatures stretched across the branches of the evolutionary tree, and picked forbidden fruit from here and there."

She felt strongly about this. "These kids should know that evolution's in crisis. They should know there's a 'family at war' saga going on. It's so gripping, underhand and dramatic that pupil boredom should be a thing of the past."

He had not seen Sophie angry before.

They left the school kids and the penguins, and walked hand in hand looking at the animals in their different enclosures - bears pacing round a pool, lions blissfully sleeping, cheetahs licking their fur, and finally the playful primates.

She was still indignant. "They're such wonderful creatures. And they say it all came about by chance!"

"What bugs you most about evolution Sophie?"

"If I'm honest, it's mainly because the Bible says it didn't happen that way."

Jon hadn't yet thought through all the arguments. "But Sophie, what if someone says it's now been proved."

"But it hasn't Jon. It's just a big deception." She pointed to a large family of chimps. "We know that all animals change within the species. That's adaptation. It's a reshuffling of the genes. But it's not the result of new genes."

"What about the similarities between the animals," argued Jon "like similar anatomy - four limbs, five toes, two eyes - sounds a good argument for evolution?"

"But it's an equally powerful argument for God choosing a common design for creatures which share the same world."

Jon added his bit from geology and the uncertainties about the fossils, but he couldn't stop Sophie.

"It used to be said that classification would produce a perfect evolutionary tree, but you know what I read about the 'cladists' - the biologists from the American Museum of Natural History?"

He listened.

"They had the courage to step out of line and say - 'Darwinism is in short, a theory that has been put to the test and found false'."

"Don't mind standing in their slipstream," said Jon. "But I bet Dawkins had something to say about that."

"He did - four words. 'Too bizarre to credit!' [78]."

They sat in the cafe drinking hot chocolate and Sophie continued.

"I get really upset, because so many of the planks of evolution that were once claimed to be important, have one by one been destroyed. In their day, they were powerful tools of indoctrination, but we now know that they were wrong. Before long, I'm sure the whole impressive edifice of evolution will collapse."

Jon smiled. He'd no idea Sophie felt like this. He knew Darwinism was in trouble. Of course, evolution was a clever idea for those who wanted to throw out God's special creation. In fact it was the only good explanation if you dispense with God, but there was an alternative.

"Maybe you're right Sophie. The impregnable Berlin wall didn't last for ever."

They had other things to talk about. He gently put his lips to her hand, and they looked again at the new sparkling engagement ring.

MOSCOW

62

CAPTAIN KULIKOV STOOD for his debriefing before the Select Committee of the KGB in Moscow. As usual they had kept him waiting for two hours in a cold corridor and now they invited him into number one committee room.

"Comrade. You have come to tell us about your mission in Britain."

His eyes swept round the room staring at these leaders of men. They held him in no fear. He was a professional's professional. In fact, some of these great men who had long records of service to Mother Russia, felt a chill in their spine as they returned his gaze. None of them would have cared to meet this sadist in the dark.

"Mohammed is dead" he said in slow staccato speech. "The China-man is also dead. The American agent Max was not obstructive. The research data was finally destroyed in postal dispatch. The two young British adventurers are in despair, and in order to be doubly safe I have it on the best of British authority that the MI5 has them framed. They will soon be put away for a very long time - until they are old enough to draw their state pension."

He was secretly pleased with his little witticism but no one's lips moved.

"I can report that the British end of this adventure is concluded."

Most of them believed him.

The Head of National Security seemed satisfied and nodded curtly. He stood to his feet.

"Sit down Comrade Kulikov. We are grateful for your usual efficiency. The Premier knows of your success. And our Chinese colleagues" - he waved a document - "have told us how they appreciated your prompt action with their defector, and they offer their thanks."

He continued - "You will be pleased to know that Mohammed's team in Baghdad has been completely eliminated and the laboratory has long been closed. Any record of past mistakes - sensitive history - is totally in our own hands. We alone posses the data on Saddam's cruelty in Iraq and we know the men responsible. Some are alive today, and that gives us tremendous power in the region, and influence with the US. We alone control the satellite programme. We may reasonably conclude that the problems caused by this dangerous research are now only a page in history."

One or two men round the table volunteered a smile, but the Head of Security had not finished.

"The work from Baghdad has been destroyed and thanks to your efficient action in Scotland, our country has been saved from many dangers. Your work has been of great importance to the State, not least because of this foolish notion of " - he paused and looked at his notes - "'time slowing down'. Extreme religious groups would have found this false research as fire for their fanaticism. We need no more trouble in Chechnya - no more disturbances in Central Asia - and even the Americans are relieved that the wings of their political Christian groups have been clipped. They will never be able to fly with this pernicious false propaganda. We can consider the matter is closed."

ST. BASIL'S CATHEDRAL, MOSCOW

And with a dramatic sweep of his hand, he closed the thick file.

There was restrained applause, praise indeed for a man who had done his duty.

Captain Kulikov had to admit however, that secretly he was just a little anxious. If the problem was to resurface - and for some reason he thought about Iraq - all those fine words would turn out to be so much sand in the desert.

INVITATION TO IRAQ

63

THEY HAD A LOT to consider - getting married, how to evade the police, and now where to set up a web-page? After a few days Sophie thought she had the answer to the last question. It came in a letter from Pastor Ibraim in Damascus. She could hardly wait until the last patient left the clinic so she could take off her white coat and find Jon.

She made her way to Jon's part of town, through crowds of wayward kids with green hair and studs in their jaws, and she arrived at his flat just as he was heating up a pizza. She pushed the letter under his nose.

"There" - and she turned up the volume of the CD. "Sometimes one's best decisions are made by someone else".

He pulled her onto his knee, kissed the nape of her neck and read the letter of invitation to join some Syrian friends on a mercy trip to Iraq, taking in food and medicine. Help rebuild a war torn country.

He saw problems - "Iraq ! It's a boiling cauldron."

She had answers - "God makes no mistakes."

"It's the last place on the planet I'd think about."

"Exactly."

"What about visas?" he said. "We'll never get in."

Sophie thought that General Kapta in the Military Hospital would help, and once in Iraq, they could find what remained of Mohammed's friends and maybe stay for a while.

"I agree it's just the place for a web site" he said - "to get Mohammed's work on-line. But there'll be enormous risks."

"No more than staying at home."

"It's like going into the lion's den. We'd have to tread carefully one step at a time." He was pensive. "It's dangerous, but who knows - some of Mohammed's Iraqi bosses may still be around and pleased to see us. And it's the last place the American, Russian and Chinese alliance would expect to find us."

Sophie thought the pieces fitted together.

"The timing's right. They want us there in eight weeks. I'll have finished my residency. We shall just be married and can disappear for a long honeymoon!"

Jon was more cautious.

"We've learnt to pray together Sophie. Let's wait till morning."

• • •

NEXT DAY THEY TALKED again. They were both sure. They couldn't risk phone or fax, but they sent an e-mail to Pastor Ibraim. Yes - they'd be honoured to join the team, and they'd bring some medical supplies and text books with them. Sophie was going to contact some drug companies - ask them to give practical help for the Baghdad Children's Hospital.

Sophie had a lot to do - fixing up the wedding day with the vicar, booking the church hall for the reception, and making the guest-list. She also sent a second e-mail to Anita in Damascus. General Kapta owed her a favour, and his favourite daughter had his ear.

Sophie explained that they planned to join a relief team from the Church in Damascus. They were taking medical aid into Iraq. Would her father accept supplies from some Western drug companies, and store them until Sophie and Jon arrived in a few week's time? There would be boxes of drip sets, catheters, syringes, needles and antibiotics. And there was the more delicate request. They needed two visas to get into Syria.

Anita was quick to reply. No problem accepting the medical supplies. Her father would also send the visas, inviting them to Syria. Once in the country, exit visas to Iraq would be routine if they were taking in medical aid. Anita also had a request for herself. Could she join the party? Her father would also loan a hospital 4 x 4. She had spoken to Pastor Ibraim who agreed it was okay.

Some party! It would be good to have Anita with them. She sent them hugs and kisses.

Jon also had a full agenda - to prepare a reading list for his research, a web site to claim and a honeymoon to organise.

"We've got to set up a web site before we leave Sophie. We need to claim a domain. Any thoughts about a name?"

They thought for many days, and then admitted that the sound of wedding bells influenced their choice.

"We'll buy it now," he said.

"One more thing Jon - the honeymoon - where are we going"?

"Tell you after the wedding !" he said grinning from ear to ear.

The weeks flew by and everything fell into place.

Three weeks passed without the police or Special Branch knocking on their doors and asking questions - no sign of anyone following them - normal routine at the hospital and in the library. Maybe the authorities thought the data had been completely lost in the post-box explosion and there was no more interest in the project. Maybe they would be left alone. Maybe....

But two weeks before the wedding day, they were 'invited' to help the police with their enquiries.

INTERROGATION

64

SOPHIE AND JON REHEARSED their stories until they were word perfect. They needed to be, or they wouldn't see daylight for a long time. They would tell the police only so much of the truth that avoided references to Mohammed's work on the 'Time probe'.

Sophie had met Mohammed in Damascus when she was doing her student elective at the Military Hospital. He had wanted to visit the UK and she introduced him to Jon. They had struck up a friendship - first in Jersey. Mohammed moved to Edinburgh, and after a meal together at Grey Friars, Jon and Mohammed had agreed to take a winter break together. They wanted to make the most of the snowy weather by going north for some cross country skiing. On Culloden Moor, Mohammed had refractured his leg and whilst Jon went for help, for some unexplained reason he must have tried to follow. He was buried in the blizzard and the pathologist said he died from exposure. Jon's story seemed secure. There was no need to say anything about the Russian and the Chinaman, nor of Mohammed's last letter.

"Keep it simple, Jon. That sounds okay."

Sophie went over her story again. Someone had stolen Mohammed's coat at Grey Friars Inn. She realised that it was the man lying dead on the pavement. It was too late to help the poor victim, but as a good doctor she had called the emergency services. They didn't retrieve the coat, because Mohammed being a devout Muslim was superstitious about wearing dead men's clothes. That wasn't her problem.

Yes, she did have the same access to drugs as does any doctor, but she didn't have a drug problem. She didn't even touch alcohol. She thought that her story was water-tight.

They were taken to the basement of the police station, and into separate windowless rooms.

"Please be comfortable Dr Tristan."

It could have been the Gestapo sitting in front of her - a small sallow middle-aged man with a drip on the end of his nose, and his rather plump female assistant.

"I will come straight to the point. We have evidence that the man you call Mohammed was a drug courier from Afghanistan. Do you know half the world's opium comes from that country?"

She did.

"He had travelled through Iraq to Syria, and had been involved in a road accident. We know you met then him at the Military Hospital and you helped him get to this country. He has a large bank account in Jersey, probably as a result of his illicit drug trafficking. We believe it's the start of a laundering process, and unfortunately your friend Jon seems to have become involved. When did you first know of Mohammed's drug running activity?"

A tape recorder was running on the table between them and she guessed the blank wall behind was a one-way mirror and that someone was recording her reactions. She began to sweat under the bright light.

She denied any knowledge of Mohammed's connection with drugs. As a doctor she could say with confidence that Mohammed was not a drug user. She couldn't comment on his account in Jersey.

Her interrogator was drinking coffee - bad coffee from the look on his face - and he put the cup down.

"Let's move on Dr Tristan. This man who was shot outside Grey Friars was a baron in one of Edinburgh's major drug rings. We have witnesses who saw him speaking to Mohammed at the bar a few minutes before his death. We believe they'd been concluding a drug deal and as part of the pay-off, Mohammed gave him this Cashmere coat."

She made no reply.

"Let's help you. Do you think Mohammed owed this man a favour for marketing his drugs?"

"I've never heard such a ridiculous set of assumptions" she said. "Mohammed was no drug trafficker."

The inquisitor leant forward "How can you be so sure Dr Tristan?"

Again there was no reply.

"Now I'm afraid there is something more serious." He pushed a box towards her. It was a carton of twenty four vials of 100mg Pethidine. "We found this in your surgeon's-room locker. Can you tell me how it got there?"

It didn't look good, but Sophie could honestly say that this was not her personal dedicated locker. She only used it on operating days, and it was also shared with two other residents.

"We thought you would say that Dr Tristan. But the circumstantial evidence is not favourable, is it? You have been friendly with a drug trafficker - Mohammed. You make a phone call about the death of one of the city's leading drug dealers. And when we investigated the theft of drugs from the operating theatre we found that a locker which you frequently use contained this box of Pethidine."

She was hot, sticky and very uncomfortable. A trickle of sweat was running down her back. She shifted in her chair. This was the frame-up she had been expecting. And it was going to work unless she could outwit them.

They pushed the box towards her. She looked at it and saw the trap. They wanted her to pick it up, but she could read their thoughts. She left the box where it was.

"What evidence do you have to associate me with this box of Pethidine. You happened to find it in a locker that I sometimes use. Why not check it for my finger prints?"

The detective replied angrily that they would take prints before she left, but he was beaten for now.

"Things look very serious for you Dr Tristan. You can have your wedding day, but you are to be here at 9 o'clock the following morning to help us further."

Jon fared no better. His two interrogators had tight smiles and no handshakes. He was grilled for two hours about Mohammed's visit to Jersey and the large Jersey account he'd accessed to help Mohammed get out of Syria. They also questioned him at length about his friendship with Mohammed. They suggested a homosexual relationship, and that it turned sour in Scotland and they had finished with a heated argument.

"We don't suggest that you intended to kill him, but that blow in the head and the fractured tibia - they must have been inflicted in anger. Perhaps you couldn't carry him down into Inverness and he died from exposure."

Jon was composed throughout. He gritted his teeth and told himself to keep performing. He stuck to his guns, and they made no progress with the interrogation.

They told him that he too would have to return with Sophie on the morning after his wedding day.

They compared notes as they travelled home in Sophie's noisy old car. They would probably be arrested next time, put before the Magistrate and spend a long time inside.

WEDDING DAY

65

THE SMALL HAMLET of Shelly nestles in a deep valley on the western slopes of the Pennines. It had not known a day like this for years. The Ladies' Flower Club had fussed about with pleasurable anxiety, decorating the little church. Sophie's formidable Aunt Maud had baked a three tier cake, and dextrous Aunt Doris had made dresses for the three bridesmaids. The men examined their grey toppers and tails to be sure of the fit. It had the promise of being the wedding day Sophie had dreamed about for years.

Phil was the best man. This tall Scottish rugby player - Jon's colleague from student days - sat at the front, trying to calm Jon's nerves. Three times he reassured him that the ring was quite safe in his waistcoat pocket. Andrew organised his team of ushers, and uncle Harry was on the organ as the church gradually filled.

Jon looked across the aisle to Sophie's mum. She was no longer young, but she was pretty. She had a charming smile and bubbly personality. Today, there was a tear in her eye, and when Jon looked at his own mother she was reaching for a handkerchief too. Why do women weep at weddings?

The big moment had arrived. Jon looked round to see his lovely bride walking towards him. It was a picture he'd never forget. She was radiant, wearing the same white lace wedding dress that her grandmother had worn sixty years before, when she had walked up this very aisle.

Today she was in the arm of her father, who turned to his prospective son-in-law and nodded his approval. Jon remembered how nervous he had been, when some weeks back he'd asked him for Sophie's hand in marriage, and this quiet unassuming man had put Jon at his ease - "She needs lots of love Jon. If you can give her that, I'm a happy man." That was now to be his promise, and it wouldn't be difficult to keep - a covenant of love.

The bearded Reverend Hopkinson-Jones faced the colourful congregation, the biggest he had seen since Easter Day. He had thoughts of his own as he looked at Sophie. He had know her from childhood, seen her blossom into womanhood, and from what he knew of Jon they were a good match. He told the congregation that this was a wonderful beginning - two young people, making their vows before the Almighty - not a certain recipe for success, but an excellent start.

"A commitment of love in marriage is a love worth working at," he said. "This is their journey."

Sophie gave Jon a knowing look.

The best man Philip, dropped the ring. The organist hit the wrong key. A nephew and niece had a minor scrap, but otherwise the general opinion was that this was the wedding of the decade.

Fifty minutes later, Sophie glided back down the aisle arm-in-arm with Jon, smiling this way and that at friends and relatives, until she caught the eyes of the two uninvited men at the back. Were they Jon's friends? Then she remembered.

They emerged into the bright sunshine with cotton-wool clouds skimming across the sky. Down the valley a brisk wind carried the sound of bells. As the wedding Rolls Royce took them to the reception, Sophie turned towards Jon and her eyes sparkled.

"Such a beautiful wedding Jon - but did you see the uninvited men at the back? They were the same guys who were in the balcony at the Procurator Fiscal's court in Inverness!"

The reception lived up to expectations. The young at heart decorated the honeymoon car with balloons, toilet paper and old tin cans. They were showered with confetti and to the cheers of scores of friends they made their departure from Shelly, and up into the moors.

Five miles down the road a Jaguar with its engine idling, was waiting in a side road. It pulled out in front of the honeymoon car, forcing an abrupt stop. The two men walked slowly back to the stationary car, and knocked on the widows, which were half obscured by wedding decorations. "Special Branch" they said, waiving their identity cards and opening the car doors. "Sorry sir - ma'am - but you're both under arrest."

The best-man Phil, enjoyed his moment as he lowered the window.

"I think there must be some mistake officer."

Sue was still in her bridesmaid dress. Otherwise the car was empty.

The men from F-Branch got onto their short-wave and called for extra help immediately. Jon and Sophie must have switched cars, but they couldn't have got very far. Unfortunately the agents had no idea what car they were looking for, and they had seriously mis-calculated. These moorland roads were Sophie's home patch. Jon kept one eye on the rear-view mirror, whilst his new bride navigated them skilfully across the hills towards the airport.

The officer in Passport Control picked up his phone.

"Yes" and he scribbled down the names. "Okay - I'll keep my eyes open."

But it was a busy evening, and he could not remember that he had checked their passports a few minutes before.

Once through Security they breathed freely. They boarded the chartered holiday flight to Cyprus and Jon relaxed in his seat. They had outflanked their pursuers.

"Can't say married life isn't exciting, Mrs Le Var."

HONEYMOON

66

THEY SPENT A FEW blissful days in the honeymoon hotel, enjoying pure happiness. Lying on the sun drenched beach, she turned towards Jon and said

"Why can't we stay here?" but they both knew they had a rendez-vous in Damascus.

"Remember this Sophie, because it will get tough from here on."

He lay back in the sunshine as Sophie leaned on one elbow looking at her handsome man.

"Don't burn Jon."

She thought a while.

"You've twelve pairs of ribs" she said "just like me. So why does it say in the Old Book, that God took one of man's ribs, and made a woman? You should only have eleven ribs."

She was teasing him.

"Tell me - my knowledgeable wife!"

"A rib was the best bone for Adam to spare. Sometimes in theatre we take a rib to use as a bone graft. Cut it out under the bone membrane, and the old rib regenerates as good as new within a few weeks."

He still had his eyes closed, but she continued.

"I asked my brother Andrew what was the Hebrew word for rib, and you'd never guess what he said."

"Okay."

" It is a word *'tsela'* -which means *'side'*. It literally says 'The Lord God made woman from one of the sides he had taken out of man.'

"So what?"

"You know that each cell in *your* body has a pair of *dissimilar* sex chromosomes (XY). In every cell - except your reproductive cells - and they've been rather busy lately - one is an X chromosome and the other is a Y chromosome."

"Well?"

"In *my* body, every cell has *similar* sex chromosomes (XX) because I'm a woman."

"And what a woman! I'm listening" he said, opening one eye.

"Women have no Y chromosomes. Genesis could be saying that the Lord God made woman from one side of man's chromosomes. He took the side of man's chromosomes that contained the X and made woman XX.

And God had to make woman (XX) out of man (XY) - it couldn't have been the other way about or reproduction would have been impossible and there'd be no little boys with XY chromosomes".

Jon sat up. "Amazing! How on earth did you think of that?" he said [79].

"It may be wrong," she said laughing. "Race you to the sea."

• • •

WHILE JON AND SOPHIE enjoyed the beach, life was no holiday for the two Special Branch men - Steve and Danny in London. These two young clean-cut agents, fresh from college, had to endure the wrath of the Director General, a woman who had a cold-eyed way of getting what she wanted. Her tentacles had extended to the court in Inverness, to the CID in Edinburgh and even to the little church wedding on the Pennines, and she could not stomach failure.

She was not impressed by their latest efforts, distinctly unimpressed were the exact words she used.

"Find them" she shouted - "and silence them.

And this Dr Tristan - what's her first name?"

"Sophie, ma'am. It's now Dr Sophie Le Var."

"This Dr Sophie Le Var then - and her husband Jon isn't it?"

They understood their instructions perfectly, and left Auntie's office quietly.

After 24 hours came a glimmer of hope. Danny picked up the phone.

"Manchester Airport - Security."

"Yes."

"The birds have flown. We've picked them up on 'face recognition'. Last night 20.30 hours - flight to Cyprus."

"They're there ?"

The new computerised video surveillance was paying dividends.

Marios was their 'sleeper' in Cyprus, and they brought him out of hibernation.

"Know anything about ornithology Marios? Your job is to identify two migrants, and not let them out of your sight. We'll collect them when they return on the 3rd. Keep watching."

Marios bought some powerful stabilising binoculars, and he made himself comfortable in the sand-dunes. He enjoyed watching them on the beach, but had not reckoned on the island's strict Orthodox morality. They abhorred 'Peeping Toms' - and he awoke in the hospital forty eight hours later, recovering from a nasty concussion.

• • •

ON THE FOURTH DAY they paid their bill and departed, carrying a heavy suit case and two cartons of state of the art lap-top computer equipment they had bought in Nicosia. The taxi took them not to the airport, but to the docks.

They sat hand in hand, in a long waiting-room. It was suffocatingly hot in spite of three large rotating fans overhead. Two hundred other passengers shared the same fate - groups of men talking together and smoking incessantly, noisy women clutching cloth bags and children running wild. One man had a cage full of birds, another was taking a motor bike, and occasionally an official looking man wandered through the room looking at passports with no sense of urgency.

"We'll get away tonight to be sure" said Jon.

After what seemed to be an eternity, the waiting-room doors suddenly opened, and the mixed crowd surged onto the dock towards the Beirut ferry. The fit dashed ahead and the lame limped behind. The ancient ship was more like a cattle boat than a passenger ferry. They struggled with their suit cases and boxes of computers and then waited at the quay-side in an endless queue to complete the emigration documents. There were papers to be filled in triplicate, asking questions only in Arabic. No one was interested in translating for them.

The man sitting behind the table didn't give them eye contact, but threw their passports and visas and uncompleted papers across to another officious character at the next desk.

"Be patient" Jon whispered to Sophie, and he was right. Eventually they were waved into the dark bowels of the ship, and then up a metal stairway to the upper deck.

They camped on a dusty old settee in the rear lounge. In the opposite corner was a television set, entertaining some of their fellow passengers with spaghetti Westerns dubbed into Arabic. A talkative steward discovered them and warned of a rough night's crossing. He explained that leaving Cyprus had been a doddle. Wait till they got to Beirut. It would be organised chaos! He recommended some good food from the galley.

"Best put sumtin into d' belly."

They tried a bowl of greasy lamb soup, but by the time they had started on the curried-rice, the ship was pitching heavily into a strong swell. "Enough Jon, let's bed down and get some sleep."

They snatched a few moments of fitful sleep huddled together under a hairy blanket, until through the porthole they saw the grey light of dawn. On the horizon was the thin dark line of the Lebanese coast silhouetted against a brightening blue eastern sky. Then the sun burst into view to herald a new day. The sea settled to a gentle swell, and Jon even found an appetite for breakfast - boiled eggs, milk and dry bread. The ferry leaned to one side as it entered the harbour, slowed to pick up the pilot and reversed gradually into the dock.

Half the city was at the quay-side. There were families anticipating reunions, business men waiting for their imported goods, customs officials expecting bribes and swaggering soldiers mingling with the police.

"There she is Jon" shouted Sophie. It was Anita running across the dock and waving frantically to attract their attention.

The talkative steward was wrong. Thanks to Anita, entry into Lebanon couldn't have been easier. A smart immigration officer came aboard and escorted Sophie and Jon down the gangway ahead of the other passengers. He had been told that these VIP's were guests of the Syrian Army, and they required preferential treatment! A few quick stamps on the passport, casual chalk crosses on the luggage and Anita and Sophie were reunited, chattering together like old school friends.

"Wonderful to see you both" she said. "Everything's arranged" and she gave them a large bunch of flowers.

"For the newly-weds" she said laughing. She held Sophie's hand, scrutinised Jon carefully and whispered approval to Sophie. They giggled. She swaggered with them across the quay to a waiting Mercedes. The driver in army uniform sporting a few shoulder pips and medals, opened the door for the three of them to sit together in the large back seat.

Jon supervised the luggage and computers being loaded into the boot, and was relieved they had entered Lebanon so easily.

It was going to take about six hours to drive to Damascus and they made themselves comfortable in this air conditioned limousine. They drove through the city and then headed east on the freeway.

"We've so much to talk about Sophie."

Yes the medical supplies had arrived and were waiting for them in Damascus. Her father was also giving them some of his time-expired drugs. A four wheel drive was ready for the run to Iraq. Anita had never been to Iraq before and she was as exited as a child anticipating her first holiday.

67 MI5

IT IS NOT OFTEN that MI5 is outwitted by a couple of amateurs, but Sophie and Jon's departure from UK was something for the book. And they were not on the flight back from Cyprus. The Director General was grilling her two young agents from F branch - Steve and Danny. She was not a patient woman at the best of times, and this was certainly not the best of times. She was very angry indeed. She was steaming.

"Two amateurs have outsmarted you" she yelled, rummaging under a pile of papers. "I don't know whether to admire these youngsters for anticipating our plans, or demote the pair of you for a total disaster."

She looked up. "The Americans only pulled their man out because we promised to have this thing sewn up in no time. You've let two shrimps slip out of the net. They'll say we're incompetent, and they're right." Her eyes were saying it with thunderbolts. When Auntie was like this, it was wise to keep quiet.

Auntie lived only for her work. She wore tweeds and woollen stockings, and believed in the great indoors. She had beaten all the men for the top job, and they knew it. Unfortunately this closeted life made her irascible. When she thought about Jon and Sophie she began to raise her voice again.

"They're cleverer than the pair of you. They've gone to ground because they know we are onto them and they know why."

She shouted to her secretary on the other side of the door.

"Get Marcus now."

Marcus was only a small man, and because the surgeon had bungled the operation, he had limped on a deformed club-foot since childhood. He came into her office, puffing and panting after hurrying up two flights of stairs. He was not often invited into the Director General's office.

She told the three of them to sit down and listen. Marcus learnt for the first time that two young people were in possession of pseudo-scientific data that suggested the world was young.

What's wrong with that he thought, but she assured them it was dangerous.

"It has the ring of scientific truth even though all the pundits know it's a gigantic fraud. It's particularly dangerous because it will be grasped by the crank religious fundamentalists as gospel, and they'll use it to recruit more fanatics to their ranks.

It didn't seem a big deal to Marcus, but the Director General explained that there were political ramifications.

"Bin Laden's men and their followers will have more information to help them wage Holy War on the decadent West. Uncle Sam's very unhappy because it gives the Christian Right something to crow about. The Orthodox Jews might have a revival that'll make the current Middle East conflict look like a tea-party. Do you want me to talk about China! Aren't these extreme groups enough to destabilise the world governments. What more do you want?"

Marcus lifted his horn-rimmed spectacles and mopped his brow. Thin wisps of hair that had covered his bald pate fell across his left ear and he looked distinctly flustered. What had all this to do with him? He was soon to discover.

"Marcus, these two young people - a doctor and a research student - are in possession of this information and will publish as soon as possible The peer review journals are closed to them but they have other plans. It'll be on the Internet. They'll set up shop somewhere and broadcast to the world that they have evidence that the world is young.

Marcus - your job is to drop everything. From now on you've only one job. Day and night you're to surf the net. I want to know when you've found their web site. We've got to trace them and shut them down. Get them off line straight away. And we need to know where they are. Is that going to be difficult?" She looked at Marcus.

Marcus was the department's IT wizard. As a child, he had no sooner dipped his first finger into computer games than he knew he had found his natural environment. Now in his late twenties, he could do with a computer what Yehudi Menuhin used to do with a Stradivarius.

He nodded and told the Director he would have a working plan on her desk by morning. He always kept his word.

"You two" she said looking at the men who had let Sophie and Jon slip though their fingers, "may yet redeem yourselves if Marcus comes up with the goods."

INTO SYRIA

68

THE TWO GIRLS TALKED incessantly as the limousine glided effortlessly up the mountain road which had been newly cut into the rocks. Jon slumped back in the luxurious seat. He left them to their girl-talk and dozed as the car climbed ever higher up the pass. To the north were the snow-capped Lebanese Mountains, and reaching up into the sky on the right was Mount Hermon ribbed with white gullies. They stopped only momentarily at the summit border post, where the driver lowered his window and the mountain air was distinctly colder. Syria's mandate to administer Lebanon, and a *bona fide* army vehicle made the crossing a non-event.

They sped down the new wide road, never leaving the fast-lane, and swept past assorted lorries loaded with fruit, furniture, fridges, even families of nonchalant camels. They were soon in the outskirts of Damascus.

Anita had organised a hospital flat for them whilst they prepared for the journey ahead. There was much to do. General Kapta had laid on a Toyota 4 x 4, just a year or two off the drawing board. One of the hospital engineers spent a few hours with Jon explaining maintenance - how to manage simple repairs. He had to watch the water, not overheat the engine on the desert roads and remember a maximum speed of 50 miles per hour.

The drug companies had turned up trumps donating several boxes of supplies, and the military hospital had chipped in with time-expired drugs. Sophie checked the inventory to make sure it was all usable. It would make a big difference to the Children's Hospital over the border.

On the final evening they had supper with Pastor Ibraim and his gentle wife, and Brother Joe had been invited. He was still chewing liquorice.

"Hi ya Anita - so good to see ya. And Sophie - our new bride!" He gave her such a big bear hug, that could have made Jon jealous. But even if this happy priest did not possess deodorant, Jon had to like him. He suspected that his flowing brown habit covered more layers of fat than was good for him, and he watched him help himself to three chocolates.

"Everything in moderation" he said, and looking at Jon. "You the fortunate young fella?"

He licked his fingers and thought of his ancient basket. "What's the news?"

Jon didn't keep him waiting.

"Good news Brother Joe. The radiocarbon analysis came out at - 2100 years BP plus or minus 160 years. It could be wood from anywhere between 260 BC and 60 AD give or take a few years. You might say 'about right' for Paul."

Brother Joe was like a little boy at Christmas. He danced round the room clutching a very apprehensive pastor's wife, and knocking over a chair.

"Whoops!"

Then he looked at Jon. "You know the States came up with some very different figures. I sent bits of the basket to two different labs and gave them no clue to what I was looking at. One said 400 AD and the other 270 AD, and now you're saying....er...100 BC."

"Not surprising Brother Joe. There's always a big margin of error. Different labs will get different results. All you can say is that the basket was old, and it might have been the one used by Paul."

> **Radiocarbon dating**
> depends on all sorts of assumptions that
> we can't be sure about - like the initial conditions.

"Now" said Sophie "Don't get Jon onto the uncertainties of dating rocks, or you'll be here all night!"

They all went out onto the veranda to watch the setting sun, and enjoy the welcome breeze after the heat of the day. Sophie watched a green lizard scuttle up the wall and disappear into the creepers.

Pastor Ibraim turned to his three young guests. "It's wonderful to have your support" - and looking at Anita -"your father's vehicle is a godsend. Life in Baghdad's very difficult. They don't enjoy even the basics, never mind the luxuries."

"Anything to build the peace," said Brother Joe.

"Our church there'll give you a great welcome," said the pastor. "In these troubled times they're growing fast - thirty baptisms in the last few months. They've lots of widows and fatherless children who depend on these things" - and turning to Sophie - "the hospital will be full, and you'll find it quite an experience!"

"If things go well, we might offer to stay on a while in Baghdad."

"That's possible. They'd never turn down an offer like that."

They looked down into the courtyard below, where the small pick-up was already loaded to the roof with food, clothes and toiletries ready for the start tomorrow.

"We've been collecting for weeks, and Brother Joe's people have helped"

"I'd have come along for the ride if I could" said Brother Joe. "Iraq is in pain. And it's the site of the Garden of Eden, of the Great Flood and the birthplace of Abraham. Tread lightly my friends. You'll see things that no one could pay to see. And you'd go a long way to find a more decent, generous and upright people than the Iraqis."

"Shame you can't come Brother Joe," said Anita. They'd have enjoyed this man's company.

"But I'll pray for you - all the way," he said beaming broadly.

Jon slept little that night, thinking of the uncertain journey ahead.

A SPIRITUAL VACUUM

69

URUMQI'S CITY CENTRE was rapidly changing, with a host of shining new buildings reaching to the sky. Street posters proclaimed that the Communist economic miracle was bringing a new prosperity to China, and the propaganda machine showed pictures of smiling young people, expressing their gratitude to the wonderful party leaders. But it was an illusion.

Xi-xi surveyed the scene from the window of her high rise flat. She lived alone in a grey box-like building. It was similar to a hundred others in the city. She could see the mass of people in the streets below, trying to make their way along wooden walkways. They were deafened by the noisy pneumatic diggers, taking care to avoid the swinging cranes, and because of the clouds of dust, most of them were wearing cardboard masks. She knew like any other careful observer that these people were not easily deceived. The new prosperity was hiding a strong undercurrent of discontent.

There were tears in Xi-xi's eyes. Some of the Chinese people were enjoying an improving economy, but it did not fill the spiritual vacuum. She thought of her own problems. She never saw her mother, and she had lost contact with her father. She'd been logging on to her e-mail several times a day, but there was still no news from him. If he couldn't come home, why hadn't he sent word?

Then her face brightened as she scanned the computer screen. There was a new message and she let out a "whoopee" when she saw the name of the sender.

"xi-xi. you don't know me, but I am a doctor in UK and I looked after your father in Scotland".

Sophie was being careful, and was only using her lap-top to fish for information.

"your father left a few belongings in his flat. not worth sending back to China. hope you don't mind. i gave them away?"

Xi-xi replied at once.

"Sophie. my father told me about you. thanks for looking after him. do you know where he is? we've not had a word from him".

It continued with quite a long message about student life in Urumqi, and asking Sophie a lot of questions. For a long time this e-mail stayed in Sophie's 'in-tray.'

DESERT ROAD

70

THE TWO VEHICLES CRAWLED out of Damascus, past the Sheraton and onto the Al Mahdi Bin Barak Street. Although it was an early start, they were trapped in the rush hour traffic. Gradually the driving became easier and they left the suburbs behind. The pastor was in front in the pick-up, every spare inch loaded with good things. Jon was following behind in the Toyota with Sophie beside him and Anita squeezed in the rear.

"The old pastor's a great guy," said Jon watching the vehicle ahead. "What a wonderful idea to help these kids in Iraq. He's pushing sixty, and what energy! He's one of the world's unsung heroes."

The foothills of the Anti-Lebanese mountains were on their left, their summits reflecting the pink of the early morning sunshine, and the road between this escarpment and the desert followed the narrow fertile crescent. It was a highway in ancient times - a thin ribbon of green that stretched almost up to Turkey, before it branched eastwards to Iraq. To their right was the desert - an endless expanse of brown and grey stretching to the horizon. Anita had been as far as Palmyra before, but the road beyond would be new. They talked, they sang, they listened to CD's and they swapped life stories.

Anita knew that Sophie and Jon had been helping Mohammed, but she didn't yet know the whole story. She leaned forward.

"Tell me what happened to Mohammed in the UK"? she said. "My father got him out of Syria and you helped him begin a new life in the West. How's he doing now?"

There was a moment's silence - and Jon came straight to the point.

"He's dead."

"What on earth..."

"They gave an open verdict. We were skiing in Scotland and he died of exposure."

Jon looked straight ahead, and Sophie said nothing. The thought of Mohammed always brought a lump to her throat. Time had still not levelled his memory.

Anita started probing. "There were two men who came asking about him. They told my father that they wanted to help Mohammed. Did they ever meet?"

It was Sophie's turn.

"Anita, we must come clean with you. Your father asked me to look after those two, a Russian and a Chinese. They said they were doctors, and they turned out to be hit guys, bent on putting Mohammed out of the way. These men were crooks. Jon and I have no doubts, and you've just confirmed it when you said they were asking about Mohammed. I don't blame your father. He acted in good faith, but we know their visit to UK hospitals was just a cover."

"It's right Anita," said Jon. "When Mohammed died of exposure he was really killed by these two rogues."

Anita covered her mouth with both hands.

"Oh - I'm so sorry."

And then after a few moments. "Why did they do it? Was he a criminal?"

They didn't reply.

"And where do you two come in? Are you both in the clear?" Anita was certainly frank.

They had agreed that if Anita asked, they'd tell her as much as possible and now was the moment.

"Yes Anita, we are unavoidably involved. Mohammed had been doing some brilliant work in Iraq. He was pursued by some assassins who mis-managed his death on the border, and that brought him to your hospital in Damascus. Your father got him back to health, and we tried to help him in the UK, but the hit squad finally caught up with him. Mohammed told us some of his ideas, and we are duty bound to get them published. The same people who were after Mohammed would like to silence us, but at the moment we're just a step ahead."

Anita thought for a while.

"So why are you going back to Iraq?"

They said nothing

"Tell me about Mohammed's research."

They agreed to trust Anita. She could be a good ally. And once in Iraq her knowledge of Arabic would be invaluable.

During the long hours on the desert road they explained to Anita how Mohammed had worked in Baghdad for both the Iraqis and the Russians. How he had developed a 'time-probe' to look back in time at least over the past decade. How useful this was to his masters, as long as they were in control.

Anita listened in silence. They told her that Mohammed had done more seminal work. He had observed features about the recent past that suggested the days were getting longer, and if true it was going to be a paradigm shift in science. It gave completely new information about 'time' itself. It had implications for a young earth. Politically this was dangerous, because it strengthened the hand of the fundamental religious people like Militant Islam, Orthodox Jews and Evangelical Christians. And for these reasons the global establishment wanted Mohammed silenced.

Anita was not lacking in intelligence. She could see that there was more to this than they were telling her.

"Then why have you come to Iraq" she asked "It must be more than charity. Have you got a secret agenda?"

"Yes there's more Anita, but we'd better stop there," said Jon. "You're a good friend, and we don't want to put you in danger."

She gave them a quizzical look.

"But I might want to be involved."

"Then read this."

He passed a crumpled letter to Anita - the copy that the Jersey bank manager had saved and given to Jon.

"I got it from the bank. It was written by Mohammed, and most of it's in Arabic. Can you translate it? We know it's authority to retrieve the discs, but we can't read Arabic!"

The two vehicles crept along the highway, as Anita read the letter in silence.

"Jon - it's to you and Sophie, asking you to do something."

"Go on."

"My two friends, if I disappear, I know you will publish the work. Also please tell my mother I've not been the best of sons, but I do love her dearly. And this is my last will and testament - I bequeath to her half of the money that remains in my Jersey bank account at the time of my death. After paying any debts, I bequeath the remainder to my friends Sophie Tristan and Jon Le Var to help them publish my research ......signed and dated, Mohammed al Harty."

"Wow!" Sophie exclaimed. "He wrote that on the day he died - in the bothey - and he was thinking of us - and thinking of his mother. We're on the right course Jon."

Jon looked straight ahead. "Baghdad, here we come!"

LIZARDS IN PALMYRA

71

THEY REACHED PALMYRA by lunch-time. The guide book described it as an ancient Roman garrison fortress that had straddled the trade route to the East. They parked under a few palm trees.

As Jon stepped out of the air-conditioned vehicle, the first thing that hit him was a temperature of ninety-five degrees F. Even dressed in a T-shirt, jeans and sneakers, he felt roasted before he'd moved a few paces. The sun was a hammer overhead. It beat down remorselessly, burning up the dusty alley ways and reflecting off the white walled houses. They walked around the ruins. Shadows dark as night were cast by over-hanging masonry where the sun could not reach, and lizards played hide and seek under the stones.

Anita and the pastor were more used to the climate, and they climbed effortlessly to the top of the amphitheatre.

"The old boy's certainly fit."

Jon and Sophie found a sheltered place and perched on a toppled white stone that twenty centuries ago had been part of a magnificent temple. They opened some Coke. Jon's thoughts inevitably turned to 'time'.

"The main thrust of our argument is that the cosmic clocks and biological clocks run at different rates" said Jon. "We need to know why. What's so special about biological time?"

He looked at the ruins around him. "If we knew the difference between these old crumbling stones and this young lizard sunning himself," he said "we'd have the answer." He picked up a small stone. "We're saying that this stone is part of the cosmos, the physical non-organic world, and the rate of radioactive decay inside it is slowing down like the rest of the physical Universe. By contrast the biological clock in this lizard is running at a steady state, quite independent of the slowing cosmos. Why should it do that?"

He looked at Sophie.

"What's different about biological clocks" he said, "that would make them independent of cosmic time and run in a different time-frame? What is unique about living things? Aren't living cells just complicated physical machines?"

She knew Jon had an idea, and she waited for him to tell her what was on his mind.

"Okay. Tell me my husband!"

He laughed and continued. "Do you think that the Second Law of Thermodynamics has anything to do with it?"

"Try me Jon."

"You know the Second Law ? It says that there's an unbreakable principle in the Universe, that all things ultimately decay. In an isolated system, order is changed into disorder, resulting in chaos and entropy. In any isolated system, there's a loss of useful energy and an increase in entropy. That's why a bouncing ball will eventually stop and come to rest. It will only continue to bounce if the system is opened to new energy, say if the ball is hit with a bat. There can be temporary reversal of the law if work is introduced, but without new energy, all the physical world is steadily running down and decaying."

He looked at the ruins around them. "These ruins are decaying.

These temples fall down, unless some Heritage Committee keeps them in repair. The Second Law infers that the Universe started with a high degree of order but steadily everything is running down, and that's a basic principle of physics."

"But is that right Jon?" She was now serious. "Sometimes the cosmic world does have a great degree of order. There's the rhythm of the solar system, the tides are totally predictable, and the wind blows a pattern in the sand."

"Okay Sophie. Sure, the physical world has a pattern in its chaos. That's why we're here, because that pattern is kindly to life. You and I think that's the signature of a wise Creator who's made a delicate balance in the world's chemistry [80], physics, mechanics and biology. But the whole physical Universe - macrocosm and microcosm - in spite of its intriguing patterns, is decaying and slowly winding down. Every physicist accepts that. It's all slowly cooling towards a very cold background radiation, with an gradual increase in disorder and entropy."

She looked at him. "So then - what's different about living things?"

"Life looks quite different. Here the Second Law seems to break down. One of the characteristics of living things is their high degree of order, and life stays the same. It's maintained from one generation to the next. Lizards breed dozens of little lizards, and these fellows running around Palmyra are as perfect and lively today as they were in Roman times. The acorn grows a mighty oak and the forest remains full of them. It's like the chicken and the egg. They just reproduce indefinitely. No entropy there, at least within the system. It is exactly opposite to the Second Law of Thermodynamics."

She listened.

"One of the founders of the science of thermodynamics was one of the first to say that life somehow circumvents the Second Law [81]. Others have said that the second law may not apply to living matter, and that we needed a new type of physical law for living things [82]."

PALMYRA

"But living cells are merely bits of physics and chemistry like the cosmos."

"No Sophie. The complicated DNA inside the cell is a set of instructions that certainly *uses* materialistic processes like chemistry and physics which are obedient to the Second Law of Thermodynamics. But that's no reason to say the DNA was created by those processes [83] nor is *obedient* to them. It's these instructions in the fertilised egg that control embryonic development and direct it to a specific outcome which just go on generation after generation [84]. And these instructions determine the pace of life. They may be independent of some of the laws of the cosmos, and be independent of the Second Law."

Sophie continued to play Devil's advocate.

"Hear the critics Jon. They'll say that life only appears superficially to contradict the Second Law. Living things receive energy from outside the system and then like everything else, they decay in the end - dust to dust. Sure, life has occupied this planet, they say for four billion years, and it may look as healthy now as ever it did, but it only appears to defy the Second Law. It has energy conserving machinery but it increases the degree of entropy in its surroundings. At the end of the day it will be part of the decaying universe [84][85]."

"But that's no problem Sophie. We're saying that within the system, as long as life has existed with its high information structures, it's been going on in an orderly state and with no *internal* increase in entropy [86]. It reproduces itself again and again with new generations of healthy individuals, whether it's lizards, lice or leopards. 'Be fruitful and increase in number, fill the earth'. And organisms just go on multiplying. If they don't fit their changing environment they just move on to a new home. Life goes on regardless. It ignores the decaying cosmos. It's dynamical. The whole planet is bursting with living things and life itself just keeps on going, with no sign of increase in disorder and entropy. 'As long as the earth endures, seed-time and harvest..... will never cease'."

Sophie took a handful of sand, and let it run through her fingers.

"So you're saying that because you think that life defies the Second Law of Thermodynamics, ever since life was created - because it continues on an even keel generation after generation - you're saying that it wouldn't be surprising if biological clocks keep to a regular beat, whilst the cosmic clocks are decaying and slowing down. You might just be right!"

Physical and biological time could be uncoupled
The physical world is steadily *decaying* according to
the Second Law of Thermodynamics.
The biological world is different. It is being constantly
renewed with no internal entropy. It is *dynamical*

Jon had the final word. "Our theory doesn't depend on life breaking the Second Law, but it would give it some support."

$$\bullet \;\; \bullet \;\; \bullet$$

"YOU TWO LOOK THOUGHTFUL" said Pastor Ibraim. They got up to join him.

"OK. Let's hit the road."

"Thanks for air conditioning" said Anita, as they pulled onto the long east road. She looked at the map.

"Another 200 miles to the border."

Much of the traffic went further north by Aleppo, but this was a more interesting route and they hoped it would be an easier crossing.

They were not trying to break the land-speed record. Fifty miles per hour would do, not only to avoid over-heating but also because oil had been spilt from lorries travelling west. These had picked up illegal loads in Iraq to sell at four times the price in Damascus. Occasionally they passed a slow moving lorry heading east, full of food that would be sold to black-marketeers, long before any of it reached Baghdad.

Jon checked his watch. They should make the crossing by sundown.

They had a clear run, with the sun beating down on an the unchanging landscape - miles and miles of flat sand. It stretched from one horizon to the other, with only the occasional cluster of palm trees or a shepherd with his goats to break the monotony. It lulled the girls to sleep, and Sophie's head kept dropping onto Jon's shoulder.

Jon drove on, occasionally glancing in his mirror. He could have been a million miles from home, but he still had the uncomfortable feeling that some very nasty people were chasing them. The road behind was clear.

They woke up just before the border, stopping behind a long row of stationary vehicles which by now were casting long shadows from the setting sun. The pastor and Anita walked ahead to the first check post. A pretty girl made such a difference. "Hi boys!" When she slapped the military documents on the desk the Syrian official knew they would not be accompanied by little red notes. They were quickly stamped with a smile and no questions asked. The pastor came back to Jon beaming.

"That's a record" he said "We should have Anita with us every time."

It was a further mile to the next custom post. This time they were inspected carefully. The Iraqi walked slowly round the two vehicles. He returned to the driver's side, barked an order which even Anita did not understand, and then waved them on.

It was now dark. The lorries that approached them from the opposite direction heading for Syria, rarely had more than two of their four headlights working, which sometimes made them appear like motor cycles in the distance, so overtaking became hazardous. Their eyes needed to be most alert for the lorries ahead of them, where even one tail light was a luxury.

They stopped for a light meal at a roadside petrol station and decided to spend the night on the forecourt, sleeping in the vans.

"We can't leave them unattended" said the pastor "they'd be stripped to the chassis by morning".

So they snatched a few hours' sleep curled up in their seats. If it was cold outside, Sophie and Jon didn't know about it.

They hit the road again shortly before dawn and travelled down the beautiful Nahral al Furdt valley which was bathed in an orange glow, from the early morning sunshine. The country people were poor, but there were still orchards, vineyards and small date plantations on the hillsides. Soon the sun was shining from a cloudless sky, which at other times would have delighted any tourist board.

It was late afternoon before they joined the six-lane highway and entered the outskirts of Baghdad. From afar, this could have been any major city in the world, with its glistening skyscrapers and modern buildings. But on closer inspection the burned-out tanks, craters, ugly scars from Tomahawk Missiles and unrepaired buildings told another story.

Pastor Ibraim knew his way into the city and Jon kept close behind, while trying to take in the sights of a country that had long been closed to the rest of the world.

"What on earth's that?" asked Jon, pointing towards the city.

Rising above the buildings and reaching for the sky, was scaffolding for four gigantic minarets."

They must each be as high of the Eiffel Tower."

"That'll be the new Mosque" volunteered Anita. "The second largest Mosque ever built! Its dome'll cover an area the size of a football field, but the money's run out!"

They drove down Freedom Avenue, across People's Square and under the Al-Nasser - the massive archway of two crossed swords still gripped by casts of the old dictator's hands - into the wide concourse, and around the parade ground with a partly demolished statue.

"Can't you still feel his presence?" said Anita. "One in five of the population were informers for the regime, and these people are still here - the old guard with new names. Armed criminals roam the streets. It's still a dangerous place."

They passed the dreaded old Makhbarat headquarters, still standing in spite of thousands of missiles. It was a fearsome witness to a generation of unbelievable cruelty. Sophie looked at the flags of state hanging limply on dozens of posts, and Jon's eyes moved up to the gun turrets on top of the Foreign Ministry. There was a military presence, but it seemed low key.

They crossed the Tigris river, and then into dusty streets, where traders plied their wares from rows of barrows and stalls, and people walked aimlessly. No one took any particular interest in the two vehicles heading towards the eastern suburbs. There was no second look. You could smell three decades of fear, manifest by the lack of curiosity.

They finally turned into a potholed cul-de-sac, and then through some iron gates into a quiet sheltered courtyard. It was bordered by semi-tropical plants growing in large terracotta pots and everything was in bloom. A small notice said 'Fellowship of Believers in Baghdad'. Sophie thought this unobtrusive advertisement was still more than was permitted outside the church in Damascus. But then there were lots of believers in Iraq, perhaps enjoying some limited freedoms.

A handful of excited staff came out to greet Pastor Ibraim and to be introduced to Sophie, Anita and Jon, and they were ushered into a cool shaded room.

"So good to see you" they said, adjusting the blinds. "We've been expecting you for days. How was the crossing?"

Then looking at Jon and Sophie. "So these are the young people we've heard about". The girls were shown their respective rooms whilst Jon and Pastor Ibraim enjoyed a long cool drink.

THE CHILDREN'S HOSPITAL

72

THE NEXT MORNING, Anita dressed Sophie in the traditional garb of Arab women. She was covered from head to toe in a black abayah, and apart from the eyes, her face was covered by a small mask.

"Is this really necessary?"

"Yes. Keep still." Anita helped Sophie adjust the black cloth. "You can't walk round these streets in jeans and tea shirt ! If you advertise that you're from the West, you'll invite trouble."

" But we set them free from the tyrant Saddam."

"You don't understand the Arab mind, Sophie. Of course, everyone hated Saddam - he was one of the cruellest men on earth. Most Iraqis - most Arabs - hated his politics. But the orthodox Muslim is angry with the West even more - for daring to invade Allah's land. That's religion. And religion has the heart of the people, not politics."

"You're saying that's why the people were slow to welcome the coalition?"

"Sure. If it's a choice between politics and religion, between Saddam's evil regime and the infidel West, religion wins every time. Your people may have removed the old regime, but anyone from the West is still viewed with suspicion."

Sophie was getting the message.

"Muslims believe that once a land has been won for Allah, it's his forever" said Anita. "You can't have foreign armies walking over this land. There's been Islamic rule here for generations, with an underground current of fear. This is the place where they behead women in the streets. They're in the middle of a 'Back to faith' campaign. If you see the dreaded Mujahidine, keep your head down. Best blend into the crowd, not to attract unnecessary attention!"

Pastor Ibraim agreed. "Saddam and his family may have gone, but you can't be too careful. His Fedayeen louts still roam the city. Under Saddam everyone knew the rules. Now there are no rules. You can't be too careful. When you're out, only speak if you're asked a direct question, and never pose a question yourself."

"I always wanted a subservient woman" laughed Jon, hiding a little anxiety.

"Ignore him Anita."

The girls stepped out into the hot dusty street, merging with the crowd. After half a dozen blocks they stopped outside the Children's Hospital. The rendered walls needed a coat of paint. The wooden sills were cracked and peeled. Broken windows had not been replaced. International aid had not reached this place.

A mass of humanity crowded around the main door. There was a sick child in a wheel-barrow, and another was being lifted from the back of a bicycle. Up the stairs and into a long dark corridor. A crying baby was being rocked by its mother. A father was cradling his malnourished son. Most looked anxious. Many had an air of resignation. Anita was just one of the crowd, but Sophie sensed that in spite of her abayah, her blue eyes attracted some curiosity.

"They certainly need help here" said Sophie.

A harassed doctor brushed past them and Anita turned to explain that they had come with some aid from the West.

"I'll be with you soon" he said and half an hour later they were invited into an office. An Iraqi rose from behind his untidy desk, a cigarette stuck between his gluey lips.

"I'm the Hospital Superintendent. Can I help you?"

When Anita explained that they had medical supplies from both the UK and Damascus, his attitude changed and he grasped their hands warmly, assuring them that anything they had brought would be welcome. After years of embargo on imports, the hospital was still struggling to provide even basic medical care.

Sophie showed him an inventory of the supplies they had brought - boxes of drugs, blood substitutes, transfusion sets, syringes, surgical instruments, and text books. He raised his hands in gratitude.

"Thank you for coming. You just don't know what this means. Come - I'll introduce you to our matron."

Sophie was given a guided tour of the hospital. It became a growing entourage as young doctors, nurses and medical students joined the procession. They wanted to hear about medicine in the outside world. In numerous medical and surgical wards where floors sagged and roofs leaked, there were scores of very sick children and wistful parents. Sophie and Anita heard about the frustration of trying to practice medicine without resources.

If the staff were defeated by the difficult conditions - limited investigations, insufficient drugs, a shortage of anaesthetics and an out-of date library - they remained cheerful. They'd planned a short visit but it extended to hours, and they left with a mixture of admiration for the staff and a concern for their little patients. They would return with their supplies.

DANGER ON THE STREETS

73

IN THE MEANTIME JON had an adventure of his own. Lawrence of Arabia would have been proud of him striding down the street in Arab dress and sandals, boasting his strong tan and a week-old beard. No one gave him a second glance. He guessed he would be not at all conspicuous unless he opened his mouth. He weaved through the bustling crowd into a noisy shopping mall, occasionally consulting his small map. He found the street he had been looking for, crossed to the other side without looking back, and half-way down he stopped before a doorway. The building looked drab. Outside was a nameplate in Arabic and Roman text - 'Number 76 - Abdul Salam and partners - attorneys'.

This was the office of Mohammed's solicitor.

He climbed the steep flight of stairs, pushed open a glass door and was faced by a woman in a black abayah. She looked straight at him with her dark brown eyes.

"I'd like to speak to Mr Salam". The eyes shifted nervously.

"Are you American?"

He didn't answer but said "I'm sorry I have no appointment but I'd like to see Mr Salam."

She spoke softly in good English. "He left three months ago. Would you like to see his partner?" As she reached for the intercom, Jon spun on his heels and made a hasty exit. Something was wrong. He disappeared into the crowd across the street and slipped into a jeweller's shop, his heart thumping as if it was trying to escape from his body.

Shortly, the wail of a siren brought the shoppers to a standstill, and through the window he saw three Iraqi soldiers rush up the stairs into the lawyer's office, the place he'd visited but a few moments before. His instincts had been right. It was dangerous to enquire about Mohammed. A gawking crowd watched the commotion as he walked slowly back through the shopping mall and to the church compound, unaware that the jeweller was twenty paces behind.

Jon wanted to know all about the girls' day at the hospital, and he learnt that they planned a return visit not only with the supplies but also to offer some practical help. It was worth coming to Iraq for this - if the two girls could help even a few kids. And if the Iraqi authorities turned nasty, they had a legitimate cover.

When they were lying in bed that night, and were watching the moving shadows on the ceiling, Jon told Sophie of his own scary adventure.

She sat up. "I can't leave you alone for a minute" she said looking concerned. "What if I'd come home and found you were in prison or worse."

"Sorry precious, but I was trying to find someone who'd worked for Mohammed, and maybe find his Mum. His lawyer seemed the best lead. But if the regime is so sensitive about this simple enquiry, I guess it means that Mr Salam has been taken out of circulation."

They were correct. Months before, Abdul Salam had been dragged to the infamous Makhbarrat Headquarters for interrogation. He could not explain his enormous Swiss Bank account. Under torture, burnt with electric wire and beaten with rubber hose, he revealed that Mohammed's data was in a Jersey bank. He had confessed to being a traitor to his country and he was seen no more. Mohammed's complete team had disappeared, and there was no obvious way of finding his mum.

"Jon, if we're going to stay on here, you've got to take more care. They don't mess about in Iraq. This is a place where people just disappear, and I couldn't bear anything happening to you."

He drew her close to him.

"We have to be up front with the Pastor Ibraim. We need his advice." And they went to sleep.

A SUMMARY OF THE THEORY

74

JON SAT WITH Pastor Ibraim on the roof terrace where purple and white wisteria ran wild along the balcony, and in the cool of the late afternoon they sipped iced-orange.

He turned to the pastor.

"They've invited Sophie to stay on for a while, and Anita too. Can you make the return trip alone?"

He understood. Neither Jon nor Sophie had mentioned the return journey to Syria, and he knew Sophie was being useful in the hospital.

"Those girls are doing a great job. I know they're needed here."

"It's partly that, but I want to talk to you about some of our other plans. It'll take a long time and I need your advice."

"Okay Jon. I've got all evening."

He asked for the pastor's confidence.

"We're involved in some fascinating work but it does carry some risk."

The pastor had learnt to respect Sophie and Jon and he knew they wouldn't include him unless it was important.

"What's it about, Jon? There are enough risks here already, but I'll help if I can."

"I'm not sure you'll believe what I going to say." The pastor sat up in his chair.

Jon started with Mohammed's work in Baghdad and how Sophie had met him at the Military hospital. He described how Mohammed came to the UK, had been chased the length of Scotland by two assassins who eventually murdered him because he had invented a 'time-probe' with such unexpected results. And now he and Sophie were carrying the flag to get the research published in spite of the big players intent on stopping them.

If Pastor Ibraim was surprised, it didn't show. He let Jon talk for a long time without interruption and he kept scribbling a few notes. Then he looked up.

"It's not easy to understand what you are saying Jon. I have a science degree from earlier years, but it's still difficult to follow you. Let me ask you some questions."

"First tell me what you mean by 'time'."

Jon began with his black box.

"If you were in a black box, and nothing moved and nothing decayed, would there be any time at all? No, it would be timeless."

He explained why time is only a measure of motion, and if motion doesn't change, nor does time.

"Like one rotation of the earth making a complete day, and the earth circling the sun in a year - we use motion and say that a certain amount of time has passed, and provided that all these clocks keep moving in pace with each other, we say time doesn't change. That's cosmic time - it's no more than the movement of planets, and in the microcosm - the movement of atoms."

> **Time**
> is an abstraction to measure motion

He thought he understood what Jon was saying and he nodded from time to time.

"So what's this about 'biological time'?"

"Sophie says that every living cell, whether a bacterium or in an elephant, has an internal clock. It can be a 24 hour cycle, or a lunar month. The pet dog knows when it's time to go to bed. You and I know when to wake up, and turtles know when its going to be full moon. That's the biological clock. We're suggesting that even though biorhythms adjust to cosmic time, biological time may run quite independently."

"Are you saying that there might be two independent time scales, physical cosmic time and living biological time."

"Right" said Jon. "The earth's circuit round the sun, the grandfather clock and the perturbation of the atom - physical time - may all be slowing down together, but we'd be totally unaware of it, unless there was another clock outside the system. Slowing down of physical time would be an untestable theory unless there was another independent clock."

The pastor replied. "So you say that's where Mohammed's work comes in. He's found a clock outside the present system, a clock of fifteen years ago. You can compare two clocks in sequence - 'then' and 'now'."

"And we are also suggesting there are two parallel clocks in the same place - 'physical time' and 'biological time', and if biological time was stable, it might give a hint that physical time was slowing down.

It means that compared with fifty years ago, there's more time in four minutes for the athlete to run his mile. It would account for people living so long in the early days of the Bible."

> ### The biological clock
> may be uncoupled from
> ### the physical clock

Pastor Ibraim nodded.

"You two've got a novel idea. I think I understand you. If cosmic time is slowing down, the universe will be much younger than we think."

He looked at Jon.

" *Now a third one Jon. Where does this leave the radiometric dating of rocks?* I thought that told us the earth was very old."

"Okay. We estimate the age of a rock on the assumption that radioactive decay has always been constant. But if we are on the right lines, and the sub-atomic world of radioactive decay like the cosmic world, is slowing down, our radiometric dating is inaccurate. If decay was faster in the past, our estimate of the age of rocks is wildly out. The earth may be young. We may be charting it at the wrong speed [87]."

> ### Radiometric dating
> is based on assumptions
> including the invariability of time

"*Number four.*" He looked at his notes. "*What about the light from the stars?* Surely that says the Universe is billions of years old."

Jon drew a few diagrams to show how parallax is used to measure the distance to nearby stars. "The star's position is recorded when the earth is at one extreme of its orbit around the sun, and then again six months later when the earth is at the other end of its orbit, it's located again. The distance of the star from the earth is then calculated from the shift in the star's position compared to the rest of the Universe. Over 120,000 stars have been reasonably parallaxed."

"So if you know the speed of light," said the pastor, "you begin to get a feel for the age of the stars." He was beginning to understand.

"If the speed of light is constant!" said Jon. "It's meant to be constant at about 186,000 miles per second in a vacuum. But just as 'time' can be slowed down by gravity and by acceleration, so can the speed of light, at least to an outside observer. The theory of black-holes depends on the fact that light slows down when time slows down, in a very high gravity field. The light is dragged back into the region and cannot escape to the outside world [88]."

He filled up the glasses with ice cold juice, and Jon explained how light is affected by gravity.

"Einstein predicted that gravity distorts space-time. Light tries to travel in a straight line, but it always takes the quickest path - Fermat's principle. It bends round on the outside of a high gravity field, in order to find a faster route. Einstein predicted that although you would not normally see a star if it were hidden behind the sun, during an eclipse when most of the sun is covered by the moon, light would be observable from these hidden stars. That's because rather than the light of the star being obscured by the sun, the sun's high gravity field slows down 'time' close to the sun's surface. So light finds a quicker route some distance from the sun's surface and it bends round the sun. This was observed in the eclipse of 1919, and was described as Einstein's greatest triumph [89]."

Jon continued "Time dilatation slows down light, and if our theory is correct that we are living in period when cosmic time is slowing down, the speed of light is also slowing down. We estimate that it takes light billions of years to reach us from far away stars, because we use the measuring rod of the current speed of light. But if light travelled much faster in the early days of the Universe, our estimate of its age is exaggerated."

Jon described the work of Setterfield who suggested that light was slowing down, and because the velocity of the electron in its orbit is proportional to the speed of light, anything that slows down light will decrease the speed of any mass-energy [90]. Setterfield argued that because light and radioactivity was slowing down, we were grossly over-estimating the age of the universe.

"Wasn't he a creationist?"

"Sure, he had a bias like you and me. But now the idea's respectable." Jon described a paper in *Nature* which suggested that the speed of light may not be constant, and it may have been faster 6 to 10 billions years ago, and that means we have to examine the very nature of time [91][92][93].

> **If the speed of light is slowing down**
> our estimates of the age of the Universe
> is exaggerated

"Last one. What about the red-shift of the expanding Universe? Does it tell us the age of the Universe?"

"Are you comfortable! It'll be a long session."

It was now dark, and the evening was alive with the noise of chirping insects, and over the next half hour, Jon described how the red shift might support the idea that time, here and now, is slowing down [94]."

> **An explanation of the red shift of nearby stars**
> could be that our current time frame
> is slowing down

Pastor Ibraim walked to the edge of the balcony and looked up at the sparkling stars. "How old are they? I think you are saying that you have a hypothesis to support a young Universe and a young earth. If you're right, when Genesis says God made the world and everything in it in six days, that could be in six days of fast cosmic time. It is interesting stuff, and really when you think about it - quite simple."

Jon admitted it was only a hypothesis. Hypotheses can never be proved, only disproved [95]. But there were lots of ideas to support it, not least the time-probe.

Jon continued.

"I know the vast majority of contemporary scientists believe in an ancient Universe. It's hardly been questioned for two hundred years, in spite of the imprecision and uncertainty and the impossibility of doing repeatable experiments. But we are now entering a new phase of a serious challenge to that paradigm."

"Keep going Jon. The very point of a paradigm shift is the challenge it brings to the older established model. You maybe only part of a minority that is raising the first challenge, and it'll be unwelcome by the majority. But if truth is on your side you'll find it will eventually replace the older, majority paradigm.

The older man thought a while, and then leant forwards - "Let me give you a word of advise."

Jon appreciated the wisdom of his years.

"What you say Jon, is welcome to those of us who believe that the Holy Scripture is just as true when it speaks of space, time and material reality, as when it speaks about spiritual things. But it doesn't really matter whether your scientific ideas are completely right or wrong. God will be God however we try to explain things. What matters is that you are prepared to ask a big question. And you've got my support."

Jon knew that they didn't have all the answers, but he thought that much of the interdisciplinary data didn't contradict their ideas.

"We want people with better minds than ours to think and talk about it, and examine the predictions."

"And how can you do that?" asked the pastor.

"Here in Iraq - we'd like to set up a web-sit and produce a cyberspace magazine."

"Here?"

"Why not?"

They were fugitives in exile and needed to find a safe house.

The pastor knew what to do.

"Jon let me talk to my friends, and I think they'll find a way to help you. You can trust them, because the believers in this place have learnt to be careful. I'll have an answer quite soon."

And he was as good as his word.

PART FOUR

CYBERSPACE

75

IT WAS TIME for Pastor Ibraim to return across the desert. His farewell party was an emotional affair, and the church in Baghdad turned out in large numbers to send him on his way. They had enjoyed his preaching - listening to a fresh voice.

"I'd like to stay, but -."

He held out his hands to Jon and Sophie. "I'm needed at home." And turning to the crowd - "when you run short, let me know and I'll be back."

As the dust settled they returned indoors, and Gorgin the church leader turned to Jon.

"We've just the place for you." And he told him about a basement flat a few blocks away. "It's been boarded up for years, and we've almost forgotten it existed."

This would be a basic home for Jon, Sophie and Anita, and an ideal cover for their web-site operation. The girls added a feminine touch to the living quarters, and Jon put together a small office, installing his two computers to the dedicated phone-line. Soon all Mohammed's work was ready to go on-line.

Anita came into the office to survey the scene. It was only a small basement room, but it had the air of efficiency.

"What do you think to our cyberspace HQ, Anita ?" he asked.

"Perfect Jon. But will the web-site be secure?"

"I'm not too sure Anita."

She looked at Jon. "If someone knew how to hack into this, it'd be all over."

"Any ideas?"

"Well, if I'm part of the team now" said Anita, "let me help"

"Sure. You're an essential player Anita. Sit down. "

He thought he knew something about computers, but Anita amazed him. She claimed the second desk and in just forty eight hours she had installed all the new anti-virus programmes. She had designed a new fire-wall programme, the like of which he'd never seen. It was professional.

"It's tremendous Anita," he said leaning back in his chair. "This site's going to grow. The data bases will build up, and we'll certainly need more memory and out-put. Thanks a million."

At the end of the second day, Pastor Gorgin came down for supper. They sat around the meal table, and Jon surveyed his team. He'd been voted the editor-in-chief, and he'd write about geology and cosmology. Sophie, when she was not working at the hospital, was to be the bio-logical sub-editor, important when they got onto Darwinism. Anita agreed to stay at home and be the much-needed computer administrator.

Jon looked towards the young pastor.

"Gorgin, we'd like to invite you to join us as the fourth team member - as Theological Advisor. We need you - because this magazine is going to interest a lot of people of different faiths. Genesis is 'Scripture' to Christians, Jews and Muslims - half to two thirds of the world's population. We need you to give us a faith dimension."

Gorgin wanted to know more, so they spent half the evening discussing the research and sharing with him their plans for the magazine. This church leader would be a good companion.

Sophie looked at him. He was small, sharp featured, with curly hair and bright twinkling eyes, and she guessed he was not short of ideas of his own. He listened to them and eventually nodded.

"I think your work is fascinating. I'm with you," he said. "Count me in."

There was relief all round. They were in business, and they started to plan the launch for June 14th.

"What's the name of your web site?" Gorgin asked.

It was Jon's turn and he glanced at Sophie.

"Gorgin, we claimed the domain in the UK. It's 'Journey to Eden.' - _www.journeytoeden.org_. All we have to do now is fill the pages !"

"Why 'Journey to Eden'?" he asked.

"It's a scientific journey Gorgin. We're inviting people to travel with us back to the beginning of time."

Gorgin was thoughtful and said "I like it."

It was praise from a man who didn't make quick decisions.

Then he saw that Jon and Sophie were holding hands.

"And there's an other reason !" he said smiling. "Yes?"

Sophie felt the blood flushing into her cheeks. He'd guessed their secret.

"Okay Gorgin - you're right. It's also because Jon and I've made our romantic 'journey to Eden'."

"And we're all on a 'faith journey'" interrupted Jon.

Gorgin wanted to pray with them before he left. He looked at Anita. She had become used to them saying a prayer before a meal. That made sense in Iraq! And now they needed extra help, because this was a dangerous country. Anita was a liberated Muslim - not really devout, but she believed in peace, charity and mercy, and she got on well with these Christians. In fact she had never met anyone she liked more than Sophie.

"Go ahead" she smiled "I'll listen."

Gorgin prayed in Arabic, and although Jon and Sophie couldn't understand a word, they asked Anita afterwards.

"What was that about?"

"He loves us all so much and he's just concerned for our safety Jon. He knows the dangers in Iraq. He was asking God to look after you. Why does this man love us so much, when he's never met us before?"

Jon admitted that it was also new for him.

76

DISCOVERED

BACK IN LONDON, Marcus hurried towards the Director General's office breathless as usual. He by-passed the secretaries, and knocked loudly on her door.

"C'm in."

"I've got it" he exclaimed, waving a five page print-out.

He had been searching every day, and this very morning he found a 'pop-up' of the advertisement of a web-site under construction.

Web-site under construction of a new Cyberspace Magazine
www.journeytoeden.org
Launch 14th June
Editor-in-chief Jon Le Var
Sub-editor Dr Sophie Le Var
First issue: 14th June **"The mystery of time."**
(1) A description of a time-probe that has used satellite mirrors to look back 15 years - history revealed !
(2) What is 'time'- is it an illusion?
(3) The biological clock in every living cell

<u>Second issue: 28th June</u> **"The slowing down of time."**

(1) Time-probe reveals that time is slowing down and the earth is expanding

(2) Carey's theory of an expanding earth

(3) We don't know that time is slowing down unless there is another time frame

(4) Evidence that Biological time may be in a different time frame

(5) The long ages of the patriarchs

<u>Third issue: July 12th</u> - **"Has there been time for evolution?"**

(1) The history of the theory of evolution over 150 years

(2) Pros and cons of evolution

(3) Biblical authority and origins - what Genesis says

contributions to the 'message board' after each issue will be welcome

"I can send them an e-mail ma'am - with a destructive virus - a time bomb. It's clever ma'am. If they're not secure, it'll wipe out their memory within 24 hours."

"Well done Marcus." At least one of her men was up to standard.

He showed Auntie three scanned photographs of the team.

"A picture of Jon and Sophie, arm in arm," he said putting a print-out on her desk.

Auntie peered at it closely.

"So these are our two young lovers! Hmm...." She expressed a mixture of delight and irritation.

"They've even dared to publish their names. Are they stupid?" she said, looking up at Marcus and tapping her fingers on the table.

"Any idea where they're holed up?"

"No ma'am - they're probably most secure. There's no way of telling where they've set up office. It could be here in London right under our nose, or thousands of miles away in some jungle hide-out."

"But these are their plans" she said, speaking to herself - "three issues of a cyberspace magazine."

Marcus pointed to a photograph of Anita. "That's their assistant." She was at her keyboard, and was smiling at the camera.

"Arabic," said Auntie.

"Maybe ma'am," said Marcus. And he showed her a picture of Gorgin.

"This is someone described as their 'theological adviser'."

"Ahh..."

"Not many clues from those, ma'am, but we'll find them for sure."

She knew he would, because this man's mind didn't work in parallel lines. This was going to be a battle of wits, and she could rely on Marcus

"Hack into their programmes" she said, "and discover where they are. And get what ever help you need.".

He turned to the door.

"And Marcus."

"Yes ma'am."

We must talk about that salary rise -"

"Well,uh, thanks."

"- next week."

He'd heard it before, and he limped away.

WORLD WIDE WEB

77

TEN THOUSAND MILES AWAY in north west China, another computer buff had seen the same announcement about the cyberspace magazine. He attended a student's meeting that night. The room was packed with nearly two hundred young people, talking excitedly and comparing notes. They sang some unaccompanied hymns, read the Bible together and someone talked about it for half an hour. They then prayed in small groups. Finally the buff asked permission to speak.

He told them that whilst surfing the internet he'd noticed that there was to be the launch of new IT Magazine _www.journeytoeden.org_ It was to present new research supporting a young earth and the Biblical account of Creation. It was a magazine that invited debate, and was particularly directed towards students and anyone who was prepared to compare the Biblical data with science.

A few of the students were interested, but it was late in the day and many let it drift over their heads. It was only when he mentioned the sub-editor Dr Sophie Le Var that Xi-xi woke up. Could it be the very same Sophie she had been writing to? She noted the address and hurried home to send an e-mail.

"sophie, i see you've got a new job as sub-editor of a cyberspace magazine. thought you were a medical doctor! didn't know you were into science. look forward to the first edition next week. how's edinburgh? any news of my father? love xi-xi"

She received an e-mail in return.

"xi-x. not in edinburgh. guess where? am doing some medical work with needy kids. let me know what you think of the magazine. not seen your father. love sophie"

Xi-xi was just one of several thousands who were waiting for the first issue of _www.journeytoeden.org_ magazine.

On the far side of the globe, Max opened the same web page. His boss was irritated that Jon and Sophie had escaped the clutches of the British Special Branch. Apologies from the British Director General were not good enough. They should have let Max the deceiver, the briber, the shameless crook, neutralise them. Now they had some of their best US brains trying to interpret the internet announcement and discover where these people were in exile, but as yet there were no clues. The plan was to find them and give Max a free hand to get them iced, like Mohammed.

Max picked up the file again from the corner of his desk and examined it again. Where would he hide in the same situation? He had his hunch. Sophie had met Mohammed in Syria, and if he were these youngsters, he'd disappear into a country hostile to the West.

The phone rang in the CIA office.

"Permission to speak to our cousins in London, boss? I bet ya - a dollar to a hole in a doughnut - they've gone east."

He explained why. And it didn't seem too outrageous.

"Yea. Okay."

Steve and Danny took the call together.

"Hi guys. I can do ya one big favour. I'm sitting here with my finger in the wind, and it's all blowing one way - to the east."

They listened to Max and agreed his hunch might be right. They told the American how the trail led to a honeymoon suite in Cyprus, and their man in Nicosia although concussed, had eventually found the taxi driver who had taken them to the Lebanese ferry. They had a problem. They didn't have anyone in Damascus.

"We do - indirectly," said Max. "I'll call him now". He spoke to Moscow.

TURNING THE SCREW

78

"GENERAL. GOOD TO HEAR you again. How is it in Damascus?".

General Kapta knew the guttural voice immediately. It was the little Russian, who earlier in the day had been told by British and US Intelligence that the problem he believed was long buried had now surfaced again. He couldn't believe it. He had failed twice, and again it was by under-rating the opposition. He had one last chance before he would be forcibly retired or worse.

General Kapta listened intently. He didn't like the Russian, and he was not inclined to say much.

"And how is your lovely daughter?"

"She's fine. What can I do for you?"

"I need another favour my friend. You helped us once before, and we buried the irregularities."

"I don't understand you."

The Russian remained silent for a few moments for effect. It was something the KGB had taught him.

"The irregularity" - said the Russian in slow gravelly tones - "about the exit visa you arranged for the Iraqi - Mohammed wasn't it? Several countries wanted that man and some wanted him alive. They have deep convictions and long memories. It would be unfortunate if they remembered you and your family. I'm sure you want to retain our silence. In return I need an other small favour."

Small beads of perspiration trickled down the general's brow.

"I kept my side of the bargain long ago and we agreed the deal was complete."

"Almost"

And there was a long pause.

"What do you want?"

"My employers believe that Dr Sophie and her new lover-boy are with you. We need to give them a message....personally."

The general had come to respect Sophie and Jon. They had many qualities he admired, openness, kindness, integrity and honesty. What sort of a man was he to betray their trust.

"Sorry my Russian friend, you are mistaken. They are not with me."

"You have twenty four hours" said the man at the other end of the phone, "and if you fail to play ball with me........ Anita is a lovely girl............ Do I make myself clear?"

And then the phone went dead - and the general sat for a long time looking at the wall.

The Russian smiled to himself. The general owed them a favour. He had been given a very nice back-hander. Let him squirm.

THE NATIONAL MUSEUM

79

THE NATIONAL MUSEUM in Baghdad is a treasure-trove of antiquities. Jon took Sophie on a Thursday afternoon when the city was beginning to wake up from its siesta. The dozey Arab in the front kiosk slowly opened one eye, took their money and pushed two tickets through the small dirty window, and they entered an enormous marble hall with a domed roof which spoke of more glorious days. They were the only visitors in this vast building.

Their feet echoed on the grey marble floor, as they followed the arrows winding in and out of side-rooms. It was an extensive exhibition, illustrating the history of Iraq from ancient times to the present day. There were faded diagrams and artefacts illustrating the long history of *Homo* species, from his first stepping out of the forest about three and a half million years ago, to the arrival of modern humans 200,000 years ago [96].

There was a glass cabinet containing a Neanderthal skeleton from the caves of Mount Carmel.

Jon bent down to read the text.

"Neanderthal skeleton, circa 100,000 years. There is contro-versy about whether Neanderthals are truly Homo sapiens, *or a*

different species- Skull capacity 1438cc."

"One of my Jersey cousins" he cried.

Sophie had noticed a curator who was lazily sweeping the floor.

"Behave Jon. You'll have us thrown out."

They moved on.

The Neanderthal was overshadowed by the next exhibit under spot-lights - an Iraqi skeleton.

"Mature male, excavated from the entrance of a cave in the Zagros mountains of northern Iraq. The body had been placed on a bed of flowers. This is the first evidence of ritual human burial - circa 70,000 years. Skull capacity 1338 cc" [97].

Sophie looked carefully at the bones in both cabinets. "The only difference I can see in these two skeletons, is that the Neanderthal has a large brow ridge on the skull. I'm no expert" she said "but from the gross anatomy I'd say they were both part of the human race."

Sophie looked at the shining brown skulls. "These guys' bones are just the same as yours Jon. You could wear the same hat! And look at those fingers - and the spines. These are identical to the modern bones I used in the Edinburgh anatomy course. They've not changed in a hundred millennia." She looked at the hips. "Those ridges are exactly the same that I see when I am assisting in hip replacements - they're identical to those of modern humans today. Isn't that odd? You'd expect lots of changes if evolution were correct!"

They moved on and saw examples of cave art from northern Iraq 30,000 years ago.

"There are similar examples of cave painting from all over the world - in Africa, Asia, Europe and in Australia - wherever people lived" said Jon.

"Here Jon," cried Sophie her voice echoing round he exhibition hall.

"What is it Sophie?"

"Look."

It was a Jurassic landscape, with abundant primordial trees, fossilised mosses, ferns, horsetails and liverworts. It was an artist's impression of the vegetation in southern Iraq long ago. They bent down to read the text.

> *"A beautifully lush and fertile country once existed between the rivers Tigris and Euphrates. It has been perhaps one of the most beautiful places on earth - from the times of antiquity. Some claim that it was like the 'Garden of Eden' described in ancient sacred Scriptures."*

"No mention of what it's like today," said Jon, standing up and shaking his head. This is Marsh Arab country where Saddam practiced his scorched earth policy - where he massacred 200,000 Shiites. Today it's a bleak empty desert - a haunt for jackals.

They came to a hall exhibiting the development of Chaldean culture - the cradle of world civilisation - 6,000 years ago - with models of the first simple baked brick houses of Neolithic farmers and then the first ancient city in Iraq with a towering Ziggurat - a terraced fired-brick pyramid with tar they used as mortar.

There were examples of the first Iraqi cuneiform writing in 3000 BC, and with that came literacy, the explosion of Babylon's public works, taxation, and the market. There was then a sudden profusion of specialists - freemen and slaves, landlords and tenants, agents and merchants, wine-sellers, priestesses, physicians, veterinarians, boatmen, herdsmen, brick-makers, tailors and carriers - doing things which were possible only because the new society could read and write. And as literacy developed so did the science of arithmetic, geometry and astronomy - civilisation had arrived.

Jon looked pensive. "Can you explain this to me Sophie? The *Homo* genus is said to have been around for three and half million years, and modern humans for 200,000 years. They say that by 75,000 years ago, biological evolution had reached a point where mankind had the genes necessary for a fully developed human life [98]. These people could paint, keep records of the phases of the moon and build Stonehenge. Why then did it take until 3000 BC for clever people to start civilisation, not only here in Iraq but simultaneously in 'three tiny patches of the Earth's surface'. - Asia, Middle Eastern Europe ?"

"Rhetorical question Jon."

"Sure, but these humans had anatomy just like ours for scores of millennia, with the same self-awareness, and yet the first sign of culture - writing, building, money, specialists - occurred only so very recently. And it blossomed simultaneously and independently in the different races. How could a fully human man have been around for such a long time, and then only in 3000 BC show signs of culture and technology? Why didn't some clever guy try to write a message to his wife when he went off for a day's hunting, or give her some money when she went to the supermarket?"

She burst out laughing, knowing him too well.

"Like you Jon ! Yes, it's odd. It's a big coincidence that the Assyrians, Chinese, Egyptians all developed their own independent pictographic styles of writing - picture words - and as a result of that, civilisation blossomed in three places all at the same time. If humans had such a very ancient history you'd have thought they'd have found ways of expressing themselves very much earlier."

> **Civilisation**
> It is surprising that modern humans
> with an identical anatomy to our own and the
> same self awareness
> *were said* to have arrived 200,000 years ago,
> and yet recorded civilisation
> appeared in many centres *only* around 3000 BC

"I guess we've a bias Jon, but the anatomy of these ancient skeletons is so like ours today, their skulls are the same size and shape as ours, they behaved as we do grieving for their dead and expressing their feelings in art. It doesn't make sense that they were so long in learning to write."

They entered another hall describing the black stones with the Code of Hammurabi, which gave the world its first law codes [98]. And finally they came to Babylon in her first glory days - with pictures of magnificent buildings, and the beautiful hanging gardens which were one of the seven wonders of the world. There were reliefs, statues and painted pottery depicting the many warriors who had mowed down the surrounding nations, and their most famous king - Nebuchadnezzar - who besieged Jerusalem in 586 BC. He breached its defences, ruthlessly butchered a third of its inhabitants, and carried the royal family and nobility in chains to Babylon. There were models of Nebuchadnezzar's splendid palace, his throne room, the Ishtar gate and the mighty walls of Procession Street.

Side by side was another impressive exhibition.

"Look at that Jon !" she said in surprise. " 'The Renaissance of the new Babylon by the favour of Saddam Hussein.' " They had suddenly jumped more than two thousand years. There was a larger than life portrait of benevolent Saddam, with quaint photographs of his earlier life.

Jon was incredulous.

"They've not updated this place since Saddam! How can they still exhibit this?"

They read the potted life-history.

"Born in the village of Tikrit, about a hundred miles north of Baghdad on the Tigris river - by the will of Allah - from the same village as Saladin who vanquished the Crusader infidels - Saddam Hussein - Leader of the Baath Party and President of Iraq from 1979 to 2003."

Finally there were two superimposed profiles of Saddam and Nebuchadnezzar, and then a remarkably ambitious statement attributed to Saddam in 1979.

"The glory of the Arabs stems from the glory of Iraq. Throughout history, whenever Iraq became mighty and flourished, so did the Arab nation. This is why we are striving to make Iraq mighty, formidable, able and developed."

There was a quote from an official state booklet.

" Today looks exactly like yesterday. After long periods of darkness that enveloped the land of Babylon, Saddam Hussein emerged from Mesopotamia , as Hammurabi and Nebuchadnezzar emerged, at a time to shake the century old dust off Babylon's face. He left his fingerprints everywhere."

"They won't forget this guy, even though he was a tyrant for 37 years!"

The new Babylon was shown to be rising again from the old ruins [99]. There were photographs of the rebuilt walls of Procession street, the new four thousand seater Greek theatre, the rebuilt Ninmach Temple on the palm lined banks of the flowing Euphrates River, and the impressive Guest House. And there was an ambitious model of the mighty new government Ziggurat.

Sophie turned away in disbelief. "Reminds you of the first Ziggurat. What did it say in Genesis. 'Come let us make bricks and bake them thoroughly. Let us build ourselves a city, with a tower that reaches to the heavens so that we may make a name for ourselves'."

Jon muttered, "The old dictator's ghost still walks this place !"

They turned on their heels unaware of that the curator had been taking notes and that the roving eye of the surveillance camera in the gallery had followed their every step.

80 PREPARING THE FIRST ISSUE

SOPHIE SPENT HER DAYS in the Children's Hospital. She helped in theatre and on the wards, and she enjoyed running seminars for the medical students. It was really no more than a repeat of what she herself had received in Edinburgh, but the students thought it was helpful and the numbers grew daily. Each afternoon she came home to the basement flat exhausted, but was never too tired to talk to Jon about the magazine.

Anita spent her days in the cyberspace office. Jon didn't want to work the girls too hard but it was June 7th, and he was worried that they may not meet the deadline. He valued talking to them about the first issue.

"The title of the first issue is 'THE MYSTERY OF TIME'. It's due on June 14th, and it is not going to be ready!"

"We'll get there" said Sophie pulling up a chair. She was an optimist. "What's the state of play?" Anita made a threesome.

"The editorial sets out our mission statement," he said - putting it one the screen. "We're saying the focus of the magazine is to discuss the relativity of time. We've one simple objective - to get people asking the right questions - trying to get them to think. We're not saying we have all the answers. But if you ask the important question you're on the right track.

We're identifying the questions, like 'What is time?' - 'Is time uniform?' - 'What are the implications of time slowing down?' - and we'll develop these ideas with each new issue.

In the first issue - we'll have three papers."

"Which are?" said Anita.

"**NUMBER ONE.** The leading article has to be how Mohammed used mirrors to look back in time - *"An optical study of the recent past"* - and we'll give due credit to his sponsors in Iraq."

"Good thinking" said Anita. "I think Mohammed would have wanted that."

"We'll publish it just as Mohammed wrote it. We're saying that this is the foundation for his next paper the following month, when we'll have something new to say about the speed of the earth's rotation and the duration of the earth's circuit round the sun, and evidence for a young earth. This first issue should wet a few appetites for the next one."

Sophie watched his face in profile as he typed quickly on the keys. She was proud of him. The man she'd married was so handsome and strong, and his every aspect was dear to her. She thought he had a wisdom beyond his age.

"What else goes in the first issue?" she asked, caressing his fingers.

NUMBER TWO was to be Jon's paper on *'What is time'?* He was quoting a lot from Barbour's work "Time is an illusion - it does not exist. Nature only creates the impression of time" and from Mach's paper "It is utterly beyond our power to measure the change of things by time. Rather time is an abstraction at which we arrive, by means of the change of things." He was also trying to remind people of Einstein's work that time is relative to gravity and to speed.

NUMBER THREE would be Sophie's paper on *'Biological clocks'*. She was describing how biological clocks tend to run with a slightly longer cycle than solar time, and that would be a springboard for the next issue when they would be looking at the possibility of different time-frames.

They forgot about food, and worked a long time into the night hours, reading and refining the papers.

"I'll put in some overtime and help you tidy up the text," said Anita.

"Promise you - come June 14th - we'll be on-line!"

LAUNCHED

81

THEY HAD BEEN ADVERTISING on the scientific pages for a few weeks, and the first issue of _www.journeytoeden.org_ magazine hit the net promptly on June 14th. It claimed that Mohammed's time-probe could look back over fifteen years, and it caused a stir across many time-zones. The scientific community refused to believe that someone had made a time-probe that could look back over a decade - it was an impossibility. Politicians were frantic - it could reveal their secrets. The security men in China, Russia, UK and the States were furious. Some old soldiers who had abused human rights began to get frightened. Theologians were frustrated. Students were fascinated. The press had a field-day.

"Twenty five thousand logged on the first day - and building up" said jubilant Jon when Sophie returned. "It's increasing as the word's getting out. So many enquiries now, we just can't cope with them all. We should have another computer and more staff."

Anita installed more memory with more power, and she spent hours just cataloguing the correspondence, checking the incoming mail and sorting out priority mail from junk.

There was now a captive audience waiting for the magazine's second issue on 'THE SLOWING DOWN OF TIME'.

"We'll have to be sharp to have the five papers ready in two weeks." said Jon.

He told the team about his plans.

"**NUMBER ONE** is to be Mohammed's important work - *'The relative change of time'* - how he recorded the slowing down of the earth's circuit round the sun by 0.5% in a decade, and the evidence for an expanding earth. This article will stand alone just as Mohammed wrote it. It'll speak for itself without comment.

NUMBER TWO. I'm writing on *'Carey's theory of the expanding earth'* and how this agreed with Mohammed's observations.

NUMBER THREE is going to ask - *"'Is the whole cosmos slowing down in unison'* - and how we would be unaware of it unless there was a gold-standard measurement outside the system. Mohammed's time probe is that independent yard-stick.

NUMBER FOUR is a paper Sophie has written on *'Biological time'* and she gives many examples of how biological clocks are out of sequence with cosmic time. She describes how most free-running biological clocks run in 25 hour cycles, and she suggests they had been programmed for a "one day" cycle in earlier times when cosmic time was faster. What used to be 24 hours of biological time in the past is now 25 hours - it's slower because the earth is rotating more slowly. The biological clocks have a lag time, and although constantly being reprogrammed, they have a delay in synchronising with the slower cosmic time.

She's also written about athletes running faster, and about young DNA being found in ancient rocks, and she says it's compatible with the idea that Biological clocks are uncoupled from physical time.

NUMBER FIVE is Gorgin's *'The Long Ages of the Patriarchs'*, describing several reasons why these people could have lived to such a great age. It could also have been predicted if cosmic time and biological time were marching to a different beat."

Jon took a deep breath.

"Good stuff Gorgin. We'll include some graphs" said Jon "to show that if we're right, then the earth is young."

"Jon, I've got to say we can't be sure that any scientific theory is a true explanation of the plain teachings of the word of God."

"Sure Gorgin. Science is only approximating to the truth."

"We must add that word of caution," said the pastor. "I'm confident that what the Bible says about the space/time cosmos is true, and then I look at science and try to make the best sense in both realms." He looked for Jon's approval and continued. "Many believers will welcome the scientific challenge you're making, without being sure this is exactly the way it happened."

"I'm with you Gorgin - one hundred percent. That's okay."

They hit the web on time. They had invited comment, but they'd never expected so much.

INTERNATIONAL AUDIENCE

82

"sophie, an e-mail to say your magazine's causing a stir here in urumqi. we'd never thought of the slowing down of time before. i know you must be terribly busy but please reply. love xi-xi"

"xi-xi, sorry not to have answered before. we hardly have time to eat. jon is working all hours trying to answer the correspondence. we have some good help. what do you think about the magazine? love, sophie"

"sophie, i haven't told you before, but i've been a believer for over a year. your articles are making us think a lot about science and religion, and we're having a meeting specially to discuss it next week. it's illegal so pray for us. my father was showing some interest, but i've heard nothing from him. i'm so afraid he might have had an accident. love, xi-xi"

Xi-xi invited some of her friends to her flat to discuss the first two issues of the *www.journeytoeden.org* magazine. They were surprised to know that Xi-xi was already corresponding with one of the editors.

"Will they accept something from us?" they asked. They worked all night, writing something for Xi-xi to attach to her next e mail.

> *"sophie, we had a great meeting last night. no problems. thanks for praying. can you consider this attachment for publication in your chat page? love xi-xi"*

Their attachment said that they believed they were typical of Chinese students who were disillusioned with the atheistic teaching they had received from school-days. They believed in God and the teachings of Jesus, and they had no difficulty accepting the truth of the Bible. It was changing their lives. They found it refreshing that someone was taking the fight to the opposition. They already believed in a young earth, in special creation of living kinds, in an Intelligent Designer God who cares, and they were pleased to see that the dogma of atheistic science was being challenged.

> *"xi-xi, Jon says he will be pleased to include your letter in the next issue, blessings, sophie"*

Sophie knew that because of Anita's 'fire-wall', incoming mail was secure. But she was unaware that in China, the e-mail server - the ISP - was controlled by government. Maybe she had volunteered more information to Xi-xi than was wise.

There was so much traffic from the 'chat room' and 'message boards' that Jon stayed up half the night sifting through the letters. He put them into four files.

- The first group said they were a bunch of foolish, ignorant amateurs who hadn't thought through their ideas about time. It was obvious they didn't have any knowledge of physics, the properties of light nor the working of the cosmos. There were obvious explanations for athletes running faster and for the biological clock being out of step with cosmic time. They knew nothing about modern theology and in fact they were dangerous and someone should silence them - permanently !

- The second group like Xi-xi were supportive. They said the magazine was a breath of fresh air. They accepted the concepts without question as an answer to some of the scientific conundrums that had plagued religion since Darwin and Lyell. They thought it was a wake-up call to the church.

- There was a third group that sat on the fence. They were cautiously optimistic, saying that these ideas were novel and were worth serious thought. They said they were open-minded people and they looked forward to more.

- There were many correspondents who had ideas of their own. Some were very ingenious.

For example a woman from Australia commented on the newly discovered extra-solar planets. "More than 70 stars are now know to have at last one planet orbiting round them - 'wobbling stars' - like two ice-skaters spinning round together - and their number is rising fast. The Frenchman who first detected a 'wobbling star' was surprised that the planets were revolving round their sun in an unbelievably fast four or five day cycle. How could a planet's circuit be so short, without being tremendously close to its star?"

She asked - "Can these stars be transmitting light from the early days of the Universe when cosmic time was much faster?"

Jon scratched his head. "We need an astrophysicist to answer that one."

An other researcher from Central Africa encouraged them to challenge the concept of evolution. It their theory about time was right, then evolution must be wrong. Sophie read the letter with interest, because she had a paper on evolution for the next issue.

This man was reconstructing *Homo* species skulls dug up from the Rift valley in Africa, and he was measuring the skull volume. "The brain of *Homo sapiens* is three times the size of his supposed nearest evolutionary relatives, and it is argued that *Homo* has developed by a slight step-by-step increment in the size of the brain. Even a little extra brain is said by evolutionists to be an advantage, and the brain size is cited as a measure of the progress of the *Homo* species, climbing up the ladder from more primitive primate ancestors. Every small enlargement is said to increase the potential to survive, and so modern man wins over his competitors in the African savannah. It's claimed that this clever primate - modern man with a big brain - finally swings down from the trees in a warm, wet clearing somewhere in Africa 65 million years ago."

He quoted some figures from Shakey [100].

GROUP	RANGE OF SKULL CAPACITY (cc)
Chimpanzees	320-480
Gorillas	340-685
Australopithecines	450-750
Pithecanthropines	835-900
Classic Neanderthal	1300-1610
Modern man	1195-1520

However, the researcher admitted to being one of the underdogs who believed in a more recent beginning on the ground, with tree swinging as a fun option. He pointed out an error in the argument, that everyone knows that brain size is not an indicator of intelligence.

"The most brilliant people can have small brain volume and much of our brain has surplus unused capacity" said the researcher, "and it's illogical to argue that a slight increase in brain volume is an advantage to survival, when so much of it is spare capacity and never used."

Sophie agreed. "He's right. A patient suffering a stroke can lose lots of brain tissue permanently - and yet still function as though there was no damage. We lose brain cells every day of our lives, but my granddad's brilliant! Let have this in the next issue Anita."

THE TRAIL IS HOT

83

"TWENTY FOUR HOURS IS up General." It was the Russian's rough voice again.

The General braced himself for an other confrontation, and listened.

"What do you have to say?" asked the gruff Russian.

Like Pontius Pilate, General Kapta had had a bad night. He had no stomach for betraying innocent people, but he had to think about his daughter. What could a man do? Best wash his hands of the whole affair.

"You could ask 'Thompson Pharmaceuticals' what they know about it, but I can tell you nothing."

That was enough for the Russian. He was on the phone immediately, and the sales-manager of one of the largest international Pharmaceutical firms was not reluctant to say how charitable his company had been. They'd happily responded to Dr Sophie Tristan's request, and provided a generous gift of supplies for her to take to the Sick Children's Hospital in Baghdad. The pursuit was on.

Within the hour Moscow, Washington and London had a three-way conversation, and the key players were called to Auntie's office for briefing. Max arrived at Heathrow on a 757 and the Russian came in a few hours later.

"Hi ma'am - how ya doin'?"

The Russian merely grunted.

Auntie shook their hands. It was cold, strong and brief, as if to emphasise a mere formality. She made a vague gesture towards two black swivel chairs, and murmured something to the two men behind her - Danny and Steve - who offered them stiff drinks.

"Good" said Max. "That's real good."

She looked at her watch and called for Marcus.

He was pacing up and down his office - troubled that the first issue of the *www.journeytoeden.org* magazine had gone on line, and he'd not been able to hack into it.

Marcus felt his pager buzz, and quickly pulled it from his pocket. "AUNTIE ASAP" A conference now - and no one keeps Auntie waiting.

He climbed the stairs, stumbled in, and assessed the scene. The place was full of professional hit men ! Auntie was in charge. She was in near panic mode. She looked distinctly unhappy as she started to spell out the gravity of the situation.

"Sit down men," she barked. " "Listen to this !" They scooted their chairs back - because she tended to spit when she spoke - and they listened for ten minutes without interrupting her.

"The allies - USA, Russia, China and our own UK government," she shouted "are agreed that we're facing an unusual situation. These youngsters have no idea how they are contributing to the a global problem. We believe they are in Iraq using the Children's Hospital as a cover. Marcus" - she nodded to him - "will tell you why in a moment."

She looked at the Russian. "And our friend - our colleague here - has traced the Pharmaceutical company that gave supplies to Sophie for the Sick Children's Hospital. It also fits with what we know about this pastor" - she looked at her notes - "Gorgin - in Baghdad - writing about his so called theological reflections."

Auntie looked up and laughed derisively - "Religion!"

She started to talk about Islam and what they already knew about Islamic terrorism, and its breeding ground.

"First the background. Central Asia is at 'boiling point' and the Republics are ripe for take-over by Islamic fundamentalists. In Xinjang north-west China, the government is rapidly losing ground. Their army hasn't been paid for months, and the soldiers are selling their uniforms in the streets. The fundamentalists are preaching to the entire Muslim world, that from Central Asia they will expand and create a powerful united Islamic empire. They want to rise up against the corrupt anti-Muslim regimes, and transform these republics into an Islamic homeland. Their long term goal is to unite with the rest of the entire Islamic world into one great super-state. And then" - she couldn't resist a short dramatic pause - "Europe will be in their sights.

At the moment it is a battle for the mind. These Muslims in Central Asia say they are not really militant ! They hope that by argument and preaching and many conversions, the sheer weight of numbers will bring them to government. More than 60 percent of the region's 50 million people are under the age of 25 - impressionable young people - many of them students who spread their ideas by text messages, e-mail and live webcast."

There was silence. You didn't interrupt Auntie.

"All across the Arab world underground extremist Islamic groups are flourishing. They have a well organised base here in London - they're linked to al Qa'eda - and they're getting impatient." She looked out of the window. "We're trying to respond on every front, and if we fail, ultimately there'll be an incredible war."

She turned to the job ahead of them, and looked at her dossier.

"To the specifics - this phoney research. It's dangerous for two reasons. First, the time probe is a propaganda coup for the old Iraq. Those old guard who have disappeared into the undergrowth. They are still out there, and they are the main bidders to rule the Islamic world. They are flexing their muscles for a marriage of terror, alongside al Qa'eda. We don't want them to get credit for this time probe."

Auntie's men were listening. The Russian was scratching his chin, and Max was examining his finger nails.

"And there's an other reason" she said - "this crazy idea they're suggesting - that the earth is young ! If such an belief gets hold, it's just the thing to tip the balance in this battle of ideas - to swell the ranks of Islamic fundamentalism."

She'd spelt it out in detail, because if they got it wrong again, her own career was now on the line.

"So it's over to you, men" she said closing the file. "We've no choice but to remove them. A bit messy - but the stakes are big. Our governments demand that these two young hot-heads with their cyberspace magazine are eliminated, and you are assigned to the task."

Max spoke first, looking at the Russian and then at Steve and Dave.

"Can I speak ma'am? If we're working as a foursome, when we're on the ground, then I take the lead."

The Russian didn't care, because he could always change the rules, and Auntie had no objection because her two men were responsible for this whole fiasco.

"We'll cope with that," she said. "How does Washington want to play?"

Steve and Danny watched the other two reach again for the bottles, and put back more whiskey than was good for them. They abstained. Auntie preferred her men to have daily viagra, because it didn't dull their wits.

Max put his glass down and smacked his lips. "My American boss wants us to join the UN Inspection team that's snooping all over Baghdad" he said. "They're still searching those factories to see whose making and hiding al Qa'eda's biological and chemical weapons. Our guys are still searching, so we'll tag along." And with a wink, "Ya - and make sure the Children's Hospital's clean - no ricin, anthrax or small pox there !"

The two British agents grinned, but it brought little change in the Russian's expression. He betrayed his strongest emotion by a millimetre raising of an eyebrow.

Max eyed Steve and Danny. "Okay - no dumb questions or excuses this time" he drawled.

Marcus had been listening to their conversation and was repressing a slight smile when Auntie asked for his comments. He thought the situation was surreal, but he played his part.

"You're right about Baghdad" he said. "These kids send e-mails between 9am and 6pm, and that means they're in the Iraq time-zone - unless they're burning the night candle at some other place!"

Marcus continued "Dr Sophie can't know that her e-mail is exposed in China. Their servers are government agencies, and my opposite number in Peking has cracked the correspondence between Sophie and a girl in Urumqi. Sophie is talking about doing some medical work. So it might be the Children's Hospital."

He then pointed to the articles by Gorgin - "This is their theological advisor. It's not a common name in Iraq - probably French extraction. And there's a church pastor in Baghdad registered as Gorgin Atlan. We tried to speak to him on the phone yesterday but his wife says he's too busy with some research. It fits together boys. I wish you success."

He gave them a full report of the first two issues of the _www.journeytoeden.org_ magazine. He had written down a few ideas of his own. They could read the ten page dossier on the plane. He had done his job well, but he didn't care for the hit men.

Until now Max had been rather disdainful of this quiet little man with the limp, but he recalled Truman's comment - often repeated in his training - about size to a Missouri student: "When it comes down to inches, my boy, you should only consider the forehead. Better to have a spare inch between the top of your nose and the hairline than between the ankles and the kneecap." Perhaps Marcus had something to contribute after all.

84

ISSUE NUMBER THREE

EVOLUTION WAS TO BE the theme of the third issue of the _www.journeytoeden.org_ magazine due on July 12th, 'HAS THERE BEEN TIME FOR EVOLUTION?' They gathered round Jon's desk in the basement office as Jon was banging away on the computer keyboard.

"Why evolution?" asked Anita as she fixed them a pot of coffee, French blend.

"Because if evolution's right - afraid we're wrong" said Jon.

Sophie stood behind him, massaging the back of his neck. She chipped in. "And lots of people will say we're crazy suggesting a young earth - it gives no time for evolution. The media leads folk blindly along, until they think that evolution's a proven fact. It's not. Darwinism gets weaker the more you look at it. We can only share the facts and let people judge for themselves."

"Right."

"That coffee smells good."

"Only three papers this time," said Jon. "Mine is historical. Sophie's on the arguments for and against, and Gorgin comes in with the theological finale. Okay Gorgin?"

Sophie pulled up a chair. "So what's your title Jon?"

"EVOLUTIONARY THEORY IN THE LAST 150 YEARS."

"I'm writing that if our hypothesis is right and the earth is young, there's just no time for evolution - not a problem for those who believe in a God of miracles - but a young earth could only mean special creation, and after living with Darwin's legacy for one hundred and fifty years, the early chapters of Genesis have to go back onto the agenda, even if this might be uncomfortable for some."

Sophie bent over and kissed his rough face.

"You've forgotten to shave again Jon. But you look good with a growth of stubble."

"Women!" he chuckled.

1. HISTORY

He wrote about the climate before Darwin boarded the *Beagle*, when most scientists believed that the earth in the vast cosmos was the work of God, and the profusion of life was created by the hand of an imaginative, intelligent and purposeful deity. Then came Darwin with his untiring advocate Thomas Henry Huxley, who turned this idea on its head. God's creative work was described as nothing more than the result of time and chance. Evolution which had previously been only speculation was now a fact, and there was no room for God unless He played dice.

They were watching the screen as he talked through his ideas.

His article described how, after Darwin wrote '*On the Origin of Species*' in 1859, evolution was thought to be responsible for everything. Darwin thought that the great variation within the species - the tall, short, fat and thin individuals - changed as the conditions change. That the environment favoured some members of the species with certain variations, and their numbers increased. It was the 'survival of the fittest'. The weak and unfit went to the wall.

"Darwin didn't know how it worked, but he thought that if there was enough time, evolution would automatically make new species. Sexual selection was important, and the strongest and fittest male got his mate......"

"He's right about that" and Sophie prodded him in the ribs.

"No reply.....and passed on better qualities to his offspring. They became distinct from their cousins in another place, and eventually a new species formed, incapable of breeding with the friends they left behind."

"That sounds okay," she said.

> **Darwinism**
> is now widely accepted
> as the explanation for living things

Gorgin looked over his shoulder.

"Say something about its effect on people's faith, Jon."

2. THE EFFECT ON FAITH AND SOCIETY

(i) *Faith* : Jon wrote that although Darwin was proclaimed in his day, as the modern Moses to guide the people through the wilderness [101], he couldn't lead them to the promised land. There was no promised land. This was the price to pay - despair and a distrust of religion. Darwin saw only struggle, temporary victory and defeat in Nature, and a complete absence of meaning. It left mankind alone in a silent Universe.

Gorgin interrupted.

"I think it was Neitzsch who said 'if you gaze for long enough into the abyss, the abyss gazes also into you'. And the French biologist Jacques Monod said 'The ancient covenant is in pieces: man at last knows he is alone in the unfeeling immensity of the universe, out of which he has emerged only by chance. Neither his destiny nor his duty have been written down.'"

> **Despair**
> It left mankind alone in a silent universe.

So Jon kept typing. He went on to describe the great battles between Darwinism and the so-called bigots. Even Lyell who made Darwinism possible by suggesting an ancient world, didn't fully accept evolution when he wrote his *Antiquity of Man* in 1863, and Darwin never forgave him for avoiding the question of man's evolved place in nature, and for holding on to his religious beliefs [102]. Many like Wallace thought that Nature was guided and the process of evolution had a higher meaning, but Darwin would have non of it. He also criticised the great naturalist Sir Richard Owen for hanging on to the idea that 'a superior being' guided Nature through evolution. They were dismissed as speaking nonsense, with an emotional attachment to their religious faith [103].

Jon kept hammering on the keyboard.

(ii) Social Darwinism: The philosophy of Darwinism eventually touched all of society - with the loss of value of individual human beings - it produced the dangerous by-product of 'Social Darwinism'."

"What do you mean ?" asked Anita.

Jon explained. "Darwinism provided an excuse for fanatics to try to engineer a super-race of humans. It started with the despair of Neitzsh, and was followed by the ethnic cleansing of Hitler - and atheistic communism - and the cruel purges of the 20th century."

Jon asked what monsters might be produced in the future, if genetic engineering is directed by evolutionary ethics?

3. NEO DARWINISM

They looked over his shoulder as he wrote that evolution was embellished by each succeeding generation, until in the 20th century, a new understandings of heredity, the discovery of chromosomes and genes, and finally the understanding that the complex DNA could mutate was claimed to be the driving force of evolution.

"Read it to us Jon, said Anita."

"Last ditch ideas were suggested by some evolutionists" he said, looking at the screen - "ideas to explain why lots of new fossils seem to make a suddenly appearance. Out went Darwin's concept of slow gradual change, and the ascent of species is now more like a game of hopscotch - short jumps every now and then - 'punctuated equilibrium' - bursts of new species and then nothing happening for millions of years."

"Anything to keep evolution on track," said Sophie.

4. DARE TO DISAGREE

"I have to write somewhere," said Jon looking at his friends, "that it's an aggressive climate for creationists. Anyone who doesn't accept evolution is said to be simple-minded, ignorant, bigoted, foolish and in a minority."

"I'm not sure Jon," said Gorgin. "The twentieth-century was built on Marx, Freud and Darwin. But first Marxism fragmented as the Berlin wall fell. Then Freud lost his No 1 rating, when he was criticised for his obsession with sex and his failure to understand women. The only one left standing is old Darwin. Now its his turn. His theory's in crisis.[104]"

> **Darwinism is in crisis**
> but it's still an aggressive climate
> for those who disagree.

Sophie chipped in. "You're right Gorgin. The climate's changing. Evolution has been in crises for all sorts of reasons since the mid 20th century. Lots of people nowadays don't really believe it. If they did, some of their values don't make sense."

"Such as?" said Jon.

"The Green Movement for one. It took off fifty years ago, and most people know it's right - conservation, looking after endangered species, saving the weak and all that. But how can you justify it if you believe that evolution - survival of the fittest - is the best way to get a good world. Why not let the weak just die?"

Jon thought of the muddled thinking of the zoos that protect endangered species, and they still preach evolution.

"But Genesis sits comfortably with the Green Movement - caring for the environment," said Gorgin.

"Exactly," said Sophie "and although the senior biologists still defend evolution - what about the philosophers ? They are rebels. They see no evolutionary benefit in morality, or love of art and music [105]. And it's not readily accepted in the grass-roots of the faculties. I've read that forty-seven per cent of Americans - and a quarter of college graduates - believe that humans did not evolve, but were created by God a few thousand years ago. Many of the general public have a healthy distrust of blinkered science, and ask for creation to be taught in the American schools [106]."

"It's fast becoming a world-wide creationist revival," said Gorgin.

Jon added as he turned off his computer.

"Wish it was reflected in the media. Thanks folks. Sophie's turn tomorrow. Let's go."

SOPHIE'S PAPER ON EVOLUTION

85

THE ROOF TERRACE WAS a secret haven the church used for thinking, reading and prayer.

"More peaceful than our basement office!" said Sophie. "Can we go up there for our next session, Gorgin ?" They'd decided that a foursome round table would help Sophie with her paper on evolution.

"Fine by me" said Gorgin. "I've a couple of free hours before the evening Bible Study. It's cool there in the late afternoon, and we'll not be disturbed."

They found a shaded corner, and pulled four wicker chairs round an old wooden table.

Sophie looked around. This quiet terrace was an oasis of tranquillity, a world away from the bustle and honking of the traffic in the streets below. The air up here was scented with some exotic sub-tropical blossoms, and small chirping birds flitted happily between the creepers, wild wisteria and the hanging geraniums.

Gorgin fetched a large jug of fruit juice and a plate of cookies.

"To keep us going - could be a long session !"

Jon chaired the group.

"Sophie's drawn the short straw" he began "and this is a difficult paper."

But Jon also knew his wife had been doing lots of reading. She knew the subject.

Sophie was beside him, and on the other side Anita was ready to take notes. Gorgin was opposite looking relaxed.

Jon suggested they had a few quiet moments, taking in the peace of the place, and then a short prayer.

"Okay Sophie, over to you. Title?"

"THE PROS AND CONS OF EVOLUTION"

"That sounds okay. Is there no third choice? Guess not."

Sophie shared her ideas. A short introduction about how the mass media seem to muddy the real issues by saying that any attack on 'Darwinism' is an attack on 'science', and that's just not true. We're saying that the observations of science are fine, but we think it's the conclusions that can be so wrong.

And now a growing number of scientists are saying that evolution - this colossal superstructure of philosophical speculation - rests on a foundation of supposed scientific fact, which amazingly, tends to vanish the more carefully it is examined."

"A desert mirage" said Gorgin, thinking aloud.

Jon looked to his left. "Pencil ready Anita?"

So Sophie started.

<u>"1. THE ORIGIN OF LIFE ITSELF - design or chance?"</u>

She said that Darwin thought inorganic chemical molecules must somehow have evolved into life, although no one since has ever explained how it happened. Some thought that if there was a primordial soup, with methane, ammonia and hydrogen, a high voltage electric spark might have produced simple amino acids, and eventually made the complex DNA. Others think that it all began in the hot underworld [107].

"But that takes a lot of faith" said Jon.

"It's not possible," said Sophie. "The double helix of DNA in the nucleus of every living cell is composed of such an unbelievably long string of nucleotides - several centimetres long if stretched out. If even in the smallest bacterium, each nucleotide of the DNA were to represent the letters in the alphabet, it'd be such a complicated sequence that there'd be enough words to fill the Bible. Even in the simplest of organisms, it is so very complex. How could this DNA have formed accidentally in a muddy swamp, with lots of specialised chemicals joining together?"

Gorgin added, "Who said 'the chance of that happening is like suggesting that a hurricane blowing through a junk yard could produce a jumbo jet'?"

Sophie nodded. "No laboratory has ever reproduced life. If you develop small protein molecules in a test tube, they're unstable and quickly denature by obeying the Second Law of Thermodynamics - from order to disorder. And if these amino acids are synthesised in the laboratory, they certainly can't reproduced themselves!"

Jon said "And if the first original life was said to be more basic, and simpler than today's bacterium, where are these very simple forms of life today? Why have these very simple organisms gone to the wall if they were so successful?"

Sophie agreed. "Evolutionists think ancient bacteria are probably the closest living thing we can find as the ancestor of all life. A recent discovery claims the prize - the hyperthermophile *Nanoarchaeum equitans.*"

"What's that?" asked Gorgin.

"It a simple bacterium that thrives at boiling temperatures near Black Smokers of the Mid Atlantic Ridge. It measures 400 nm, and only consists of 500,000 base pairs. Simple indeed !"

She continued. "What's more, the DNA molecule in every living cell is always a right-handed double helix, although it could work just as well if it were a left-handed spiral. If you believed in a pre-biotic soup, you'd think it would generate equally 50/50 right and left handed forms. Why then are there no cells with left-handed DNA, and left-handed amino acids and right handed sugars ?"

Anita was trying to keep up.

"Not so fast Sophie," she said slowly, scribbling the entire time. "So you're saying that if life is so easy to create anyway, it should have happened many times in the supposed long history of the planet with equal right and left handed molecules?"

Sophie nodded.

"Then slow down a bit Sophie. I want to get all this down."

Gorgin poured them some more drinks, and they were quiet for a few minutes.

"And you know" said Sophie "the complexity of even the simplest of cells is just mind-boggling. It much more than even the incredibly complex DNA in the nucleus. The DNA controls processes like taking food, using energy, disposing of waste, self repair, reproduction. The cell can't live without all these complicated cell components, packaged within the cell membrane."

"How can anyone think it all came together by chance ?" said Anita.

Sophie nodded. "The most complicate telecommunication system is not as complicated, and that didn't come by chance. The cell can only function if there are a large number of proteins present at the same time. We get down to the place of 'minimal reduction' which makes anything less than we've got, quite impossible. No individual polypeptide has a Darwinian selection advantage, only the completed ensemble. It's like an orchestra that can play a beautiful symphony, but only if all the instruments play together."

"It takes a lot of blind faith" said Jon "to say flippantly, that such a complex system as a living cell just happened to occur as a result of a bolt of lightning and the right chemical recipe. It takes a big leap in the dark to believe that life formed spontaneously.

> *Q. Which makes better sense - that even the minimal components of a living cell could (a) arise by accident or (b) come from intelligent creation?"*

"So that's the first point" said Anita. "What next?"

"TWO" said Sophie "THE THEORY OF EVOLUTION - Is mutation and adaptation the springboard for evolution?"

Jon had introduced this in his editorial, as an attractive concept explaining how simple forms might have developed into complex life.

"Unfortunately for evolution" Sophie said, "when it comes down to real life, mutations aren't much benefit. Mutation alters the genetic material. It can duplicate it, invert, move it to another place or loose it. Some mutations occasionally give a survival advantage - like having a new genetic structure that protects against specific infections - from loss of information. But no one has seen random mutation gathering new information-creating material that can push the organism towards a new species [108] ."

"So evolution by mutation is a theory and not a fact" said Anita.

Sophie nodded. "It might be a good idea, but there are no facts to prove it. No one has seen it happen."

"No one was there," said Gorgin.

"Can mutations be harmful?" asked Anita.

"You can say that again! Mutations are downhill changes. They loose information and often cause diseases - like the tumours you've seen in those kids at the hospital. For evolution, we need new information - uphill changes - and we don't see that happening today."

"So what's this about adaption?" asked Anita.

"Okay. Adaption. That's all around us. These little birds..."

And she scattered a few more crumbs.

"Are adapting to their environment all the time. There are adaptive changes in every species. It's just moving the genes around - shuffling the existing genetic information - producing different varieties within the species. But adaptation is not evidence for evolution."

"Didn't Darwin say that the individuals with the best adaptations survive in the changing environment ?" asked Gorgin.

"Yes, and it's true. Natural selection eliminates the unfit. But there's no evidence that it creates the fit. It only produces 'horizontal' change within a species. It is not a 'vertical' change like evolution creating new kinds or organisms."

"But hasn't there been research ?" asked Anita.

"There's no research that proves evolution." said Sophie. "Some research claims to support evolution, like the old peppered moth story - but frankly - it was not only very poor science, it was fraud ! Doesn't it make you angry? [109]."

"Calm down precious."

"It comes down to a simple question" said Sophie.

> Q. *"Is the change that we see in nature, like the breeding of domestic dogs, merely variation within a pre-existing type, or is it evolution - a genuine creative process that over time can produce new complex organs and new kinds of organisms'?"*

"3. HOMOLOGY AND MORPHOLOGY - is this proof of evolution?"

"What's that?" asked Anita, chewing the top of her pencil.

"It's the striking similarity you see between different species, with lungs that breathe in oxygen, hearts that pump blood round the body, and lots of bilateral symmetry and similar formation of the bones."

Anita said "You'd expect the good Lord to know the winning design formula, and stick with it - a pattern that best fits creatures which share a common environment - its atmosphere, temperature range, ultra-violet light exposure and its gravity."

"Are you a biologist?" said Jon grinning.

> Q. "If similar design is a good argument for evolution, isn't it also an equally powerful argument for a Creator?"

"4. SIMILAR GENETIC STRUCTURE - does this mean the same ancestor?

It's fashionable to say that because many creatures have similar genes - like humans and chimps sharing 97% of the genes - they must share the same ancestor.

> Q. Is this the same argument as similar morphology - that similar genes mean no more than similar design?

"5. FORM AND FUNCTION - does it or does it not match?"

Sophie said that before Darwin, biologists said that the body's form perfectly matched its function. It was the wisdom of the Creator. Then Darwin thought that the body's form has developed to match its environment, and it never quite caught up. He thought that there were imperfect parts that didn't match function, and so vestigial structures were left behind by the tide of evolution.

Sophie said this is now known to be wrong. You can't improve on nature. No surgeon had ever managed to design a body part that's better than the bit he's going to replace.

"If it can't be done by an clever bioengineer, how can it happen by chance?"

> Q. Does the body's form match its function?

"What about backache?"

"That's an old unfounded idea - that back pain is a throw-off from being upright. Not true. The human spine is just perfect for the job [110]. I guess we all do stupid things - we either fail to keep fit or overuse our bodies, and then things go wrong."

"We forget to have a siesta !" said Anita yawning. "How much longer Sophie?"

"That makes me think of the Sabbath" said Gorgin. "One day's rest in seven is good advice."

"No Gorgin, not now - another time" said Jon.

"Keep going Sophie. We're listening."

<u>"6. THE TREE OF LIFE - should the gaps not now be filled?.</u>

Evolutionists try to classify animals and plants. They draw a hypothetical tree of life, beginning with one primitive stem, then with branching trunks and finally present day creatures are left at the growing tips of the tree. In Darwin's day, they tried to put the fossil record in a hypothetical tree, but there were enormous gaps. They confidently claimed that one day fossils would be found to complete this tree, but 150 years later, the gaps are still there."

"Aren't they digging up more and more early humans' bones in Africa?"

"Maybe, but they're no nearer constructing even the human branch of the tree. You just can't classify living things like a tree. The gaps are so big and inconsistent that the imagined tree is always being changed. In fact many biologists now like to say that because these gaps exist, there are no connecting links between the basic types of living things. Some are prepared to say that the theory of evolution has no real basis in scientific fact."

"But what about the skeletons that are half man - half ape?" asked Gorgin.

"The Piltdown Man?" asked Sophie - "The so-called important evolutionary bridge between the apes and modern man - was years later exposed as a gigantic hoax - a mixture of bits of a recent human skull and the jaw bone of a female orang-utan [111]."

"But it convinced millions that we've evolved from the apes," said Jon. "What about Archaeopteryx?"

"They're fossil birds - genuine ! You're thinking about the missing link called Archaeoraptor. It was a fantasy that the experts said was the link between reptiles and birds. It was no more than the body of a bird, cleverly stuck to the tail of a dinosaur by some enterprising Chinese peasant [112]. I suppose any expert can be deceived!"

"I guess we have a bias too Sophie" said Jon.

"Sure, but I get very nervous when so-called 'experts' put small bones together in an arbitrary way and reach all sorts of different conclusions, depending on their preconceptions [113]. Their discoveries get high profile publicity, but they are sometimes the wrong interpretation of authoritative people. They can't help it because they have a bias towards evolution."

"We all have a bias" said Jon. "But it's remarkable what you can do with a jawbone and a few other bits and pieces. It ends up on the telly with legs and long hairy arms, and with its own family and community in its own hour-long prehistoric soap!"

"Do you know about Trilobites?" he asked them. "A fascinating group of fossils from 600 million years ago."

"Didn't they have complicated multifaceted eyes?" said Sophie.

"Absolutely amazing. Complicated is not the word," Jon said. "They are remarkably beautiful fossils. They came from nowhere, had no ancestors and no sequence. They should demonstrate evolution if it exists, but they don't [114]

> *Q. Are the big gaps still present in the fossil record compatible with evolution?*

They waited for Anita to sharpen her pencil.

<u>"7. FOSSILS - don't they show an evolutionary sequence?"</u>

It was Jon's turn.

"I was told as a geology student that fossils are evidence for evolution, that the primitive invertebrate organisms lie in the deeper layers of sediment, and the later more complicated creatures are found in successively younger rocks - first fish, then reptiles and finally mammals - as if they were buried during a long history of slow graduated processes, in a finely graduated organic chain."

"The old idea of uniformitarianism?" asked Sophie.

"That's the theory."

Gorgin looked at him. "How do you answer that Jon?"

"In real life it's not always as simple as that Gorgin. And its a circular argument. A date is given to the sedimentary layers because of the fossils they contain, but those fossils have already been 'dated' by evolution ! How can you then go and date other fossils by the age you've given to the sediments?"

"I've a question for you. How can the skeletons of these enormous fossil dinosaurs remain intact whilst they are slowly buried in sediment over thousands of years? Bones that are exposed to the elements decompose very quickly. It makes no sense."

> *Q. Is the fossil sequence proof of evolution, or does it allow for an alternative explanation?*

<u>"8. EMBRYOLOGY - evidence for evolution?</u>

We've got to hit this one for six."

"Sorry?" said Anita.

"Oh it's a cricket expression - to hit the ball out of the ground."

She still looked puzzled.

"Never mind," said Jon laughing. "We'll explain later. Go on Sophie."

"Embryology used to be the great argument for evolution. Hear what

Darwin said." She opened a book to get the quote right - "animals that are widely different as adults may resemble each other, even to the point of deception as embryos.......Mammalia, birds, lizards and snakes are in their earliest states exceedingly like one another, both as a whole and in the mode of development of their parts".

"They taught me that at school" said Anita.

"But it's nonsense" said Sophie. "Some of my text books still show Haeckel's 19th century drawings of human embryos with tails. It's totally false. He said that as embryos, all species resemble each other - fish, salamanders, turtles, chickens, pigs, and humans. He said all creatures start life with the same simple shape and only later form their individual characteristics. His book sold 100,000 copies and the drawings were copied into successions of textbooks - 'ontogeny recapitulates phylogeny'".

Wait a minute" said Anita. "I've got to write this down."

"You even find Julian Huxley quoting Darwin about the embryonic human spine - 'the os coccyx projects like a true tail extending considerably beyond the rudimentary legs' - which is just crazy. It's just not true. Sure, we have a few bones at the end of the spine - the coccyx. It'd be hard to spend a penny without a good anchor for the posterior muscles. And Huxley said that the human embryonic 'great toe is about an inch in length and projects at an angle from the side of the foot, thus corresponding with the permanent condition of this part in the quadrumana'[115]."

"Meaning what?" said Anita.

"That before you were born, you had a toe like a monkey !"

"It's almost humorous, but anyone who has looked at a foetus knows it's totally untrue. The misinformation about the so-called human tail is about the worst case of scientific fraud you can find [116]."

> Q . Is there any evidence in embryology to support evolution - if not, why not?

"9. VESTIGIAL, RUDIMENTARY OR SO-CALLED USELESS ORGANS - do they exist ?"

Sophie said that this had been a key argument for evolution. Darwin wrote, and it's still quoted today - "Organs adapted to one set of conditions may persist when a new and quite other environment has rendered them useless".

Anita looked up. "Which means what - in simple language?"

"That we carry about a lot of useless baggage from some previous evolutionary stage."

"And that's not true?"

"Years ago we were quite ignorant about the function of some organs which we now know are absolutely essential to life. One by one we've found out what they're for, until now there are no vestigial structures left."

"Let's have some examples" said Jon.

She listed the human thymus, now recognised as the most important organ in the immune system, the knee menisci [117] the pineal gland [118] the tonsils and the appendix.

"And there's a similar fashion to describe some genes as 'junk genes' and vestigial because at present, their function is unknown [119]."

> *Q. Are there any vestigial structures - if not why not?*

Anita put her pencil down. "I've got all that" she said. "I think you've convinced me."

Jon concluded. "I hope there's enough here so that our audience won't close its mind to the possibility of a young earth. I think we're there."

The daylight began to fade quite suddenly as the sun dipped towards the horizon. Across the city, from scores of minarets, Moslems were being called to prayer. The drone of the traffic became subdued.

Jon looked across to the high rise towers and mosques in the city centre, and he felt uneasy.

"We'll call it a day" said Jon. "We've covered a lot of ground. Thanks guys."

NOT WITHOUT RISK

86

JON HAD A LONG relaxing shower, put on a bathrobe and came into the bedroom. The window was open and the thin curtains were blowing in the breeze. Sophie was sitting up in bed, watching the Iraqi news.

"My beautiful wife. I'm the luckiest man alive."

She turned off the TV.

"No - not luck Jon."

"Darling - seriously - I want to talk to you."

He'd postponed this heart-to-heart until now. She listened.

"On the surface - everything's going just fine - perhaps too well."

"I'm okay at the hospital, and the web site's taking off. What's the worry?"

"Don't know."

"Hey - be thankful, Jon."

"I'm getting a bit scared for you precious. The Iraqis have their informers, I guess even in the church, and they could soon discover our little enterprise. I had that near miss when I was looking for Mohammed's lawyer."

She moved close to him.

"Don't worry Jon, I'm sure we'll be all right."

"But there's an Iraqi secret service out there. It may be hidden but it exists. So far, no one's come round this place - but for how long can it last? And we're on the wanted list at home."

She knew he wanted to protect her.

"Relax Jon - we've got to ride this train as far as it'll take us."

"I made a promise to take care of you my love - for a lifetime - and I'm not doing that."

"You are - my handsome Prince charming. What would life be without a few risks?"

She was right, but he was a long time going to sleep.

THE SILK ROUTE

87

XI-XI HASTILY WIPED THE memory from her computer, and put a few things into her shoulder bag.

She had been visited by one of her father's men bearing bad news. He worked for the head of counter-intelligence and advised her to depart - now.

He told her that her father who had been sent on an assignment to the West had been given a second chance by the Party, but he'd betrayed their trust. He'd been planning to defect. They had no choice but to eliminated him.

The family had been investigated and they now knew that Xi-xi associated with dissidents. They knew that she attended the Christian meetings and because of family connections, she was a security risk to the Party. The police were planning to take her in.

It was distressing, but no surprise. She had half suspected that she'd not see her father again, and she had to admit that she was now very afraid - afraid for her life. Best get out whilst there was time. She would probably never be back.

She spoke to herself audibly. "It's time to go."

Trembling, she swung the small bag over her shoulder and slipped out into the dusty street, looking right and left and she dodged across the potholed road through the noisy traffic. A bus took her to the suburbs and then she struck out on foot on the western highway. At a wayside stop for lorrymen, she had a bowl of rice and vegetables and she sat down to think about the long journey ahead.

This Silk Route had been the main artery to the West for generations. It was nothing new for a lone traveller to try their luck. She was young, healthy and wasn't there a God up there keeping an eye on her? She bowed her head oblivious to the chatter around her, and asked for a safe journey.

A scruffy truck-driver sat down beside her and poured rice into his toothless mouth, giving her a sideways glance from time to time.

"Where you from miss?"

He was one of the thousands of lorry drivers earning a meagre living on this road. Was he an honest guy? It was difficult to tell from appearances, but she could look after herself. She paid for his meal and yes - he would take her beyond Alm Ata and up to Tashkent. It depended on the state of the road, but it might be a ten day journey. She jumped in and they were off on a painfully slow bumpy ride.

BIBLICAL AUTHORITY

88

GORGIN WAS WORKING HOURS that began before the sun rose and ended long after it had set, to have his paper ready for the third issue **'ON ORIGINS AND BIBLICAL AUTHORITY'** [120]. This was the important one. He wanted to discuss it with the team, and he invited them to another round table on the roof terrace.

It was late afternoon and the city was beginning to stir from its siesta, but on the roof terrace the noisy traffic was a world away. Jon took the chair again.

"It's going to be another long session" he said "but it's important we get it right."

Gorgin was holding several sheets of A4.

"I've written down what I'd like to have in the web magazine."

"Over to you Gorgin, and maybe we'll interrupt now and then."

"Right - here it is.

INTRODUCTION

I start by saying that for 150 years evolutionary science has tried to explain religion in general, and Christianity in particular, on naturalistic assumptions. Now's the time to return the favour, with theology explaining why science is so reliable in some ways, yet so disappointing in others and why Darwinian science has come to such a dead end [120]."

Anita was doodling with her pencil. Gorgin had a rather tight style, but it was good. There was not much for Anita to write down. She just listened.

"I describe that it's important, because evolution is now the foundation of much of the intellectual life of our society. Without a theory like evolution, the secular world can't account for itself. It needs a natural explanation for everything. Whatever the difficulties in accepting evolution, they are less than the problem of rejecting it. The alternative - special creation - would imply God. Evolution is the greatest hypothesis of modern science, because it's the source of man's secular self-understanding.

It's really important whether it's true or false, because behind the power play stands a cold philosophy that stops religion from claiming there's a supernatural Creator, much less one who was incarnated in Jesus, a divinely infused soul, a life after physical death or a source of divine revelation such as inspired Scripture."

Gorgin said he was going to examine from a theological perspective not what God might have done, but what God and Father of our Lord Jesus Christ had done."

This was just what they hoped Gorgin would write.

"I'm not looking at this as a scientist like the rest of you, but in the light of Scripture, the revelation of God."

"Why's that important Gorgin?"

"Because science is speculative, when it tries to test a theory about things that happened so long ago. Scripture on the other hand speaks about them. The big theological question is - 'does the theory of evolution fit in with what the Bible has to say about the subject?'

"I'm saying in the introduction, that the theological answer about evolution is 'no'. And that might be difficult to accept. It puts the Christian - and also the Muslim and the Jew - in an embarrassing position, facing intellectual ostracism, incredulity, sneers and mocking. It may mean standing at odds with the world. Yet that's a price the believer has to pay on every other important question. Truth is never decided by majority verdict."

He looked at them to see if they were with him.

"Gorgin. That's okay" said Sophie, "keep going".

"1. 'WHAT IS THE BIBLE ?'

It's a unique book. It was written by dozens of different people over more than a thousand years. They came from different cultural, linguistic and historical circumstances, with a richness, variety and complexity. It also claims to be inspired by God, to be in-breathed. That's how Jesus used the Old Testament, it's how the early Christians used it and how the church has accepted it over two thousand years. It speaks with the authority of God."

He had their rapt attention.

"This 'high view' of the Bible suffered in many parts of the church, when 'historical criticism' began to march in parallel with the teaching of Darwinism. The confidence in a reliable Bible was undermined, and many people now think the question of origins and the earth's early history can be put aside and they can still keep the Bible as a devotional book. It is now fashionable to be more concerned about personal feelings than factual truth. The absence of objective truth, which had its origins in the earlier era, now tears away at the core of Western culture.

The modern world asks the Christian to convert their belief into feelings, with no basis in the real universe. It's a heavy price to pay for peace with the materialist who claims to speak for science. However, objective truth can't be based on subjective feelings and speculation. If theologians are to teach, they must have a source of knowledge independent of that possessed by science. And if they are going to assert the existence of such a cognitive territory, they must be prepared to defend it [121]."

"Where did you learn all this Gorgin?"

"Some from reading - more from praying."

Have you shared it with your church."

He nodded.

"Fortunate church" said Jon.

Gorgin continued. "Inspiration must be full or not at all. It means that the right people, wrote in the right places, at the right time, with the right endowments, impulses and acquirements to write just the material that was designed for them.

Ordinary unaided men and women can, on occasion, write a narrative free from mistake.

> **Inspiration means**
> that the writers of the Bible with God's sovereign help got it right,
> and it's a trustworthy word of God to every generation -
> so that men and women might come to know Him
> and be built up in Christ.

If the revelation was made through the history of Israel, how could an error in that history be unimportant? It would give a false aspect to the revelation of God and reveal a false God. A historical error of fact, would distort the picture of God and His will, no less than a spiritual or moral error. The book is not partly right and partly wrong like a mere human work. The Biblical theologian says it is wholly right and reliable."

This was quite new to Anita. She was wide eyed, and was learning a lot.

"2. THE PROBLEM OF INTERPRETATION

If the Bible is inspired it should be allowed to interpret itself. The Holy Spirit breathed into the writings, and as the Holy Spirit works as the interpreter, God reveals himself. We should ask, 'what is the meaning that the writer was expressing?' and the reader doesn't have the freedom to give it any other meaning. If the interpretation is a matter of subjective fancy, then authoritative revelation is nonsense."

The Bible interprets itself

"We are unfair to the text, and we miss God's word if we resort to figurative or metaphorical understandings, when they have been demanded not by the text, but by the presumed claims of modern culture and science."

He looked up. They didn't interrupt him, so he continued.

"There are lots of difficult passages in the Bible, but there's also a unity. Critics may suggest there are two accounts of creation in Genesis 1 and 2, but readers for thousands of years have seen them as complementary, part of the whole sacred narrative. The New Testament is the key to the Old, and when it speaks about Old Testament interpretation, it's the final authority."

"That's right" said Jon. "How did Jesus see the Old Testament?"

"And you know the answer" said Gorgin - "literally."

Jon was looking over Gorgin's shoulder, and Sophie went down to the kitchen to get some mugs of coffee shouting - "wait till I get back."

"My," said Jon "this is what we've been waiting to read, Gorgin."

"Well, the dear Lord is my teacher. I just hope I get it right, and can express it properly."

"This is just what we need to complement our other papers."

They discussed Gorgin's paper until long after dusk, and Anita scribbled lots of notes for herself.

"Gorgin," said Jon. "I've got an one last question for you."

His friends listened.

"There are lots of Christians who'll log on to our magazine who take different positions on Genesis[122]. Some already agree that evolution is wrong - it doesn't sit comfortably with either science or with theology - but they hang on to the idea that the universe is ancient - billions of years old."

Gorgin nodded.

"These people are thinkers," said Jon "and they try to be biblically minded. They struggle with Genesis and come up with the idea that the 'days' in Genesis should be interpreted more freely as 'epochs' [123] . They hang on to the special creation of humanity but over a long period of time. What do you say to them?"

"It's not new Jon, but you have to stretch the text to make it fit. We're inviting these good folk to think with us that the 'days' in Genesis are really 24 hour days - to examine the resurgence of a 'young earth theory'.

"Okay" said Jon. "Make sure they feel included."

Sophie's mobile bleeped.

"Jon, I'm needed in the hospital."

"Then we'll look at the rest of the paper tomorrow" said Jon.

REFUGEE

89

SOPHIE WAS IN THEATRE helping put together a nasty open fracture, when the nurse said there was a young woman asking for her.

"Can she wait? I'll be another half an hour" she said and she completed the plaster.

Who wanted to see her? She didn't know many people in Iraq. Perhaps it was someone from the church.

Outside in the surgeons' room sat a diminutive Chinese girl. She didn't look well, was rather undernourished and her sandals were heavily worn. She clutched a small shoulder bag.

"Hi. I'm Doctor Le Var. Don't get up."

But she rose to her feet with some effort.

"I'm Xi-xi."

Sophie sat her down, took her hand and listened to the story.

It had taken four long weeks - first on the Silk route into Afghanistan, then into Iran, through the mountains and across the deserts of Iraq. She had crossed borders in ways that was nothing less than miraculous, hidden by lorry-men.

"Do you believe in angels, Sophie?"

Sophie smiled. "Why have you come so far?"

She explained that her father had not returned from the West. He had been killed for deserting the Party. They did not tolerate defectors.

"Xi-xi, I am sorry! I -"

"Hear me Sophie. They know I'm a believer ...."

Her lip trembled and she put her hand to her mouth. "And oh, my Dad!".

Her eyes were moist and distant - " I had to move out."

Xi-xi felt guilty about leaving her mother-country, but she'd decided to get out while she could. Sophie was the only person she knew in the West. The e-mails had mentioned working in the Children's Hospital in Baghdad.

"And here I am. I don't want to be a trouble to you. Can you get me to England?"

Sophie had never dreamed that Xi-xi would travel to the West, and certainly not overland to Iraq.

She took her home to meet Jon and Anita.

"One more's no problem."

DARWIN AND THEOLOGY

90

NEXT MORNING EVERYONE was working overtime in the basement office of the _www.journeytoeden.org_ magazine. They needed the large rotating fan overhead. Books were open and there were papers scattered everywhere. Jon had his head down and was trying to complete the editorial and decide how much of the correspondence should be included in the next issue. Anita was at the other desk putting the material onto CD's ready for going on-line. Sophie had stayed at home to revise her paper on Evolution. And Gorgin was in full swing with his Theological Reflections.

"Don't disturb Xi-xi," Sophie whispered. "Poor girl'll sleep for weeks."

They left her curled up on a camp bed.

After a snack lunch, Sophie turned to Gorgin - "Shall we use the roof terrace again?"

"No problem."

They were looking forward to this afternoon session, which had now become a regular feature of their busy day. A different venue, at a different pace with lots of time for reflection. They climbed the stone stairs and sat around the table. There had been a shower of rain in the morning that made the terrace look particularly beautiful.

"Let's complete the second part of Gorgin's article" said Jon.

Anita handed them a print-out of the first part from yesterday. Gorgin now continued.

"3. WHAT GENESIS SAYS

I'm asking whether the early chapters of Genesis should be taken as being literally and historically true, as opposed to being figuratively or poetically true. We have to ask that question, because any literal reading of the early narratives of Genesis is in conflict with modern evolutionary science. Some try to harmonise evolution and science, but it's very difficult unless you abandon the Bible's authority, and its important doctrines. You can't reconcile a literal reading of Genesis with evolution and to accept evolution means abandoning the traditional structure of Christianity, and the foundational knowledge for Christian teaching."

"That's pretty challenging Gorgin."

"Well let's go on."

"Sub-section one. The perfection of God's work.

One of the most important messages of Genesis, is that it teaches about the perfection of the original creation. When God created the world, everything was 'good'. That's repeated seven times, and it finally says that when God saw all that he had made - everything - all the variety of life in a beautiful ecological harmony - it was 'very good'. It couldn't be expressed more strongly. The existence of evil in the created world is absolutely denied."

"But that's not what evolution says" said Jon interrupting.

"Exactly. You're there before me. Evolution describes a very different process. It claims that nature has always been 'red in tooth and claw', and that only the fit can climb the tree. It claims with millions of years of bloodshed, the weak went to the wall. Can a Creator who used mutation, natural selection, survival of the fittest, pain, suffering and death in order to work out His plan - can a God who presided over such a cruel and wasteful process - then call it very good'? I don't think that is the God of the Bible."

Sub-section two - The problem of evil.

This is the next big teaching of Genesis. Anyone who suffers will ask - 'If God is all powerful and loving, why is there evil in the world? Either He's not powerful enough to do anything about it, or not loving enough to care'. At the beginning of the Bible we have a statement about the problem of evil. And the Christian response is based on the story of the Fall and its New Testament interpretation."

"But how can you explain all the evil in the world?" asked Anita. She was thinking of the little children in the hospital, and the cruel violence across the world.

"It's there right at the beginning of Genesis. The loving God gave humankind free-will. It risked a rebellion, and that's what happened. All the evils in this world begin with Adam and his fall. It says that evil came into the world not from a good God, but because this man with his free will, chose to sin. And after sin, came inevitable death, pain and suffering which affected the whole of nature."

Anita fell silent. She had not thought that mankind was basically sinful, and responsible for evil.

"Down the centuries, Jews and Christians alike have understood evil, sin and death from the truth of Genesis. On the other hand, evolution is silent about the Bible's account of the problem of evil. Evolution has nothing to say about it. Either we're in an amoral world, or you say God is not good. But in Genesis, the Creator is free from blame. His work was absolute perfection.

None of them spoke, so Gorgin continued.

"Sub-section three - the cause of death.

Paul was unambiguous when he wrote about the early chapters of Genesis. He said 'since by man came death', and 'through one man sin entered the world' and 'as in Adam all die'.

And more than that, all creation was affected by the fall of human beings. It was never again as it should be. You can't read the Old or the New Testament in any other way and be true to the text. Without man's fall, we have no reasonable defence for the goodness of God. The alternative is that the world was created not by a good God, but by an ogre."

Sub-section four -the redemption of the world.

The mirror picture of Adam is the coming of Jesus, God's Son, that a fallen world might be saved. In love He comes, and with such love, that He paid the redemption price Himself on the cross. It's the story of the Bible. 'As in Adam all die, so also in Christ shall all be made alive.'"

Anita interrupted. "That's what Paul preached after his turn around in Damascus." She was thinking of Straight Street, and how Paul had to escape for his life in Brother Joe's basket.

All this was new to Anita.

The Redeemer
The warp and woof of Christian theology is the redemptive work of Christ as a response to the fall of Adam, and a historical reading of Genesis.

"Jesus spoke about Genesis, about the Creator who 'from the beginning of Creation made them male and female'. The genealogy of Luke's gospel goes right back to the historical man, Adam. We might like to read it some other way, but that is not how Scripture interprets itself."

"So you're saying it's all or nothing" Gorgin. "We shouldn't pick and choose, and either the New Testament writers got it right - or wrong."

Anita was wide-eyed.

"We can't improve on that" said Jon, leaning back in his chair thoughtfully. They were learning a lot from this man.

"Now to the final section." he said.

"Sub-section five - reckoning with the Creator."
Gorgin was looking at his last sheet of his A4.

"The atheistic cosmologist is in a dangerous place, failing to reckon with the Creator God, who has revealed that He made all things by the word of His power in Christ Jesus, and created human beings as his crown and joy. He doesn't recognise a personal God who cares for His creation, with implicit moral requirements and an inevitable judgement. Nor that the world will end just as it began, at the word of God, and at this moment everything depends on Him.[124] "

He looked up.

"I'm going to finish the paper by saying that the enormous success of Darwinism owed much to the contemporary need for a theory that would explain nature apart from God. A few generations of Christians have followed, trying unsuccessfully to embrace both Genesis and Darwinism, but now is the time to say 'No'. Many Christians in science are trying to interpret their data more in line with Scripture. They may or may not have reached the right conclusions about science, but they say that theologically they've no option but to accept the witness of the Bible."

Making the best of both realms
We may have no answer to some of science's problems
but we begin and end with the Word of God
which cannot be broken.

He sat up in his chair and looked at his small audience which gave him a round of enthusiastic applause.

The unexpected noise disturbed Xi-xi, who for one frightening moment thought she was in China. She got up quietly and she slipped into the kitchen.

Anita found her looking through the cupboards. "Can I help you Xi-xi?"

"I'm going to cook something for you."

"Not now - take it easy."

"No, no, no - I'm here to help."

However, the next day they gave her a free hand with the cooking. She discovered the market, and they didn't object to a meal with new oriental flavours.

"You like Chinese food?" she said, in her high pitched shaky voice.

"Xi-xi, you're a god-send."

"I've something to share with you" she said "but it can wait."

Xi-xi's help gave them time to re-edit the text for the Third Issue, and it hit the web as planned on July 12th. They held their breath.

The response was again extraordinary. It was impossible to read all the correspondence as hundreds of thousands logged on. Sophie's evolution paper was generally appreciated, and Gorgin's 'Biblical authority' hit the mark for many people. There were thousands from Korea, Japan, the Pacific Islands, across China, India and the Middle East, the cities of Africa, Europe and the Americas. It was a global audience.

NON OVERLAPPING MAGISTERIA

91

MARCUS LIMPED ACROSS to his office window to look again at the old grey River Thames, an ever-changing scene flowing beneath him. Today it was surging downstream under Westminster Bridge, making turbulent waves as it met the incoming tide. He admired the boatmen who from early times had so skilfully navigated their small crafts across this powerful stream. Today he could identify with them.

He was unsettled. When he thought about Jon and Sophie, he recognised that his work was conflicting with his personal life. He'd never allowed that to happen before, but now the going was distinctly rough. He'd always kept his religion to himself. No one at work knew that on Sundays he went to church. He'd kept his job with MI5 in a different compartment. One file for work and one file for faith - keep them separate. He was a 'Sunday Christian'.

Marcus liked the phrase 'Non-Overlapping Magisteria' (from the Latin *magister*, or teacher). Keep the domains of authority quite separate - one compartment was for the church and the spiritual life, and one authority was for work. One for religion and an other for science[125]. It didn't matter if they disagreed because they never met. That's how he had lived in peace with himself - so far.

Few could match Marcus in his grasp of Information Technology. He knew all about bytes and glitches, but he admitted he was no scientist. What he knew about Cosmic science and Biology came from surfing the web and from the television. However, this science was kept securely in a magisterium that didn't overlap with his religion. Keep life simple and avoid conflict.

But this cyberspace magazine *www.journeytoeden.org* had opened his eyes. While he was scanning it carefully for clues about Sophie and Jon, he was captured by their material, especially the last issue. He read it again and again and it challenged all his pre-conceptions.

Marcus had always believed that the Bible was for guidance on living a decent life - no more. He never thought you couldn't trust it to say anything relevant about history, because the writers were fallible people like ourselves. He had been told that science had proved the earth was incredibly ancient and that evolution was a fact, and why disbelieve that? He kept the Bible and science in two separate compartments, and with this philosophy he had sailed calmly along on the river of life.

But now this web-magazine had come like a strong wind, challenged and refreshing his mind. What if they were right and the Bible was inspired in such a way that it was speaking God's word truly from cover to cover, right from the early chapters of Genesis and through to the New Testament? What if it was saying true things about origins, and it was correct about God's nature, about the creation being good, and about the source of evil in the world? If so, it was going to turn his life upside down.

He saw for the first time that there could be a unity between science and the Bible. No more need he have a fragmented life. It could also mean a harmony in every area of his life - not just between religion and science, but also a consistency between worship on Sunday and his work on

Monday - a united life, a surrendered life with everything open to God.

Now he knew why he was having a troubled conscience about Jon and Sophie. If he took a big leap of faith - and that would mean taking a big risk - would he be able to swim? The waters looked very rough indeed.

CHINESE WRITING

92

XI-XI THOUGHT SHE KNEW why the magazine had such a big impact in China where students were logging on in their thousands.

"There's a lot of despair in my country, and when you say that Genesis is true, you've found something that matches our ancient Chinese traditions" she said. She had an engaging way of tilting her head to one side and smiling.

"Tell us more."

She explained that the Chinese writing had been invented by the Yellow Emperor *Huang Ti* around 2205 BC. The characters were simple drawings of familiar objects - picture words. Their ancestors learnt to write a story by adding characters together, and these characters had sacred meaning.

Jon interrupted "Like the ancient Egyptian scribes inventing hieroglyphics, a word that means 'sacred writing'."

"Sure" she said in her high pitched voice. "At the heart of the Chinese script are religious concepts."

CHINESE TEMPLE

"It's not a hit-or-miss calligraphy depicting any old object of every day life, but rather the early Chinese had a real plan for their writing. We think it was based on their knowledge of the God *Shang Ti*. This early writing is picture language about the beginning of human history, with the first created human couple, and their relationship with God."

She started to draw the early Chinese characters - God with arms upraised in blessing, God as personal, His creative hands, the first two humans being more than ordinary people but flames of fire, the second human emerging from the first, their being created in a holy garden, two trees in the garden, warnings, forbidden fruit, greed and sorrow, sin, sacrifice and the beautiful lamb of God [126].

Some might think it fanciful but Jon and Sophie could see how the Chinese students compared Genesis with the Creator-God pictured in their earliest writings. Was God telling the Chinese 4,000 years ago about His perfect creation, His loving relationship with human beings and entrusting them with a glimpse of that primeval earth through the medium of well-stored pictures? Were these ideas remnants of memories of Genesis?

Xi-xi thought that this simple foundation was one reason why so many Chinese students were logging on. They already saw the Bible as God's complete trustworthy revelation.

"Wow" they murmured in unison.

THE DESERT FEAST

93

"WE'LL CELEBRATE IN IRAQI style" said Gorgin "with a night in the desert."

The day before he had gone with a few young men into the desert to dig a deep hole - six by six. In its base they had piled wood and charcoal, set it alight until the flames roared, spat and changed direction with the wind, and then having prepared two yearling lambs, they placed them on the burning embers. The carcasses were covered with herbs and spices and with another layer of hot coals. This desert oven was then buried under a mound of sand and left to smoulder for 24 hours.

The whole church was invited. About fifty people came, some in trucks and old cars, others on motor cycles and pedal bikes, and one family on a donkey cart. They brought with them vegetables and salads, sweets, fruit and drink. Someone had organised live music, and they celebrated under flare lamps and beneath a sky full of sparkling stars.

Sophie looked at Jon, his face glowing in the firelight, and his mouth dripping with roast lamb the like of which he had never tasted before.

"They certainly know how to enjoy themselves, in spite of their poverty."

"That reminds me Jon. Tomorrow a team of International Inspectors are coming to the hospital."

"I thought they were looking for weapons of mass destruction."

"A hospital laboratory would be a good place to start, but I can tell you it's clean" she said.

"Keep your head down Sophie. We don't want to advertise our presence."

THE CAPTURE

94

JON WAS BUSY AS usual on the computer when Sophie was ready to leave for work. It was not a good day. Everyone seemed jumpy, even Jon.

"Love you darling" she said, kissing the back of his neck and sensing the tension in his muscles. "Relax Jon." He turned his face upwards. She laughed and he pulled her onto his knee for a few minutes.

She was getting a sore chin. "Don't you ever shave? That stubble's like a newly harvested corn field!"

"Sorry - so busy I forget. You take care precious. I'll die if anything happens to you. We've been so fortunate, and I'm afraid it's all going to go wrong. Once we've got the next issue on line, I think we should get out of Iraq. We can't keep below the radar screen for ever. Who knows what this government is up to. If they know about us, we could be in deep trouble."

"Only the Lord can keep us safe. We'll talk about it tonight" she said, and with shouts of farewell to the others, she flew through the door.

Anita was scanning through the correspondence, country by country and she came to the UK. Jon was talking to Gorgin. Xi-xi was making the coffee. And Anita burst into the room, with an e-mail print-out.

"Look at this Jon" she said with a trembling hand.

From *marcuswood@premier.co.uk*
"jon and sophie - PERSONAL and URGENT. advise get out now - now. they are on to you. watch inspectors. from a friend"

For a moment Jon couldn't think, breathe, feel, hear. His bronzed face went distinctly pale.

Gorgin looked over his shoulder.

"You two okay?" Then his blood froze.

"What's the date Jon?"

It had been sent three days ago, but because of the volume of work Anita had not seen it before.

"I must run" Jon said, and he sprinted down the road towards the hospital.

A few heads turned, because Arabs don't run in the street. There was no time for protocol. He had to warn Sophie.

As he arrived at the hospital there were armed soldiers everywhere. Three white Mercs were parked at the hospital entrance, with 'International Inspection Team' written in bold blue letters on each side. The Arab drivers were leaning on their vehicles, smoking and talking to each other lazily in the hot morning sunshine.

An inquisitive crowd was gawking at the proceedings.

Jon summed it up quickly. The vans were empty. The inspectors were inside.

He pushed his way through the crowd but was stopped roughly by a guard at the door.

"I have to see my wife urgently" he said. "She works here."

The security man smiled but did not understand. It was clear to Jon that he was barred.

He went round the back to find another entrance - and then his heart stopped. Three men were bundling Sophie into a mini-van. He stepped back into the shadows.

There was a sharp prod under his ribs, and he felt a simultaneous snap on his right wrist.

"Come with me son. We didn't expect to pick you both up today."

There were three rows of seats in the van. Sophie was in the rear beside one of the British MI5 men, and Jon was pushed into a middle seat beside the second. His mind was racing. They had been warned, but it was too late. At least he was with his wife. He knew Max but who were the others? They weren't Arabs.

Sophie's worst fears had come true. She'd seen all these men before. There were the two British agents who had been at the Procurator Fiscal's Court in Inverness. They were the same two men in the back seat at her wedding. Then there was the Russian sitting impassively in the front seat. He was no stranger, but she had hoped never to meet him again. Max, chewing in the driving seat was the surprise.

"Sorry ma'am" he said in his southern drawl.

"Nice to meet you again" he said turning his head and nodding at Jon. "Told you in Edinburgh this was a dangerous game, and you wouldn't listen."

Jon was trying to work out what they intended to do with them. A flight home to face the law? But they were not heading towards the airport. They were taking the desert road.

"Where are we going?" asked Sophie.

The Russian snuffled and spat out of the window.

Max said "Have a nice day" and whistled "Abide with me."

The two British agents glanced at their captives and looked rather sad.

The negative body language didn't look good.

They turned off the desert road, and drove over a rough track into the dunes for about fifteen minutes, coming to a halt in a small valley.

They were ordered out of the van and Sophie thought it reminded her of the place where they had the banquet the previous night. They were marched a short distance towards a deep hole, but it was no desert feast. There was no charcoal and wood. What about the lambs? Jon also saw the irony of the situation, and he pulled Sophie towards him.

"Need a blindfold?" asked Steve, but the Russian pushed them forwards towards the edge of the gaping hole in the desert floor. They stood impassively clasped together aware of each other's pounding heart.

"I didn't expect our journey to end this way my darling" she said trembling.

He remembered other sands where he had played as a boy in Jersey, and where he had walked carefree with Sophie. He tried to be strong for her.

Although his legs felt like jelly and he was sweating, there was also an inner peace

"Precious, we shall be together forever."

Sophie remembered holding this same strong hand on their wedding day. She was not afraid.

Several shots rang out in the silence of the desert, and bodies tumbled silently into the grave.

MEETING THE PRESIDENT

95

A 4 x 4 SPED OVER the dunes. It was packed with elite Iraqi soldiers shouting and waving their automatics.

They pulled up bedside the hole in the sand and talked excitedly in Arabic, and the officer spoke to Jon in broken English.

"That was very close. You are most fortunate."

They covered the four bodies with sand, and Jon and Sophie were taken into town. Only minutes before they were standing at the threshold of eternity, and it took some time to understand what had happened. There were a number of questions. Why had these Iraqis followed them from the hospital? Had they been saved because the Iraqis objected to a bunch of foreign inspectors taking the law into their own hands, or had Jon and Sophie been under surveillance for some time? They waited for events to unfold.

They were waved through the gates of the old Mukhbarrat head-quarters, escorted up the white stone steps, through enormous cedar-wood doors and into a large marbled entrance hall.

"Follow me" said the officer, his voice echoing as he guided them down a labyrinth of corridors. He extracted a plastic card that unlocked an enormous door and he invited them into a large thick-carpeted room.

They were taken aback by its sheer opulence. How had it survived the war? It was brilliantly lit by three beautiful chandeliers hanging from a painted ceiling. They were surrounded by large mirrors between heavily draped windows, and round the walls were ornate gold seats - delicate French style - upholstered in red velvet. On one wall was a large oil painting of the Hanging Gardens of Babylon and on another an enthroned Nebuchadnezzar. At the far end of the room was a raised platform and a large padded empty arm chair.

"Be seated please and we'll get some refreshment."

Sophie had no appetite, but the portents were good.

"They don't plan to dispose of us just yet if they are offering us food" she whispered.

The large panelled door opened again and Anita, Xi-xi and Gorgin were ushered in. They stood with them in a lonely circle and compared notes.

Gorgin was particularly anxious and Anita had goose pimples down the back of both legs. They both knew the score. Sophie put her arm around Xi-xi who's slender frame was shaking. In an authoritative regime there is no place for discussion. You must take what is coming to you on the chin. But Jon and Sophie's rescue was a good omen, and they were not in a prison cell.

The food arrived and it was good. Then a senior officer and his deputy came, and invited them to sit at a large circular table. He pulled up a chair and looked at his notes.

"Our government knows all about your activities" said the spokesman, in Oxford English.

He looked at Jon. "The jeweller followed you back to the church and we have been monitoring everything you have done since then."

He turned to Sophie. "You've done a good job at the Hospital Doctor Le Var. Thank you."

He continued. "Li Xi-xi, you arrived in this country illegally but we can overlook that. You have been part of an exercise that has enhanced the reputation of our country."

He looked up at a large picture of the President.

"We were happy to let your project run so far. It has also given the infidel West a bloody nose."

He looked at Gorgin. "We allow religious freedom in our country. We have always been tolerant of the Christian church even though we don't agree".

Gorgin had his own ideas about this but it was not the time to interrupt.

"We have been pleased to see Mohammed's research get international acclaim - this revolutionary new hypothesis on time and the universe. It's a triumph for Iraq. As we try to rebuild our country, this will remind the world that we are a great people. Neither does it do any harm to Islam. Some of our faithful brothers across the world are rejoicing that the science of the decedent West is being rocked. Islam will be vindicated !"

Again looking at Gorgin.

"However we are not happy about your so-called theological reflections - not happy at all. Our government's decision is that your cyberspace magazine must now be closed down."

"You must wait a minute or two. You are fortunate that our busy President wishes to give you an audience."

This man, educated in UK no doubt, was still only a ventriloquist's dummy. Every word had been chosen by his seniors. But it didn't sound too bad. The man glanced up again at the portrait of his President, and he turned quickly and left.

There was some relief in the air, and Sophie regained her composure and some of her appetite.

The few minutes extended to over an hour, but then there was a flurry of activity and the President of the Iraqi Council, stepped from a rear door and onto the platform. Instinctively they all stood to their feet and there was a hush of expectancy. They were beckoned towards the platform.

There was no smile, and the important man wiped his upper lip. He sat down, looked at his notes on a table in front of him, and then read slowly a prepared speech, in broken English.

"We have followed your work here in Iraq with interest," he said. "The great nation of Iraq has conducted unparalleled research which for the first time in history, allows us to look into the past. It also has provided information about the age of the earth. Unfortunately Iraq has had its troubles." He shuffled his papers. "Hmm.... The chief research worker was the only person with the complete data. He was trailed by our enemies and killed before we could publish anything."

He looked at Jon and Sophie.

"We are grateful to you British people who rescued this valuable work and returned to Iraq to publish it. That was honourable. We would have preferred to have co-operated with you, but we are a tolerant peace-loving people, and we share" - he paused - "hmm....some of your objectives. We have permitted you to continue with your work unhindered and uninterrupted."

The great man continued.

"I have read each issue of your magazine with great interest, until you unfairly promoted Christianity above the true faith of Islam. For this reason your magazine will close. We shall give you a free passage home."

"The Chinese girl Zhang Xi-Xi, can return to any country that will accept her. General Kapta, Anita's father, has been told to collect his daughter tomorrow at the Syrian border. We wish Mr Le Var and Dr Sophie to return home with 'The Iraqi Certificate of Merit'. Pastor Gorgin....."

They all looked at Gorgin. What would become of him?

"Gorgin, we shall confiscate your computers".

He paused.

"But as a token of our benevolence, we want your church to receive a personal gift."

When he had finished the last sentence he was gone.

FINALE

96

GORGIN'S CHURCH WAS INCREDULOUS, when they heard what their pastor had been doing in the last few weeks. They were unsure what to do with their gift - an enormous picture of the President. The computers were confiscated and the office again gathered dust, but it could have been much worse. Gorgin was given the address of Mohammed's mother. She received lots of friendship and the promise of a very large legacy that would keep her in her old age.

Anita received a good telling off from her very relieved father. She'd learnt a good deal, and she began to visit Brother Joe. He enjoyed her company, and wondered if celibacy was really a good thing. He was surprised to receive unexpected gifts of after-shave and an electric tooth-brush !

Xi-xi was given a student's visa to the UK. She applied for a place at university. She kept in touch with her little church in China which continued to grow. If things improved, she'd go home one day with a post-graduate degree.

The Director General's plans had misfired. The PM was not pleased.

Auntie had messed thing up very badly indeed, and she had to take early retirement. The usual veil of secrecy descended on her department, and the names of two good men were quietly removed from the payroll. The US denied that Max Bellman had ever existed. Overseas relationships had not improved, and there was still a world crisis.

However, Marcus was baptised. He didn't get his salary rise, but he stayed with the firm, and for the first time he began to enjoy his work. He told his friends that he'd discovered a 'unified magisterium'. When they asked what that meant, he said that his life was no longer fragmented, and for the first time he had a purpose in living.

Andrew the theologian read the magazine carefully. He thought again about his interpretation of Genesis, and didn't change his mind.

Frank the astronomer was also unconvinced. He was amused that his friend Jon should cause such a furore. He kept looking at the night sky through his telescope, and he remained an agnostic.

The press had a story that would run for months, that new science about time, refuted evolution. Some very angry words were exchanged by people in ivory towers. A media debate began that might go on for ever.

What about Sophie and Jon? They returned to Jersey and kept their heads down. They shared the best news of all with their proud parents - "We're going to have a baby!"

REFERENCES AND COMMENTS

1.Chesterton GK. (1927) _The everlasting man. Hodder and Stoughton_ Chesterton says that nobody can imagine how nothing could turn into something. It is really more logical to start by saying "In the beginning God created the heaven and the earth". For God is by very nature a name of mystery, and nobody ever supposed that man could imagine how a world was created, any more than he could create one.

2.Gould SJ. (1988) _Time's arrow, time's cycle. Penguin Books, London, New York_ Gould makes interesting comparisons between the biographical details of the 'fathers' of uniformitarianism - Hutton and Lyell.

James Hutton (1726-97) the farmer/physician turned geologist, began with the premise that there must be a process whereby the earth renewed itself, or else the world was intentionally made imperfect. His preconception was that the earth was constructed with infinite power and wisdom, and that there must be a restorative force rebuilding the continents, sustaining a steady state of benevolence. His first paper to the Edinburgh Royal Society in 1788 was about erosion, with soil being washed down to the sea, and then sedimentary deposits being eventually uplifted to form new rocks. He described a "succession of worlds... with no vestige of a beginning - no prospect of an end". This beginning of the idea of deep time, was built on scant evidence. Although he has traditionally been described as the founder of geology, breaking formally with religion-shrouded tradition, James Hutton recognised that the earth was constructed for a definite purpose - to be a habitable world contrived in consummate wisdom. Gould says that this notion of purpose which was pivotal to Hutton's logic, is alien to modern science. It shows a major change in scientific methodology between Hutton's time and ours, and suggests the arrival of intellectual bankruptcy.

Gould then writes about _Sir Charles Lyell (1797-1875)_, who took Hutton's mantle and is remembered as the father of geology. Lyell's earth was immensely old, ever moving in a stately cycle of slow and continuous change. For him there had never been any universal catastrophe. The earth had always looked and behaved just about as it does now. The catastrophists like George Cuvier, who believed that dramatic events were responsible for the abrupt changes in strata, were ridiculed and eventually silenced by Lyell's clever legal mind and his withering rhetoric. He caricatured them as vain and foolish people, "armchair speculators" who guessed and invented theories. Lyell on the other hand portrayed himself as inquiring, investigating, patiently exploring, undertaking laborious enquiries, and representative of people with growing intelligence !

3.Lewis CS. (1970) _God in the Dock. Wm B Eerdmans Publishing Co., Grand Rapids, MI_ Lewis, Fellow of Magdalen College Oxford and Professor of English Literature at Cambridge, challenged the logic of atheists who believed the universe was an accident. He was himself for many years an atheist. He became a reluctant convert to Christianity, and points out that our ability to reason would be called into question if atheistic beliefs about origins were true. "If the solar system was brought about by an accidental collision, then the appearance of organic life on this planet was also an accident, and the whole evolution of man was an accident too. If so, then all our thought processes are mere accidents - the accidental by-product of the movement of atoms. And this holds for the materialists' and astronomers' as well as for anyone else's. But if the thoughts - i.e.of materialism and astronomy - are merely accidental by-products, why should we believe them to be true? "I see no reason for believing that one accident should be able to give a correct account of all other accidents."

He also wrote about creation, "I do not maintain that God's creation of Nature can be proved as rigorously as God's existence, but it seems to me overwhelmingly probable, so probable that no one who approached the question with an open mind would very seriously entertain any other hypothesis."

4.Balleine GR. (1970) The Bailwick of Jersey. Revised by Joan Stevens. Hodder and Stoughton, London This is a classical book about Jersey, telling of the island's long and varied history. It describes the cave at La Cotte St Brelade, which was a camping site for prehistoric hunters in about 110,000 BC and for a second group - probably Neanderthals - practising the Mousterian culture in about 65,000 BC. (Much more has been added to the Palaeolithic records since 1970 which is now well documented and displayed in the Island's museums).

The book describes the forest of Brequette, and an old document saying "The manor of the Fief of Morville and Robillard, was in the valley off a village called L'Etac, and was known as the Manor of Brecquette. Near it was an oak forest to the east and north. This valley and house for many years have been covered by the sea; howbeit at low tide one can still see the ruins of the manor." In 1669, Phillippe Mahaut, aged 80, testified on oath, that when he was young, he had seen at low tide some stone walls, which the old men who were with him declared to be the ruins of the Castle of Brecquette. The word "Becque" means gap, opening or break.

This book also quotes an old guide book as saying "You who love Nature in her wildest beauty, you pious souls who seek utter solitude to muse on godly things, come to St Brelade's, and you will find the object of your search."

5.Stringer C, Gamble C. (1995) In search of the Neanderthals. Thames and Hudson, New York This is a well illustrated book describing the current thinking about Neanderthals. They describe the last interglacial period with mega-fauna - hippopotami, straight-tusked elephants, narrow nosed rhinoceros and giant extinct cattle around the British Isles.

Neanderthal man lived in rock-shelters like La Cotte de St Brelade on the island of Jersey, from between 250,000 years ago until the last glaciation. They used stone tools and left large collections of Middle Palaeolithic artefacts. The book illustrates piles of mammoth and rhino bones which were found on two levels at La Cotte, probably from separate hunting episodes in which small herds were stampeded over the cliff. They comment on this rich and complex site yielding flake tools like side scrapers dated about 238,000 years ago. They leave the question open whether Neanderthals were close kin or distant relatives.

6.Shackley M. (1980) Neanderthal man. Duckworth, London This is an interesting volume describing Neanderthal Man who was said to have lived between 35,000 and 90,000 years ago. Most primates would avoid caves, for fear of being trapped by predators, whilst Neanderthal Man used fire as protection. Their tool-making traditions were taken over by modern man. Shackley thinks they were not an off-shoot of evolution, but maybe true ancestors of *Homo sapiens*.

7.Le Gros Clark WE. (1965) History of the primates. Trustees of the British Museum, London He described the anatomical features of Neanderthal Man, from parts of skeletons from caves including St Brelade's Bay in the Channel Islands. He thought Neanderthal Man coexisted with *Homo sapiens* and was not a distinct species, but rather an aberrant side-line of evolution, some sort of evolutionary regression with an exaggerated development of certain features. The Neanderthal brain was not any smaller than the modern human brain.

8.Gould SJ. (1991) Ever since Darwin. Penguin Books, England This is a collection of reflections on the importance of Darwin. He credits the anthropologist Charles Oxnard with research showing that there are three coexisting lineages of hominids (*A Africanus*, the robust australopithecines and *H habilis*) none clearly derived from another, none displaying evolutionary trends during their tenure, and none brainier or more erect as they approach the present day. He denies that Neanderthals were stooped or a 'missing link'. He observes - though many anthropologists will disagree - that there is no trace of the evolutionary ladder among early African hominids. Species seem to appear and later disappear, looking no different from their great-grandfathers. However, he cringes because creationists will say "sounds like special creation to me." Gould is irritated by creationists whom he says distort his theory of punctated equilibrium and incorrectly think he is writing about special creation.

9.Cuozzo J.(1987)Earlier orthodontic intervention: a view from prehistory. Jour.N.J.Dental Association, 58:No 4. Jack Cuozzo is head of the orthodontic section, Mountainside Hospital, Montclair, New Jersey, USA. He writes an interesting account of his PhD research describing the examination of teeth and skulls of Neanderthals in Berlin. He was troubled that when fragments of Neanderthal skulls had been recons-tituted, they seemed to have been 'adjusted' to suit preconceptions. He also thought that the Neanderthals who had inhabited Europe and the Near East were more recent inhabitants that the widely accepted idea of two hundred thousand to thirty thousand years ago.

He made the startling claim from his anatomical studies and a series of standardised radiographs, that some of the Neanderthal skeletons in south-western France were from people had had lived for a great age, up to 250 - 300 years, and that Neanderthal children had later maturation times than do children today.

10.Albritton CC. Jr. (1989) Catasrophic episodes in Earth history. Chapman and Hall, London, New York This is a well researched and balanced volume promoting the controversial theory of catasrophism. It describes the birth of uniformitarianism beginning with Hutton, and the writing of Playfair who made Hutton's work understandable. He quotes Lyell's popular *Principles of Geology* suggesting that because of the slow nature of geological change, our planet must be inconceivably ancient. He describes the 18th and 19th century debate between uniformitarianism and catastrophism, the antagonism not always coming from the religious quarter. Some believed at that time, that the geological evidence pointed to two major deluges, compatible with the creation story and Noah's flood in Genesis.

He says that Whewell argued against Lyell that "the degree of uniformity and continuity must be collected not from any gratuitous hypothesis, but from the facts of the case. And we are in danger of error, if we seek for slow and shun violent agencies further than the facts naturally direct us, no less than if we are parsimonious of time, and prodigal of violence."

Though Lyell won the argument in the 19th century, the debate continues. He quotes the Nobel laureate Urey who in 1973 proposed that the extinction of the dinosaurs and other organisms at the close of the Cretaceous period, was the result of the earth's collision with a comet. This was not taken too seriously until in 1980 a geochemical anomaly - the iridium spike - was found at the contact zone between Cretaceous and Tertiary strata (the K-T boundary).

Albritton thinks that Hutton and Lyell's uniformitarianism although refreshing at the time, needs modification. He thinks it is likely that there have been sequential catastrophic crises in the earth's history. He thinks the increasingly popular ideas about catastrophe, places us in the midst of a new revolution of thinking about the earth and planetary sciences.

11. Ager D. (1995) The new catastrophism. Cambridge University Press, Cambridge Ager was a geologist who believed in catastrophe. He thought that episodic and rare "catastrophic" happenings dominate over the gradual and continuous processes that we see in the record of the history of the earth. It is an entertaining book, illustrated from his travels in which he describes how hurricanes, colliding continents and asteroid impacts have shaped the planet. He wrote that for a century and a half, the geological world has been dominated, one might even say brain-washed, by the gradualistic uniformitarianism of Charles Lyell, and any suggestion of 'catastrophic' events has been rejected as old-fashioned, unscientific and even laughable.

He described a tree standing 10m high in the strata of the Lancashire coalfield where contrary to traditional views, sediment at times must have been incredibly rapid. The Natural History Museum and the Swansea Museum also exhibit similar trees which had been standing vertically in the Carboniferous strata.

He concluded that he did not support the views of creationists whom he refused to call scientific.

12. Walworth RF, Walworth-Sjostrom GW. (1980) Subdue the Earth. Panther Granada Publishing, London, Toronto, Sydney, New York This book is a critical examination of the conclusions of mainstream geology. The authors suggest that catastrophic ice ages have been responsible for the abrupt changes in geology and life forms. They say that the book is not an attempt to propose a new age for the earth, but it explains how changes may take place in tens, hundreds or thousands, but not in millions of years. They think that geologic clocks could be reset to a more realistic speed.

13. Allan DS, Delair JB. (1995) When the earth nearly died. Gateway Books, Bath These two authors explain why they think that about 11,500 years ago there was a tremendous conflagration, a great flood and bombardment from outer space. They say there were terrible earthquakes and volcanic eruptions with upheaval of mountains and warping of the earth's crust. They think for example that these changes are supported by the rapid refrigeration of Siberian animals. They question the commonly held assumptions about the Ice Ages, particularly the great Pleistocene Ice Age which is said to have lasted until about 9,000 BC.

They quote Egyptian, Greek, Eskimo and Chinese writings that the heavens turned upside down, and settled in a lower position. They believe that the difference in the earth's and Moon's orbit is one piece of evidence that the axis of the earth tilted. They think that the earth is a rotating muti-layered visco-elastic system, and slippage has caused a change in the length of the day.

14. Burke D. (1985) Creation and evolution - when Christians disagree. Inter-Varsity Press, London Seven Christians, highly respected in their own scientific fields, take part in a debate about creation and evolution. In the first chapter Fraser describes what he thinks is the evidence for an old earth, with the large granites needing millions of years to heat sediments to a temperature consistent with mineral formation. Andrews in reply believes that temperature rise can occur quickly, and gives the example of the volcanic island of Surtsey, off Iceland, that was produced during an eruption in 1967. This island now has beaches, pebbles, sand and vegetation, with all the appearance of a great age. He thinks that given sufficiently large forces, the rates of geomorphic development may be speeded up by orders of magnitude. He criticises the assumptions used in radiometric dating. He quotes other authors who say it is "impossible to establish unequivocally that the ages reported reflect the time of original crystallisation or emplacement", and "the isotope age is not necessarily the geological age of a rock."

15. Gould SJ. (1988) Time's arrow, time's cycle. Penguin Books, London, New York As a writer of geological history, Gould gives little credence to creationists who think the earth is young. But he does champion those opponents of Lyell who were catastrophists whilst also believing in an old earth. Gould says that for more than a century, many geologists have been stifled - their hypotheses falsely channelled and limited - by the belief that proper methods must be based on gradual change, that everything had always moved at the same rate and intensity.

16. Barbour J. (2000) "The end of time". Phoenix, London . He quotes Leibniz who suggested that God - the supreme rational being - could have no other alternative but to create the best among all possible worlds, with as much variety as possible, and with the greatest order possible in order to obtain as much perfection as possible.

17. Peacock RE. (1989) A brief history of eternity. Monarch Publications Ltd, Bungay, Suffolk Peacock writes as a scientist and a convinced Christian. He describes the long historical procession of world scientists, whose faith in God was their primary motivation for scientific study.

Galen, a second-century Greek physician said "The purpose of a deity could be ascertained by detailed inspection of the assumed works in nature."

Copernicus in 1500s declared his faith in Christ. "The Universe has been built for us by a supremely good and orderly Creator."

Kepler in 1609 recognising a Sun-centred system and a moving earth said "O God, I am thinking Thy thoughts after Thee." He constantly prayed to God. He thought the cosmos was "a sacred sermon, a veritable hymn to God the Creator."

Galileo in 1609 described a Sun-centred system, writing of Jupiter's moons - "I have faith in our blessed God that just as He showed me alone the grace of discovering so many marvels from His hand, He will also concede to me to find the absolute order of their revolutions." He believed his work to be "lifted up to the ultimate goals of our efforts, that is to the love of the Divine Artifactor". In 1633 he wrote that the book of Nature and the Book of Scripture were complementary and not contradictory since they emanated from the same Author.

Newton in the 1600's said - "It seems probable to me that God in the beginning formed matter in solid, massy, hard, impenetrable particles, of such size and figures, and with such other properties, in such proportions to space, as most conduced to the end for which he formed them; even so very hard as never to wear or break in pieces."

Blaise Pascal (1662) who was one of the greatest mathematicians of history, had a piece of paper sewn into his coat, which was found at his death - "Righteous Father, the world hath not known Thee, but I have known Thee - joy, joy, joy, tears of joy - total submission to Jesus Christ."

Robert Boyle (1691) was the greatest physical scientist of his generation, and the Father of modern chemistry. According to his physics, the immediate efficient causes of phenomena were entirely mechanical, and their ultimate and final causes were seen as entirely supernatural.

Michael Faraday (1821) - was able to generate an electric current with either a moving wire loop or a moving magnetic field. The Secretary of Royal Institution said of him - "His standard of duty was formed entirely on what he held to be the revelation of God in the written word." He believed that the book of Nature that we have to read, is written by the finger of God. Faraday was missing from the Royal Institution when the Prince Regent was giving him a vote of thanks. He had slipped off to a prayer meeting.

Lord Kelvin (1851) was the founder of thermodynamics. He began the first lecture of each day with prayer to God

James Clerk-Maxwell (1855) interpreted light in terms of electrical and magnetic radiation. He understood that the electro-magnetic field took the form of waves moving at the speed of light. Visitors to his laboratory were invited to share in, and were impressed by the morning prayer meetings.

Albert Einstein (1879-1955) was convinced that even in a quantum event, there is a further level of understanding from which an occurrence may be dictated. He said "God does not play dice", which from a believer in a pantheistic God, is open to various interpretations.

Stephen Hawking. Keeps an open mind, without believing in a personal God. He thinks that the behaviour of the universe on a very large scale seems to be simple and not chaotic. He thinks that so carefully were things chosen that "it would be very difficult to explain why the universe should have begun this way except as the act of a God who intended to create beings like us"

18. *Preston R. (1996) The search for the edge of the universe. Corgi Books, London* He writes "I was surprised to see how chaotic, amusing and passionate science is. Scientific facts are often described in textbooks as if they just sort of exist, like nickels someone picked up on the street. But science at the cutting edge, conducted by sharp minds probing into nature, is not about self-evident facts. It is about mystery and not knowing. It is about taking huge risks. It is about wasting time, getting burned, and failing. It is like trying to crack a monstrous safe that has a complicated, secret lock designed by God. Some of God's safes are harder to open than others. The questions may be so difficult to answer, the safe so hard to crack, that you may spend a lifetime playing the tumblers and finally die with the door firmly locked. Science is therefore about obsession. Sometimes there is a faint clicking sound, and the door pulls wide open, and you walk in."

19. *Daily Telegraph, 16.06.01* "Russia and China forged a new regional alliance yesterday to combat rising fears over the spread of Islamic fundamentalism into the nations of central Asia. President Jiang Zemin said he had signed an agreement with Russia to fight ethnic and religious militancy, whilst promoting trade and investment in an area whose big oil reserves have revived international competition for influence." He had signed the pact, to crackdown on terrorism, separatism and extremism to safeguard regional security.

20. Preston R. (1996) The search for the edge of the universe. Corgi Books, London His book makes enjoyable reading. It is written in the style of a novelist about the development and the use of the Hale telescope - seven storeys high with a two-hundred-inch mirror. He describes eccentricities of cosmologists and their day to day experiences, as they are seen searching into the farthest recesses of space, searching for the answers to the riddle of the beginning of time.

21. Panek R. (2000) Seeing and Believing. Fourth Estate, London This delightful little book is the story of the telescope - from the time of Galileo to the contemporary surveys of the sky across the electro magnetic spectrum. It explains how the telescope has changed our understanding of the universe.

It is a historical journey, bringing us up to date at the end of the book. We see light from a star which was there two million light years ago, but it may not be there now. Where we are in space is relative not to what is, but what was. Our position is where we are in time as much as in space.

George Gamow in 1950s described a beginning of the universe which "blew up". Fred Hoyle called it a 'Big Bang'. If correct some of the energy from the initial expansion would still be present - light that had red-shifted along the electromagnetic spectrum into the far end of the radio waves. Alpher and Herman correctly predicted that these radio waves should exhibit a wavelength corresponding to around 3 degrees above absolute zero. The discovery of this 3 degree background radiation also validated invisible-light astronomy.

The Hipparcos satellite survey 1989-97 has given us a size to the universe. It determined the once elusive parallax for 118,218 stars and proved the position of more than one million others. Red shift surveys measured the distances to hundreds of millions of galaxies, clusters, super clusters billions of light years across, and larger structures of walls or filaments.

In the 1970s astronomers found that the outer rims of galaxies were spinning too fast. This could be explained if there was other invisible matter - a missing mass - "dark matter" which might account for 90 to 99 per cent of the universe.

Visible light is only a small part of the electromagnetic spectrum. Infra-red, ultra-violet, x-rays, gamma rays are all transmitted by matter out in space. Many of these waves such as those from quasars (quasi-stellar radio sources) can only be recorded from satellites, because they are blocked by earth's atmosphere. The universe is full of information far more extensive than the naked eye can see even with optical telescopes. It is a turbulent, convulsive, violent and expanding universe.

He says that whenever we can't conceive what's out there, whenever we can't guess, it's not because we don't have the technology or lack the information, but we don't understand that our preconceptions might be restricting our view.

22. Gribbin J. (1979) White holes. Paladin, Granada Publishing, London, Toronto, Sydney, New York Gribbin writes with an easy style about how the universe may have begun as a white hole, a cosmic gusher, and he suggests that there may now be a oscillating state.

23. Ferguson K. (2000) Measuring the universe. Headline Book Publishing, London A fascinating little book, very easy to read. It is a historical record of man's attempt to measure the universe, and the role religion plays in the motivation and conclusions of the researchers. One interpretation of Galileo's trial (although he believed in the Bible) explains it as a clear contest between two authorities - religion and science. Eventually from the mid-19th century onwards it was out of fashion to include God in any scientific statements.

However in the 1920's the red-shift was recognised, suggesting an expanding universe. Belgian astrophysicist and theologian, Abbe Lemaitre, first described something like what was soon to be dubbed the 'Big Bang'. There must have been a time when everything that makes up the present universe was compressed into a space only about 30 times the size of our Sun - a 'primeval atom'. Some of his colleagues greeted his idea with derision. "It smacked too much of Genesis." The recognition that the universe was expanding, meant it almost surely had a beginning. That seemed to say to many scientists that the universe required a Creator, and it was difficult to accept.

Thus in the 20th century, those who had thought science had won that contest long ago were chagrined to find science seeming to uphold a religious point of view. Anyone for whom the idea of a God was anathema now had to face the unthinkable - a beginning - a moment of choice about whether there would be a universe - a Creator's choice.

Ferguson quotes Robert Jastrow "For the scientist who has lived by his faith in the power of reason, the story ends like a bad dream. He has scaled the mountain of ignorance, he is about to conquer the highest peak; as he pulls himself over the final rock he is greeted by a band of theologians who have been sitting there for centuries."

She also quotes Alpher and Herman who predicted in the 1940s that there ought to be left-over radiation surviving from about 1,000 years after the origin of the universe with a background temperature of about 5 degrees above absolute zero. This it is now known to exist at about 3 degrees above absolute zero.

The universe is now in a highly desirable condition of flatness, desirable because that is the only sort of universe that eventually allows intelligent life to emerge.

Although the universe looked so uniform when it was about 3,000,000 years old, it has now become diverse and clumpy. Somewhere back there must lie the seeds of those developments.

She describes the Hawkin and Penrose theory of the Big Bang - unimaginable density, extremely rapid inflation, slowing down of expansion, thinning out, cooling, virtually uniform but with faint wrinkles, clumping, stars, galaxies and clusters gravitationally bound together. But this discovery has not put an end to attempts to devise an origin-of-the-universe story that would be more palatable to those unwilling to accept the impenetrable obstacles and hints of a Creator.

She describes how the red shift measurement of the star's or galaxy's spectral lines indicates how rapidly the object is increasing it's distance from the earth, and how it is measured in supernova - exploding stars at great distances - an increasingly useful yard stick.

The degree of red-shift observed suggests that some galaxies are receding at 37% speed of light. She discusses how the red shift might be caused by a gravitational field, because gravity as well as acceleration can stretch the light waves, but such a degree of red-shift would need a very great gravity.

The Hubble constant is the rate at which the universe is expanding. Freedman thought the Hubble constant was about 80 and therefore Sandage said that the universe was only 8 billion years old. But other measurements suggest that some stars in Milky Way are 14 billion years old!

The Hubble Constant may be 50, but if it is paradoxically suggesting that the universe is younger than some of its stars, then there is a two-way tug-of-war between gravity and expansion energy. It revives Einstein's "old mistake - the cosmological constant." She concludes the present rate of expansion is an unreliable indicator of the age of the universe.

The January 1998 meeting of American Astronomical Society was shocked to hear from the Supernova Cosmology Project that younger galaxies (close to us) were fleeing from us faster than older galaxies (further away). Their data indicated the expansion of the universe was actually speeding up.

In March 1998 a second group described similar findings reporting that the expansion rate is approximately 15% greater now than it was when the universe was half its current age. It suggests some weird form of repulsive energy - the cosmological constant.

24. Barbour J. (2000) "The end of time". Phoenix, London Modern science is in the remarkable position of possessing beautiful and very well tested laws, without really being able to explain the universe. He says either the universe was created in a highly special state and its initial order has been degrading ever since, or it has existed for ever, but the so-called Big Bang makes that improbable.

25. Atkins P. (1992) Creation revisited, the origin of space, time and the universe. Penguin books, England Atkins an atheist, attempts to investigate the nature of the cosmos and the existence of time, but he is reluctant to accept a purposeful universe. He thinks that although the fact that the universe did emerge with exactly the right blend of forces seems to favour a miracle, it does not require an intervention. He says that we are awake now amid benevolence, but this does not require a purpose. He thinks we can still be the children of aimless chance. He thinks the question of biological function is extremely difficult, and will remain so for a few hundred years, but he is blindly confident that the fundamental nature of the world will soon be qualitatively and quantitatively certain.

26. Chown M. (1993) Afterglow of creation. Arrow, Sydney, London He writes in a language that laymen can understand, about the different models of the universe (1) a universe forever oscillating (2) a steady state and (3) a unique Big Bang and the "unsettling problem" of a beginning.

He also describes how the discovery in 1992 of "cosmic ripples" - slight variations in the temperature of the ancient radiation leftover from the Big Bang - meant that there were early irregularities. They were described by some as suggesting purpose and "seeing the face of God."

27. Hoyle F. (1955) Frontiers of Astronomy. William Heinemann, Melbourne, London, Toronto The possibility of an expanding universe and the implication that there was a beginning with a superdense singular explosion was "uncomfortable" to Fred Hoyle. It suggests an origin, and perhaps an Originator. He said that a beginning was valid only if all the matter now existing in the universe was also existent in the past. To avoid this possibility he therefore introduced in 1948 the concept of "the continuous origin of matter" and admitted his emotional preference for a "steady state theory." He thought that by eliminating arbitrary starting conditions, then everything was still testable by processes still operating.

28. Davies P. (1995) About time. Penguin Books, England The date of the Big Bang hinges on the use of the red-shift. However there are other mechanisms that produce a red-shift such as gravity, acceleration and changing time. He asks if those discrepant red-shifts are real after all?

29. Gribbin J. (2000) The birth of time. Phoenix, London

He traces the story of how scientists have recently reached a consensus that the age of the universe is about 13 billion years old. He starts with Hutton's paper to the Royal Society of Edinburgh in 1788, after which scientists began to think the earth and the Sun were at least millions of years old. Then in the 1920s Edwin Hubble and Lemaitre discovered the expanding universe, and combined with Einstein's general theory of relativity, it was concluded that the Universe was born at a definite period in time with the Big Bang, and that is was billions of years old.

He says that while many astronomers accepted the new idea that the Universe had a definite beginning a finite time ago, and secondly because entropy (the tendency for things to wear out) suggested that the Universe was probably in a state of perfect order when it was created, they were "uncomfortable" with these ideas of a structured beginning. He says that Lemaitre pointed out that however repugnant were these new ideas, science did not depend on personal taste, and the results of experiments and observation had to be taken seriously.

He describes the pursuit of the Hubble Constant where red-shift is proportional to distance. Using many different methods - studying cepheid variables, nebulae, quasars, gravitational lensing, background radiation, rotating galaxies and supernova the Universe seems to be 13 to 15 billion years old which matches the estimated age of the oldest objects in the universe from other techniques.

Finally he mentions the new results of studies of very distant Type 1a supernova. They all have the same maximum brightness, and therefore their distance is known. Measurement of the red-shift suggests that those closest to us are accelerating away faster than those at further distances (which are older). This means that the current expansion of the universe is actually getting faster and is not slowing down, probably as a result of the springiness of space, explained by Einstein's constant, lambda. The real time from the Big Bang may therefore be different from the apparent time, but he concludes that the Universe is about 13 billion years old.

30, Pickover CA. (1998) Time - a traveller's guide. Oxford University Press, New York.

Pickover asks a number of people if time-travel is possible. He quotes Roger Ebert of the Chicago Sun Times 1997 " There is one invention - a time probe - revealing the past and everything that has ever happened. When you think of the implications of that, it's pretty appalling. Could we as a human civilisation survive such a thing? I just don't know. I don't think it's possible, but I can't rule out that a time probe could be created. All the mysteries and all the secrets that have ever happened would be revealed. Total transparency. That's the most terrifying invention I can think of."

Craig Becker said "I believe that time travel to the past is impossible. On the other hand, I don't rule out the possibility of some kind of 'time-viewer' that allows one to see into the past."

Mike Hocker is quoted. "Personally, I would like to have a viewer into the past. The time-viewer would blow away the revisionist historical accounts of past events. A lot of 'heroes' would have clay feet."

Brad Pokorny said "The time-viewer would have little effect because events are subject to interpretation. People will believe what they want. If people viewed Christ rising from the grave, it would not change much. Those who don't want to believe would think it a trick, and would doubt the viewer."

31. Feynman RD. (1985) QED- The strange theory of light and matter. Penguin Books, England This book is a series of lectures for laymen, attempting to describe quantum electrodymanics, the theory that won him the Nobel Prize, the strange theory that explains how light and electrons interact. Light which has a finite speed, is made up of particles - photons - which follow the path which takes least time. This path is not predictable but is governed by the probability of the event. The speed of light is different in different media.

32. Barbour J.(2000) "The end of time". Phoenix, London Barbour says that there is an undoubted tendency for scientists to work within a so-called paradigm, and pay at best fleeting attention to ideas that do not fit within the existing established patterns of thought.

33. Le Grand HE. (1994) Drifting continents and shifting theories. Cambridge University Press, Cambridge and Melbourne This is an introduction to modern geology, describing the history of the theory of plate tectonics. He describes how some scientists have believed that the earth has not always remained the same size. Holmes in 1925 believed that the earth was cyclically expanding and contracting by the build-up and release of radioactive heat.

Then in 1958 Carey made a strong case for 'expansionism' because the jigsaw fit of the continents matched best if the globe was smaller at an earlier time. The mid-ocean rises and ridges have tensional features. Carey remained a tireless proponent of expansion. He thought the degree of subduction which is claimed to occur at the continental boundaries is a myth, and that the continents were permanently fixed to the mantle below them. He concluded that the earth's crust is divided into a hierarchy of polygons allowing a rigid crust to expand. The expanding earth theory had a small following up to the 1970's since when it has continued to gain a few recruits. There is an increasing number of supporters, especially amongst palaeontologists, like HG Owen, Neil Archbold, Steiner, Ahmad and Saxena.

34. Walworth RF, Walworth-Sjostrom GW. (1980) Subdue the Earth. Panther Granada Publishing, London, Toronto, Sydney, New York They suggest that there is a relationship between the speed of rotation of the earth and the formation of heat, and that a change from rotational kinetic energy to heat will cause the earth's revolving round the sun to slow down . They say that "some propose that the day was once about 21 hours long in the Cretaceous period."

35. Hoyle FA. (1982) Chilling scientific forecast of a new Ice Age. New English Library, Kent, England In a book where Hoyle says he thinks a new Ice Age is on the way, he describes the history of plate tectonics, and Pangea - one supercontinent - 200,000 million years ago

36. Allegre C. (1988) The behaviour of the Earth. Harvard University Press, Cambridge Mass and London This is an introduction to modern earth science, reviewing particularly the history of Wegener's concept of continental drift and sea floor spreading. JT Wilson is described as defending S Warren Carey's theory of the expanding earth, although he says this has not been supported by objective observation.

37. Kunzig R. (2000) Mapping the deep. Sort of Books, London Kunzig writes about the history of marine science. In three excellent chapters on the sea-floor he describes the rift valleys extending around the world from the Mid-Atlantic ridge, across the Pacific, up the west coast of the Americas, into the Indian ocean and branching into the Red Sea and to the south into the African rift. It goes north through the Arctic Ocean, past the North Pole and vanishes in eastern Siberia. It is like the seams of a baseball, and like a wound that never heals. Magma rises up into these ocean rifts, cools and solidifies, spreading out and pushing the ocean floor away from both sides of the rift. He describes how when the sea-floor runs into a continent, it is so old, cold and dense that the floor sinks down under the continental shelf.

He notes Wegener's observation that that the coastlines of Europe and Africa fit like a jig saw with the Americas, as if they had previously been joined together. He accepts the general view that the ocean floors are like conveyor belts, the floor sinking under the continents, and that the earth stays the same size. However he acknowledges that the continents on either side of the Atlantic are separating at a speed of an inch or two a year, the Pacific is spreading at nine inches a year, Australia is moving away from Antarctica, and the Indian ocean is widening. He then casually dismisses the idea of Hess in 1960, that the whole planet is expanding, as "a wild idea."

38. Ager D. (1995) The new catastrophism. Cambridge University Press, Cambridge He mentions that if it is correct that in the past the earth rotated more rapidly in 15 rather than in 24 hours, then at that time many of the uniformitarian presumptions would not have applied. Also a variable gravity constant could mean that the world was very different in the past, and it would have been much smaller than it is today. He sees a great deal of evidence for an expanding earth especially in the fossil distribution. Even though this is ridiculed by many or most geologists, with the notable exception of Carey, he says he cannot otherwise see how the oceans could widen simultaneously, and subduction does not solve the problem.

39. Gribbin J. (1998) Watching the universe. Constable, London He considers a number of intriguing facets of modern astronomy, including "the curious case of the shrinking sun". He describes the various studies of the sun's size over the last three hundred years. In 1715, the position in England of the northern and southern edges of the total eclipse of the sun were identified. Comparable measurements in Australia in 1976 and 1979 suggested that the sun had shrunk in 260 years by 0.02 seconds of an arc. Similar conclusions about a shrinking sun are supported by transit time data when Mercury sometimes crosses in front of the sun. The Royal Greenwich Observatory measured the sun's angular diameter in 1836 and 1953 and noted a similar reduction in size. Measurements were less accurate in the past and not everyone agrees that the sun is shrinking. However it is generally accepted that the sun does change in size, and there is probably a cyclical rhythm every 11 and 76 years and possibly also a longer cycle. Gilliland believed "One is not inexorably led to the conclusion that a negative solar radius trend has existed since AD 1700, but the preponderance of current evidence indicates that such is likely to be the case". If this is correct it questions our assumption that the earth and the sun have existed with essentially the same relationship for at least 4 thousand million years. A rate of shrinking by 0.01 per cent per century would imply the total disappearance of the sun in a million years ! Gribbin says that current monitoring programmes should provide the answer within a decade.

Particle interaction in the sun should produce lots of neutrinos but in practice very few can be detected. A shrinking sun would explain the mystery of the sun's missing neutrinos. Perhaps the sun is "going off the boil". Missing neutrinos could be resolved if the heart of the sun is ten per cent cooler than standard astrophysical models imply. Rouse suggested that the sun may have a cooling core and a contacting outer layer. It makes sense that the sun which is using up unimaginable amounts of energy might be losing mass and getting smaller.

40. Heidmann J. (1989) Cosmic Odyssey. Cambridge University Press, Cambridge, New York, Port Chester, Melbourne, Sydney Heidmann takes the reader on a journey through space and time, with a broad-brush view of the Universe as we understand it today. He explores relativity, the quantum theory and the inflationary universe. He ponders the question of whether the gravity value G is a constant of nature, immutably fixed, or whether in the remote past history of the universe, G could have been different.

41. Gribbin J. (1979) White holes. Paladin, Granada Publishing, London, Toronto, Sydney, New York He says that decreasing gravity should produce observable effects allowing our planet to expand which Hoyle and Narlikar calculate as 10km in 100 million years. He thinks however that the rigid crust makes the old idea of an expanding earth no longer tenable. He describes his favourite but wrong idea, that a previously low gravity might have made it possible for dinosaurs to flit gracefully across the plains instead of staggering under gravity's burden.

42. Gould SJ. (1991) Ever since Darwin. Penguin Books, England He says animals respond to changes in gravity by altering their shapes. A large mammal with poor supporting structures would collapse into a formless mass under the influence of large gravitational forces. The crustaceans - lobster and crab - for example, can be of larger size in an environment where a buoyant force counteracts gravity, than say comparable organisms like insects on land.

43. Barbour J. (2000) "The end of time". Phoenix, London He says that because clocks run at different rates, what justification is there for saying that a minute today has the same length as a minute tomorrow? What do the astronomers mean when they say the universe began fifteen billion years ago? Conditions soon after the Big Bang were utterly unlike the conditions we experience now. So how can hours then be compared with hours now?

44. Davies P. (1995) About time. Penguin Books, England Time is relative. It depends on motion and gravity. We are caught up in the general expansion of the universe, and all astronomical bodies posses gravitational fields with drastic time-warping. He asks how can we talk of the universe as a whole marching through history to the beat of a single cosmic drum? The universe changes its rate of expansion with time and probably time itself is related to that expansion, and has not been constant. He thinks that there is good evidence that at least a one million-solar-mass black hole lurks at the centre of our own Milky Way.

45. Hawking S. (1998) Black holes and baby universes. Bantam Books, Toronto-New York-London 1998 This is a collection of Hawking's essays. He writes about Einstein's greatest triumph - that time is not a universal quantity which exists on its own, separate from space. You can only go in the future direction in time, but you can also go at a bit of an 'angle' to it and therefore time can pass at different rates.

46. Price H. (1997) Time's arrow and Archimede's point. Oxford University Press, New York, Oxford This is a philosophical book about time. Like many other authors he comments that Einstein's theory tells us that there is no such thing as objective simultaneity between spatially separated events. Simultaneity differs from observer to observer, depending on their state of motion. He tries to stand outside time and view the passage of time objectively. He argues that there is no physical law why time should not flow backwards. He thinks there may come a time when with a contracting Universe, there is a reversal in the flow of time. Though most authors including Hawking, agree that there are no physical laws to contradict that time could flow backwards as well as forwards, they think that in practice such a concept is impossible. He does not comment of the possibility that if the flow of time reverses, it would reasonably be preceded by a slowing down of time.

47. Novikov ID. (1998) The river of time. Cambridge University Press This Professor of Astrophysics gives a Russian perspective on the study of 'time'. He quotes Leibnitz who rejected the Newton's idea of absolute time. Rather the world is described by a sequence of phenomena following one after an other which we call 'time', but it is relative to space and motion.

He also quotes Alexandrov about Einstein "His greatest discovery was that nature knows no absolute time". Einstein's theory means "that when one's velocity approaches that of light, time stands still".

To the uninitiated it may seem that an individual space traveller cannot get too far away from the spot where he or she was born since nothing can move at a velocity exceeding the speed of light. Hence, one cannot escape by more than say, a hundred light years over a lifetime. This, however, ignores the slowdown of time for the space traveller. If the slowdown of time is taken into account, the ship can go to the distant corners of the universe.

When approaching a black hole, gravity becomes so great that for the external observer, time slows down and eventually stops. For the individual going into the black hole, the speed eventually reaches the speed of light and once in the hole, nothing can get out, not even light.

48. Poole MW and Wenham GJ. (1987) Creation and evolution - a false antithesis? Latimer House, Oxford Poole is a Christian physicist who believes in evolution. He discusses what he thinks is woolly thinking of both creationists and evolutionists and what he thinks is shaky science to support a young earth such as the (i) the shrinking sun (ii) the unexpectedly small amount of meteoric moon dust (iii) the decaying earth's magnetic field (iv) small quantities of compounds found in the oceans (v) claims that gas and coal can form rapidly. He says that even though these are surprising if the earth is old, it is not logical to employ backward extrapolation from the presently observed rates only when it suits one's arguments. However, he admits that the science is at present uncertain about the age of the earth.

49. White AJM. (1985) How old is the earth? Evangelical Press, Bath, England The author, an academic chemist, finds no contradiction between the Bible and science, and he described biblical and scientific arguments which favour a young earth. He discusses the ambiguities of radiometric dating, and the circular argument that rocks are dated by the apparent age of fossils. He thinks that scientific data supports the earth being less than 20,000 years old, and if this is correct then there is no time for evolution, and the biblical six day special creation is correct.

50. _Hawley D. (1995) Oman and its Renaissance. Stacen International,London_ This is an account of Oman, its history and its present culture. It describes the tomb of Nabi Ayyoub - Job of the Bible - which lies on the rolling hills of Dhofar, north of Salalah. It is a place of importance for Islamic, Christian and Judaic pilgrims, conceivably 3000 + years old. It says on the tomb that Job lived for 287 years.

51. _Johnson MR. (1988) Genesis, Geology and Catastrophism. The Paternoster Press, Capetown_ Johnson is a Christian geologist who does not believe in a literal interpretation of Genesis. He thinks that there are insurmountable difficulties between the scientific account of origins and the Genesis account of pre-history. He argues that the Bible is primarily a religious book which was not intended to provide us with scientific and historical facts _per se._ He thinks that the biblical revelation was written to accommodate the level of pre-scientific understanding of the people to whom it came.

He says catastrophic ideas were widely debated by scientists in the first half of the nineteenth century and decisively rejected. He differentiates between what he says is the eternally valid, infallible, theological message of the Bible, and the elements which are time and culture-conditioned. These are part of the vehicle through which the message in conveyed. He thought, when he wrote in 1988 this was the most popular view held by Christians, and he claimed it was legitimate to abandon a literal understanding of the early chapters of Genesis.

52. _Kelly DF. (1997) Creation and Change. Mentor,Great Britain_ Professor Douglas Kelley, a theologian argues for a literal interpretation of the seven day account of creation, and says that God who is our Maker would have no difficulty making any literary form match exactly the very way He created everything.

53. _Chesterton GK. (1927) The everlasting man. Hodder and Stoughton_ Chesterton thinks that evolution is really mistaken for an explanation. It has the fatal quality of leaving on many minds the impression that they do understand it and everything else; just as many of them live under a sort of illusion that they have read the _Origin of Species_. But he says that the notion of something smooth and slow, like the ascent of a slope, is a great part of the illusion. It is illogical as well as an illusion; for slowness has really nothing to do with the question. An event is not any more intrinsically intelligible or unintelligible because of the pace at which it moves. For a man who does not believe in a miracle, a slow miracle would be just as incredible as a swift one.

54. _Catchpoole D, (2002) The Koran vv Genesis. www.Answers in Genesis.org_ This paper explains the various Islamic views about creation.

55. _York D. (1997) In search of lost time. Institute of Physics Publishing, Bristol and Philadelphia_ York is a physicist who helped set up the radioactive dating technique in the Department of Geology at Oxford. He admits to being obsessed with the concept of time and its measurement. He says the earth is about 4.5 billion years old - unless there is something wrong with our understanding of the radioactive process and the meaning of time itself. He argues that if there is something wrong with our concepts of radioactivity and the rate of decay, one could strike at the very heart of all dating methods simultaneously, and many non fundamental scientists would love to do this, for it would require a revolution - a paradigm shift - in our understanding of time, and the earth would be young. He says Einstein's theory of relativity, where time is interwoven with gravity, means that in principle one could cross the galaxy or the universe in a day.

56. Pickover CA. (1998) Time- a traveller's guide. Oxford University Press, New York This is a book of science mixed with science fiction. It tries to probe the mystery and the nature of time. If you start out moving slower than the speed of light and go faster and faster, time runs more and more slowly until, at the speed of light itself, it comes to a stop relative to stationary observers.

57. Barbour J. (2000) "The end of time". Phoenix, London He makes the case that time is an illusion - it does not exist. Nature creates the impression of time. To say time has passed, we must have some evidence for it. That means things must move. Outside the universe there is nothing that can be timed because nothing is going from one place to another. We reckon time by the totality of changes. A single 'now' contains only positional information. Two 'nows' give information about change of position. He quotes Mach "It is utterly beyond our power to measure the change of things by time. Rather time is an abstraction, at which we arrive by means of the change of things."

Speed is not distance divided by time but distance divided by some real change elsewhere in the world. Galileo measured change by water escaping from a tank. No sooner do we present some measure that is supposed to be uniform than we are challenged to prove that it is uniform. For example the rotation speed of the earth could change if the earth could expand or contract, but he says this is prohibited by a rigid earth. There are many different motions in the universe, all equally suitable to measure change but they may not be uniform.

There are several clocks and no motion in one system necessarily marches in step with any motion in the other.

- · sidereal time (the stars)
- · solar time (the sun and planets)
- · atomic time (relies on quantum effects)
- · inertial time (the movement of a body in space in a straight line)

Barbour says time is meaningless, unless expressed in relation to another body. All bodies are affected by forces of other bodies. He asks how can we tell the time if we cannot find any bodies free of forces?

58. Davies P. (1995) About time. Penguin Books, England In spite of the decades of progress unravelling the mysteries of time since Einstein's revolution, Davies thinks that the answers remain tantalisingly incomplete. He confronts tough questions about time. He describes how Einstein's views that time is affected by gravity was confirmed by the echoes of radar signals being bounced off a planet behind the sun. The echoes were delayed when their waves travel close to the solar surface because with increased solar gravity time runs slightly slower at this site. The shortest path and the selected path is at some distance from the surface of the sun where time runs at a faster rate. Time on the sun's surface runs about two parts in a million slower than on earth.

He says that the pace of time will affect radioactivity. Excited atomic nuclei emitting gamma rays at the bottom of a tower where time is slower, will have a lower frequency than a similar nuclei at the top.

How do we know that a super accurate caesium-beam atomic clock, if left for a few million years, won't tick a little bit faster or slower than it does today? Can we be sure that the great clock in the sky has been ticking away evenly from the beginning of time until today? He thinks that if the cosmic clock itself were changing with time, this would completely compromise our estimates of the age of the universe. We know that time can vary from place to place. Why not from time to time? Might this be a possible solution to the time-scale problem? If time is something measured by clocks, and if clocks vary with time, how can we be sure we ever know what time it really is?

He quotes Arthur Milne, of the Rouse Ball Chair of Mathematics at the University of Oxford, who thought that there are two time-scales. Certain physical processes operate according to one time-scale like atomic processes and light and atomic clocks. On the other hand gravitational and mechanical processes like the earth's rotation have another time-scale. These get gradually out of step. Atomic clocks gradually march ahead of astronomical clocks, although it might take a thousand years for the difference to add up to one second. He thought that light frequencies gradually decrease with time explaining the red-shift. This is not generally accepted today, but the idea that there might exist two or more scales of time in the universe cannot be dismissed lightly. There is no logical imperative nor a known law of physics that compels all varieties of clocks to agree.

Paul Dirac, one of the founders of quantum mechanics and Nobel prize winner, reached similar conclusions to Milne. He thought astronomical clocks get out of step with atomic clocks, (and presumably with our biological clocks). The theories of Milne and Dirac are thought to be flawed but Davies argues that the intriguing question remains open - 'how many time-scales exist'? There are many clocks - astronomical, pendular, atomic, sapphire crystal, super-conducting resonators involving different physical principles. Some may lose their synchrony over cosmological time. Perhaps cosmic time is different from earth time, but the rebels who think like this are in a small minority.

59. Cuozzo J.(1998) Buried alive. The startling truth about Neanderthal man, Master Books, Green Forest AR. USA.

Jack Cuozzo the orthodontist, who wrote about Neanderthals, quotes data to show that over the centuries, children have been maturing earlier and earlier. For example, one of the staff of the Natural History Museum in London wrote to him about the Spittalfield Collection of skeletons, (1759-1859), which contains many infant skeletons with dates of death from the church records. The letter about the Spittalfield children reads -"often no teeth had erupted in 11 or 12 month children." This contrasts with the eruption of teeth of modern children beginning at 6-8 months. He also describes well documented evidence of increasing rates of tooth development from 1883 to 1936. Cuozzo thinks that it is unreasonable to claim that earlier milestones are merely the result of better infant nutrition.

(On a personal note, I agree. I was privileged to examine over a hundred of the Spittalfield adult and children's skeletons, recording the prevalence of spinal stenosis. Adult spinal stenosis is an excellent marker of infant nutrition, because the spinal canal matures very early in life with no catch up growth. If there are a lot of adults with spinal stenosis in a population, it suggests that their children were poorly nourished in utero and in infancy. I observed that the prevalence of spinal stenosis in the Spittalfield collection was identical to its prevalence in three other archaeological populations and also in spines today. (Papp T and Porter RW. (1994) Changes of the lumbar spinal canal proximal to spina bifida occulta. Spine 19: 1508-1511) The conclusion is that there is no evidence from examining spines, that children today are better nourished than they were in the past. On the contrary, many children are born today with low birth weight and they become adults with spinal stenosis because of poor nutrition in utero and maternal smoking. Their infant dentition was not obviously delayed. I suggest that it is difficult to attribute this degree of delayed dentition in Spittalfield bones two centuries ago, to poor nutrition.)

Cuozzo, in support of his view that Neanderthals matured late and lived to a very great age, describes a continuing trend towards lower ages of the onset of the menarche over the past two centuries. In 1880, the average of the menarche was 17.3 years, compared with 13.0 years today. He says that the average age of voice change in boys in 1750 was 17 years, compared with 13.5 years today. He also quotes Professor Wente who examined royal mummies of the Cairo Museum, that 'the pharaoh's ages at death as determined by the biologists are generally younger than the written sources suggest.'

60. Ritchier W. (1971) The living clocks. Mentor book from New American Library, New York and Toronto This is an interesting little book about biorhythms. Birds and bees use an internal clock to maintain a given direction throughout the day. They use the sun as a compass, and compensate for the movement of the sun with the aid of an internal 24-hour clock. Starlings will continue to use the clock in continuous dim light using a circadian oscillation. They have a free-running period independent of sunlight, of about 25 hours.

The circadian changes can be measured precisely in many organisms. This rhythm that persists in darkness is not precisely the same as the Earth's rotation. Individuals within a species will have a different free running period. A few have a periodicity of less than 24 hours but usually it is more, with an average of 25 hours.

61. Aschoff J. (1965) Circadian rhythms in Man. Science, Vol 148 pp 1427-32 When Aschoff spent time in a carefully controlled bunker, isolated from the world, he said the days seemed shorter than 24 hours, but most of his subjects had rhythms of more than 24 hours.

62. Hamner KC et al. (1962) The biological clock at the south pole. Nature, Vol 195 pp 476-80 Hamner was not sure what would happen to the biological clock at the south pole. Rhythmicity may cease, or be altered to new frequencies, or the rhythms might continue as before. He therefore took hamsters, fruit flies, bean plants and fungi to the Antarctic, and examined them on turntables. "It can be stated that the external environmental variables of diurnal nature associated with the rotation of the earth have no detectable influence on the basic mechanism of the biological clock" He thought the clock was unrelated to geophysical stimuli.

The smallest and simplest animal cell in which circadian rhythms have been clearly shown is the ciliated protozoan Paramecium. It has a rhythmic capacity to mate normally in the daytime. Under constant darkness the rhythm continues with a circadian period a little more than 24 hours.

63. Hardin P, Hall J and Rosbask M. (1990) Nature 343, 536 They suggest that there is a feedback loop through which the activity of *per*-encoded protein causes cycling of its own RNA, as an important mechanism of the circadian rhythm.

64.Schibler U and Sassone-Corsi P, Cell, 111: 919-922, 2002. There has been an explosion of interest in circadian rhythms in the last three years, and in 1998, the American Association for the Advancement of Science recognised circadian rhythms as the runner-up in their list of breakthroughs of the year. *(see Edery I, Physiol Genomics 3:59-74, 2000. Rajaratnam S and Arendt J, The Lancet 358:999-1005, 2001.)*

65. Coveney P and Highfield R. (1991) The arrow of time. Flamingo, London This is written by a physical chemist and a science journalist. They examine why time is irreversible, and flows in only one direction. There is a long section about biological time, and how the dominant rhythm does not tap out an exact 24-hour cycle, but actually a 25-hour one. The circadian body clock is constantly reset. They describe the spectrum of different biological rhythms, from nerve impulses in microseconds, to the heart beat, the hormonal and metabolic oscillations, the daily cycle and the woman's monthly rhythm.

66. Fish SA, Shepherd TJ, McGenity TJ andGrant WD. (2002) Recovery of 16S ribosomal RNA gene fragments from ancient halite. Nature 417(6887):432-436 They reported finding small inclusions of bacterial DNA in salt crystals that ranged in ages from 11 to 425 million years. Surprisingly the sequences differed by less than 2% from know bacteria today, but in spite of this, they concluded that the DNA was not a recent contaminant, but rather that the salt had preserved the DNA. If the inclusions were very ancient, they would have expected that mutation would have resulted in more than 2% difference from current bacteria, especially in organisms with a short generation time, because the DNA of these organisms would have been separated from living organisms for millions of years. To explain the anomaly, they argue therefore that in certain phylogenetic lineages the molecular clock must be slow.

67. Paabo S. (1993) Ancient DNA. Scientific American 269(5):60-66 He wrote that water would completely break down DNA within 50,000 years, and background radiation in the absence of water and oxygen, would eventually erase all DNA information.

68. Sarfati J. (1999) Refuting evolution. Master Books,Green Forest AR. Sarfati describes research by M. Schweitzer and T.Staedter (which was published in *Earth*, 'The Real Jurassic Park', June 1997, p55-57,) that blood cells and haemoglobin which could not last more than a few thousand years, had been found in some dinosaur bones thought to be 65 million years old.

69. Jones M. (2001) The Molecule Hunt. Archaeology and the search for ancient DNA. Penguin Books London England. Martin Jones is professor of Archaeological Science at Cambridge University, and chairman of the Ancient Biomolecules Initiative research programme. He describes the exiting search for ancient biomolecules and the anomaly of finding fragments of DNA in ancient fossils. Paabo had reasonably estimated that DNA would not survive longer than 8,000 years and yet others claimed to have identified its presence in 17-20 million year old fossil leaf and in a 400 million year old brachiopod, in insects trapped in ancient amber and in a 50,000 year old mammoth tooth. He describes how Mary Schweitzer detected what seemed to be nucleated blood cells in a 65 million year old *Tyrannosaurus rex*. He believes that some preservative properties may explain the long survival of the remnants of these biomolecules.

70. Peacock RE. (1989) A brief history of eternity. Monarch Publications Ltd Peacock expands on his views about time and about two time frames. Time does not have an absolute quality; it depends upon the frame of reference in which it is quoted. We as observers, view the creation event and subsequent history in a detached sort of way from our frame of reference, outside of this history, since we are at the end of it. Our measurements give us a possible age for the universe of 15 billion years. However in the frame of reference of the creation event, there was no observer - except, perhaps, a Creator.

Peacock invites us to assume that, since God was at work at the beginning of the universe, he recorded the events of creation as he moved in the framework of the creation process - a different time frame from ours. Then let us suppose that he filed his report with a scribe who is resident in our framework. The time dilation effect due to speed alone can be 20,000 to 1. It increases further when we take into account the contribution due to gravitational time-warp. A convergence begins, between the two extreme ages of 15 billion years by science and 6,000 years in the Bible. He says "we must not build a set of dogmas on the assumption that time has the absolute quality inferred by the Newtonian system. We only need to assume Einstein to be believable and that the two frames of reference exist. He says that it is astonishing that Einstein the Jew, has unconsciously given credence, from a scientific perspective, to a set of Jewish writings which are part of what we call the Bible!"

71. Humphreys DR. (1997) Starlight and time. Master Books, Green Forest, Ar Humphreys writes as a convinced creationist, who works in nuclear physics. He attempts to solve the puzzle of distant starlight taking billions of years to reach the planet, in a universe which according to creationists is young. He describes how according to Einstein's general theory of relativity, gravity and velocity dilate time. He argues that by gravitational time dilation - when clocks tick at different rates in different parts of the universe - God could have made the universe in six ordinary days as measured on earth, while still allowing time for light to travel billions of light-years to reach us by natural means. He thinks that the relativity of time also appears to explain the red shifts of light from distant galaxies.

Humphreys thinks that it is reasonable to hold to a young-earth cosmology and be consistent with Einstein's general theory of relativity and astronomical observations. As measured by clocks on earth, the age of the universe today could be as small as the face-value biblical age of about 6000 years. He believes that the relativity of time could harmonise the apparent conflict between Genesis and traditional cosmology.

72. Johnson PE. (2000) The wedge of truth: splitting the foundations of naturalism. InterVarsity Press, Illinois He asks whether one particular viewpoint should be presented as fact, which tolerates neither scepticism nor competition; and whether sometimes the authority of 'science' is used to validate claims that are based largely on speculation. He says that it's not a matter of letting a tiny bit of religion into a science-dominated world. If heaven exists, the authority to determine how to get there is vastly more important than the authority to say how the mundane cosmos works, because the latter deals with earthly knowledge that will soon pass away.

73. The Bible, book of Proverbs, Chapter 18 verse 17. Living Bible translation Proverbs is a book in the Bible ascribed to King Solomon and to a circle of wise men. Solomon was said to have 'wisdom greater than the wisdom of all the men of the East, greater than all the wisdom of Egypt. He was wiser than any other man. He described plant life...... he also taught about animals and birds, reptiles and fish' 1 Kings 4, 30-33.

74. Gould SJ. (2201) Rocks of Ages, Jonathan Cape, London He says that his concept - that science and religion can live harmoniously together - precludes a loving God who must show his hand by peppering nature with palpable miracles, or that God could allow evolution to work in a manner contrary to the facts of the fossil record. He believes that Creationism is a partisan and minority view of religion that has transgressed into the magisterium of science. These zealots still find ways to impose their will and nonsense. He says that young-earth creationism offers nothing of intellectual merit. It is just a hodgepodge of claims conclusively disproved more than a century ago. It maybe as American as apple pie and Uncle Sam, but no other Western nation faces such an incubus as a serious political movement, apart from a few powerless cranks at the fringes. He says that virtually all professionally trained scientists regard creationism as nonsensical, based on either pure ignorance or outright prevarication, and any who digress cannot recognise the cutting edge of their own subject.

75. Zacharias R (1996) Deliver us from evil. World Publishing, Dallas, London, Vancouver, Melbourne He says that there is a philosophical attack upon the moorings of contemporary society, apparent in the polemical overtones of the writings of Steven J Gould of Harvard and Richard Dawkins of Oxford, who ridicule a theistic framework. Science claims to have vanquished theology, and reason has embarrassed faith. To speak from a Christian perspective is frequently to become a target for abuse and hostility. The religious are thought to be bigoted and prejudiced, and seek to crush the culture under their tyrannical heels. Those who believe in God as the author of the universe, are dismissed as intellectual dinosaurs who have outlived their usefulness. He says that students entering college are very guarded about their religious beliefs, for fear of being outcasts in the world of learning.

76. Jones S. (20 March 2002) Creationists spread pure poison, Daily Telegraph Steve Jones, professor of genetics at University College London, contributed to a lively debate in the Daily Telegraph. He was angry that a leading British school was teaching Creationism, suggesting that evolution was merely a theory, and that they dared to encourage their students to question the age of the universe being other than billions of years old. He was joined in a media frenzy by an eclectic mixture of atheists, bishops and scientists.

Professor Richard Dawkins of Oxford arch apostle of Darwinism, had written in *The Telegraph* on March 16th that such questioning by the school propagated 'ludicrous falsehoods', because he said there was no scientific position stating that the universe is a few thousand years old.

Professor Andy McIntosh of Leeds University also entered the debate on March 16th, by criticising Darwinism, and pointing out that there was no possibility of Darwinian evolution at the biochemical level because of the irreducible complexity, down to minute details, in the workings of living organisms - details that will not go away even with all the heat generated by professor Dawkins' evident atheism.

Professor Jones waded in, saying that anyone who teaches biology without a belief in evolution is like someone teaching English without confidence in grammar. All science unites to prove these people wrong. They are described as teaching garbage and pure poison, they are clowns, cranks, primitivist, stupid, grubby and like the Taliban.

It was one of the shortest PM Question Time queries on record, as Prime minister Tony Blair tried to lower the temperature. He plunged his pointed finger to attack the despatch box, as he defended the excellent academic record of the Gateshead College, to the howls of disbelief from the scientific, religious and educational establishment.

77. Uttley T (16 March 2002) God knows what Professor Dawkins is talking about. Daily Telegraph Tom Uttley in his Saturday Column (March 16th) was worried at the hysterical outbursts from Professor Dawkins, and his refusal to admit even the slightest possibility that anybody else might be right. He wrote - "it strikes me as thoroughly anachronistic - and unscientific - of anybody to believe that the author of Genesis had the same concept of time as we have now." He thought it odd that Professor Dawkins should be so hung up on the difficulty of squaring time, as it was understood by Genesis, with time as modern science understands it. If there "is no absolute *now*, and no absolute *then*, why does he find it so difficult to stomach what Genesis has to say about time?"

78. Dawkins R. (1986). The Blind Watchmaker. Longman Scientific & Technical, UK Ltd Richard Dawkins has the reputation of being one of the most brilliant of this generation of Biologists. In this book he says that animals are the most complicated things in the Universe, but that is no reason to believe in a Designer God. He says Darwin described the origin of this complexity without God - by natural selection which is unconscious, automatic and blind. According to Dawkins it explains the existence and form of all life, and why we exist. He says that for a biologist to doubt evolution is almost too bizarre to credit. He claims that Darwinism is the only theory that is capable of explaining certain aspects of life. Like Julian Huxley fifty years earlier, he says "even if there were no actual evidence in favour of the Darwinian theory, we should still be justified in preferring it over all rival theories", because there is no acceptable alternative. He has no time for fundamental creationists.

79. Burkitt D. (2002) Personal communication Dennis Burkitt was one of medicine's great original thinkers. His trek across Central Africa and the discovery of 'Burkitt's Lymphoma', the first cancer found to have a viral aetiology, is an epic story of pioneering research. He was also the first to observe that many Western diseases like appendicitis, diverticulitis, bowel cancer, varicose veins and cardiovascular diseases are related to low fibre diet, and he toiled tirelessly to share his views.

He came to me in 1986 with his usually enthusiasm, saying he had discussed Adam's rib with Stanley Brown - an African missionary who had introduced the sulphone treatment for leprosy. They both had the novel insight that in Genesis 2:22 when it says "The Lord God made a woman from the rib He had taken out of man", the word "rib" might be better translated "side", accounting for the XX chromosomes in woman and XY chromosomes in men.

80. Atkins P. (1995) The periodic kingdom. Weidenfield and Nicolson, London This is a delightful book for a reader with no knowledge of chemistry, who is taken on an imaginative journey through the periodic table of the elements. Atkins sees the one hundred or so elements - the materials from which everything tangible is made - as finely balanced living personalities. He describes the real world of rocks, stones, rivers and oceans as a jumble of awesome complexity and immeasurable charm, and says that if you add to that the ingredient of life, the boundless wonder is multiplied almost beyond imagination.

81. Zotin AI. (1978) in Thermodynamics of Biological Processes p 19. edited by I Lamprecht and AI Zotin, de Gruyter, New York He says that the German physicist Hermann von Helmholtz, one of the founders of the science of thermodynamics, was one of the first to suggest that life somehow circumvents the Second Law. It is a linear process that avoids an increase in entropy.

82. Schrodinger E. (1944). What is Life? p 81 by Cambridge University Press, Cambridge He examines the Second Law of Theromdynamics and says that it may not apply to living matter. He argues that there is need for a new type of physical law for living things.

83. Johnson PE.(2000) The wedge of truth: splitting the foundations of naturalism. InterVarsity Press, Illinois He describes what he thinks is a common fallacy, and argues that the instructions in the cell which control embryonic development and direct its outcome, only "employ" material processes, but they are not "created" by those processes. He thinks the big question is not whether miracles are required once theinstructions are in operation, but whether intelligence is required to create the instructions in the first place.

84. Coveney P and Highfield R. (1991) The arrow of time. Flamingo, London They describe the important work of Paul Nurse in Edinburgh who showed that the molecule responsible for triggering cell division is the same from yeast to man. They say that cells can be thought of as ticking clocks oscillating through two states. First the cell grows whilst division is inhibited. In the second state, although it continues to grow, the cell divides. First the 'tick' and then the 'tock'. The blueprint of this living timepiece is in the fundamental genetic programme of every cell, from yeast to starfish and to humans. The trigger for replication, is a DNA instruction to one protein that 'suits all'.

The authors say there has been an attempt to interpret 'evolution' at a macroscopic level as transgressing the Second Law of Thermodynamics - that evolution shows an increase in order, rather than the decrease in order which is seen in the cosmos in general. They think this is confused thinking. They say that individual living systems are dissipative with increasing entropy, but admit that because of their immense reproductive power, living things are dynamical.

85. Dawkins R. (1986) The Blind Watchmaker. Longman Scientific and Technical, Longman Group, UK Ltd He says that Dollo's law - which says that 'evolution' is irreversible with increasing order and less entropy - is nonsense. Evolution does not transgresses the Second Law of Thermodynamics. He says that the half of the population who know what the law is, will realise that even the growth of a baby doesn't violate the Second Law, but he gives no reasoning for this statement. He thinks evolution does not transgress the second law, because the fossils show that the earlier organisms had as much perfection as there is in living creatures today. Living things show neither decrease or increase in entropy - (exactly !).

86. Maddox J. (1998) What Remains to be Discovered. The Free Press. New York. Maddox argues that living things are sustained in an exceptional condition. They are an aberration, by not conforming to the Second Law as it applies in isolated systems.

87. Kelley DF. (1997) Creation and change. Christian Focus Publication, Great Britain Professor Kelley writes is a theologian who argues persuasively for a literal interpretation of the seven day account of creation found in Genesis chapters 1 and 2, and that the earth is young. He looks at the biblical details and the scientific data, especially the concept of time, and makes a convincing case that this position is scientifically viable.

88. Hawking S . (1998) Black Holes and Baby universes. Cox and Wyman Ltd Reading, Berkshire He comments on the speed of light at 186,000 miles a second which is always the same no matter at what speed the observer was moving. He graphically describes "Einstein's greatest triumph" - how gravity distorted the light from a star behind the sun, so that it was visible during an eclipse of the sun.

He describes black holes which have immense gravity and how they affect space-time. The gravitational field is so strong, that any light or other signal is dragged back into the region and cannot escape to the outside world.

89. Atkins P., (1992) Creation revisited, the origin of space, time and the universe. Penguin books, England He describes light appearing to try all the paths, and then eliminating all traces of having done so, it selects the briefest - Fermat's principle of least time. We can see light from stars behind the sun because the star's light curves round the periphery of the sun - a fact which was predicted by Einstein - because light selects the path of the shortest time. The gravity close to the sun slows down time, but time is faster in the lesser gravity at a distance from the sun. Light from behind the sun takes this quickest path.

90. Setterfield B. (1985) The velocity of light and the age of the Universe. Creation Scientific Organisation, Adelaide, Australia Setterfield thought the speed of light is now slower than it was in the past, and because the velocity of the electron in its orbit is proportional to the speed of light, radioactive decay is also slowing down. This effects our estimates of age by radiometric dating.

91. Davies PC, Davis TM, Lineweaver CH. (2002). Black holes constrain varying constant. Nature 418(6898), 602-603 Paul Davies the theoretical physicist at Sydney's Macquire University and his colleagues argues that because light that has been travelling for 12 billion years from giant stellar objects violates the accepted laws of physics, the speed of light may not be constant. They say that a reasonable explanation is that the speed of light was faster 6 to 10 billions of years ago than it is now.

92. Magueijo J. (2003) Faster than the speed of light. William Heinemann, Cambridge Varying speed of light is also examined by a theoretical physicist, who claims that many of the big cosmological problems will simply melt away if one breaks the rule that the speed of light never varies. He examines the implications of the primordial speed of light being 32 zeros added to its current value. He describes how in 1992 John Moffat, a theoretical physicist at the University of Toronto, also proposed a variable speed of light as an alternative to inflation. Magueijo thinks that a group of Australian astronomers led by John Webb, may have discovered evidence that spectral lines of light from distant stars supports the theory of varying speed of light.

93. The Times. Einstein's famous equation doesn't add up, expert says. The Times, 9 August (2002) The article in *The Times* quotes Paul Davies' paper about the slowing down of light (see ref 91), and says "we will need to examine the very nature of time".

94. Novikov ID.(1998) The river of time. Cambridge University Press The velocity of any electromagnetic wave like light, is constant, though dependent on the medium. It is independent of the motion of the source. He says that the red-shift in the fast jets of hydrogen gas emitted from a binary stellar systems, is due to time slowing down.

95. Bolles EB, (1997) Galileo's Commandment. Abacus London This book which is a collection of classical scientific writings, contains Karl Popper's paper *Replies to my* *critics* (1974), where he says bold ideas and new daring hypotheses must have the ability to be refuted, and it is essential that they should generate predictions to be tested.

96. Johanson DC and Edey M. (1981). Lucy. The Beginnings of Humankind. Granada London,Toronto Sydney New York In this book Don Johanson examines the supposed evolutionary history of humankind. He described his discovery of a partial skeleton of 'Lucy', approximately 3.4 million years old, in a remote part of Ethiopia. He claims it is the oldest best-preserved skeleton of any erect-walking human ancestor ever found (see Leakey - ref 97 - who says 'Lucy' was not upright).

97. Leakey R. (1999) The Origin of Mankind. Phoenix, Guernsey CI He says that the significant changes that occurred with the evolution of the genus Homo over 2.5 million years, was in brain size. It probably also marked the beginning of a change in the level of consciousness. - a sharper consciousness - to higher and higher levels - gradually unfolding into a new kind of animal, with language, conscious awareness, artistic expression and burial of the dead. He describes the first evidence of human Neanderthal burial 100,000 years ago, and a little later some 60,000 years ago, ritual human burial in the Zagros mountains of northern Iraq. He says the cave drawing from 35,000 years ago were not art for art's sake, but images that were mediated by cognitive reflection, like the elaborate ritual burials.

He thinks that 'Lucy', a mere 3 feet tall primate, was entirely ape-like with long arms and short legs. The inner ear anatomy gives a clue to uprightness and 'Lucy' was probably not upright (see Johanson (ref 96) who says 'Lucy' was upright.).

98. Redfield R. (1966) The Primitive World. Cornell University Press. Ithaca, New York He examines human society before urbanisation, saying that 75,000 years ago mankind had reached the point when fully human life had been attained. He quotes Childe, that it was only about 3000 BC at a time when writing was invented, that civilisation appeared simultaneously in three tiny patches of the earth's surface. He describes Harper's translation of the Code of Hammurabi when there appeared many different types of specialists in Babylon.

99. Dyer CH. (1991) The Rise of Babylon. International Bible Society, USA Dyer says that Saddam Hussein and the ancient world conqueror Nebuchadnezzar not only looked alike, but Saddam Hussein claimed to have had the same mission - to control the world. He describes how Saddam Hussein attempted to rebuild Babylon to the exact specifications and splendour it had in the days of Nebuchadnezzar. Dyer believes that the Middle East is the world's time bomb, and Babylon might be its fuse.

100. Shakey M. (1980). Neanderthal Man p 25. Duckworth Surrey, England He describes a progressive enlargement of the brain from Austalopithecus to Neanderthal, after which there appears to be a slight reduction. He says it is difficult to infer psychological development from cerebral volume, (See ref 97).

101. Carter WB (1886) Isaac Marsden of Doncaster, Woolmer, London This is a compilation of the correspondence of Isaac Marsden, a nineteenth century Methodist evangelist. He wrote in 1863 "I am reading the works of Sir Charles Lyell. The testimony of Moses on the antiquity of man, is but yesterday, compared with the 'Antiquity of man' according to the deductions of our modern Moses. In which have you the most confi dence, the stony pages of antiquity, or the pages of the five books of Moses? Nature and revelation are in agreement, and that will be demonstrated eventually."

102. Gould SJ. (1988)   Time's arrow, time's cycle. Penguin Books,London,New York It is of note that after a lifetime of trying to destroy the arguments of so-called religious bigots, Lyell said "There is only one great resource to fall back upon - trust in God - that the intelligent ruler of the universe has given us this great volume as a privilege, that its interpretation is elevating."

103. White M and Gribbin J. (1995)   Darwin - a life in science. Simon&Schuster, London, New York,Tokyo, Singapore, Tornoto The authors believe that in his day, Darwin received more antagonism than accolades, but since then, his seminal work has become a fact not theory. It now impacts on modern physics, astronomy and above all on biology. They describe Darwin's scientific legacy as being as influential to modern thought as Newton's or Einstein's.

104. Denton M.(1986) Evolution: A Theory in Crisis. Alder & Alder,Bethesda Md. This is a critique of evolution by a non professing Christian, who claims - "that there can be no doubt that after a century of intensive effort, biologists have failed to validate it in any significant sense. The fact remains that nature has not been reduced to the continuum that the Darwinian model demands, nor has the credibility of chance as the creative agency of life been secured."

105. O'Hear.(1997) Beyond Evolution. Human Nature and the Limits of Evolutionary Explanation. Oxford University Press, Guildford and King's Lynn Anthony O'Hear, is Professor of Philosophy at the University of Bradford, and although he thinks that evolution may be successful in explaining the development of the natural world in general, he says it is of limited value when applied to human nature. It offers no explanation for our reflectiveness and rationality which have no survival-promotion or reproductive advantages. He thinks that the distinctive facets of human life, like the quest for knowledge, moral sense and the appreciation of beauty, transcends evolution.

106. Johnson PE. (2000) The Wedge of Truth. IVP, Illinois Johnson quotes the results of a gallup poll conducted in USA in June 1999, which showed that 69% of Americans favoured teaching creationism in public schools along with evolution, and 40% did not oppose replacing evolution altogether with creationism.

107. Davies P. (1999) The Fifth Miracle. Penguin Books, London Davies a physicist, writes in his usual interesting style about the mystery of the origin of life. He noted that Oparin and Haldane in the 1920's suggested that lightning in the primitive atmosphere might have created the chemical building blocks of life. Davies describes how themophilic bacteria can live on the periphery of black smokers in the ocean depths where temperatures reach 350 degrees Centigrade, and this suggests to him that life might have started in the hot underworld.

108.Spetner L.(1997) Not by chance: shattering the modern theory of evolution. The Judaica Press, Brooklyn,New York This is an anti-Darwinian book about mutations, written by a biophysicist. He says that all point mutations that have been studied on the molecular level, reduce the genetic information and do not to increase it. Sometimes mutations duplicate material - make copies of *existing* nucleotide sequences - but they do not add new information. It is theoretically possible that information adding mutations might arise, but to date, no one has discovered mutations that specify for increased complexity. Some believe that there are rare examples of information adding mutations, but these claims are disputed. One would expect a vast number of such mutations to make evolution plausible, and this is not being observed.

109. Hooper J. (2002) On Moths and Men. Fourth Estate, London Judith Hooper writes about Dr Bernard Kettlewell who in 1953 had a pre-conceived idea, that the changing industrial environment favoured the black variety of the peppered moth, and it thrived because it was camouflaged on dark trees and was protected from its natural predators - birds. He went into the woods with a mission - to catch evolution in action. He was going to prove it. He wrote a paper that was to be the flag-ship for evolution - "Darwin's missing evidence". His work was then cited by two generations of biologists, as proof that evolutionary change can occur quickly. Now it has been exposed as research that was seriously flawed.

Unfortunately, if Kettlewell didn't get the data he wanted, he often altered the experimental design. No similar piece of work would be accepted in any scientific journal today. The cause of pigmentation is complex, but it is not because of the result of the "survival of the fittest" in a changing environment. Peppered moths are not a model for evolution.

"Kettlewell's colleagues didn't want to shoot him down because they loved the idea" even if it was wrong, because it claimed to be "an example of Darwinism." The author who is an evolutionist writes "Even if it is a little bit wrong, some say, we should stick with the basic story!"

110. Porter RW. (1992) Upright Man. Aberdeen University Review, 187: 201-219 This is a transcript of my inaugural lecture given on 23 April 1991 in the presence of the Duchess of York. The lecture examined the biomechanics of the human lumbar spine, its protective role for the nerves of the spinal cord and the important function of the intervertebral discs. It concluded that the human spine is excellent in its design, and its form ideally matches its function.

111. Millar R. (1974) The Piltdown Man. A case of Archaeological fraud. Granada Books Ltd. Bunghay, Suffolk, England A real historical who dunnit, recording the fraudulent exhibit that was in the Natural History Museum London from 1912 for 41 years, and was claimed to be an important missing-link between apes and humans.

112.www.answersingenesis.org/docs/4208news3-2-2000.asp This describes the fraudulent Archaeoraptor, originally claimed as a missing link between dinosaurs and birds.

113. Porter RW. Personal observation I have personally examined many hundreds of specimens of the human lumbar spine and also of the lumbar vertebrae of other primates, and I can confirm that the photographs I have seen of the vertebrae of 'Lucy', are more ape-like than human.

114. Fortey R. (2000) Trilobite ! Eyewitness to evolution. Flamingo Publishers This beautifully written and well illustrated book, says everything about Trilobites. It is claimed that the complicated eye structure of this little creature watched evolution unfolding over a period of 300 million years. However the book does not provide convincing evidence for evolution, because Trilobites suddenly appeared in the rock formations complete with their multifaced eyes. There are different species without obvious transitional forms, and once a species arrived, it endured, often for a long time with little change.

115. Huxley J. (1942) Darwin. Cassell and Co. London, Toronto, Melbourn and Sydney He described Darwin's theory of evolution in a book to help the layman. He said we can be sure it does occur even if we don't know how it occurs, because the only alternative to evolution is special creation, and he said that there is no one with the least pretension to biological knowledge who does not accept Darwinism. He believed that thousand of new facts were being added each year to support the theory. He made much of two "facts" that he said supported evolution - (1) useless, rudimentary, vestigial parts, and (2) organisms recapitulating their evolutionary history in their embryological form - two ideas that are now known to be wrong.

116. Hawkes N. The Times August 11 (1997) Nigel Hawkes writes in *The Times* that Ernst Haeckel was an embryonic liar. This man was admired as a giant amongst German biologists in Darwin's day, and his popular work "The riddle of the Universe" sold 100,000 copies in the first year. He wrote that embryos of all species look very similar in the early stages of their development. He argued that embryonic growth is a rerun, fast-forward, of the evolution of the species. "Ontogeny recapitulates phylogeny." It was a central plank in the theory of evolution.

He drew pictures of embryos of different species to show their similarity, and these illustrations have been repeated in successive textbooks of biology. His drawings of human embryos with tails have survived even into current anatomical textbooks. Hawkes said that because modern embryologists don't do comparative work and are sometimes ignorant of the facts, some of them still cling to the wreckage of Haeckel's theory.

Dr Michael Richardson, a lecturer at St George's Hospital, reviewed Haeckel's work and found that embryos of different species are not the same. Haeckel's drawing could not have been done from life, and they are fakes. Richardson described this as one of the worst cases of scientific fraud. "It's shocking to find that somebody one thought was a great scientist was deliberately misleading. It makes me angry."

117. Wright V. (1985). The origin of man. in Creation and Evolution. ed Drek Burke, Inter-varsity Press, London Vernon Wright, Professor of Rheumatology in Leeds, writes about one of the most striking about-turns in evolutionary teaching - so called vestigial structures. They were said to be "leaves blown off the evolutionary tree". At one time the menisci in the knee were described as vestigial in man. Wright's own work showed that these cartilagenous discs in the human knee joint carry 60-90% of the body's load during the walking cycle, and when they are removed surgically, the patient is prone to develop osteoarthritis. The existence of vestigial structures was thought to be a firm plank in the platform of evolution, but it has now been shown to be rotten.

118. Porter RW . (2001) The pathogenesis of idiopathic scoliosis: uncoupled neuro-osseous growth? European Spine Journal, 10: 473-481 This is a review article about a possible mechanism for scoliosis. It considers a review on the importance of the pineal gland in secreting melatonin, its role as a calmodulin antagonist and how this gland may be essential for normal spinal cord growth.

119. Gould SJ. (2001) Rocks of Ages, Jonathan Cape, London He thinks much of our genetic material (so called 'junk DNA') serves no apparent function, and because we are ignorant of its use, it must be a throw back to earlier evolutionary times.

120. Cameron NMdeS, .(1983) Evolution and the authority of the bible, The Paternoster Press, Australia, South Africa Cameron, who held a high view of biblical authority, examines the doctrinal issues raised by the theory of evolution. I am indebted to many of Cameron's ideas, some of which have been included in chapters 88 and 90 of this book.

121. Johnson PE. (2000) The Wedge of Truth. IVP, Illinois This university Berkeley law professor is a leading figure in the Intelligent Design movement. He identifies logical flaws in the evolutionary theory, and he describes the key philosophical assumptions that constrain the ways data is allowed to be interpreted in the physical sciences.

122. Wilkinson D. (2002) The Message of Creation. IVP. Nottingham David Wilkinson is Fellow in Christian Apologetics at the University of Durham. He is both an astrophysicist and a theologian. He believes that it is a misreading of Scripture to take a literal meaning from the early chapters of Genesis and he describes the different views. However, he encourages us to challenge long held assumptions and maintian the highest regard for biblical authority.

123. Kelly DF. (1997) Creation and Change. Mentor,Great Britain Kelley, a theologian who believes the truth of a literal interpretation of Genesis, describes how some people avoid a literal interpretation of Genesis, by using the 'Framework hypothesis'. This is a concept that the beginning of Genesis has literary character, a poetic   quality, but it avoids the force of the normal sense of day during creation week, and also the chronological sequence of six twenty four hour days. Kelley argues that this hypothesis evades realism and truth.

124. Stott J.(1990) Issue Facing Christians Today. Marshall Pickering, London John Stott writes about the importance of developing a Christian Mind, and having a right understanding of the four basic presuppositions of Scripture. He describes them as the four epochs of human history - (1) Creation (the good) , (2) the Fall (the evil), (3) Redemption (the new) and (4) the End (the perfect). This supplies the true perspective from which to view the unfolding process between two eternities, the vision of God working out His purpose. It enables us think straight even about the most complex issues. These four events when grasped in relation to one another, teach major truth about God, human beings and society which gives direction to our Christian thinking.

125. Gould SJ. (2001) Rocks of Ages, Jonathan Cape,London Gould has invented a principle he calls NOMA 'Non-Overlapping Magisteria' that he thinks should allow science and religion to co-exist peacefully in a position of respectful non-interference. Science defines the natural world, religion the moral world. He says that their spheres of influence are separate. Christian beliefs are relegated to the realm of subjective feelings, with no basis in the real Universe, (a heavy price they are expected to pay for peace with the materialist who claims to speak for science). He has no room for miracles, and enjoys having a regular side-swipe at creationists whom he says refuse to live at peace with scientists.

126. NelsonER BroadberryRE Chock GT. (1997) God's promise to the Chinese. Read Books Publishers,Dunlap,TN. These authors have studied the most ancient forms of Chinese writings on 'bronzeware' and 'oracle bone'. They compare the stories depicted by the primitive ideographic symbols with the Hebrew Scriptures, and conclude that these Chinese characters of antiquity have a deep and hidden meaning that mirrors the Genesis story. They think that the writing was built on the ancient knowledge of their world, and a loving relationship between early mankind and their Creator-God, *Shang-Ti.*

Visit the website

www.journeytoeden.org

ADDENDUM

If you would like to explore in more detail some of the
questions that arise in this book, you are invited to visit the
web site